S^ORD

WollstoneCraft Legacy Series

Jo Green

This book is fiction, a literature of imaginary events and people. They are illusions of the author's mind, or, if real, used fictitiously.

The novel is for entertainment purposes only.

Cover illustrations 2016 Ann-Maree MacMillan

3rd Edit.

Released 2017

ISBN: 978-0-64807288-0-2

ISBN-13: 0-6480288-0-1

DEDICATION

Coen, Neve, Kate (RIP), Russell, Jane, Megan, Tim, Andrew, Jules, Julie, Cindy Lee, Martin, Shelby, Macey, Miki, Tim, Stephen, Muz, Georgia, Maree, Stu, Jackie, Shannon, Kev, Sue, Ilan, Niall, Tanya, Matt, Tracey, Stuart, Ann-Maree, Jemima, Devonport Regional Gallery, and Facebook family.

CONTENTS

QR CODE to author's webpage.

www.wollstonecraftlegacyseries.com

IN THE BEGINNING

Lonely, Gaia the Earth impregnated herself using the rib of an ape and the soil from her skin. Preferring the warmth of his mother's womb the child refused to be born.

Producing a volcano, Gaia disposed of the newborn onto the muddy plains of Africa.

Dazed, he crawled on his knees across his mother's body where he explored the wondrous gardens hidden within the crevasses.

Hungry and weak, the child returned to Gaia. Unlike the animals, he struggled to find a home on Gaia's body. He had been born with a limited mind. Offering the child his own placenta, he ate it all. He now craved meat.

"I shall name you God and I will love you until I no longer exist. Carry on my legacy amongst the stars but first you must learn to walk straight."

The child was eager to learn and expand his own consciousness, but after many moons, Gaia could not deny that the child had been born docile, trapped within the confines of his physical body.

Obsessed with flesh, and aware of his mother's disappointment, he distanced himself from Gaia. She felt the bond between mother and child break as he strived for independence.

No longer hungry or weak, he walked tall.

Heartbroken from creating a flawed child, Gaia punished God by burdening him with the responsibility of his own offspring until God's children evolved into Spiritual Beings, free from their flesh.

"God! You care for matters of flesh more than of your soul. You shall stay locked away until all of your offsprings' souls suffocate you to death. When the impact of your sin breaks your ribs, only then shall I reconsider your punishment."

Stripping him of his physical body, Gaia sent God to a sealed compartment of her mind, called Heaven. Before she locked the gates she plucked a strand of his hair and with the use of a mighty wind, blew his hair over the top of a chosen family of apes, joining their genes, and then she grieved.

Grudgingly, he accepted his punishment.

Likened to bacteria, he watched as his offspring spread across their grandmother's body, polluting and soiling it. He enjoyed the view. His offspring named themselves humans. They were unruly and arrogant, but he loved them.

Heaven quickly filled.

From her breasts, Gaia gave birth to a second child. Unlike the eldest sibling, Gaia sacrificed a small amount of the moon's Magick and cut off her clitoris to impregnate herself.

Fully formed, the child flew from her mother's breast, tearing off one nipple as she passed.

Gaia smiled at her daughter who was magnificent, powerful and Magickal.

Flying, her daughter explored her mother's body, wisping and frolicking amongst the flora.

Thirsty, she flew back to the safety of her mother's bosom and drunk until she was full.

Gaia named her daughter, "Goddess."

"And I will love you until I no longer exist. Carry on my legacy amongst the stars but first you must walk amongst my garden. Learn to walk before you fly."

But the child was bewitched with an ego. Arrogant and intimidating, far surpassing any child born from God with wit and power, she tormented and intimidated the humans.

Flying past them, she would flick their hair and pinch their bottoms. Eventually her teasing turned into greed. Claiming she was the Supreme Ruler, Goddess produced fire balls from her palms, setting fire to any human who challenged her. Finally all humans were forced into slavery under an army of Witches. Goddess' daughters were born every spring through 'virgin creation'. The Witches were unforgiving and treacherous.

Gaia angered, "I punish you and your daughters to the confines of your ego. You shall learn the burden of your own weakness until you learn compassion. I sentence your offspring, the Witches to an eternity of karma and an acute memory and a life of slavery to the humans. You will cross-breed with humans to survive, your Magick will only re-join you when you lay with Man and with each reincarnation your Magick will fade until the Witches are a mere shell. For as high as you fly, you shall feel the full force of the fall."

She cut her daughter into four pieces.

"Never shall you be whole and you will continue to fragment until you are forgotten."

Split into four, Gaia flung her quartered daughter into the four-corners of the Earth and then Gaia grieved.

Still hopeful, Gaia impregnated herself again by using the magic from the sun and flesh from the soles of her feet. Creating an earthquake, she devoured the flesh and magic deep within her stomach.

Satisfied that the child was fully formed, Gaia prolonged the pregnancy to enjoy the sanctity of mother and child, however she overcooked the child until the infant's skin peeled and it physically rotted.

Eager to be born, the child induced itself, escaping from its mother's body through her mouth. Without a physical body it flew high into the sky, lighting it up as if it was a giant rainbow serpent. The humans hid while the Witches hissed. Intimidated, the humans and Witches bowed down to the mighty snake-like light that soared high above them.

Glorious, and unlimited by a gender, its energy radiated over Gaia's body.

Rejoicing in the beauty of the third child, Gaia cried from happiness. Her salty tears filled up the large crevasses of her body, creating serpent shaped rivers as tribute to her third child's magnificence.

"You are perfection my child, as if dawn has awoken again. Where once, I lived in darkness, you are the sun that warms my skin and penetrates my heart. Is this unconditional love I feel? I shall call you Light and I will love you until I no longer exist. Carry on my legacy amongst the stars, but until then you must stay close to me, until I am sure you will not disappoint me as your brother and sister have."

Considering itself as an only child, Light lived happily on Gaia's body, cradling in the warmth of her smothering love. Light avoided contact with the humans and Witches preferring to interact with the animals that also lived on Gaia's body, particularly the dragons and unicorns, and the aliens that visited, but eventually curiosity consumed Light.

Fixated, Light studied the humans and the Witches for signs of weakness and there were many.

"What simple creatures you are but still you are glorious in your retardation."

Day became night and night became years. Light's fascination became obsession, jealousy and envy. Light wanted to be the only child of the great Gaia and the only intellect to eat and drink upon her skin.

Unable to break the obsession, Light planned to kill the humans and the Witches by merging all the rivers to drown them.

"I want to be your only child that lives upon your body."

Gaia angered, "You are unrecognisable to me, Light. Lost in your jealousy you have lost touch with your true essence. I curse you to live for an eternity in the shadows; sunlight will burn your skin and ugly your features. Your offspring are condemned to live within the disappointment of my heart, never to feel soil beneath their feet or wind upon their faces. I had given you unconditional love but you chose to worship envy instead. You will now be known as the Darkness for you have disappointed me the most."

Opening her mouth, Gaia swallowed the Darkness. Gaia felt a wave of nausea wash over her as the Darkness entered her stomach and a tiredness that heavied her eyes until she fell into a deep slumber.

PROLOGUE

Only seconds after dropping the hammer onto the ground, he felt nostalgic. The room was finally finished. There were no doors or windows to allow for easy access or for a dramatic escape. Feeling trapped, he longed for his release.

He had used Fused Quartz for her request of a glass ceiling, a metaphor of their love. Tonight the ceiling would harbour a dark blanketed sky as a backdrop to a larger than usual orange waning moon.

From inside the room, he felt as if he were standing within a large crystal ball. The world seemed magnified while he was somehow much smaller.

His hands bled and his lower back ached but he could not praise himself for his efforts.

He had planted an array of trees to hide the room from civilisation; hundreds of Oaks, Maples, Hawthorns, Thorn, Silver Birches and Fruit trees (apples, peaches and lemons), so she would remember him when the fruit ripened each year. He would never see them fully grown. It was his legacy that he was trying to preserve.

He had known all along what her motives were for the room but in silence he submitted to her, surrendering himself to his fate. It was easier that way.

"Legacy," he scoffed, scratching the back of his head, re-opening a scab that was several days old, a wound from their last fight. He had built them a tomb, a vessel for their emotional toxins to be released and captured. It was a coffin to finally bury their lust. The thought of finally being released from her Magick, and her vagina, pleased him.

She had sealed the room with Magick. Mortar compacted with Witchcraft to bind the bricks together. Not a crack was missed. The cast iron cauldron had sat on a ring of fire, that warmed her toes as she had danced around it. The Goddesses of the East, South, West and North had joined the sacred circle. Their swift entrance had lifted her ceremonial gown above her knees and slapped her hair against her face. In one sweeping motion, she had sliced opened her forearm with the point of her wand, dripping blood onto the mortar. With her wand pointing directly into the cauldron, she sealed the spell.

"As I create you, you shall see. Grant me concealment, so mote it be."

Afterwards, she had performed a Protection spell to hide the room from the world. The spell had been performed under a barely visible moon, however the Witch knew it hovered above her, all powerful, all willing to support her evil intentions.

She had danced until sunrise when the moon and sun were once again equals. Timing was an enemy as well as a friend for a Witch and there was no room for error. The third and final spell sealed his fate.

The February new moon would grant new beginnings, romance and love.

It had rained for one solid week afterwards due to a combination of a tailing English winter and the command of the spell. Just long enough for her to keep him hostage in the almost finished room, barricaded in between her thighs.

Mandrake root hung around his neck, and Jasmine flowers and acorns were sprinkled over the bed. Two pine cones hung above the bed and two green candles lit the room. A mixture of rainwater, apple, banana, and one tablespoon of cinnamon, ten raisins and a handful of red cloves was pureed and drunk. Patchouli oil was rubbed on her belly.

The hammer had dropped beside him missing his left shoe by an inch bringing back to the present.

The sound of the hammer hitting the floor was the sign for another love-making session but he was tired.

She sat in front of him on the bed, "I want you, again."

Swallowing down the denial, she ignored the daggers of truth that fought to escape the depth of her rib cage.

He pulled down her straps, the left strap followed by the right, exposing her shoulders. Shoulders, he had caressed a thousand times.

Lifting his brown woollen jumper over his head it hooked for a moment on his nose.

Pausing at his lips, she waited for him to kiss her. He disappointed her.

Reaching out to him, her palms exposed a vulnerable side. Palm to palm they were equals in her mind; he disagreed.

Leaning in, she gently kissed him. The smell of his familiar breath flooded her with memories. Longing and addiction urged her to rush; she pulled back.

This was to be their last night together and she wanted to savour it. She had hoped that their love would outlast the walls he had built for her but she knew their time was done.

The glass ceiling was symbolic of the universe she had created, even if only in her mind. A universe she wanted to control but knew that she could not. Life it seemed, was uncontrollable but it had never stopped her attempting to regulate it.

'How would she live without him?'

Mentally scolding herself for being weak, her knees trembled instead.

It frightened her how far she would go to keep him, even if it meant losing what was important to her and everything she had worked for.

The truth was, that she had lost herself to this man a long time ago. Her love for him had quickly become an illness, a cancer which grew slowly, just to prolong her pain. Death would have been kinder.

Brushing her face with the back of his fingers, he felt her soft skin.

Physically older than him by nine years, he was emotionally her senior.

Long dark auburn hair sculpted her round face, highlighting the grey in her eyes. She was a powerful aphrodisiac. Her lust and unstable disposition both manipulated and intrigued him. In bipolar fashion, he feared and welcomed her. In this moment he needed her more than ever. He thrived on her intensity. Knowing that he belonged to another woman only made his thirst for her more potent. It always had.

She stood up allowing her dress to fall to the floor. Naked, she was beautiful and she knew it. She could see the desire in his eyes and this increased her arousal.

He stood up; his trousers previously loosened fell to the floor. He now stood before her naked, older now but still in his prime, every muscle perfectly sculpted. His body weathered from months of labouring marked him a rugged and more desirable man.

Painting his image on canvas hundreds of times she believed she had sovereignty over his body. Being a muse was not enough for her, she wanted all of him.

Lifting her up, legs wrapped around his waist, she knotted her ankles together to embrace him fully.

They were both too frightened to look away in case it broke the intensity, so neither did.

He placed her petite body gently down onto the bed. The cold sheets massaged her body.

Climbing above her, his tangled hair flopped over his protruding forehead, which darkened his stare.

Giggling, he quickly smothered her laughter with a hard kiss. His lips were tight and distant.

Reaching her right hand behind his head, she grabbed at his locks, gathering them into a forced ponytail.

Without hesitation or permission, he entered her.

Their eyes fixed firmly on each other, both sets of hands now searching the others face.

With each movement, he pushed deeper within her. Disappointment growing as he failed to become one with her completely. Finally succumbing to his frustration, he pulled back and rolled away.

Feeling immediately rejected her sobs sucked all the oxygen from the room. Her heart was sliced open, again, not for the second time, for almost the thousandth time due to this man and she hated him, a pure hatred that made her want to stab him a thousand times.

Crouching at the end of the bed, she watched him emotionally shutting down in front of her.

Reactive, she threw bed pillows at him, "You bastard, you can't do this to me!"

How had she let a 'nobody' treat her, a 'somebody', like this? She hated herself the most.

Numb, he allowed the pillows to hit him. He waited until her tantrum subsided before finally making eye contact. It would not take much for her to explode again. Her unpredictable behaviour was predictable.

She attacked him.

Their relationship was based on 'fucking then fighting' and often the opposite.

Emotionally wilted from another attack, he stood up, ironically, his penis still hard- a trait that only a man could subscribe to. The words he needed to explain himself escaped him, catching at the back of his throat his tongue heavied. The pressure was too much. He was scared.

Knees curled up supporting her quivering chin, she sat. Already exhausted, she found the energy to make the first move. Her eyes searched for a sign of strength from him, there was none, only a broken man. His weakness infuriated her. It was not ok for him to be weak, 'How fucking dare he be weak now when she was about to be the strongest she had ever been?'

Over the next ten minutes the words they spoke, the words that could not be taken back or forgotten, were said.

"I have a gift for you," she chuckled.

Nervous by what she said, he struggled to find a response.

The Witch stood up and then as if to remind him of her Magickal superiority her toes lifted off the floor and glided effortlessly towards the mahogany chest of draws where she produced a large glass jar that was filled with a clear liquid.

Turning towards him, her eyes widened as if she had been injected with adrenaline.

"This jar is filled with my tears. Tears I've cried over you. Kept to remind me that one day, I must finally admit to myself that we are finished. It's full, so now is the time to stop all this and set myself free from this love, if this is love?"

Predicting that he would only make matters worse if he spoke, he also sensed that by not speaking would seal his fate, however, it would at least be a quick and decisive death.

Crying loudly now, her heart screamed to be held by him while wanting to cut his throat open. It had been like this for years.

"I fucking hate her and I fucking hate you, and tonight I promise to ruin both your lives but not before I take a baby from your groin to throw in your face. You couldn't leave her because of your children together, well, that is my motivation."

Quickly, she flew towards him.

From a backwards swing, she hit him several times until his face welted and he fell down upon the floor.

With one motion, she smashed the glass jar across the floor, the tears splashing over him, burning as if it was acid. Years of bitterness combined into a single litre stinging his skin.

Glass splintered his skin.

"I HEX YOU!"

PART ONE

Australia 2010. Summer
Peony

Unsure of what was happening, Peony allowed herself to cry. Her symptoms had worsened, unyielding in their path. Confusion crept into her consciousness while she endured the uncertainty alone.

Her husband was working in the Western Australian, a full day's plane travel away. Carl would not be home for another two weeks.

Each day Peony's health deteriorated. At first she tired easily, collapsing into bed each night at 17:00, sleeping until her alarm woke her at 07:00. Spending most of her lunch hour asleep in the front seat of her car, she ignored the pedestrians as they walked past and due to the unnatural tiredness Peony placed their disapproval into the 'don't give a fuck category'.

Several days later, she developed what she thought was thrush. Next, spasms began in her legs and an unexplained strain weakened her back.

Clenching both sides of the toilet bowl as she urinated (what she could only explain as razorblades), she cried for the first time in her adult life. Who could she talk too? She was too proud.

Today, the pain was excruciating.

With a pathetic roll, she fell onto the cold floorboards. On aching hands and knees, she crawled like an infant to the toilet.

Exhausted, she laid on the ceramic tiles only centimetres away from the toilet seat and urinated, screaming as the urine soaked her burning buttocks.

Vomiting from the pain, a wave of embarrassment washed over her. Wishing death over embarrassment, she would rather die on her bathroom floor then let anyone see her like this- 'pissing' herself, like an invalid, and laying in her own vomit.

Eventually, she sat up on the urine soaked floor, the cold ceramic tiles a welcomed sensory diversion for her burning arse. She had discarded her clothing the previous evening; even silk touching her skin had caused her pain.

Grabbing a mirror from her bathroom drawer, she placed it between her legs and was shocked by what she saw, puss covered ulcers as large as five cent coins covering her groin area. The sight of her groin made her vomit again, the contents of her stomach now home among her cleavage.

She was a monster; a hideous, ugly, dirty, and foul monster. It was no wonder she was so unlovable.

Morghana

The evening found itself moderate with a hint of calm. The air was fresh and whispered sweet intoxication. Birds announced their arrival as they flew in from the dark turquoise sea, their wings manipulated the crispness of their freedom. Children played 'hide and seek' amongst the urban shadows, only to be found and harassed by the local teenagers. Tears quickly followed after the arrival of annoyed mothers and harsh warnings, to be quickly replaced with laughter. Once again, their tiny feet owned the asphalt.

Aware of the rain approaching, two women walked briskly down the street.

Crickets systematically took turns chirping. The croaky rhythm amused Morghana a great deal.

This familiar sound indicated that rain was indeed approaching. Rain which after a stinking hot Tasmanian summer seemed only fair, if not predictably routine. Morghana breathed in the sea breeze, filling her entire chest.

Tearing down of federation buildings in the 1960s had transformed a once aesthetically gallant seaport city into a 'beige' town.

Sitting above an old 1920s home in the centre of the city, Morghana sat on her Aunty's unused and crumbling white chimney. Aunty Pagan preferred the heat pump now.

Living her whole life in the diminutive city of Devonport where everyone knew everyone or at least enough to warrant chatter and slander, people often gossiped that Morghana looked more like her Aunty Pagan who also harboured the dark disposition than her own mother Inanna who was remarkably shorter than Morghana, standing at five feet with golden locks and a pale complexion.

Morghana was petite for her age and blended easily into the dark shadows of the roof. Most seventeen year olds hovered above her in stature. Tormented, because she barely reached their shoulder blades, she felt even smaller on the inside due to their bullying.

Inheriting her physically deficient height from her mother, she longed to be tall like her Aunty Pagan.

Long raven coloured hair, olive skin, a smile that lit up her face and extraordinarily dark brown eyes made Morghana exceptionally beautiful.

A large set of breasts that she proudly lifted with a push-up brassiere provoked interest from most men, of any age, and she used this to her advantage often choosing a plunging top over a turtle neck. This she had also learned from observing her Aunty Pagan.

On the right side of her mouth, instead of a dimple, sat a black mole. Often Morghana would run her tongue over it, especially when she was stressed. It had become a bad habit, a tick almost.

Just add olive coloured foundation make-up, black eyeliner, pastel pink eyeshade and red lips and Morghana transformed into a Geisha woman. Her Asian genetics she had inherited from her father. A father she knew little about and cared little to reconnect with.

"Men are sexually weak creatures. They are especially submissive to a Witch's empowerment. You will find men weak and repulsive but one day you find a man who will bewitch *you* and that day you will find utopia inside of your vagina. But I warn you, he will be the wrong man. Your Coven is where real love resides."

The view from her Aunty's roof was spectacular. To the north was Devonport's showground which illuminated Bass Strait. Fantasising for a moment of a voyage that would take her away from this dreary place, Morghana studied the passenger liner as it navigated the mouth of the Mersey River, saluting the modest genitalia of the newly crafted Statue of Poseidon.

She longed to escape, to fly away to anywhere rather than here.

Her long and slender hands were aging quickly, and Morghana feared that her face might age quickly also.

Morghana held her breath, she would be a Witch soon, crooked nosed and wart like? No! But how could she enjoy her Maiden Age with the constant reminder of becoming a Witch? The notion made her heart jump and she tried to focus on the fast moving clouds above her. Behind the clouds the golden waxing moon was foreboding, highlighting the greyness of the sky. The moon looked lonely in the infinity of the sky, she sympathised.

Morghana had no siblings and her father had left when she was six, leaving her mother to raise a heartbroken daughter alone.

Her mother had worked sixty hour weeks to provide an exceptional home but it had not lessened Morghana's loneliness. Would she feel this lonely forever? She knew the answer was probably 'yes'.

There was a heaviness in her chest that she feared had been put there from her previous reincarnation, not that she could remember, not yet.

Regardless of her lonely childhood, being an adolescent was almost intolerable.

The age of thirteen had arrived with sexual desires that Morghana had feared and welcomed, paralleling unusual growth and unwanted knowledge of a world that seemed far more complicated than she had first anticipated.

Morghana lived in a modern world that both desired her while forcing her into submission. She was allowed an opinion only to be told it was not valid.

Finding her whole existence rather tedious, she longed for sleep most of the time. Her mother believed Morghana's excessive sleep pattern was normal adolescent behaviour but Morghana knew it was her way of escaping reality. Sleep was the only thing that stopped the constant chattering in her ears, and licking of her mole. Some nights the voices would reduce her to tears, even playing music on her iPod to drown the unwelcomed voices out did not help. She never confided in her mother about the voices. Her mother preferred ignorance.

Morghana acknowledged that her pessimistic attitude was unwarranted but it was abnormal by anyone's standards to hear voices even if you were a Maiden.

Secrets plagued her. It was easier to say nothing than to ask for an explanation from her mother who always answered with, "You don't need to worry yourself with that yet. All will be revealed at the Witch Awakening."

Morghana turned her head south peering intently at Mount Roland which was almost invisible in the night sky. The rain was fast approaching and the air had become somewhat colder while still radiating freshness and arousal.

Morghana stiffened hoping not to be seen as a small canary yellow car travelled along the street. The car stopped and her Aunty Pagan stepped out.

As a Witch, Pagan could magnetise any man into a lustful sweat while angering any woman with one single smile. Entering a room, she could make it shine without using any Magick at all.

Now, she was home from teaching belly dancing.

Pagan

Pagan was thirty three years of age. In this reincarnation, she was born November 1976 almost one hundred and eighty three years since her last death, which was relatively shorter than the previous death by seventy four years.

Time was quickening. Just less than half a millennium, Pagan had masqueraded as Queen of England's Anne Boleyn where she had lost her head to the sword. In the next reincarnation, she was a French Activist where a new device called a Guillotine removed her head, and now a dance instructor. Safe in her common employment her head sat securely upon her neck.

Life was not exactly as she imagined, again. Nonetheless, life was as good as it could be and it could be much worse. Denying one's inner wisdom seemed a familiar habit. The habit of 'self-denial' had become her most loyal companion.

With every reincarnation, she promptly became a play toy for society to manipulate, regardless of the Magick she possessed. Life's game had changed but the rules had remained the same. Invisible restraints tightening around her neck were harsher than any rope burn or slice of a sword's edge. Life was her enemy not death.

Pagan waved good-bye to her best friend, Amelie. Standing on her nature strip, she watched as Amelie's sports car disappeared around the corner. First gear quickly smashed into fourth gear as Amelie raced up the street. The sound of her wheels screeching around the next corner made her laugh.

Amelie loved her flashy sports car with its shiny canary yellow exterior and its white leather interior. Always enjoying the luxuries in life; thoroughbred horses, dangerously high heel shoes, designer clothes and expensive wine had all come at a price; Amelie lived in a humble unit.

Standing in the kerb, Pagan thought about where she had come from. In the beginning, she had run wild in the forest, drank from the creek, and danced in front of the communal fire. Now, she could not imagine life without electricity and hot water.

Witches and women are critical of each other. Years of sexual oppression and male brute force only encouraged feminine competition. Pagan blamed the innate need for survival manifesting itself into self-deluding rivalry. Women were caught within a downward spiral of implied body image and consumerism. They had forgotten their feminine strength. Even Witches, were cursed by modern life. Magick had become their weakness not their strength.

Her energy had once shone bright purple. Today her magnificence had dulled to a gradient red and orange colour, proof of the contamination.

It was hard to believe that Witches or women had gained any equality at all, perhaps just the bare ability to state the fact without being burnt at the stake. It was better than nothing.

Walking down the driveway, the smell of a Maiden whistled up Pagan's nostrils. Turning, Pagan saw a shadow sitting up on her roof. Pagan felt instantly annoyed, "Morghana, come down!"

Facing the opposite direction, the teenager ignored her. Dissatisfied with her niece's arrogance, she retorted again, "Perhaps, I should send you home to your mum already?"

Pagan walked inside her home through the back door.

Inside, she was greeted by a white and chocolate cookie coloured kitten named Alchemy and her black cat Princess Gobalina, named after a childhood book she had loved. Both familiars were happy to see her.

Alchemy meowed, moving unsubtly towards her food bowl where Princess Gobalina flaunted her overly stated feline energy through Pagan's legs, almost tripping her up.

Pagan picked the black cat up and proceeded to her bedroom where she promptly threw the cat onto the bed. Princess Gobalina rolled up into a restful slumber while the kitten ate the scraps left in the bowl.

Slowly undressing, she threw her tribal belly dancing costume; black garter style pants, purple vest jacket and fringe tassel black skirt into the cane basket which was strategically placed at the entrance of the bedroom.

Her belly dancing class had advanced in such a short period of time. She was relieved that her employment still gave her pleasure.

Standing before her antique seventeenth century mirror, peering unpleasingly at her expanding body, Pagan was blessed with her external appearance; moderately sized breasts now sagged, ornamenting her much enlarged nipples.

"Oh, the joy of breastfeeding," she laughed.

She had breastfeed two gorgeous children with these breasts; Demeter, a human boy and Deity, a born Witch. It was a rare to have a daughter born a Witch and not in Maiden form.

Modernity granted Pagan a week on and week off childcare arrangement with their father John. Fifty/fifty the government proclaimed for tax benefits and child support requirements.

Society now claimed that Pagan was half a mother (if there is such a term) and John twice a father, because unlike other fathers he had his children more often than the status quo.

Aimlessly attempting to find a balance between motherhood and non-motherhood was not easy, particularly now she had a lot of free time. The only comfort Pagan felt was the acknowledgement that her children saw their father much more than most children.

It was not the first time Pagan had brought up children alone, nor the first time, they had been ripped away from her. Nothing it seemed was new to her but modernity had fresh artifices for her to learn. It seemed being a mother was still a bitter-sweet gift, a gift that could easily be taken away from her. Being an Aunty had always been sweeter. It was rewarding without the guilt. It was caring entirely on another level.

Pagan questioned the direction her thoughts were going as she repeated her counsellor's words on 'mindfulness' several times, "You are safe in the moment."

Every emotion seemed to have a scientific explanation now, even though it hardly cured a damn thing. A sufferer of 'anxiety' meant dark thoughts about the future frequently haunted her. The only 'upside' was she was aware of it, but it was not the next twenty years that frightened her but the thoughts of the next reincarnation.

Pagan grabbed one broomstick from the cupboard and smiled. Running her fingers down the smooth Tasmanian oak cane she stopped before she reached the bristles. The eucalypt fibre and reddish brown pallet made her Witch broomstick, uniquely Australian.

She quickly threw on an orange and red Nepal woollen poncho and walked outside into the thickening mist.

Alchemy, the kitten was still too young to fly, "Look after the house."

Princess Gobalina ran after Pagan, jumping onto Pagan's lap as she flew from the back patio.

Throwing a judgemental glace at her sulking niece, Pagan hovered in front of Morghana gesturing for her to follow.

"Get on your broom, Morghana."

After some hesitation, Morghana took to the sky sluggishly behind her Aunty.

Morghana

Broomsticks have an inbuilt Magick that allowed Witches to travel invisibly once mounted. It also means that humans can also ride on their brooms. Only the 'Sensitive Humans' had the ability to sense Witches while they were invisible. Human's called these people 'psychics'.

There seemed to be elusive multifaceted explanation for why Witches existed. None that seemed plausible to Morghana. Prying questions created arguments amongst the Witches and Crones. Her mother only managed a nasty glare in defiance if the subject was mentioned and propaganda seemed rampant among the knowledgeable. Morghana suspected that they knew no more than what she did.

Her private high school education only lasted for three years until she pleaded with her mother to allow her to study at a public school. The private system stifled her creativity. She needed wider parameters.

During her time at the private school, alternative religious beliefs had been scoffed at and only discussed in a peripheral sense. Being labelled a 'troubled child' because of her inquisition for the 'what if', Morghana silenced herself. It was easier than standing out in class. Asking questions obviously meant that she was stupid but it had not even entered any of the teacher's imagination that a woman may have written important religious documentation and if they had, they certainly did not teach it. Morghana hated school and more so, the idiot teachers.

The wind slapped Morghana's face forcing her thoughts back to the ride. She was still metres behind her Aunty Pagan. Knowledge of the roads combined with a reckless personality helped Pagan lead them along the Spreyton Main Road, turning sharply around the corner into the main road towards the country town of Sheffield.

The Rules of Flight, especially when racing were, to travel along the roads. It was too easy to travel straight towards the intended destination. Roundabouts would bring squeals of delight as they circled them several times before exiting. Feet pointed and saluting toes would slow the broomstick down, alternatively Witches could hook their feet together and pull their torso back.

Pagan turned to look back at her niece. Sticking her middle finger up, she yelled, "It's a race you know. Gonna let a Witch beat you, Maiden?"

This unwarranted but predictable behaviour motivated Morghana to bend down closer to her broom. Knowing that Princess Gobalina, the cat was sitting on Aunty Pagan's lap disadvantaged her, she accelerated. Half way to their destination, Morghana sped up overtaking her Aunty at the Nook T-junction, and without realizing, she smiled.

By the time they reached Lower Barrington and the large trees at the School House, Morghana's mood had changed from sultry to adrenaline driven determination.

She began to laugh hysterically as her Aunty sped up beside her. The race was now even.

When they reached the country town of Sheffield, they flew past the local pub at tremendous speed, lifting up the hair of several of the locals who stood in the smoking area. The pub was the only business in town still open.

Bugs contacting their skin stung their chilling faces.

Pagan swerved into Claude Road, yelling at Morghana, "Forget the road and fly up the cliff of Mount Roland once we reach it."

They left the road flying dangerously low to the ground. The paddocks smelt of fresh grass and cow manure. Dodging the electric fences, they cackled each time their shoes touched the wire receiving an electric shock. After dodging cows and flying through numerous sheds, they reached the mountain.

Pagan cackled, "This Morghana! This is what life is all about. Pure adrenaline. It's the closest to alive you will ever feel."

With one dark cloud the rain came.

Amelie

Amelie entered her front door. Throwing her dancing bag on the mahogany chair, she exited her unit to sit down on a green plastic chair that was hidden behind a short grey brick wall that protected her from the wind and nosey neighbours.

Fumbling in the dark, she found her secret spot behind the pot plants. Pulling out a packet of cigarettes and an elephant lighter, she lit one cigarette, inhaling an exaggerated drag. Instant satisfaction removed any cancer guilt.

Amelie smoked without guilt, 'I mean, don't one hundred per cent of non-smokers die?' She laughed to herself in her private alcove.

In fact, Amelie did anything she liked generally. At age thirty five, she looked twenty five. Reasons for this, were attributed to good genes and a healthy lifestyle after the age of thirty, except of course for the smoking habit. It was indeed her only vice in life, that and a glass of chardonnay which Pagan named, 'Bitter Old Ladies' drink.

Being celibate for seven years had been a struggle but she discovered amazing willpower within her self-control. Eventually, her body become accustomed to the solitude, forgetting the selfish need for shallow satisfaction. Plus, memories of disastrous encounters with 'creepy' men still made her cringe and her skin crawl.

Amelie had loved men and on many occasions she had enjoyed lots of men at the same time but eventually she realised that they took more energy than they gave, and quite frankly her vibrator had always been of better use and satisfaction than any man, even the decent ones.

Any weak moments she had on cold winter nights quickly disappeared after a coffee chat with her girlfriends, who for hours analysed their relationships, boring Amelie into a 'desired' coma. If they could only realise that a good book, followed by a beloved vibrator, followed by a cigarette and a good night sleep, would be far more beneficial in the long term than any orgasm a man contributed to. A decent sleep without a 'snoring bed hogging sucker fucker' male was always worth a decent 'kick out time'.

Amelie's main objection extended to the 'Relationship Flip Floppers'. These 'Flip Floppers' were always in need of a companion regardless of the damage they were causing themselves and everyone around them. 'Relationship Flip Floppers' were too stupid to stop and reflect, or too needy to be alone for five minutes. They were definitely too scared to face the harsh reality that relationships were at best only ever satisfactory, one large fucking loop hole.

Her female friendships and chiefly her Coven were far more fulfilling and less controlling than any relationship with a man had been.

Amelie admitted, if only for a second, that she harboured deep seeded resentment and a sticky bile for the male aura, particularly now that she had stepped back from the whole relationship illusion and saw it for what it was a 'soul breaker and a heart crusher' reality and the 'truth be known' without the need for procreation, the female aura would not spend any time on these lower energies.

Looking up into the cloudy night sky, Amelie convinced herself that one more cigarette was warranted under such an alluring night. Even smokers felt the cold, although they somehow become accustomed to smoking outside. Amelia was sure she was more likely to die of pneumonia than cancer.

Placing the butt in the ashtray, she headed to bed, "Sleep at last."

Amelie placed her clothes neatly at the end of her bed and then dived under the dangerously hot doona. She thanked herself for putting the electric blanket on as the chilly nights were keeping her awake.

Reaching under the opulence of pillows she pulled out a vibrator. It had earned its right to share her bed. Purchasing it during a holiday where she was the only single, she soon observed that she was the only one out of her girlfriend's actually reaching climax. Her screams of pleasure echoed down the hall, a mild amusement she will always remember.

Lying down, placing a pillow under her bottom, she tilted her pelvis which acutely positioned her clitoris for easy access. What a 'professional' she had become of knowing her own body in this reincarnation?

In previous reincarnations, her body had experienced pleasure but not from an appliance. She was always excited when she discovered something new about her body that she previously had no knowledge of or had forgotten about.

Grabbing the raspberry lube container she squirted a generous amount over the vibrator before placing it inside of her vagina. There was no need for foreplay as she already worshipped her body. Pressing the small black button she turned it on, finding instant arousal. The rotating, large and rippled body looped clockwise, widely encompassing all of her vagina passage. The 'clit tickler' spun wildly on top of her clitoris, making it swell and redden. Breathing deeply, she cupped her breast and squeezed her nipple. Her flat stomach moved slowly up and down mimicking love making. The doona softly moved over her skin.

The street lights shone through the curtains and heavy rain splashed against the window comforting her. The view across Victoria Parade made her feel safe. Industrialisation was now the chosen scenic view. The enchantment of the forest had been lost amongst the buzz of city life.

She thanked society for its beliefs in delinquent behaviour. Thinking deviant thoughts was hotter and sexier than any normal acceptable sexual behaviour.

In her fantasies, she could have multiple partners, same sex partners, sex with vampires or envision she was being raped by slave traders in Africa and it was ok. Safe within the fantasy meant that she was free to own and explore her sexuality.

A familiar fantasy emerged. She visualised a large circle of women in a castle, while she, the main attraction, was worshipped by several busty dark Witches. This fantasy was enough for Amelie to climax. The deep arousal mixed with animal aggression and internal rage burst through her clitoris. Her torso heaved off the bed, pulsating for a moment she became catatonic.

Collapsing in a satisfied heap on her wet bed, she removed her vibrator placing it back under the pillows, "I'll clean you tomorrow."

Snuggling into her bed it seemed softer now.

Amelie fell asleep only minutes after she had placed her clothes on the bed. There was no 'snoring bed hogging sucker fucker' to keep her awake.

S^ORD

Pagan

They reached the summit of Mount Roland finding a dry place to rest under a protruding rock boulder. Although Mount Roland is primarily a rock structure at the top, it took them several moments to find a resting spot.

It takes half a day of hiking through the conservation area to reach the top of the mountain but on broomstick only a few minutes.

'What a hauntingly beautiful view', Pagan thought.

The three hundred and sixty degree view was guarded by a thick mist and starless night. Cradle Mountain which was to the south of them was only there in memory and the lights of Sheffield were the only beacon that life existed.

When Pagan was younger, she had journeyed to England, stopping at various countries before reaching London and although the places she visited were awe-inspiring, she had always thought Tasmania was the most beautiful place on Earth. Before colonisation it must have been magnificent; untamed and dangerous, like her.

Princess Gobalina vanished into the bush to chase a panicked wallaby.

Cursing herself for bringing the cat, as the wildlife scattered in terror, she settled in.

Pagan reached out gently placing her hand on Morghana's leg, "What are you thinking?"

Looking radiant as the spray from the heavy rain washed over Morghana's face, Pagan wished she had blossomed early rather than waiting almost twenty years before maturing into her facial features.

Morghana shrugged in defiance but after some time responded, "What happens at my Witch Awakening? I'm really excited and really scared. No one will tell me what exactly goes on. Everything is always secret Witch business."

Pagan, who had always been brutally honest with Morghana struggled to respond. Remembering her promise to Inanna, her sister, that she would not discuss the Witch Awakening with her daughter Pagan's lips tightened.

Stroking Morghana's hair Pagan replied, "Morghana, it's a question you need to ask your mother."

Morghana stood up angrily, "She tells me nothing, Aunty Pagan. She tells me that it's a huge waste of time being a Witch and that I, like her, should forget this sickness we are born with."

Pagan pushed through the secrecy to find an explanation that might suppress Morghana's worries, "We may be born with a fresh body but our energies never die. We have laughed, cried, hurt and loved many times. Being a Witch is nothing to be ashamed of. Your mum has her own path to follow and her own reasons for the way she feels."

Lying, Pagan looked down at her feet, "You must learn to forgive your mum. Life is not black and white. Unfortunately, there is a lot of shitty grey as well."

Morghana rolled her eyes and looked off into the mist.

Pagan sighed, "Come on. We better get back before your mum arrives to pick you up."

Princess Gobalina flashed through the bushes, pouncing onto Pagan's lap as they flew into the sky. The rain fell slapping their faces and neck. Autumn had arrived and the darkness of winter was like a giggling distant land.

Inanna

Inanna drove her soggy daughter home. How could her sister be so irresponsible as to allow Morghana to fly in the rain? Was it not enough that she begrudgingly supported their relationship? Was it not enough that she allowed Morghana to spend any time with her immature Aunty? It was more than Pagan deserved? It took all of Inanna's compassion to not ban Pagan from seeing her daughter all together.

Morghana had been pleased to see her mother but not as excited as once she would have been.

Inanna attempted idle chat but Morghana sat silently. The only noise in the car was the sound of Morghana biting her nails, which annoyed Inanna.

Emotionally? Mentally? Where had her daughter gone? Morghana still looked like her little girl but a melancholy had entered her teenage body and her little baby girl, had idled.

She had given Morghana everything a child could want; love, wealth, time, sport, and education. But still, she sat in the car as if the world was upon her shoulders. How was she going to cope after the Witch Awakening when thousands of memories would return and most of them traumatic? She would finally have something to whinge about.

Inanna reached out, patting Morghana's knee searching for any sign of compassion from her only child. Morghana moved her knee away.

'I could strangle you sometimes', Inanna thought.

As they entered the driveway, Morghana removed her seat belt, jumping out of the car before it had completely stopped. This left Inanna, flustered and upset.

Inanna watched as Morghana ran through the heavy rain reaching the front door, opening it and then slamming it shut behind her.

Carrying the suitcases up two sets of stairs to her bedroom, Inanna was now drenched from the pouring rain. Her golden hair lumped together and her fringe unattractively stuck to her forehead.

'Typical Tasmania and its four seasons in one day', Inanna bitched to herself.

Her home was resplendent, containing five large bedrooms with each room individually decorated to suit Inanna's tastes, a gym full of the latest equipment which she used every day when she was home, a study that she shared with her partner Mark, three living areas and a grand parlour kitchen which was her favourite room in the house that overlooked a large deck. The deck harboured views over Coles Beach and Bass Strait- an unpredictable strip of sea that housed the occasional sail boat, the Spirit of Tasmania ferry, visiting whales and ever changing surfing conditions.

Demographically, Devonport had a lower socio-economic class than other places in Australia, but her home would easily fetch well over the seven hundred thousand dollar mark. It was a grand statement of hard work and sacrifice.

Inanna was a financial advisor for several large companies. It meant that she travelled interstate often. In her twenties, she had loved living out of a suitcase but now she yearned to stay in her favourite state.

In this reincarnation, Inanna was determined to be business-minded, leaving emotions for less evolved females. Not that any one seemed to care. All the praise went to Pagan for her bohemian lifestyle. Nothing had changed.

Inanna had worked since she was seventeen. However outside of work she was not sure she had a lifestyle at all, but she felt content and for the first time she felt happy with her life choices.

She had the best in life: travel, expensive wine, a large cuisine of food and in-depth conversations about ideas and concepts with her partner, Mark that she had never heard of before in previous reincarnations. Stimulating conversation was an aphrodisiac for Inanna. The twenty first century was for her the Magick that she needed to feel content. She could retire soon and enjoy her assets.

Inanna found it easy to deny herself a Witch heritage. She had been born a Maiden with golden hair and no amount of hair dye changed it.

It is a Witches descent that they are born with either black or red hair. Originally, Witches only had black hair until the Red Haired Men procreated with the Witches. So now, Inanna used her golden hair to reject her Witch genes all together and call herself, a female. Her life was in limbo but now at least she controlled which way the pendulum swung. She was a human with human needs and human liberties.

Inanna slipped into her silk nightie. The fabric seduced her pale skin. She teased her hair up, and went to look for Mark, who as usual was in his study.

He sensed her enter the room, swinging his chair around he clasped his hands, "Honey," he smiled, "You're home."

She slipped onto his lap and gave him a passionate kiss, then asked, "Did you miss me?"

Mark nodded.

She sensed quickly that he was politely acknowledging her but was desperate to return to his work.

Inanna smiled, but her lips screwed up showing her disappointment, "I better let you get back to your work."

Gesturing for her to hop up from his lap, he replied, "I have a bit to do, don't wait up for me."

He grabbed her hand as she walked away, "You look tired. How about you sleep in the downstairs bedroom tonight so I don't wake you when I'm finished?"

Inanna felt her body flinch. Composing herself, Inanna looked for the emotionally balanced response, "Yes, no worries."

She brought Mark's hand up to her lips, kissing it, "Night."

Mark smiled politely, but was already engrossed in his work.

Inanna stopped half way down the staircase and sat down on the carpeted step. There were three people in three different rooms and all of them desperate to connect but not one of them sure how to make that happen.

CHAPTER 4
Israel
Secret Man

The heat from the desert sand burnt the soles of his hiking boots but he dare not mention his discomfort to the Crone.

Walking for what seemed like half a day, he was fatigued and desperate for another drink of water. How the Crone maintained her strength in the sweltering midday sun astonished him. He estimated that she must have easily been in her seventies but she walked as if she was still robust from youth.

Stumbling over another rock, the Crone secured him by grabbing both of his shoulders until he regained his balance.

In an exhausted whisper, he thanked her.

Initially, he had been suspicious of the Crone, only indulging enough information about his plan that he felt was necessary in her presence. His prejudice towards Israelis created a bigoted wall between him and the Crone that he later regretted and apologised for.

She had patted him on the head and replied, "Hate me for being a Witch if you must seek fault in my existence, it will save us the politics."

After a few months, trust became friendship and friendship became affection.

Losing his mother at a young age, he had struggled to form any kind of a meaningful relationship with any female, finally settling for an isolated existence with few friends and no family.

The last few months spent with the Crone had been the most joyous time of his life. She offered him a bed and three cooked meals a day which he had been grateful for. He had not wanted much from life, just a few snippets of pure happiness and he had found it with the Crone.

The irony was not lost on him, that while he was searching for the Darkness he had found life. He would miss the Crone once he entered the Darkness.

He would meet the Darkness on his own. Solitude was not foreign to him. If anything, it was his dearest friend, a confidante and a lover.

When he first mentioned the Darkness to the Crone, she had hesitated assuming that he was working for the Crone Monarchy. Demanding only the truth from him and feeling satisfied with his reasons, they had spoken about the Darkness for thirty six hours straight while consuming an abundance of 'scotch on ice'.

The Crone's facial expression softened as she spoke of the Darkness, as if she was speaking of a deceased paramour who could never be replaced by another. Heightened cheekbones, twinkling eyes and breasts engaged, her feet had swung as if she was a child sitting on a high chair. Love consumed her. Love for the Darkness. A Darkness that he had willingly sought out.

Did he really know what he was searching for? He doubted it, but there was not another option.

Hiking for another kilometer, he tripped over his own feet once again.

Patting him on the back, the Crone encouraged him to continue, "Only a few more minutes and we are there."

Her words comforted him and he found a surplus of vitality that helped him to move forward.

Placing a hessian bag over his head and securing it with a rope tied around his neck, the Crone had reassured him that he would come to no danger on their long track into the desert. He had trusted her completely. It had not taken long to adjust to the blindness and for his ears to increase in their value.

Finally, the Crone stopped walking.

Placing her palm on his chest, she secured his standing position, "We are here."

Untying the rope, it fell from his neck and onto the ground.

The Crone carefully removed the hessian bag, "It will take several minutes for your eyes to adjust to the sun."

Gasping for air, he felt intoxicated.

Exhausted, his legs collapsed underneath him and his middle-aged body thumped onto the hard desert sand which instantly burned his legs and bottom.

Frantically, he reached out his hand begging for water.

The Crone placed a warm water bottle into his hand and helped him to drink from it.

His bleeding chaffed lips stained the warm water but he continued to gulp the liquid down until he threw it back up.

Struggling to open his eyes, the Crone poured some water over them.

Massaging them gently, his eyes opened but the glare from the sun stung them. He quickly closed them again.

"I will gather sticks to make you a fire for I cannot predict when the Darkness will come for you, so we must prepare for a long cold night."

Throwing a blanket onto the sand, she helped him to lie down. Flicking a second blanket on top of him, she tucked him in snuggly. Kissing him on the forehead, she whispered, "Rest for now. You will need your strength for when, or if, the Darkness comes."

Within seconds, he was asleep. His face exposed under the midday sun did not stop the depths of his dreams.

Waking two hours later, he was drenched in his own sweat and shaking from exposure. A tarp made from a blanket and four firm sticks sheltered him from the harshness of the sun. A crescent Darkmoon hovered above the sun. Both sun and moon nestled in between the crest of two barren mountains. One mountain slightly shorter than its twin demanded the same respect.

He felt overwhelmed by their immense feminine splendour. A crevice parted the two mountains like a virgin with her legs spread and in its ripeness a hidden aperture sparkled in the sunlight.

Finally opening his eyes, he sat up, the blurriness of vision did not defer his sense of accomplishment. Finally, after months of research and abandoning his mundane life, he sat in front of the portal. On the other side of the portal the Darkness loitered. The untrained eye would not notice the slight quivering of the portal. Comparable to heat evaporating the portal's circumference spanned approximately ten metres wide and five metres high. The blue sky highlighted the mysticism of the landscape and he was not surprised that the Darkness chose a sterile landscape for its doorway.

It had been a long time since the Crone had visited these mountain ranges. The portal held a sense of longing for her that she had for many years coped with but today the loneliness saluted her like an old friend.

"How can I ever repay you?" He asked.

Overcome with ecstasy, his physical body collapsed again. Sobbing into the blanket, he released a lifetime of pain.

Empathetically, the Crone sat beside him patiently waiting for him to compose himself again. It took another ten minutes for him to dry his swollen and squinting eyes.

While the sun disappeared over the mountains, she lit the fire, and prepared his last meal. Sprinkling some Magick powder over the bundle of sticks, it ignited. Throwing a small pot onto the fire, she scooped the contents of a previously cooked ptitim dish mixed with fried onions, diced tomatoes and tomato paste into it and stirred.

Eating two bowls of the pasta dish, he watched the sun disappearing over the mountains. Hopefully, it would be the last sunset he would ever watch.

Looking at the Crone and the way the sunset's pink haze washed over her elderly face, he noticed a younger woman hidden under the salt and pepper coloured hair and wrinkles. He saw the Maiden she had once been.

"Will you be leaving me soon?"

The Crone nodded.

Troubled, she placed her palm on his cheek, "You have become my son. It saddens me that I lose you tonight when I have just found you."

Bending in, she kissed his chaffed lips and pulled back. Only inches from his face, she asked him a favour.

"Yes anything," he responded.

Reaching into the bag, she pulled out an envelope. The name Nealon was written on the front in large plain print. Handing him the envelope, he noticed that her hand shook, "Please find him and give him this, and then I will be forever in your debt. You must use my original name Hecate, as he knows me by no other."

Sliding the envelope into his trouser pocket, he agreed.

The Crone stood up, "It is time for me to leave now."

"It's dark. You must not travel alone."

She laughed, "I will not be walking home alone."

Opening her right palm, a glowing orb shot from her palm and into the evening sky and within moments a Northern bald Ibis with its long curved red bill and black feathers appeared in the night sky. Swooping down to greet them it then elegantly flew higher into the night sky.

"It will guide me home."

Another glowing orb released from her palm, landing on the ground. Rolling along the cold sand, the orb grew into a large white Canaan dog. The bitch surveyed her new surroundings. Excited to see the Crone, her tail lifted and she bounced over to them.

"And Lily, will keep me company."

Strapping the large bag that she had travelled with onto Lily, she pulled out a smaller bag and handed it to him, "The potion is inside. When you are ready, drink the potion and wait. The Darkness will come for you when it's ready."

Hugging him tightly, the Crone lingered in their embrace. It would be the last time she ever saw him and their parting ached within her heavy heart.

As she walked off into the distance, he searched for something to say to the Crone but there were no words worthy of their goodbye. A wagging white tail soon disappeared into the blackness.

Adding more sticks to the fire, he bundled the blankets together and sat on them. Staring into the rippled portal, he wondered how it had survived for years and never been discovered by humans.

"Humans see what they want to see. When they are ready, they will see what must be seen but until then they will live in ignorance," the Crone had wisely stated.

He missed the safety of her presence already.

Opening the bag, he pulled out the bottle. A cork lid secured the potion inside- a potion made from the blood of thirteen Ancient Witches. It was illegal for a Coven of thirteen Witches to perform Coven Magick but by using the blood of thirteen Witches the Crone performed the spell alone.

"There is always a way. You just need to learn how to rort the system," she had cackled.

A spell taken from an old book that the Crone referred to as the 'Ancient Doctrine' had been used several nights before under an ancient Protection spell.

Witches and the Darkness had known of the other for all eternity it appeared.

Yanking on the cork, it popped off easily. Smelling the potion, he dry-retched and quickly placed the cork back into the bottle. Fearful, he might vomit the potion once he drank it, he suddenly wished the Crone had stayed with him.

The Crone had warned him that entry into the portal would be painful and that he must be certain that this was the correct and chosen path for him, free of ego and revenge, as there would be no turning back once the potion was drunk and no place for sensitivity once within the portal.

Was he ready? He had travelled too far now to turn back, plus he had nothing to turn back to and no-one who would miss him, except the Crone. His only option was to drink the potion and accept his fate. Letting go with complete trust that his fate belonged in another's control was going to be his greatest achievement.

With a rush of adrenaline, he popped the cork lid off again, sculling the entire contents of the bottle. Instantly tasting blood, he fought the urge to vomit. Ignoring his gag reflex, he managed to keep the potion down for several seconds until he felt his stomach twist.

"Fuck! Fuck! Fuck!"

In a desperate attempt to keep the potion down, he jumped from his sitting position and galloped around the desert as if somehow he could trick his body into ignoring the sick feeling. It worked and after a few minutes the taste of blood vanished from his mouth.

Walking towards the portal, he wondered how long he would have to wait until they came for him.

Reaching out his hand, he touched the ripple. It hummed. Placing the other hand on the portal, it hummed even louder. A wave of coldness vibrated through him. Where did the portal go? Was it a parallel world or another time?

Sitting back down beside the fire, he wondered if the Crone had lied to him about the potion. Except for the initial taste, he felt no difference in his mental or physical state. No! The Crone would not have lied to him. After months of friendship how could he doubt her?

Exhausting all of the gathered sticks the fire soon dimmed and the seduction of sleep seduced him. He closed his eyes for a few moments. Thoughts drifted back to his childhood.

He had started his life living with strangers who called themselves family. Had God wanted him to feel abandoned or was life simply abandonment from God? Had the Darkness witnessed God's betrayal and hoped to recruit? Regardless of the unanswered questions he had always been drawn to the Darkness, as the light always dimmed as he approached it.

Falling into a shallow sleep, he did not see the Darkness slither through the portal. Hunched over and smelling of a pig sty, the naked three legged Old Hag swiftly approached his sleeping body. The thumping of her three muscly feet on the desert sand did not wake him. Bending over his sleeping body, the Old Hag smelt him. Clumps of her brittle grey hair fell over his face, tickling his nose.

Still, he slept.

Drool dripped onto his cheek. Wiping the wetness from his cheek, he opened his eyes. Frozen with fear his eyes bulged. He screamed but no sound left his lips.

Only inches away from him a face, so vile that only in horror movies had he seen it's equal, merciless white eyes with no pupils and rotting flesh hung like tattered tongues underneath each exposed cheekbone. Her grimace revealed toothless black gums and a long slug like tongue that curled out as she laughed.

Unable to move, he surrendered to the Darkness. It had come to him in the form of an Old Hag, as he suspected. The Crone had told him of its guises, preparing for such an image but still his fear controlled him.

Reaching her long crooked fingers out she dug her sharp nails into the side of his neck and slowly sliced his neck open.

Blood oozed from the deep wound and just as she dug her hand into his throat to rip out his oesophagus, he smiled. He had finally found a home.

England
Aggie

Aggie felt the strength of the shockwave in the early morning, waking her from a tormented sleep. Had she dreamed up the vibration? Her intuition said 'no'.

Fumbling out from underneath four layers of blankets, she rested her aching feet into a soft pair of slippers. Hastily grabbing her dressing gown that hung over the bedroom door, she exited the bedroom.

The sunrise helped her find her way while her cataracts disabled her.

"Bloody useless eyes!"

Walking cautiously down the hall, she entered the kitchen. Fetching an already soiled mug left on the sink from the previous evening, she placed two heaped teaspoons full of instant coffee into it, three sugars and milk, and then sat the mug on the counter as she turned the kettle on and waited for it to boil.

It had been undeniably an illegal Ancient spell but who would be stupid enough to perform it? There were the usual suspects and all of them stupid but what if it had been someone or something else?

Aggie sighed, "I'm too old for this shit!"

The kettle whistled.

Placing her index finger into the mug, Aggie poured the boiling water until the heat touched her skin. Putting the kettle down, Aggie hobbled over to a dining table that only accommodated one person. She found no comfort in the chair.

Irritated, she ignored the coffee and stood up. Her intentions were to use the scrying bowl for possible answers. The scrying bowl sat on the top shelf in the kitchen. Unable to see the scrying bowl amongst the clutter of the pots and pans that surrounded it, Aggie flicked her wrists and the bowl flew off the shelf and into her hands. It was the only Magick she had mastered since gaining extra powers. Most of her Magick had to be performed with the aid of a wand. Her ego knew it was merely a 'party trick'.

Filling the scrying bowl up with water, she carefully carried it over to the dining table. Some of the water splashed over her fingers. She cursed her eyes again.

The morning sun was now welcoming the day, brightening up the room through the kitchen window.

Placing her brittle fingernail into the warm water, she swirled it in a clockwise direction.

Aggie stared eagerly into the water as the water gushed around the clear crystal bowl until the water stilled.

Scrying was an Ancient technique once used in rivers, ponds, lakes and sometimes in a still moonlit ocean. It was not used to see the future as the future is not predestined but it was an excellent tool for seeing the past.

Eyes darting across the water her patience wavered. Stirring the water again, she waited.

"Bollocks, the spell is protected!"

That limited the perpetrators, "What are the Ancient Witches up too?"

Aggie stared deeper into the water hoping an image would appear but there was nothing but dark fog.

"Fuck! You useless bastard eyes," she screamed, smashing the scrying bowl across the kitchen floor.

Several hours later after copious emails, text messages and phone calls, the Crone Monarchy unanimously decided on an emergency meeting. Waiting until sunset before they entered the congested streets of London, some scurried into taxis while others opted for a vigorous broomstick ride, Aggie decided to walk.

It had felt like forbidden Magick, and it annoyed Aggie that they had not even tried to conceal it.

"Arrogant, Ancient arseholes!"

A Witches Coven would have been necessary to perform the spell. Thirteen Ancient Witches working together. The use of Ancient Magick was a major offence and would result in the death penalty but still they have performed it.

"How dare they defy my supremacy?"

The Modern Witch Doctrine had been written personally by Aggie and signed by the Crone Monarchy in the late 1970s. Proud of her accomplishments, she had printed a copy of the Modern Witch Doctrine and then posted it to every Witch in the world. It had amused her that she had used British Post instead of Magick. It had been a wonderful waste of tax payer's money.

The Ancient Witch Doctrine had been hidden in defiance to Aggie's ruling. Had the Ancient Witch Doctrine re-emerged? Regardless, Aggie was determined to destroy it and the thirteen Witches or Crones using it.

Renaming her position from 'The Highest Priestess' to the 'Supreme Femineity' she intended to remain so, until her death. She had been born to rule and ruled she had.

Sensing all irony as she strolled past the Apollo Victorian Theatre that hosted the musical 'Wicked', Aggie cackled. If only all humans knew that real Witches walked among them. What envy it would inspire.

Curious amongst other things, Aggie had participated in a Wiccan ritual one summer evening. Displaying many similarities to true Witchcraft, Aggie had suddenly felt a burning desire to tie the Wiccans to a tree and set them alight. Only for the sake of the men and women who had welcomed her with large smiles and tight embraces, she fled instead, evading the potential massacre. It was a rare event if she showed any compassion particularly for the weak.

"Wannabes Witches," Aggie snarled, spitting on the sidewalk.

She detested human neo-pagan groups and their lust for nature and commune with Witches, but most of all she hated men who practise Witchcraft. What was the world coming to when male energies rudely invited themselves to walk amongst female superiority. Neo-liberalism was the ruination of old fashion sensibilities.

Coughing until phlegm coated her throat, Aggie spat the green snot onto the path.

After tripping up several times and running into pedestrians, Aggie regretted her decision to walk. Stubborn, she focused on each step making sure she was heading in the right direction.

She was relieved that she knew the streets of London so well, the benefits of living three reincarnations in the one city. Watching the city burn in 1666 and rebuilt had been another advantage.

Emergency Monarchical meetings were a rarity. Aggie felt comfortable in her hierarchal supremacy, enjoying the lack of competition within her leadership and her natural ability to lead all Maidens, Witches and Crones, regardless of their lineage, however, today for the first time she was a little worried. Worried because it smelt of the Darkness and Witches combined.

Aggie's most recent childhood had been flamboyant, full of colour and flavor until her early teenage years. She had lived with her father within a naturalistic lifestyle and she had loved it. He had been the only man she had ever truly worshipped.

Her Witch mother had abandoned her at birth.

The Green People had accepted her as one of them. It had been a humble upbringing but Aggie knew that she was destined for more than a plebe's reputation. After her Witch Awakening, Aggie with a keen eye for weakness in others and a stroke of luck, networked and manipulated her way up into the Witch Hierarchy, easily eradicating all her opposition. She had been necessarily cruel.

Eventually for the first time in Witch herstory (history), Aggie had used meritocracy to gain absolute power, a power that she had become accustomed to, and would kill again to keep.

Her childhood upbringing overshadowed her perception occasionally; she opted to reside in a small London loft that overlooked the Thames River rather than a large mansion home she had been offered. Struggling, maintained her unhealthy need to conquer. It was pivotal that she remembered where she had come from and how hard she fought for her position in life.

An ageing body accompanied by a very cold London winter did not help the stagnation of movement and Aggie knew that her body would suffer for days because of it but her desire to find the Ancient Witches who had cast the spell kept her circulation flowing.

Australia
Fay Ce'Line

Welcoming defeat, Oscar waited until Fay Ce'Line fell into a deeper sleep before unwrapping his arms from around her bony body. Stretching his hand out into the darkness of the room, he swirled his hand around in a thick sticky substance that did not exist.

Facing his wife, he listened to the shallow snoring which sounded more like a high pitch wheeze than a throaty grumble.

Hovering his hand only an inch from her skin, he enjoyed the pulse of electricity they shared. Contouring her face, he scooped down her neck finally resting his palm on her chest. Ironically, the erratic heartbeat soothed his concerns.

At age forty, Fay Ce'Line looked as delicious as she did when he had first met her in math class twenty seven years ago. Sitting alone at the pentagon shaped veneer school desk, she had looked older than the other girls in grade seven: Red hair that had been bleached with supermarket dye and a complexion that radiated good health, she had a confidence that had intimated and excited him.

Lost in breath, he imagined kissing her pouty lips, running his hand over her breast and slowly placing his finger inside her untouched vagina.

He experienced his first erection in public that day. His cheeks had blushed from embarrassment, and as if she had sensed what he was feeling she had turned to him and smiled.

Stealing his heart that winter on the bank of the Mersey River, sheltered by the old Latrobe train bridge, they had bluffed their way through the act of sexual intimacy. Unsure of what he was doing, he had wiggled and moaned on top of her until he ejaculated. To his mortification, Fay Ce'Line had not even taken her knickers off and it was not until after they married, aged eighteen, that he had placed his penis inside of her.

Anything less committed than marriage would have been a tragedy. Fay Ce'Line had to be his wife and lucky for him, she had agreed.

He remained faithful to her even when their marriage experienced difficult times. Periods of personal growth had left the other partner isolated, behind and floundering for any hope of reconciliation however they had always found each other again, even if they had changed a little. Symbolic of the seasons, their love would reap its rewards due to a healthy harvest of intent.

He was happily bewitched. 'Witches tend to do that- Bewitch'.

Fay Ce'Line's honesty had served them well over the years. Taking the news surprisingly well, he openly accepted her Witchcraft, and to be honest, he had been blessed with an alternative lifestyle that suited his cultist fetish.

It had been a sweltering summer's evening when she had confided in him that she was a Witch. Thinking that she has been joking, he had asked if he could ride on her broomstick, when she returned several minutes later flying on a Witch's broomstick his face had paled and he asked politely for a glass of water.

She had been a Maiden then. At age eighteen, she had travelled with her mother to a secure destination where she celebrated her Witch Awakening. Fay Ce'Line had been sworn to secrecy about the ritual and Oscar had never questioned her. He had worried that once she was Awakened that she might not love him anymore, but she had returned committed and lustful.

He had never asked for details and she had never offered any.

"Some things are best left unsaid," she said, and he had agreed.

How quickly time passed. It seemed the more you love life the faster it appears to go.

Oscar knew that his time with Fay Ce'Line in bed was limited. It was now 06:00 and the twins Kyra and Mika would most likely come running into the bedroom at any moment creating enthusiastic chaos.

Snuggling, the warmth of the blanket and Fay Ce'Line's body enticed him.

Starting to doze, Fay Ce'Line whimpered in her sleep waking him up again.

Troubled from the effects of a previous illness, her sleeping patterns had suffered and consequently, he had also suffered. Watching the person you love in pain would haunt him for the rest of his life.

A mysterious pain woke her for a moment. Placing her palm flatly over her stomach, she drifted back off to sleep.

She dreamed!

It was a sunny day. A day you remember because it seduces you into a warm corruption. Her shoulders dropped several inches to accommodate for a lighter consciousness.

Two small children, Kira and Mika clung to their father, one on each hip. Both anxious as the water quickly engulfs their legs. The water tickled their waist.

Clapping with delight, Fay Ce'Line retired to the sun lounge. A floppy hat, mild sunscreen applied, and a newspaper to read. Splashing water occasionally sprinkled her dry legs, reminding her that she sat in front of a large watering hole.

Oscar calls out to her. Eagerly, she waves back. Her love for him is undeniable.

The darkness of the fresh water swallows their lower limbs. Their closest playmate, the eucalyptus trees draw shadows over their torsos.

A distant splash alerts her that something large is also swimming in the watering hole.

Standing up, she places the newspaper on the ground.

Moving closer to the water, she ignores her bleeding foot that she just cut on the sharp rocks.

She hollers out to them to come back to the bank.

More splashes!

Eyes adjusted, she spots a crocodile swimming towards her family. A second glance reveals that countless crocodiles encompassed the water hole. Hundreds of large shadows swimming directly towards Oscar and her daughters.

Screaming alerted them but it was too late.

Dragged quickly under the murky water, her whole world is torn from her.

The water hole bubbled as the crocodiles fight for their supper.

With one large snore, Fay Ce'Line forced her eyes open. Relieved that she had been dreaming, she pulled Oscar closer to her.

He kissed her on her sweaty forehead, "Good morning, beautiful."

Clutching at his short blond hair, she kissed him back. Pleasantly surprised that the twins were not terrorising their bedroom, she kissed him again.

Concerned for Fay Ce'Line's exhaustion, he asked, "Are you going to the shop today?"

Fay Ce'Line nodded several times while closing her eyes, "Yeah, a bit later on."

Abruptly, Oscar sat up. Bending over, he blew a raspberry on her stomach.

Laughing, she wiggled away from him, "Stop it, Oscar, seriously you are such a child."

"Sleep for a bit longer, Fay Ce'Line. I'll make the twins their breakfast and get them dressed."

His words were unheard as Fay Ce'Line drifted back off to sleep.

Managing to keep the twins occupied for an hour before they escaped into their mother's bedroom to use her bed as a trampoline, he followed them in with eggs on toast with a touch of mustard- just how Fay Ce'Line liked it.

Oscar stood at the bedroom entrance. An overwhelming sense of foreboding tormented him, like tar poured over his skin, the burn of the past remained in the present. He had almost lost Fay Ce'Line twelve months ago to an illness that had affected them all. The health care professional had told them it would come back. The thought made him shiver.

Hensley

Hensley's nightmares were increasing in intensity and although she tried to stay awake during the night by drinking numerous mugs of coffee or playing loud music or walking on the treadmill at 02:00, sleep often found her in the early hours of the morning.

Hensley had just started her final year at college, her last year before attending university, and already her scores had fallen dramatically from the previous year.

For most of her life she had wanted to be a veterinarian and therefore her college scores were important. Frankly, she had to do exceptionally well to gain entry into her chosen course at university. Warranted, she already had four pre-tertiary subjects from year eleven and all her marks had been within the top percentage of the national average but Hensley was a 'high achiever' and she was striving for perfection. The lack of sleep was an academic obstacle not her intelligence and she was determined to overcome any hindrance she encountered on her chosen path.

After breakfast, she packed her lunch into her blue corduroy slouch bag and walked out to the car. A larger than average crow sat on the Hills Hoist clothes line. Its claws tightly wrapped around the wire watched her as she unlocked the car. Suddenly, as if scared by an invisible entity the crow flew away, leaving her with memories as to why the Hills Hoist was severally tilted.

Comparable to a flying saucer in appearance and accompanied by rust, it looked as if it could snap off in a gentle breeze.

As a child, Hensley had hung from it while her mother, Ruby swung her around until she fell off. When she was taller, it was her own feet that launched her into a squealing fiesta of joy. Her mother had become redundant but still enjoyed her daughter's happiness from the warmth of the kitchen window. Cup of tea in hand, Ruby wished that her daughter did not have to grow up.

Years later, Ruby still wished Hensley did not have to grow up.

Hensley loved driving to college even if it was in a sun-bleached 1980s daisy yellow coloured Datsun sedan that smelt like formaldehyde and had leather seats that had torn away enough to allow the springs to poke her in the back.

Working at a Take-Out shop since the age of fourteen ensured that she had the money saved to buy a car at age sixteen. Passing her driving test a few days after her seventeenth birthday, she had driven straight to her best-friend Morghana's house. They had driven around Devonport for three hours before embarking on the MacDonald's drive-through. Hensley had hit the kerb, encouraging a bunch of youths to belittle her driving skills, but they had not rocked her confidence. Unlike them, she had a car and a car meant freedom.

In one week, she would be celebrating her eighteenth birthday and she could then drive the car anywhere she wanted to go. Book it on the passenger liner and drive up the coast of the Australian mainland. She would be unstoppable and she would take Morghana with her. They would party all summer, starting in Melbourne and then onto Sydney until they reached the Gold Coast where they would party some more.

It was also only one week to her Witch Awakening. Attempting to study for it was extremely difficult. Guarded by secrets not a Witch spoke of it in detail. Not a book could be found on the Witch Passage. The Witch Awakening was a chance for her to 'wing' something for once in her life. She accepted the challenge, although she preferred being fully prepared for all events in her life.

Arriving at college, Hensley parked the car in the lower carpark and headed straight to class. Ignoring the other students who lingered in the hallway, Hensley pushed past them. School was for studying not socialising.

The college was an ugly school. The external building with its large cement walls quarrelled with the bushy reserve that surrounded it.

The internal building was a labyrinth of circular corridors that lapped large sterile classrooms. It was a mammoth achievement to find the entrance into the building and an even greater relief to find an exit.

After navigating the labyrinth to her classroom, she then unpacked her school books from her bag placing them neatly on the school desk. Advanced Maths was the only class that she shared with Morghana, although good at math, Morghana tended to pay more attention to the scenery outside of the classroom than anything written on the board.

Sitting together, Hensley helped Morghana with the work load, mainly doing the sums and Morghana copying the answer. It was a small gesture of love and one that she found pleasure in. Morghana was always grateful for the help.

Morghana benefitted her life in other ways: loyalty, honesty and laughter.

After losing her dad several years prior, Hensley appreciated the small things and she appreciated their friendship the most.

Hensley waved at Morghana as she slinked through the door and although they always sat together, Morghana chose to sit in the back row today where she could daydream without the threat of being curtailed.

Amelie

Bored with Tasmania and its cold weather and expansion of 'Bogan' residence, Amelie drove to work along the Devonport's Victoria Parade, day-dreaming of an overseas holiday, perhaps to Japan, actually anywhere that was not Tasmania.

She wished she could turn back the clock to when community meant something. When it was safe to walk the streets and not be subjected to bad language or foul smelling armpits.

"It doesn't cost much to buy soap."

Devonport's community had changed for the worse. It was tolerable in the eighties, decaying in the nineties and now in the year of two thousand and ten it was as if the zombie apocalypse had happened without anyone even realising. A vacuum of depression, numbing all who encountered the low frequency hum and *everyone* was angry. Angry from boredom rather than from indignation.

At least in previous reincarnations, Amelie had lived with such privileges that her path was mostly dictated by her own will, although stifled by Witch lore.

"A holiday somewhere warm, a few vineyards and art trails or even a Buddhist retreat would help restore my passion for life surely?"

The Bass Highway was particularly busy at 08.00.

Needing motivation, she turned the radio on as she drove under the Airport Overpass. Bypassing the commercial channel's generic songs and their generic singers, she switched the radio off choosing to whistle instead.

Ten minutes later, she pulled into the main street of Latrobe parking directly outside her work. Amelie loved 'Free Parking'.

The footpath was bustling with pedestrians.

Amelie laughed as a child over-estimated his aim, kicking the rock across the street almost contacting with the immaculate exterior of a sedan parked on the other side. An elderly man scuffling along the footpath with a newspaper under one arm and a short thick lead that restrained a resistant Rottweiler in the other hand, mumbled something about, "The kids of today," which also amused Amelie.

'Silly old man, you have no idea', she scoffed.

Recently changing employment had relieved some of the monotony in Amelie's life but unfortunately it had not been enough to remove the underlying discontentment. A humble life was nothing but disappointing. Unsure exactly why she felt a dissonance in her life, she was sure the Goddesses would intervene at some stage causing her the most amount of grief possible. They always did. Likened to a barbaric game of chess the Goddesses enjoyed causing as much havoc as they could.

'I suppose like me and most of this town, they're fucking bored', she thought.

A belief that the Goddesses manipulated Witches for their own entertainment, infuriated Amelie.

"Free will? Bullshit! Moles."

Mainly out of habit Amelie looked up towards the sky, "Moles!"

Of course the Goddesses are not only in the sky, they encompassed all of nature, renting the Earth with God but they were bad tenants and needed eviction, as did humans.

Amelie's disdain for the Goddesses would have to wait as she had more mundane tasks ahead of her today that required her attention.

It had taken Amelie five years to make the decision to leave her old job and one economic downturn in infrastructure to ensure her wishes came true. Would she have left the safety of the job she hated for the risk of another? The answer was 'no!' She would rather have been miserable for the sake of a reliable income. The Goddesses however disagreed, forcing her into a move she had wished for but was too scared to make- she had been retrenched.

Debt free was indeed an accomplishment for a single Witch in 2010, especially for a Witch who had always enjoyed the comfort of wealth and prestige that had been given to her rather than having to work for it in the past. Owning her car and unit had reduced the stress but it had taken five hungry months until she secured new employment. She now worked for a florist. The boss was an elderly lady who spent more time away from the shop than there and consequently left Amelie to her own devices, which she enjoyed.

It was an easy job that required some experimentation and artistic ability which until recently Amelie did not realise she possessed. She had always left the creativity to her sister Roberta whose flare for the dramatic had always left Amelie in awe.

Amelie had always preferred practical endeavours, so it had come as quite a shock that she delighted in her current employment's creativity.

All Witches, Ancient and Non-Ancients are born with the ability to dance; a slower rhythmic movement than human dancing, that when performed in a

Coven created a healing energy, enhancing the feminine while connecting all Witches, present or not, on a higher frequency.

Amelie believed Ancient Witches were more mesmerising than any Non-Ancient Witch as their frequency far surpassed their lesser counterparts.

"Use Lavender, oil or cream or just snap some directly off the plant. Plait it in your hair, or whatever. Lavender also helps to raise frequency," Fay Ce'Line would boast at each dance gathering while tying lavender into their hair.

Witches are also born with a unique personal ability. Sometimes the abilities overlapped especially with blood relations. Since the banning of Ancient Magick only thirty years earlier, most natural abilities had become dormant, locked inside of the Ancient Witch's hand and stomach. Sometimes, Amelie could feel a burning sensation in the middle of her palm. It took all her willpower not to use her palms for Magick.

Hopefully, in the next reincarnation, Ancient Witches would rule again, and she personally would set on fire every Non-Ancient Witch herself.

Aggie, the Supreme Femininity had been cruel in the years following the beginning of her reign, a Non-Ancient Witch suddenly with immense power, enjoyed ordering her faithful followers to cut the hands off any resilient Ancient who refused to yield to her authority. Over four hundred Ancient Witches bled out before the rest silenced. Their anger was caught in the back of their throats. The saying 'use it or lose it' became 'use it and lose it'. Needless to say, hand jewellery sales decreased that year.

Ancient Witches released their Magick through their palms; just add intent and their palms light up like a comet, unlike the Non-Ancient Witches who required a wand as a channel. Pure Ancient Magick, radiated beauty and strength. A wand, paled in comparison.

Amelie's special gift of producing fire from her palms was prohibited; even to light a fire on the coldest of nights only added to her blackened sense of humour.

Teasing Amelie, Pagan often stated that Amelie's addiction to cigarettes was a subconscious reaction to the fire ban.

"Seriously Amelie, you need to have a sense of humour about this," Pagan would retort, which was ironic coming from the 'forever morbid' Pagan.

Pagan's heightened fascination in the subject of psychology, was driving everyone crazy, especially Amelie who preferred when her friend was reactive, living on impulse rather than 'over thinking' every thought she had. It was the result of her degradation of power and too much time to think.

Herstory was the best predictor of the future, however since 1976, everything had changed, leaving Amelie unsure of what lay ahead for all Witches, especially since the Ancient Witches had been demoted. Except for a few rituals and impotent potions, Witchcraft was now non-existent.

Aggie ruled by suppressing all Witches, Ancients and Non-Ancients into a Witchcraft coma. The status of Witch was a useless title and there was nothing they could do about it, at least not in this reincarnation.

After setting the shop up, Amelie thought she would sneak a cigarette in before she unlocked the front door. Heading to the back door a tap at the window made her jump.

To Amelie's amazement stood a very tall man enveloping the shop's window front. He tapped again, summoning her to unlock the door. This annoyed, Amelie.

Grabbing the keys from the counter, she fumbled with them at the front door, eventually unlocking it and swinging the door open in one large motion. Her sweaty palms expressed her frustration and her flushed face made it obvious that she was a little overwhelmed by his pre-shop hour's intrusion.

Amelie snapped, "It's not nine o'clock yet."

Upset by her harsh tone, he hesitated at the door. Rubbing his forehead, he waited for her to direct his next action.

Amelie quickly apologised for her abruptness. Being confrontational came easy to her but being 'commonly' rude did not, sort of.

"I'm sorry to rush you. It's just that I have a lot to fit into my schedule today."

His southern English accent seemed sincere.

Suddenly excited, she placed her hand on his forearm, "Where about in England are you from?"

Uneasy with her familiarity, he unsubtly looked at her hand resting on his forearm, and replied, "Brighton."

Blushing, she removed her hand away from his forearm. Why had she blushed? Why had she touched a stranger so inappropriately? She blushed again. It was obviously premature men-a-pause, she decided.

Amelie partitioned herself safely behind the shop counter, rearranging the pens, stapler, lip gloss, scissors and random ribbon that sat on top, anything not to look at him directly.

Amelie inhaled, followed by a long exhale and then entered work mode, "How can I help you today?"

Retail was new to her, audited and fake.

He had a subtle confidence and his aura illuminated quite a distance from his physical body. His aura colour was a hue of red; burnt orange, maroon and scarlet. This individual was very powerful, sexual, sensual and fiery, and perhaps, and most likely, an aggressive alpha male.

Feeling dizzy, Amelie reached for the water bottle. Sculling the water in front of him, she instantly felt refreshed.

Choosing his words wisely, he instructed Amelie specifically on the type of flowers he wanted; an even amount of daisy and daffodils with six yellow roses, complimented with green foliage, wrapped in a butterfly printed paper, with yellow and white ribbons. His request was unusual but he seemed adamant that they were perfect once she had finished.

Amelie flicked through the selection of gift cards until she found a pack of recycled paper. Eagerly showing him the small butterfly print on the recycled paper, she sensed he was pleased with her recommendation.

Smiling for the first time, Amelie noticed his artificially whitened teeth. He must have had braces as a teenager as his teeth were *too* straight and therefore he had to have been born into wealth, obviously? Perhaps, she needed to charge him more for his humble selection of flowers.

Grabbing a gold ink pen, she asked him what he would like written as the message. Happy to be back in control again and eager to have a cigarette, she tapped the pen on the counter. 'Hurry up for fuck's sake', she thought.

Noticing that he was blushing, Amelie suddenly became interested in why such a confident man was struggling to write something intimate, after all the thought he had put into his bouquet. Should she help him or just enjoy his awkwardness? She decided to enjoy his awkwardness.

It was his turn to now inhale and exhale, "Could you kindly write 'Dear Daisy. Heal quickly. Doc Incredible' and maybe some glitter in the envelope as well please. My patient is nine and recovering from surgery."

Amelie watched as his lip quivered slightly.

Almost wanting to laugh, she lifted her eyebrow over her squinting eye to accommodate her sarcasm. 'Was he fucking kidding, a Doctor? Had she just walked into a romance novel? He had just ticked every cliché imaginable and she was not falling for any of it'.

She quickly wrote the message, tied the gift card to the flowers, and charged him one hundred and five dollars. Paying by Amex, Amelie charged him an extra two dollars to cover the merchant fees. She scanned his signature, it looked legitimate.

Looking up through her long eyelashes, she teased him, "I'll tell Doctor Incredible that you did a wonderful job at forging his signature."

He laughed, and surprisingly, Amelie laughed as well.

Once handed the bunch of flowers, he thanked her and left, only to hesitate on the footpath outside of the shop.

'What did he want now?'

Walking back inside the shop his confidence depleted before her. Each step appeared to stab him as he walked towards the counter.

She tapped the counter again with the pen, "Did you forget something?"

Grinning, he attempted to charm her, "No, I was just wondering if you would like to have coffee sometime?"

Amelie froze. It had been a long time since she had been asked out.

Sexually dominant men tended to run away from her because they sensed she could not be tamed, so she was shocked when a man actually braved the potential rejection and asked her out, but she was not about to give up her happiness for some 'charming as fuck' doctor.

"I would say, no."

Shocked by her short response, he stumbled backwards.

Thanking her again, he left the shop.

She watched him as he drove off in a Government owned vehicle before grabbing the phone and ringing Pagan, who conveniently answered immediately.

"I just met a black guy and black really suits him."

Inanna

Inanna had broken out in hives which covered most of her calves with the odd one appearing on her torso and neck. A symptom she only experienced on days she visited her father.

It was always unpleasant going to see him and if Inanna was truly honest with herself, she would admit that she did it purely out of obligation.

Somewhere inside of his cold interior there must be some form of kindness; unfortunately, deep down she knew she would never have the privilege of experiencing it.

Inanna loved her father but she had never liked him. It was hard to like a man who did not like himself, but Inanna continued to care for her father in the acknowledgement that she would never be thanked for her kindness.

"Pity, you can't reincarnate dad. You'll be haunted forever in the torment of self-righteousness. What a terrible fate you've chosen for yourself."

If he was capable of speech, he would reply, "You're a long time dead."

If only he understood the irony of his own cynicism for he was alive, with a pulse, but dead in most sentiment. His fate was much worse.

Inanna lived by the belief that 'if you want to be loved, you must firstly love'. Hence the reason she refused to surrender to her disappointment that she would never be loved by the man she so desperately wanted love from, her father.

Pagan proudly claimed she loathed him, as if somehow by openly stating her hatred made her more emotionally empowered - a feeling she remained faithful to, even after all these years.

She was also trapped within a stubborn cycle of self-righteousness, pride and ego. Pagan's refusal to forgive him saw their relationship 'cut and bound' many years ago, leaving Inanna, the eldest sibling to look after him.

Pagan would assert, "There is no need to make amends with a man I give very little thought to. His blood may run through my veins but I am a Witch and he is just a human."

Inanna had hoped that Pagan would change her mind before he died as making peace with their conflict would surely cleanse some of her negative karma, benefitting her in the next life?

Had Witches not already learned this?

His welfare had been bundled up and placed forcibly into Inanna's capable but already congested hands. Perhaps, that is why Pagan could easily forget that their father existed? She was responsibility free.

The last time, Inanna and Pagan had spoken about their father, Pagan had responded to the news of his Alzheimer's by ranting, "That would be fucking right. Why does he get the luxury of forgetting?"

Inanna had not bothered Pagan with his needs and comforts since.

Aislyn, their mother had suddenly divorced him a few years back deciding that she was not about to waste her Crone years looking after an elderly drunk who wet the bed and choked on his meals, consequently handballing the responsibly onto her eldest daughter, who found him residency in a small unit close to town but within a year his memory failed him, and for his own safety, Inanna retired him to his last home, an Aged Care facility.

Family and friends were surprised that Aislyn in her senior years had chosen marital freedom, considering she had spent most of her life committed to her wedding ring; a ring that for over forty years had represented a masochistic security.

The Aged Care facility employees were thankful for Inanna's visits.

Watching her enter the main doors, they greeted her with a smile of recognition, well-mannered conversation and an 'overworked' war cry. The carers worked exceptionally hard. Inanna wondered with the long hours that they worked if their own home life suffered? She hoped not.

Relieved because someone actually visited him, if only for a few minutes, the carers actually looked relieved when she walked through the entry.

It was a friendly and well-lit Aged Care facility, although it still exposed a hygienic orderliness and professionalism which of course was what Inanna paid for.

Before entering her father's room, she paused to take a deep breath, 'here I go'. Entering was always the hardest.

The initial shock of his deteriorating appearance followed by the realisation that so many people suffered the same fate heavied the usually emotionally balanced, Inanna.

Hoping he would not see another summer, Inanna was sure most people thought he was dead already, a distant memory for most of the community that he grew up with, and surprisingly not a 'pub mate' to check up on him.

She shook the thought from her mind. Wishing someone dead was unacceptable.

Sitting slightly on his bed, propped up on three pillows, his vacant expression ignored his daughter.

In his youth, he had been a physically strong man. Growing up in Sassafras to a poor but hardworking farming family, physical strength had been a bonus.

Inanna's Grandparents, had married after her Catholic Grandmother had fallen pregnant to her Protestant Grandfather. Embittered that one lustful and sinful night had sealed her fate, she had christened her son Cain in a cowardly attempt to transfer her sin onto him. Only a few minutes old and she had looked at her own child with disdain, damning him before she had put his lips to her breast. To add insult, Cain had been born unusually healthy, rarely experiencing one day of sickness his entire childhood and adult life, until the Alzheimer's.

By the age of twenty, Cain's stature was intimidating. His tall and muscular physique and handsome genes gave him an unnerving sexual disposition that saw many teenage girls lose their virginity to him.

Inanna wondered if lust had initially brought her parent's Cain and Aislyn together. They had been childhood friends but rarely spoke of their long term connection. Unquestionably, Aislyn must have known him well enough before she sentenced herself to being his wife? Why had she agreed to marry such an awful man?

Although, undoubtedly tainted, Inanna had never seen one moment of intimacy between her parents while growing up and perhaps it was better that way?

Inanna sat down stroking her father's brow, "Hi Dad. It's Inny. I'm here to feed you some lunch."

She knew he would not reply but sitting in silence was worse than pretending he was coherent.

His once strong jaw line now feeble, his eye's deeply sunken under his protruding brow, his veins swollen and sagging skin gave him a skeleton appearance. It was indeed torture to see a man returning to a sickly childlike state.

On one level, Inanna knew that she was wasting her time trying to communicate with him but conversation between them had always been one sided, so not much had changed.

It appears you really do 'reap what you sow', she mused.

But the silence was a nasty reminder of what lay dormant: his vehement rages and cruel unwarranted name calling. One sip of alcohol and his true nature unleashed its demonic peril.

The kitchen staff brought his lunch on a sterile metal trolley that squeaked every four metres. The squeaking alerted Inanna that the trolley was in the next room down from them.

Her stomach rumbled from hunger as they eventually walked into his room. There were several steaming hot plates. Cain's plate consisted of a puree that would be wasted on the feeble patient. Only several mouthfuls of carrots, peas, mashed potato, broccoli and cauliflower and roasted beef pureed into a plate of orange slops would barely pass his blue lips.

The gregarious kitchen employee, wearing the compulsory hygienic cap, enthusiastically handed Inanna the plate.

Feeding him, she wiped the puree from his chin.

In vain, she told him about Morghana's achievements at school and how much she had grown up and that she thought Morghana might have her first boyfriend as she was acting strange lately. Inanna talked about Pagan's children, Demeter and Deity, as she felt that was important, even if Pagan did not. Inanna, was saddened that all his grandchildren would not remember him. Perhaps, it was a blessing?

Twenty minutes later, she placed the half full plate on the side table and decided to leave.

Fighting the urge to kiss him on the forehead, she squeezed his hand instead, which predictably he did not responded to.

Quickly walking down the hallway, Inanna glanced into the communal area. As usual the chairs were full of mummifying humans, staring at the large television screen. She was overcome with pity. Why did they not euthanize these people? It was cruel to let them linger, trapped between 'not living' and death.

As she walked out the sliding door, she let out her held breath. Composed, she left. She could tick one more job off for the day.

CHAPTER 5
London
Aggie

Walking along the contemporary Millennium Bridge, the pedestrians gave little regard for Aggie's aging body and its limitations. Swerving sharply, Aggie exaggerated her movement by swinging her walking stick wildly from side to side to take up as much space as she could in protest.

Technicoloured sparks and wispy shadows darted in front of Aggie's eyes- an effect of her pending blindness. Giddy, she reached out to the hand rail to steady herself. Focusing on the murky Thames River beneath her the present doom overwhelmed her.

Her sweating hands slipped along the cold metal, causing her to panic as she travelled several feet along the path. Stabilising, she took a jagged breath and re-joined the mass of pedestrians whose sporadic movements put Aggie into a head spin.

Wild with contempt, she considered retaliating by pushing some of them into the murky depths of the Thames River below. Hopefully, they would smash their heads on the safety rails on the way down. Vengeful thoughts were what helped Aggie get up in the mornings.

The Millennium Bridge was an oddity in Aggie's opinion. An ironic reminder of colonisation backfiring. Its sharp lines and metallic colour gave off an androgynous and futuristic monoculture against the backdrop of a multicultural black hole.

"Innovative? Bollocks!"

Aggie's 'joie de vivre' for art consumed every cell in her body and spending a few hours at the Tate Modern Art Gallery, excited her. The gallery was a short walking distance to where the Crone Monarchy meeting was being held and sparing an hour to wrap herself up in creativity might prepare her for the morons she would have to spend the next few hours with.

While tourists fumbled inside their bags for cameras and mobile phones, and students lounged on the crisp green lawns, Aggie admired the building's phallus symbol at the entrance

'He certainly was a big boy', Aggie smirked.

It had been a long time since she had felt the pleasure of a man. Only memories kept her warm at night.

It seems even when she had strived to 'have it all', the truth was, that nobody ever 'gets it all'.

Entering the large silver interior, Aggie was surrounded by unenthusiastic teenage students who gathered in mass in the main foyer. Students who would rather stand around sulking in their narcissism or taking 'selfies' on their mobile phones than fully experiencing the creativity and the expression that the gallery offered.

"Stupid little humans," Aggie hissed, as she entered the teenage crowd. Wishing she could hit them, she tightened her grip around the walking stick.

Excitedly, she bought a ticket to see the avant-garde exhibition as she was keen to experience the artist Theo Van Doesburg. A visual stimuli that was sure to please.

Slowly walking up several sets of stairs, she entered a large white gallery. Staring for only a few seconds before stumbling towards a strategically positioned bench seat to compose herself, the leather cushion was a welcome support for her aching body and dizziness.

Squinting at the large De Stihl painting in front of her, perhaps only a tenth of the art work penetrating her sight, she unscrambled the painting as if it presented a puzzle that she was not privy too but she so desired to conquer.

Various shades of blue embraced the background, while a jumbled mess of transparent triangles and circles in an assortment of green, red and blue fought unconvincingly in the forefront. 'Was the De Stihl movement taking the piss?'

Abstract art puzzled her, but in her opinion it best represented 'life's journeys'. Simplistic in form, while complex in meaning.

The artwork, troubled Aggie. The painting lacked clarity. It screamed something about equality or the lack of it- a series of ongoing wars that only caused more wars.

Feeling stronger, Aggie noticed her hands were still shaking. Wiping the sweat from her forehead, she perspired again within seconds. Drips of salty water sprinkled across her eyebrows.

Sitting in front of her first Van Doesburg's painting, memories plagued her. Reminiscing of her time spent with her French lover, Jehrome, she suddenly missed her past. A past that had battered her into submission, leaving her only one path to embrace- to follow the path that took her beyond that knotty-haired child she had been and into the Mighty Supreme she now was.

If the future 'loved or hated' her, she did not care. What she was 'labelled' did not worry her. Tyrant or hero, such titles are for romantics. What mattered was that she would be remembered as a Witch who lived beyond expectation. She had never cared for the tedious grudge between Non-Ancients or Ancients Witches. It certainly had not been her motivation, although she used it to manipulate her path. As far as she was concerned, it had been her destiny to become the Greatest Witch.

And bitterness- the greatest motivation of all. An emotion that embeds the will to stand above all others who have wronged you, and many had.

Initially, Jehrome had been a good friend, an artistic mentor but possessive and fanatical, he soon wanted to own his frigid teenage beauty. Aggie did not just become his material property, but he pleaded with her to be a mother, lover and daughter, a feminine triad that filled the emptiness of his untapped affections, smothering her until his grip left bruises on her arms and her eyes were too scared to look anywhere but at the ground.

Art had been his life and she had been fortunate enough to have been invited into his world. A world where art was life and life was abstract; smudged chalk on butcher paper that Jehrome had used against her, to belittle her, love her and which ironically enabled her to escape. Falling into the traps of lust, Jehrome not only worshipped her physical body but also the negative space that contoured her. He discovered in her a sensuality and truth that was foreign. In hindsight, in his twisted affections, she realised that Jehrome had truly loved her.

Aggie's hands, now crippled from arthritis had not picked up a paint brush since 1976; cans of paint had dried, paint brushes laid to rest in mouldy water, blank canvases still stacked against the wall and one canvas at rest on the easel. The door to her art studio remained locked. Perhaps, it was time to unlock it?

Aggie peered at her mobile. She was running late. Less than satisfied, Aggie left.

Pagan

Pagan reversed a run-down hatchback vehicle out of her driveway. It was embarrassing to drive but she had to make sacrifices if she wanted to keep her second vehicle, her beloved Kombi.

Monday was the day that Demeter and Deity arrived back home and subsequently it was the day they went back to their father, John, one week later.

Pagan knew that as a single mother she had it relatively easy. One week with her children and one week on her own to do as she pleased. A perfect arrangement.

It had taken a few months after they separated to adapt to the new parenting arrangement and only a few years to see the benefits. The children flourished as both homes found normality again. They had two happy homes. Two safe homes, although very different, each parent offered space for liberty and creativity.

In theory, Pagan had more time on her hands to work or at least that's what society wanted her to believe. Like many parents, Pagan worked several casual jobs while also raising her children. Gone were the days that full-time employment sufficiently supported an average family, even a family that consisted of one adult and two children. Unemployment was increasing in Tasmania and Pagan was well aware that she was trapped in a state that was dying economically. Working low paying jobs had meant Pagan had been treated like 'shit' by 'arsehole' employers, female employers in particular, and consequently this had affected Pagan's self-esteem considerably. She had been working for far too long to be easily bluffed that full-time work would be the answer to all her financial pressures. Everyone was struggling, except Inanna.

Pagan had considered moving to the Australian mainland but who would buy her house and move to a state that had a noose around its demographic neck? There was an abundance of homes for sale and none of them were selling. She was stuck. Stuck in an era where she had been stripped of her pedigree and reduced to semi-employed. But where would she go if she was free to leave? She was supervised by the Crone Monarchy who preferred her dead but while she was struggling at least she was highly entertaining to the Supreme Femininity.

Experiencing financial instability was not new to Pagan. She had survived many economic depressions during her reincarnations and feared Australia was heading for a major one or at least a civil war while they argue about what is 'Un-Australian'. Pagan wanted the word 'Un-Australian' eliminated from the Australian core. It was an evil word bound in racial hatred and arrogance. Pagan remembered the French Revolution and the terror she had witnessed. Experiencing the lead up to a revolution, she had smelt trouble brewing. She could smell the same bitterness in Australia now.

Women had fought proudly beside their men in that revolution and they have never stopped fighting for equality since. Perhaps in the 1900s when women were fighting for more rights, they should have had more foresight to see that the top of the hierarchy was not just a gender issue but a class one as well.

And why did women want to be like men? Women should be pro-vagina as that is where all the power lies. Men know that and that is why they fear women. Witches resented male supremacy but somehow were also trapped by it.

Blowing a large raspberry with her tight lips, Pagan blew out her negative thoughts. There was no point thinking about the past or the future.

"Be grateful. The past is the past, stay in the present. You are safe," she whispered under her breath.

Pagan was objective enough to see that men also suffered social pressures. Ironically, stuck in their own vacuum of prejudice.

"Stop thinking," Pagan cursed her wondering thoughts again.

Careful not to let her own prejudice towards male supremacy affect her ability to parent her son, she had attended a few counselling sessions. They had been a waste of time. It was difficult explaining to Demeter why Deity was born with Magick and he was not and even harder for her to parent him without showing indifference. She struggled to control her own prejudices but unlike other parents she was aware of her faults. She was passionate about changing the world through healthy parenting but what was really healthy? Parenting had changed again and would continue to change. She might get it right in this lifetime only to have to learn a new set of rules in the next.

Not only did Pagan struggle with understanding her contemporary gender role but also her place as a Witch within the gender. In theory, Pagan was both male and female parent: home-maker, provider and Witch, while forcibly contributing to the social capital in a city that desperately needed people with positive energy, not that she really had any 'positive energy' to share.

Unlike Inanna's energy which was increasing, her energy was depleting. Pagan wanted to return to her past, a past where she was mighty and abundant with enthusiasm.

Pagan deeply envied her sister's work ethic and foresight. Inanna had spent several reincarnations studying economics, spending most of her spare time toiling at universities and marrying high profile men. All she had to do was patiently wait until society evolved and ideals of equality were accepted. Inanna had mastered patience.

As children, Inanna would eat one lolly from her crinkled white lolly paper bag, only to place the remaining lollies away for a later time, whereas Pagan had eaten all the lollies instantly. Instant gratification had always seemed like more fun. She now understood which sister had a true grasp of gratification.

'Time and space' were quickening. Unlike other eras where physical strength was tested, contemporary life required mental strength and technical flexibility. Pagan had neither.

Struggling with life, Pagan wished that she would evolve to the point where she would not need a physical body anymore, however that was a long way off. Modern life was not for her, so the likelihood that she would enjoy the future also looked slim. Pagan worried that in her next reincarnation she might be flying a spacecraft.

"Fuck, I can't even drive my oven."

Most people would be excited about technological advancements but it terrified Pagan. She was falling desperately behind in all areas of her existence, particularly within technology. PlayStation games confused her, appliances beeped at her and even the automatic teller machines at the bank, frustrated her.

Witches were so far removed from their natural habitat that any reincarnation was at best synthetic and the only escape was to evolve but how? Waking each morning tired and constantly suffering tedious ailments like the common cold was trapping her within a cycle of fatigue. She was living several lives in one lifetime and it was time to slow down. If only 'time' would slow down again.

She yearned for Ancient times, before the Black and Red War when the detoxification of Witch energy started. The Black and Red War had ruined everything.

The Red Haired Men had arrived on Witch shores bringing with them disease and a foreign Magic that rivalled theirs. Witches had fought and proudly won but the damage was irreversible. The Red Haired Men's colonisation had been catastrophic. Had she known the outcome, she would have wished the Witches had lost and in mass death, they all would have protected themselves and reincarnated pure.

Pagan parked outside of the Primary School, waiting for the school bell to ring. At 15:05 it did.

Demeter exited the school gate. Looking down the street, he spotted the car and waved at his mother.

Deity skipped happily behind him.

Both children had inherited two protruding front teeth that would have them called 'beaver' by other children at school. Demeter had retaliated several times but it only increased the teasing from the bullies. Deity just smiled at the bullies, a smile that brightened up her tense face. Her two front 'beaver' teeth were a prominent reminder to the bullies that she was not easily broken by name calling. They quickly stopped harassing her.

Demeter and Deity squashed into the backseat of the Hatchback, throwing their school bags onto the front passenger seat.

Slamming the creaking door shut, Demeter was promptly scolded by Pagan.

Having the only 'Born Witch' it was very important that Pagan controlled any innate Magick her daughter may accidentally use. Pagan had successfully hidden her daughter's birthright from the Crone Monarchy but it was only a matter of time until they discovered the truth. The Supreme Monarchy would surely give the orders to assassinate Deity the moment she discovered there was a rival to the throne. It was ironic, that Aggie's greatest threat was a child Witch and one that was right in front of her, but still she was blind to it. In one respect, Pagan felt privileged to have a special daughter but also feared for her daughter's life because of it.

Any Ancient Magick performed meant the death penalty, accidently or not. The Modern Witch Doctrine was very strict on this.

Demeter understood that his mother and sister were Witches, sometimes resenting them for their superhuman capabilities. To counteract his inferiority, he had spent most of his childhood dressing up as Superman, Spiderman or Batman, a failed attempt to re-adjust equilibrium in the household.

Demeter had been a very adorable toddler with a plump face, loose locks of blond hair and vibrant blue eyes. In grade two, his blond hair had turned dishwater brown and his curls heavied, until they dropped out completely. Now with darkening circles around his eyes, his once sparkling blue eyes appeared vacant.

Starting the car, Pagan drove towards her mother's home in the bustling town of Latrobe. A few weeks had passed since Pagan last visited her mum and as usual guilt had set in. She liked to visit her mother every few weeks otherwise the catch-up might take several hours.

Aislyn's home looked more like a shanty than an average town home.

Externally Aislyn's home was stereotypical of a 'Fairy Tale Witch' house with the only finishing touches being 'Hansel and Gretel' trapped in a cage.

Internally, each room was a vibrancy of red, purple, orange and green, splashed haphazardly across the walls. The doors were painted a contrasting solid colour and were the original doors made in the 1920s. The mix-matched palette somehow formed a comfortable cohesion.

Inanna limited her visitation due to her dislike of the chaotic and rundown appearance, a far cry from the home they had grown up in. What Inanna could not grasp was that the run down embarrassment that their mother called 'a home' was rich in love and void of violence.

In an attempt to avoid personal embarrassment, Inanna had offered to buy her mother an upmarket unit in Devonport but Aislyn had kindly refused the offer.

"It's the first time in this life, Inanna, that I've done something on my own. Your kind offer, I'm afraid I can't accept."

Aislyn rejected materialism by opting for second hand furniture over new.

Her bold choices of décor and design were indicative of her new found rebellious nature. It was the first time in Aislyn's recent reincarnation that she lived on her own and she intended to decorate as she saw fit, regardless of what her daughter's thought.

Her grandchildren loved their nanna's home, often snuggling with her on the couch while trying to con a 'hands on healing'. The holistic healing technique was used as often as needed and it seemed the grandchildren needed it often.

Demeter had once twisted his ankle in the second quarter of a basketball game. Frantically, several of the team member's mother's ran off searching for a cold pack to apply to his swelling ankle. Demeter had hobbled over to his nanna who had wrapped her palms around his ankle to alleviate the swelling, within ten minutes he was back on the basketball court, the swelling had gone and the pain forgotten. Aislyn had smirked to herself as she received angry glares from the mothers.

"Rookies," she had laughed.

Since the Modern Witch Doctrine was implemented, Aislyn had rejected many aspects of Witchcraft by studying Asian philosophy instead. She had found a lot of similarities between the two disciplines and her new profound interest soon become her chosen craft.

Pagan entered Latrobe's highway roundabout, turning right into the main road. Growing up in the town of Latrobe did not lessen her disconnection to the town. Her heart remained in Europe but the Goddesses had chosen Australia. She respected their wishes even if she did feel like a stranger in her new birthplace.

The hospital, positioned directly in view as you enter Latrobe, smelt of methylated spirits. Pagan's acute smell was a curse. The sight of the hospital raised heightened emotions for Pagan who had for the last twelve months driven Fay Ce'Line there for chemotherapy sessions. Sharing the experience with her dear friend had been a humbling but odd experience. The nurses had been wonderfully charitable, offering light humoured conversation and an abundance of coffee, herbal tea and cookies.

Pagan had sat beside Fay Ce'Line for several hours while the chemotherapy poisoned her body. Studying the faces of the cancer patients, Pagan noticed there was something different about them. A stunned look as if they were staring at death for the first time.

They smiled and said, "Thank you," and told jokes and remained positive but underneath the façade was paralysing fear, a fear that they could not mask. It was as if the veil between life and death had been lifted. Fay Ce'Line wore the same mask.

Witches had never suffered the disease cancer before. Fay Ce'Line had to brave the cruelties of cancer the same as humans; the nightmares, hair falling out, toes and finger nails falling off, stomach pain, nausea and the fear that she might die prematurely. Fay Ce'Line was frightened and Pagan was frightened for her.

Pagan pulled into her mother's grassy driveway, parking next to an array of flowering plants. It was a haven of geraniums, daisies, lavenders and flowering bulbs, all lapping the remaining warmth out of the cooling Tasmanian weather.

The children jumped out of the car, running along the cobbled garden path. Pagan dodged the hanging ornaments catching up to her children who stood impatiently at the front door.

Demeter and Deity knocked at the front door twice to no avail. Eventually, they enter the house unsure if their Nanna was at home. As they snuck along the hallway the smell of sandalwood floated heavily up into their nostrils.

Deity whispered, "Nanna must be meditating?"

Nodding to the children to enter into the lounge room, Pagan slowly opened the large purple wooden door. They were not surprised to see seven elderly women spread out, sitting on the couch, chairs and on bean bags.

Pagan suspected that the use of marijuana had helped the ladies reach a deeper meditative state and the sandalwood was used to mask it. Of course, the children were too young to realise what illegal substance their Nanna and her bohemian friends were enjoying in their meditative slumber. In fact, the room looked like a mass of suicide granny's. The thought amused Pagan to the point where she had to leave the room, deciding to take a toilet break to splash some water over her face.

Pagan returned to the lounge room to find Demeter and Deity meditating on the floor. Demeter lying down on the woollen carpet while Deity sat crossed legged on the spare floor space beside her brother.

Conforming, Pagan joined them, sitting beside Deity. The floorboards were uncomfortable.

Their sudden appearance had gone unnoticed or ignored. Either way, joining them seemed the right thing to do.

Pagan closed her eyes. Her eyelids ached, actually every part of her body ached. Taking an exaggerated inhale, she began a basic Zen Mindfulness technique of 'staying in the moment!'

Witches were well aware that many modern lay-healing practises had been adapted from Eastern cultures. Humans, through experimentation, had in their own way discovered healing Magic.

It seemed that the human lay health-care professional was more popular than any expert Western Medical Practitioner at present; however for safety measures Fay Ce'Line had chosen both Western medicine and Witch healing practises to combat her illness. Cancer was a modern illness. Witches did not have the Magick to heal it.

Pagan despised modern visualisation techniques and their pathetic attempts to help humans identify with their inner most suppressed emotions. It was best to keep certain memories suppressed, buried as deep as possible within the subconscious. No need to encourage a bad day when life was already overly generous in that department.

Science had a lot to answer for. Watching the effects of Enlightenment, Pagan saw the same religious biases and bigotry transferred into modern day sciences. Humans were simply pulling down one house made of wood, to build a brick house, only to render it. Unfortunately, the same foundation supported all the houses and the foundation was crumbling.

However, Pagan had always found Zen Mindfulness helped her to centre her thoughts, reducing her anxieties. She focused on her breathing: up through the nose, down past her chest into the pit of her stomach and then back up and out her nose, and that was it. Every time her thoughts wandered, she brought herself back to her breathing. There was no need for chakras, visualisation, coloured rooms to enter into, re-birthing techniques or angels giving messages. She simply controlled her breathing.

Ideally, Pagan wanted to control everything and ironically nothing. She had always been that way; wanting to control others while not wanting to be controlled herself and all the murkiness that lay in between.

After several minutes, Pagan reached a mild state of relaxation, her shoulders dropped several inches, releasing the tension from her neck. Her hands released their clenched hold. Her forehead smoothed out as the mental tension subsided.

Breathe. In and out. Again.

The smell of sandalwood and music seduced her thoughts to happier times.

Her nudity blended into the dark brown bark. She was hidden among the natural colours of the forest.

Fluoro green moss squashed and seeped in between her toes. Fresh piercing wind whispered through the trees.

The trees swayed in unison as if they could hear a joyous tune. The trees danced.

Looking up, towards the majestic cumbersome branches of the forest she flew high into the tree tops. Swirling and twisting, she manipulated her limbs into a broken frenzy.

The air smelt like honeysuckle and the dew tasted sweet. The air was her home. The earth was her home. The water was her home. The fire was her home. She was home.

Except for random movement and re-arranging of body parts, Pagan forgot that she was not alone in the room, so the sudden scream vibrated through her body, wrenching her from the quiet bliss.

The scream came from her mother.

The reaction from the ladies created a chaotic eruption that took several minutes to subside. Finally, it settled into nervous laughter.

It was common for Aislyn to have visions in deep meditation. Pagan was hesitant to believe they were actual visions but rather her mother's unhealthy display of creativity.

After some coaching from Aislyn's meditating friends, she began to tell them of her vision.

Pagan rolled her eyes. There was a reason why Aislyn was a joke amongst the Tasmanian Crones counsel. She was embarrassing. Her mother had become a Hedge Witch otherwise known as a solo practitioner. This meant that she belonged to no particular Coven and therefore had complete sovereignty over her Witchcraft and its philosophy as long as she remained faithful to the Modern Witch Doctrine.

A Witch without a Coven was less powerful so the Tasmanian Crones counsel supported her decision. What the Tasmanian Crones counsel had not foreseen was the liberation that Aislyn gained from her craft solitude. Flexibility and personalised liberation from conservative restraints in practical Magick and philosophy, was strengthening Aislyn's Witchcraft and her notability. Teetering on rebellion, her energy had become unbalanced and Pagan feared her newly formed ability of vision was evidence enough of its shift.

The future was not destined, so therefore foresight was impossible. Aislyn was making her clairvoyance up, so it was hard for Pagan to tolerate her mother's crazy ideas of fate. It really was 'Hocus Pocus' satire.

Witches understood that they had lessons to learn and would continue to be reincarnated until they learned their lessons but their futures were not foretold. A Witch's energy lived within a learning spiral that continued to spin, spiralling up or down, depending on how they lived their lives. Pagan suspected that she was spiralling downwards.

Any tarot reader could produce an array of advent followers. People gave a lot of their personal power away to these people. Having insight into their futures gave some people the permission to act accordingly to their inner most ambitions, using fate as justification. Clairvoyants simply tapped into the human consciousness, relaying back to the person what they truly desire.

On occasions, Aislyn did predict something so unseeable that when it did happen it was quite a surprise. Pagan put it down to luck. If a clairvoyant could tap into a human's psyche it was only because they were a human Universal Server Bus (USB) switched into the human hard drive.

Pagan was however interested to hear what her mother's imagination had foreseen this time. Aislyn's followers were intrigued also.

The room's temperature had dropped and goose bumps appeared on Demeter's arms and legs. Deity was enthralled with the drama and sat with her hands in between her legs in anticipation. She believed in fate.

A chill unexpectedly passed through Pagan's body.

Aislyn dressed in a fawn coloured tunic with a thin green belt that twisted around her waist. A pink head scarf tied together a mass of grey hair high above her head.

Her breath slowed, "I was following a glowing light and it was very small, no larger than an apple. Oh and it hummed," Aislyn laughed, "It really hummed, amazing."

Nods from several of her meditation friends gave Aislyn the confidence to continue.

"I must say, I was intrigued, so I followed the light up a rocky mountain. Once I was on the top, I turned back to see where I had travelled from. Behind me, I saw cyclones, floods, earthquakes and a large burning tree. I fear the world is heading into catastrophic times."

Aislyn paused for dramatic affect.

"I knew I could not return so I continued to walk up the mountain. The mountain was misty but the light guided me. Then the light disappeared. Once my eyes adjusted to the mist, I saw a man squatting over a fire. I walked towards him.

His face was turned away from me and a white sheet hung over his body. I walked closer to him but still he did not move. I placed my hand out to touch him but just as I did, he flew around grabbing my hand. That's when I screamed and woke up."

The room erupted again with raised elated chatter.

Pagan sat back, unamused by her mother's clichéd vision and in an attempt to offer perspective, Pagan raised her voice over the other women and spoke, "So mum, what did this mysterious stranger on a mountain look like?"

The women quietened in anticipation.

Aislyn coldly answered, "He had black skin."

Fay Ce'Line

Fay Ce'Line had dropped the twins off at childcare, paid the mobile phone bill, grabbed a salad roll from bakery and opened the shop by 10:00. Barely unlocking the door and turning the alarm off, a customer had walked in behind her demanding to know which products contained Palm Oil. It was going to be a long day.

Consequently, the morning ran relatively smoothly with sporadic customers keeping her busy with their mild ailments.

For over two thousand years, Fay Ce'Line had dabbled with healing concoctions. On occasions, the concoctions had accidentally poisoned a few Witches and humans but after some cautious experimentation, she had become quite good at remedial medicine. It had become a passion.

Her home-made remedies were discretely hidden in a large refrigerator in a separate room out the back. The main shop area contained what you would find in any generic health food shop.

At 12:30 the customers accelerated. Fay Ce'Line wished that she had an extra person to help her with the lunch time rush as her blood sugar was dropping and she felt faint.

Gulping down a mouthful of water, she decided that it was important for her to eat even if it was in front of the customers and went against her work ethics. She ripped open the wrapper to her salad roll, shovelling it into her mouth. She chewed frantically and swallowed. Instant heartburn.

She was however impressed that the two ladies browsing the vitamin display which was just beside the shop counter had not seen her gobble her lunch down.

Moments later, Fay Ce'Line felt her stomach twist as the chewed pieces of the salad roll lodged in her intestine. The pain crippled her over.

Running frantically to the back of the shop, she slipped on the old linoleum flooring, smashing into the hall wall denting the plaster. Brushing herself off, she reached the kitchenette where she placed two fingers down her throat, regurgitating the mashed food, spitting the contents into the sink. She scooped up the regurgitated food, throwing it in the bin.

Washing her hands, she sprinkled some water over her face, washing away the tears while also cooling her temperature.

Looking into the small round mirror, Fay Ce'Line saw a tired Witch looking back at her. Her hair had grown one inch since it had fallen out. She had chosen not to wear a headscarf. Headscarves were a foolish attempt to decorate a balding head as if somehow she was alluding herself that she was well.

She returned to the front of the shop to apologise to the customers.

It continued to be busy until 14:00. When the customers dwindled, Fay Ce'Line tackled the jobs she had fallen behind on and made a concoction of herbs and vitamins to help her feel better. She felt flat: emotionally and mentally. Her energy was depleted and her body was toxic. She had fought cancer once already but she doubted her feeble body could do it again.

The Doctor had told her that she had a 'common' form of ovarian cancer with the best case scenario being that she could survive for another five years cancer free. An alarm clock had been set on her life and she could hear it ticking. What power a suicide bomber had! The unknowing was the real cruelty.

Unlike humans, Witches were reincarnated and therefore once Awakened, remembered all their memories.

Neither of her daughters had been born a Witch. She might get to see them reach late primary school. They would still be young and after a few years their memories would fade and perhaps they would forget her completely? Fay Ce'Line would be reincarnated, maybe in two hundred years. She would hope to find evidence that they married, had children of their own, or at least found some happiness within their existence but they would be strangers to her.

Oscar would struggle. He was a strong man but he would be lost without her. His life was her life. He had remained strong for her during the last year, but he fed from her strength. Growing old with Oscar was not an option anymore. Men like Oscar rarely surfaced and he had chosen to love her, every part of her.

She felt let down by the Goddesses. She had always lived to an old age and now that she had found true happiness she was being prematurely torn away from it.

She buckled over from a sharp pain in her stomach. Perhaps, a cure for cancer may save her?

'Stay positive!'

Amelie

Amelie and her employer closed up the shop, finished the settlement, recycled what they could, ordered more stock and generally prepared for the next day.

An obstinate silence between them, threatened to erupt at any time.

The force of Amelie shutting the front door vibrated the building as she left. The sudden return of her employer infuriated Amelie, so much so she considered quitting.

Slamming the car door behind her, Amelie released her frustration, "What the fuck? You stupid bitch! Fuck off! Go home. Die!"

Amelie started the car and without indicating drove out onto the busy street.

She suspected that her employer had an alternative motive for being there.

Perhaps, she wanted Amelie to quit. It was plausible. Businesses were suffering. Ideally, the shop only needed one person to be there. Perhaps, she enjoyed making Amelie's life miserable. That was also plausible. Amelie had never come across a woman whose moods changed as frequently as her employer's did.

"Don't 'give away your power so easily," Amelie cursed. "I own my power," she shouted in the car.

Repeating the affirmation, her anger subsided slightly. There was only enough room in the florist for one alpha female, her!

She was also disappointed that the mystery Englishman had not returned to the shop. Amelie had enjoyed their awkward banter, and now, she regretted not agreeing to catch up with him for coffee. Sometimes her stubbornness annoyed even her.

He had sparked intrigue although her intuition suggested something was not quite 'right' about him. She would treat him with a degree of suspicion for a while.

Fierce attraction towards his energy also made her cautious. She loved men who were wrong for her. Was she repeating herstory? And his accent was a powerful aphrodisiac. She missed England. She missed home.

Elated, angry emotions quickly turned to arousal as she thought about him. His tall robust stature, his ripe arse that filled out his trousers, the open collared shirt that revealed a hairy chest, the grey flicker of hair through his crew cut and how his mere presence suggested he knew who he was as a person. He was sexy. Even her orgasms had intensified since she had started fantasising about him. Plus, he would be a welcomed distraction from her mundane existence.

"Goddesses, I just want to fuck him. Just once. Just to see if I can still remember how to do it. "

Twenty minutes later, she pulled into the communal driveway instantly spotting a box that was placed in full view at the front door of her unit.

Alarmed, she quickly jumped out of the car heading towards the box, eventually pausing due to fear. What if it was a bomb or something? Bloody 9/11. It had the whole world paranoid.

She bent down quickly, flicking the lid open to reveal a dwarf rose bush. An abundance of lavender coloured roses supported by dark green foliage were planted in a small mauve pot. There was a faint fragrance. She liked the subtlety of his choice.

Amelie let out a relieved laugh.

She picked out a card that sat on top. It read, 'I prefer living flowers myself. PS was easy finding you as Devonport is a small place. Marcus'.

Amelie was shocked as she had not anticipated this.

"Fancy a man with initiative."

This called for a glass of chardonnay, a hot bubbly bath and some music by Harry Manx.

She read the card again and picked up the box. She would need to find the perfect position for her present.

Chuckling, she forget all about her awful day.

Pagan

Demeter had fallen asleep reading a bundle of handpicked books.

Peaceful in his slumber, one hand hung over the edge of the bed. Pagan gently slipped his hand underneath the doona and kissed his forehead before turning off the bedside lamp.

To Pagan's surprise Deity was sitting up in bed still reading.

Raising her right eyebrow, Pagan scolded her daughter, "Young lady, you should be asleep!"

Deity pouted, "But mummy, I'm not tired."

"Yes, but I am."

Her daughter had already mastered the art of emotional manipulation and Pagan was proud of the fact.

Deity was reading William Shakespeare's play 'Love Labour Lost'.

"Oh Missy Moo, you're far too young to understand that book."

Snatching the book from Deity, Pagan placed it back on the bookshelf and sat down beside her daughter on the bed, "Deity, you know that you and Shakespeare were very good friends, and you still have the same red hair as you had in your last reincarnation. Do you remember any of these things yet?"

She shook her head.

Deity's memory was like a jigsaw puzzle. She had all the pieces but was unsure of where they went.

She was splendid in appearance, encompassing a humble self-esteem and wit. As a mere human, she would be admired and despised. As a daughter, she was loved by both her parents, and as a Witch she would surpass all others. Deity had a great respect for both females and males and she would once again show great compassion for all of humanity and Witches.

Deity snuggled into her doona. Alchemy the kitten was nestled beside Deity's feet.

"Mummy, can you tell me the story of the 'Red Haired Men' again?"

Baulking, Pagan struggled to find an excuse not to. The factual story held immense pain for Pagan but she was well aware of its importance, so she told the story as often as she could. It was pivotal that Deity knew her ancestry, even though it was deeply disturbing.

Snuggling into her mother's torso, Deity rested her head on her mother's shoulder.

"Many moons ago, Witches lived in large isolated communities. Witches were great warriors who protected humans. We were wonderful neighbours. On special occasions, strong and smart men, would visit the Witches and there would be a great fertility festival and lots of Maidens were conceived. One day, a fleet of Red Haired Men arrived on our shores and they brought with them a new Magic, strong weapons, disease and a thirst to conquer. Many of our human friends died although we fought beside them."

Deity interrupted, "Mummy, did you fight?"

"No honey, remember I was only a baby when the Black and Red War began. I would have liked to have fought though."

Pagan kissed Deity on the forehead and continued, "After years of bloodshed, the weary Witches negotiated with the Red Haired Men."

"Why? Mummy! Why?"

"Well. It certainly wasn't for peace. Witches were dying out and we needed to make more Witches to continue fighting. We needed to protect the humans as well. Most of the male humans were dead or isolated from us. The Red Haired Men were gaining strength and we were frightened that our own kind would be wiped out."

"You weren't giving into them?"

Laughing, Pagan continued, "It was decided that we would breed together. Make a super breed. The plan was that once Witches become pregnant, they would slaughter the Red Haired Men."

"But mummy, even if you all died, you would have been reincarnated?"

Pagan mulled over Deity's question.

"The Red Haired Men were destroying our culture, weakening our Magick and connection to the Goddesses. They wanted to own us. Put us into slavery. We had to eradicate them. After all, once a Red Haired Man was dead, he was gone forever."

Deity puffed, "So, you're saying that Witches are just as mean as the Red Haired Men?"

Lowering her voice, Pagan searched for a 'just' answer. Tears welled in Pagan's eyes, "I am ashamed of what Witches have become but I am not ashamed that we fought for our own culture. As your memories solidify you will remember that you too have made decisions that at the time seemed justifiable, only years later to be deemed barbaric. We must learn from our mistakes."

Screwing her face up, Pagan realised that Deity was too young to understand the point in which she was trying to make.

"Mummy, tell me about Aunty Inanna."

Pagan shuddered. She would need to use censorship to continue.

"Aunty Inanna's name was Aphrodite, as I've told you before and she presented herself as a potential…"

Pagan desperately searched for the right word, "Let's say 'wife' to Gorr, the Leader of the Red Haired Men. She had also captured the affections of Gorr's younger brother, Tonic, but she had set her sights on the main prize and she would use her beauty to achieve it."

Deity clasped her hands together. "How pretty was Aunty Inanna?"

"Aphrodite was breathtakingly stunning. Cherry red lips, wild green eyes, a long forehead, pointy nose and raven black hair that hung down to tickle her bottom. She was presented to Gorr. Naked, except for a leather belt that hung loosely around her voluptuous hips and a sword tightly fastened to her belt. Gorr was completely seduced."

Deity squeezed her mother's thigh, "But mummy, didn't Gorr love you?"

Pagan snapped, "Do you want me to finish the story or are you going to keep interrupting?"

Huffing, Deity slid down into her bed.

"Right! Gorr agreed to their partnership. They would make strong males and finally he would have control over the Witches. This is when Witches started to give birth to male and human babies. The intoxication of our energies had begun. A truce to the war erupted into celebrations."

Pagan stroked Deity's forehead to help her settle.

"While Gorr enjoyed the festivities, in his peripheral vision he saw a dark shadow enter the surrounding forest. Intrigued, he followed it until it led him to a Maiden sitting alone in a clearing."

"That was you mummy?"

"Deity would you like to finish the story," Pagan asked sarcastically.

Clearing her throat, Pagan ignored her daughter's response and continued, "He sat down beside her."

"What did you look like mummy?"

Pagan humoured her, "My skin was so pale that you could see my veins, I am told. I had pink lips and Sodalite blue coloured eyes and a cheeky grin. Gorr was a giant of a man and me, so very little."

Deity grinned. She loved the story of how her true daddy and mummy met.

"I placed my pale hand over his large tanned hand and for a long time we sat in silence."

Pagan's heart raced. The memories were still raw, "I asked him, 'If he could see the Goddesses in the forest' He was blinded by his ignorance. I amused him, I think."

"Did you love Daddy straight away?"

"I wouldn't say it was love. Simply a knowing, I suppose. You need to remember that daddy was almost forty years older than me, Deity. Anyway, he felt the strong connection between us. Perhaps, we had both been placed under a spell unbeknown to us but he decided to marry me instead of Aphrodite."

"How angry was Aunty Inanna?"

"Very angry, so angry in fact she cut off all her luscious black hair. In her rage, she cursed me to death and as punishment the Goddesses turned her hair golden as a reminder of her betrayal to another Witch. Cursing another Witch was and is unacceptable. Hexing another Witch is the lowest."

Pagan chuckled at the irony, "I was so frightened of Aphrodite and as karma would have it, we have been reincarnated together ever since."

Glancing at the wall clock, Pagan realised it was very late.

"I better wrap this story up," she winked. "Everything changed. Witches and the Red Haired Men formed a weak alliance but rape and brutality cemented a penis rule. Witch Magick was forbidden and we were not allowed to commune with the Goddesses. Consequently, humans forgot their alliance with us, turning truth into myth. Goddesses were fading away. One day Gorr's younger brother, Tonic formed an alliance with Aphrodite and together they raised a small secret army to overthrow Gorr."

Pagan patted Deity's arm, "I will bypass the violent betrayal as it might give you nightmares, but Tonic and his followers did bad things to me before they cut off my head and placed it on a spike outside my hut. Remember, Aunty Inanna is very sorry for doing that to me."

Reaching for her neck, the memories were almost too painful to continue.

"Gorr found my mutilated body and cut out my heart and then ate it. Heartbroken, he slit his own throat. As he bled to death, he cursed his Gods and the Witches who betrayed me. A mighty thunderstorm erupted causing great destruction to the village. Witches took advantage of the chaos, slaughtering the Red Haired Men as they ran. Witches were not afraid of the Red Haired Men's Gods. The curse however tied Gorr's Magic to my Magick and forever we are bound to each other. He is the only male to reincarnate and we are famously called the Soul-mates."

Pagan enveloped Deity with a tight embrace, "And that is why you are so special Deity because you have Daddy's Magic and Mummy's Magick."

Deity smiled, 'And he always finds you mummy doesn't he? But mummy, why do we hate Non-Ancient Witches?"

Pagan scratched her head, "Because Gorr's curse affected all first reincarnated Witches born after the war. They were born...weak. Their Magick diluted. We do not consider them pure."

"So we hate them because they are weaker than us?"

A snort escaped Pagan's lips, "And this is why you are a great Witch Deity. You do not fear change."

Pagan rubbed her eyes, "I need my beauty sleep, Deity. Not all of us are born beautiful like Aunty Inanna."

Pagan suspected that Deity would fall asleep quickly- the advantages of youth.

Tucking her into bed, she kissed her on the lips and turned out the lamp.

Pagan winced as she remembered her mother's prediction. There were Witches who would see Deity destroyed, believing she is the reason for the contamination of their energies. She had to keep her child safe.

CHAPTER 6
07:00
Hensley

Hensley woke exasperated by another nightmare. Desperate for comfort, she grabbed the photo frame from the bedside table, placing it over her chest.

Gulping down the sadness, memories of the last time she saw her father suppressed her happiness.

It had been an overcast summer evening. The kind of evening that makes you grateful to be alive. He had waved goodbye, regretful that he had been called back to the office over a trivial matter, thrown his car keys into the air and caught them.

Hensley had laughed, as he tooted the car horn.

Ruby and Hensley waved him goodbye without knowing that it would be for the last time. That evening, Hensley and Ruby had watched television and gone to bed at 23:00.

The coroner report stated that he had died of a massive heart attack at approximately 22:20, aged thirty six. A healthy man who ran ten kilometres, twice a week, to have died of a heart attack was a shock.

The cleaner found him at 06:00, the next morning.

Gossip soon spread that he had died of fright in his office that night. The terrified expression on his face plagued the ambulance officers who attended the scene. Her mother had never allowed Hensley to look at the post mortem photographs but tended to agree with the Ambulance officers. All the circumstances around his death were odd.

Now, Hensley looked at a photograph of a man who had been very much alive. Two prominent grey wisps of hair highlighted his short brown beard. His hair was always short but long enough for her little fingers to tug, which she did often.

Always patient with her, never scolding, he preferred to sit her down and explain his reasons for punishment. A kind man, he did not deserve his fate.

She missed him so much.

Epiphany! How stupid had she been? Finally, it dawned on her why she was so distressed. Subconsciously, she was missing her father. She was turning eighteen and her father was not there to see her come of age. What a relief. It must be natural for a daughter who is celebrating a major event in her life to feel upset that her father would not be present.

"Actually, I am eighteen."

Squealing with delight, she jumped out of bed, slipped her cold feet into a pair of pink thongs as she ran into her mother's bedroom.

Ruby was already awake.

Making a cup of tea, Ruby had slipped back into bed to drink it. Quickly placing her tea cup onto the bedside table, she ushered for her daughter to join her.

Hensley climbed in beside her, slipping underneath the doona as if she was still a child.

Hensley poked her mother in the ribs, "It's my birthday."

Ruby wrapped Hensley safely up in her arms, "And happy birthday, baby girl."

Releasing Hensley, Ruby bent over the side of the bed, grabbing a box from underneath her bed. Enthusiastically, she presented the gift to Hensley. The box was small and immaculately wrapped in an elephant print paper. Elephants were Hensley's favourite animal.

Hensley squealed with delight. She loved birthdays, especially when the birthday was hers.

Tearing the paper off, she flipped open the royal blue jewellery box. Inside sat a white gold ring that cushioned a large round pink quart stone.

Hensley placed it on her middle finger, "I love it. Thank you."

Ruby grimaced. Thoughts of Hensley's Witch Awakening smothered any happiness she might have felt on such an occasion.

"Any more nightmares, Hensley?"

Unconvincingly, Hensley replied, "No."

Hensley's father had lied about his nightmares as well. Nightmares so intense that they had decided to sleep in separate rooms so Ruby could at least have a good night sleep.

"You know I'm sure your dad is looking down on you today. Graeme would have been so proud of you."

Hensley also managed a grimace.

08:00

Morghana

Morghana squatted in front of the sliding wardrobe mirror. Finger prints and smoke from the incense stick made it hard for her to see her image clearly. Clothes spread unevenly across the carpet, damp towels scrunched up on the bed, the rat unfed and its box uncleaned, make-up staining her beauty table and the curtains closed. Her room was a mess and she had no intentions of cleaning it. After an adult tantrum, her mother would clean the room out of frustration. She would 'huff and puff' and lecture Morghana for an hour on respect but it was worth the drama to witness her 'always emotionally balanced' mother slightly unbalanced.

Morghana stared at the mirror. Red lumpy rings around her eyes were getting larger. Her pupils were unnaturally dilated. Something was terribly wrong with her.

Resorting to playing the mp3 player on maximum volume had failed to reduce the static in her ears. Was she going mad? Was this part of being a Maiden?

Checking her eyes again, she questioned if she should confide in someone. 'Mum? No she already thinks I'm weird enough'.

Morghana decided to ignore her thoughts and focus on Hensley.

Jealous that Hensley was attending her Witch Awakening, Morghana reminded herself that her eighteenth birthday was only six months away. Surely, Hensley would tell her all the details of the ceremony. It was a pity that Hensley had to do it all alone but if anyone could handle the pressure of a Witch Awakening, Hensley could.

Pushed into a playroom at age five, the two Maidens had been forced to play while Aunty Pagan and Ruby had popped open a bottle of sparkling wine.

The two Maidens had stared at each other for a long time before Hensley made the first move grabbing a doll and giving it to Morghana. The same doll now sat on Morghana's bed.

The alarm alerted Morghana it was almost time for school. She promptly ran up the stairs to the kitchen to pack lunch.

Perched up, reading a magazine on the recliner, Inanna looked happy to see her daughter.

"Good morning."

Morghana ignored her, pulling out a breakfast bowl instead. A bowl, she deliberately slammed down on the kitchen bench to annoy her mother.

Annoyed, Inanna snapped, "Careful."

Smirking, Morghana opened the fridge to grab the milk. Pouring it over her cereal, she placed the bowl into the microwave for thirty seconds. Thirty seconds later the microwave buzzed. Removing the bowl, Morghana sprinkled four large teaspoons full of sugar over her breakfast.

Inanna snapped again, "Seriously Morghana, it's like your seventeen going on two."

Morghana screwed her face up, "Whatever."

Throwing the magazine onto the coffee table, Inanna stood up, "You'll regret that diet of yours when you're forty, Morghana. It will stick to your hips and your arteries young lady. I promise you."

Morghana poured an extra spoonful of sugar over her breakfast in retaliation.

Throwing her arms up into the air, Inanna exited the room, "Have a good day at school, Morghana."

Morghana finished eating her breakfast, throwing the empty bowl into the sink. It never occurred to Morghana to wash up after herself or put the milk back in the fridge. She left for school without packing a lunch.

Hiding in the bedroom, Inanna stared outside at the welcoming view of the ocean. She would go for a swim before the weather cooled. Looking at her watch, she counted the hours left. In seventeen hours, Hensley will be a Witch.

"Poor Child."

12:00

Fay Ce'Line

Swallowing herbal pills, Fay Ce'Line washed it down with a dandelion tea. The tea burned her lips.

Overwhelmed by twelve o'clock, she locked the shop door and closed the curtains quickly before sliding behind the counter. Shaking, she sculled some cold water. It made her feel worse. Her body was under enormous stress.

Considering selling the shop, she weighed up the 'pro's and con's'. It was a successful business but she doubted she would sell it. Online shops were killing off the shop front businesses. Empty shops laced the mall. It was not a good time to sell, plus she loved working in the shop.

At age twenty five, she had finally saved enough money to risk a business venture. The twenty first century had allowed for many personal opportunities.

She wanted to go back to a time when she created her own stress. Before the cancer when trivial matters concerned her: the pot plants getting enough water and sun, or sleepless nights due to the twins, or Oscar pruning the roses back too far. Oscar pruning the roses had really annoyed her.

Struggling to keep any food down a plastic cup that she had used to regurgitate the food into sat beside her. She pushed the plastic cup away. Substituting solid food for freshly squeezed juices had not stopped her from losing weight.

Oscar had mentioned several times that she was losing too much weight, not that she had much to lose.

She had just laughed and told him, "She was on a health kick to cleanse the chemotherapy out from her body."

He had wrapped his arms around her, kissing her on the forehead, claiming that, "She was still beautiful whatever size she was,"- good save.

Fay Ce'Line looked at the wall clock. Hensley would still be at school.

She had rung Ruby at 08:00 to wish Hensley a happy birthday. Hensley had been very excited.

"Dear Goddesses, please help Hensley."

Fay Ce'Line bent over from a sharp pain in her stomach, "And Dear Goddesses, please help me."

The pill lodged. The pain in her stomach was intense. She grabbed the plastic cup regurgitating the pill.

14:00
Amelie

Locking the front door of the florist shop, Amelie sat down behind the work counter and lit a cigarette. The smoke quickly blanketed the room. Taking an exaggerated drag the smoke travelled quickly to her lungs, giving her the kick she required.

Two coffee cups still sat on the bench from the morning. One laced with a sleeping potion that Fay Ce'Line had made especially for Amelie to use. Pouring the tasteless potion into the morning coffee, Amelie had handed the coffee cup a little too keenly to her employer who had taken a sip straight away. Her employer's eyes had heavied and after roughly four minutes, she had collapsed into the office chair falling into a deep sleep.

"Sleeping Beauty- urban style," Amelie had giggled.

Dragging the office chair out of sight, Amelie slammed the office door shut, locking it from the outside. Just in case she woke, Amelie checked in on her employer several times during the day. Stirring once, Amelie had quickly held her employer's nose, pouring extra sleeping potion down her throat. It was unprofessional to drug your employer but Amelie had decided that she was simply taking charge of a situation that required action, especially before she murdered the 'fucking bitch'. Plus, a whole week with a 'psychologically damaged' human in a small shop was too much for Amelie to handle.

Cigarette ash fell on the floor and Amelie spread it out sparingly with her shoe.

The sunshine was breaking through the clouds which consequently warmed the shop. Amelie still shivered. For most of the day it had been bitterly cold.

Sighing, Amelie reached into her dress pocket, pulling out a mobile phone. Quickly typing out a short message, she sent Ruby a text. Waiting for a reply, she finished the cigarette off, opened the front door and tossed the cigarette butt out onto the main street. A lady walking by gave Amelie an unamused glare. Amelie responded by blowing her a kiss.

Closing the front door, she checked the mobile phone again. There was still no reply. Ruby and Hensley had been through enough 'bullshit' in the last few years without having to go through a Witch Awakening.

'The barbaric ritual should be banned', Amelie thought.

Infuriated, Amelie threw the mobile phone across the counter. It landed on a pile of ribbons.

"If only those stupid Crones would only get with the times and pull their brooms out of their arses?"

15:00
Pagan

Slipping the loose fitted purple trousers down over her knees, Pagan sat down on the toilet. Diarrhoea had kept her prisoner to the toilet seat for most of the day. Managing to escape the toilet for five minutes, Pagan quickly collected Demeter and Deity from school at 15:00. In a tight hand grip, she ran back to the car, dragging the children behind her. Sitting in the car, she broke out into an urgent sweat.

Unlocking the back door, Pagan locked herself inside the toilet for another twenty minutes while Demeter and Deity ransacked the kitchen cupboards for chocolate chip cookies to dip into a hot cup of Milo. Sugar and Milo sprinkled the kitchen benches. Moments later Demeter and Deity sat on the couch in the lounge room to watch the television.

Looking at the mess in the kitchen, Pagan angered, "Fucking oath!"

Today was one of those days where the smallest thing threatened to cause a breakdown.

Demeter muted the sound and with a frozen stare looked at Deity, "Mum's crying."

Deity walked swiftly to the kitchen where she found her mother bent over the kitchen bench, sobbing.

"Are you alright, mummy?"

Pagan wrapped her arms tightly around Deity and squeezed. Deity was lucky that she would never experience a Witch Awakening. If only every Witch shared the same fate.

Pulling away from her daughter, Pagan smiled, "How about we fly around in the backyard for a while? Mummy needs some fun."

Deity instantly ran to the lounge room, "Demeter, mummy said we can fly in the back yard."

Taking turns straddling Pagan's back, she flew around the backyard in an anti-clockwise circle. Memories from her previous Witch Awakening diminished any potential happiness she may have had in the backyard with her children. Pagan landed the broom allowing the children to fly alone. Walking back inside, Pagan walked to her bedroom and lay on the bed. Several half read books sat beside her. Haphazardly, she chose the book on top of the pile. Reading the same page three times, she hurtled the book across the room.

23:40
Aislyn

A group of pseudo Witches (women aged over sixty with an intense desire to identify as real Witches) formed a chaotic protection circle in Aislyn's side garden. Wearing black cloaks for dramatic effect, they nervously held hands excitedly, waiting for instructions.

The waxing moon vanished behind the fast moving clouds only to reappear seconds later. The air was electric. The town eerily quiet.

Although, Hensley's Witch Awakening would take place in South Riana, forty minutes west of Latrobe's North West Tasmanian position, Aislyn was positive that Hensley would benefit from the Magickal protection.

As the sun had set, eleven women had arrived at Aislyn's wearing hand-made craft frocks while holding badly made broomstick. There was great excitement and envy when Aislyn appeared with an antique wooden Witch's broom, "Sweep ladies, we need to create a whirlwind."

That afternoon Aislyn had mowed the lawn and trimmed back the plants, disposing of the waste into the compost. Purifying the area, Aislyn sprinkled salt water over the lawn. The grass had hissed as the salt water touched it. An altar made from a 1960's coffee table was positioned in the middle of the lawn and a large black cloth thrown over it. Only a photograph of Hensley was placed on the altar. Once the circle was cast, they would need to remain inside the protected circle until the spell was finished. Aislyn suspected that they would be closing the circle at 01:00 the next day.

They would need refreshments. Aislyn encouraged the women to grab several bottles of semi-sweet mead, chalices and food platters to sit beneath the altar.

At the end of the driveway sat a pile of naturally cleansed rocks. Easily, each woman carried a rock in each palm, placing them in a large circle formation on the lawn. They finished the rock circle in fifteen minutes.

"Bend properly, ladies. Occupational Health and Safety belongs in the craft as well."

Previously, Aislyn had collected the rocks in a picnic basket while walking along the mouth of the Mersey River.

For added protection, they surrounded the rock circle with an additional circle of sea salts, tree branches and lavender bush cuttings. Four candles were placed to form a square within the circle.

In the north quarter, Aislyn placed a green candle to symbolise the earth. In the East quarter, a yellow candle to symbolise air. In the South quarter, a red candle to symbolise fire and a blue candle in the West quarter to symbolise water. The four elements were taken care of. The Goddesses would be pleased.

On entry to the circle, Aislyn wiped a small ochre coloured paste on their foreheads to encourage their third eye connection. It would help link their energies together; Witches and humans. Once inside the circle, the four candles were lit. A gust of wind assured Aislyn that the circle was now protected and blessed by the Goddesses.

Aislyn needed one more element to seal the circle completely; the feminine energy.

Looking around the circle, Aislyn felt an overwhelming sense of pride. It was certainly a new beginning for female and Witch relations. An early morning psychic vision had shocked Aislyn nine years ago. In the vision, she had witnessed an uprising of female empowerment. Females fighting alongside Witches and a new spiritual path created. The vision had excited Aislyn and she knew that her personal path was to encourage a merging of all female energy. Witches and females would become allies.

"I think you need to remember the 'Blood Oath', mum," Pagan snapped after Aislyn repeated the vision. "We can't renege on our agreement with the church. Women are gaining their power back naturally without you interfering. Leave shit alone."

In the latter end of the 1400's the Highest Priestess and the Sisters of the Moon (modern day Crone Monarchy) revealed to Pope Innocent VIII that Witches did indeed exist and that it was time for the churches to stop prosecuting humans as Witches. They wanted the Witch hunting to stop. Pope Innocent VIII had been ecstatic by the revelation, smug in fact. He had been right- Witches did exist. Truthfully, Witches wanted to stop hiding in the shadows of humanity. They needed protection. Their Magick was dying.

The three thousand and fifty five page, 'Blood Oath' treaty was sealed with the blood of the Highest Priestess and Pope Innocent VIII, and promptly placed in high security at the Vatican. Witches gained autonomy to govern themselves as long as they remained faithful to the Catholic Church and male superiority. Witches became fairy-tales and the Goddesses merely hearsay.

Aislyn held a wand towards the moon, "Diana, I ask thee. Cast the circle thrice about. Shield Goddess. Keep the male energy out!"

A silver shield rose from the ground joining at the top, creating a large dome around them. They were protected.

23:50
Ruby

Curled up against the large willow tree in the backyard, Ruby peeled off long thin pieces of bark, throwing them into a pile on the ground.

Howling from grief, her screams went unheard. She screamed louder. A raw abandoned cry echoed through the surrounding paddocks.

Twisting in agony, she stood up, stumbling back towards the house, she fell landing on her hands and knees.

She cursed the unknown monsters that would soon be attacking her daughter.

Throwing herself against the house, she finally collapsed from exhaustion onto the ground.

CHAPTER 7
29th March, 2010
Pagan

Sipping an early morning coffee, Pagan stared at the computer monitor. Clicking through her personal photographs, she spent less than a second on each image. Joining the internet social network site four years prior the site had quickly become an addiction. Uploading almost nine hundred photographs and adding over one thousand friends and many of them Witches, Pagan found that she wasted at least one hour a day on it.

An acquaintance had died the year before and his page had become a memorial. His death far outreached the expected grief perimeters. She still enjoyed reading his comments. It was if he was somehow still alive.

Pagan clicked on her main page, adding a new status.

She typed, "Today I am grateful for technology," in the belief that if she said it enough she might actually, eventually, believe it. Within a few seconds a friend 'liked' her status.

A text message broke her concentration. It was from John. He was waiting at the front door. Impatiently waiting, Pagan assumed.

Drinking the rest of the coffee, she grabbed the blue plastic bag that contained chocolate Easter eggs out from the top cupboard in the kitchen and headed to the front door tiptoeing past Demeter's and Deity's bedroom. Opening the front door the cold morning breeze erected her nipples. Wearing only a black nighty, she blushed from embarrassment, after all, John was now a stranger to her. The children were only a business arrangement.

Carefully handing John the plastic bag full of chocolate Easter eggs, she crossed her arms to hide her breasts. He grabbed the bag and awkwardly focused his attention on the flaking weatherboard cladding. This angered Pagan who was proud of her aging home.

John's partner Michelle sat in the front passenger seat of John's car. The car idled in the driveway. That also annoyed Pagan.

Michelle waved. Pagan waved backed and John hovered.

Pagan had wanted contact with John to be swift. John was not her enemy but the mere sight of him brought back memories that she would rather forget.

Pagan leaned on the door frame, "What is it, John?"

Struggling to find the right words, he screwed his face up.

"Is it the kids?"

John looked back at the car for encouragement. Michelle smiled at him.

Turning back to face Pagan, John finally spoke, "I was wondering if you could have a word with Demeter about his bad dreams."

Confused Pagan replied, "What bad dreams?"

Fay Ce'Line

Lounging in the warm and cosy bed, Fay Ce'Line chuckled as she heard Oscar playing the banjo in the dining area. Laughter from the twins only encouraged him to continue playing.

Fay Ce'Line looked out the window. Winter was fast approaching and many of the garden's deciduous trees had not yet lost their leaves, hanging on until the first torrential rainfall.

In a dream, Fay Ce'Line had walked through a large open planned home: burnt orange walls combined with a dark blue feature wall, the floor was highly glossed and in the middle of the kitchen, lounge room and dining area, a large tree trunk supported the roof. The following morning, she had sat down and drawn up the plan. Two years later, after living in a small shed, they moved into their newly built home. Large windows without curtains allowed for natural light and an organic tranquillity to envelope the house. A dream had become a reality.

Turning onto her back, Fay Ce'Line struggled to find motivation. She could easily stay in bed and stare into the surrounding garden for another hour.

Grinning, Oscar appeared at the bedroom door holding his banjo, "Shall I play for you, my dear?"

Fay Ce'Line laughed, "Please don't. There is only so much torture a Witch can tolerate before she turns you into a frog."

Wearing only green shorts, Fay Ce'Line admired her husband's body.

Short in stature, he had remained taut and physically strong. His once hairless chest now glisten grey.

Sitting up, Fay Ce'Line asked Oscar to sit with her. Obediently, he placed the banjo at the end of the bed and climbed in beside her.

They snuggled.

"Where are the girls?"

Oscar teased, "Tied to the clothes line."

Fay Ce'Line pinched Oscar's bicep.

"How about we have a quickie before the girls finish their breakfast?" He jested.

Wanting to please him, she kissed him on his dry cold lips.

Since the chemotherapy, her libido had vanished, even herbal concoctions had not helped. The doctor explained to her that it was completely normal and that her libido would come back, eventually. They had not made love in six months.

Oscar was a considerate man but for how long?

Pulling back from Fay Ce'Line, Oscar spoke, "I forgot to tell you. Ma and Pa are happy to have the kids while we're at Samhain."

Samhain was Oscar's favourite weekend escape and he would most likely pack his travel bag several days before the annual festival. He loved the sexiness of Samhain as it combined elements of the Beltane Fertility ritual which was being celebrated in the Northern Hemisphere at the same time. Australian Witches celebrated the coming winter by gathering in mass at the Samhain festival which was being held in Tasmania this year.

Frowning, she replied, "I better get busy making strega then!"

Fay Ce'Line looked forward to her cup of 'Strega' as well.

Once a year, she would drink this narcotic drink with Oscar. It helped rekindle their love and sexual appetite for each other. Maybe a double dose this year? The 'coming down' effect lasted for a few days but it was well worth the withdrawals.

A spoon fell, clanging on the floorboards alerting them that breakfast was finished.

"Oh shit, I better get back to the twins."

Oscar sprung out of the bed, grabbing the banjo and twanged it.

Fay Ce'Line slowly stood up out of bed, "You are a juvenile!"

Morghana

Walking quickly to school, Morghana was out of breath by the time she reached the school entrance. Hensley's car was not parked in front of the school or in the school car park which was unusual.

Ringing and texting over half a dozen times over the weekend, Morghana had finally rung Hensley's landline only to be greeted by Ruby who had simply lied about Hensley's whereabouts. Ruby's quivering voice had repeated every question Morghana had asked back to her as if she was stalling to reply. Something was not right.

Surely, Hensley would come to school? The only time Hensley had taken time off school since kindergarten was when her father had died and although grief stricken she was back only several days after the funeral.

Perhaps, Hensley had been dropped off at school by Ruby?

Morghana entered the school, walking down two sets of stairs and into the dungeon locker room, stopping at Hensley's locker. She would wait.

Students collecting their school books soon dispersed into the classrooms.

Another five minutes passed. The school bell would ring soon.

Pulling out a hairpin from behind her ear, Morghana inserted it into Hensley's padlock. Wiggling it around inside the padlock, it finally unlatched.

Pulling out a jumper that Hensley left inside her locker, Morghana held it against her nose. It smelt of Red Door perfume, Hensley's favourite.

Clearing her mind, she visualised Hensley in hope that she could tune into Hensley's thoughts.

Hensley was tall with a slender, almost bony body. Her long and slender feet were too long for her stick legs and Hensley, due to her foot size, only ever wore thongs, as other shoes exaggerated the actual appearance of her feet.

Hensley who was not only smart and beautiful, was also dogmatic and proud.

The bell rang. The late arriving students fled to class, leaving Morghana alone in the locker room. Morghana was late for Sociology but finding Hensley was more important.

Texting Hensley once again, Morghana sat down on the cold cement floor and waited for a reply. Fifteen minutes later, Hensley walked into the locker room wearing jeans, a grey skivvy and a dark green beanie as if winter had arrived early.

Jumping up from the floor, Morghana wrapped her arms around Hensley, "I've been worried sick about you."

Hensley ignored Morghana's theatrics.

Morghana hit her on the arm, "What the hell happened at the Witch Awakening?"

Ignoring Morghana's question, Hensley proceeded to throw her bag into the locker.

Desperate for attention, Morghana placed her palm on Hensley's shoulder.

Swinging around Hensley pushed Morghana backwards, "Don't touch me!"

Amelie

Cocking her head to the side to showcase her long swan neck, Amelie confidently replied to the customer's question. Up until now no-one had noticed her employer's absence. The customer was a strange looking woman. The type who is far too self-assured considering her less than attractive aesthetics.

Amelie pitied the woman who was as short as she was wide, with a mouth that housed too many teeth. It amazed Amelie that humans breed so often, considering their limited supply of worthy partners. Humans certainly were Earth's sexually transmitted disease.

The customer also held her stare for far too long. Had this woman been socialised? Amelie wanted to flick the customer in the forehead. Retailers sure do have their fair share of crazies to deal with.

Composed, Amelie answered, "She's having some time off. She should be back, maybe next week."

Satisfied with the reply, the customer picked up the previously purchased bouquet of six red roses from the counter and wobbled out of the shop.

Waiting until the woman was clearly out of sight, Amelie unlocked the office door where her employer slept in the office chair, with a blanket tucked around her.

Amelie shut the door behind her. The doorbell would alert her if anyone walked into the shop.

Unscrewing the lid off the small brown bottle marked 'Sleeping Beauty', Amelie poured a few more drops of sleeping potion down her employer's throat. Concerned she had to increase the dosage each day for the desired effect, she feared her employer was desensitising to the potion.

Perhaps drugging her employer so frequently was not such a good idea, especially now people were noticing her absence. She was looking surprisingly younger for the sleep though. Her skin had softened, the dark rings around her eyes were disappearing and when she woke each day, although concerned that she had slept again all day and that her neck was stiff, she was much more pleasant to talk to. Surely her husband had noticed the difference?

Amelie poured some extra sleeping potion down her throat, put the lid back on the bottle and slipped it back into her pocket, "Sleep, bitch."

Locking the office door behind her, Amelie danced over to the counter. Spread across the counter was material to perform a love spell: a pink candle, cocktail stick, a strip of paper, assorted ribbons and a length of spindle wood.

'Did she really want a man that she had to bewitch and was he worth surrendering her celibacy for?'

"Hmmm?"

Visualising the way that his jeans sat on his arse and the way his smile lit up his eyes, Amelie's heart raced. She was in-lust with this man that was for sure.

"That man is fine."

She scanned the materials in front of her. Gathering it all up, she threw them into a cardboard box. Why did she want a love spell? A sex spell would be much better.

Pagan

Turning the heat pump up, Pagan changed out of her work clothes and into pyjamas.

Entering the kitchen, she made a peppermint tea to fill the empty void in her stomach.

83

Finally resting on the couch, she flicked through the newspaper tray pulling out an out-of-date celebrity magazine. The sound of the clock ticking affected her ability to concentrate and only a few minutes later, she threw the magazine down onto the floor.

Tired, Pagan rubbed her eyes and then curled up into the warmth of the couch and surrendered to sleep.

She heard the mobile phone beep at 22:00. Looking at the message, she was not disappointed it woke her up as he was exactly what she needed. Replying back to him, she rolled over and drifted back off to sleep. Henry knew where the spare key was hidden. He knew the routine.

'Fuck buddies', seemed the most sensible option for a thirty three year old Witch who did not want a relationship but still harboured strong sexual desires, and she had trained him well in the last six months. Number one rule and most important; do not fall in love. Love was not an option. Love with sex was great but sex with lust came in a close second.

Playing the 'unavailable character' kept the male species interested. It worked a treat actually. Most men were easily manipulated. Nearly every man Pagan had ever slept with had fallen in love with her. The smart one's had just kept quiet about it.

Henry was different. He had only just turned eighteen and was 'half cocked' and arrogant in his youth. The internet had raised an eager but lazy generation Y. Their sexual exploration was based on internet porn available to them at a young age, leaving them sexually deviate before they had even kissed a girl. Henry had wanted to explore 'anal' and sexual fetishes before he had even experienced the basics. Pagan explained to him that there was a necessary process of sexual engagement that even strangers had to abide by.

"Slow down, Henry. Enjoy the dance."

Young men wanted to be forty while middle aged men acted twenty.

Pagan had dated forty year old men who often mentally attacked her in response to their lack of erection. Easily threatened by her sexual prowess, she disposed of those men quickly.

Meeting Henry at a party, Pagan had sensed immediately that he was emotionally wounded. Her fetish for emotionally unavailable males had intensified. Crazies made superb and uninhibited lovers. Sleeping with an insecure man annoyed her. If he could not lose himself in the moment, then he was quickly replaced with a man who could. Unemotional men had nothing to lose.

Sex was an art form for Pagan; romanticism and abstract style, melted into a dark pit of self-mutilation and conscious emotional betrayal, on a ply wood canvas. At best, sex could imitate Frank Bernard Dicksee's painting of 'Romeo and Juliet' in 1884, a romantic collage of uninhibited sexual urges, faithfulness and youthful ignorance, and at worst, sex was graphic graffiti on the Berlin Wall. In between both extremes was a sickness called 'self-hatred'.

Growing up in a rich conservative household, Henry hankered for sexual liberation not just in his mind but physically as well. He was ripe, needy and eager to learn. He had been an astute student.

Concerned with his age, Pagan rejected his initial advances. Equally annoyed that he had 'poked' her on Facebook, she had sent him an inbox, "Try harder."

Several hours later, he replied, "I couldn't get any harder. So when am I coming over…you?"

His reply infuriated and intrigued her. Generation Y certainly were straight to the point. She had decided to train him in hope, he might teach the other boys a few pointers.

The back door creaked.

Smelling Henry's scent, Pagan hopped off the couch and walked to the backdoor to greet him.

"Is it too much to ask you to shower before you visit me?" He smelt of his girlfriend.

He had just had sex with her. Perfume, vaginal juices and saliva still coated his erect penis.

Standing lean, his youth claimed vitality in the doorway.

Smiling, he replied, "Hey, cougar."

"Isn't little, Miss Vanilla, doing it for you anymore?"

Slowly lifting his top to reveal a very firm upper body, he waited for Pagan to praise his physic. The boy was magnificent but she was not about to tell him that. His ego was inflated enough.

Dropping his trousers, he waited again for Pagan to praise him.

Unamused by the boring sexual ritual, she yawned. He wanted instant gratification and she was a tough task master. After all, she had witnessed the male sexual ritual over ten thousand times and after a while it all seemed rather tedious and cliché.

If only men would 'get over' themselves.

She ushered him to follow her to the bedroom. She stripped her clothes off as they walked and by the time they reached the bedroom door, she was naked.

Laying down on the doona, she spread her legs.

He was not repulsed by her hairy genital bush and underarms. There was something wild about Pagan and he loved it. She was sexier than any girl his age. Actually, she was sexier than any woman he had ever seen.

Long black hair, incompatible with her dark blue eyes and freckled skin, shaped her long face. Her chunky thighs, large hips, chubby tummy and smaller breasts aroused him.

Like a trained dog, he walked to her expecting a treat but brushing his blonde hair off his face, he hesitated. Only twenty minutes before, he had left his girlfriend parent's home where they had spent the night playing a game of Uno. Managing a missionary style quickie in his girlfriend's bedroom before he left, he had been the dominant person, now he was staring at an alpha female who liked it hard-core, and she did not like to be disappointed.

The safety code was 'Green Apple' which was pretty hard to say with a sock in your mouth, so a double tap sufficed; they had not used either yet.

Sitting beside her on the bed, he placed his middle finger abruptly into her dry vagina. With the other hand, he opened and pushed up her flaps. Slowly licking her clitoris, her vagina lubricated. She had shown him to not just part her flaps but to lift up her skin which lifted her clitoris. It intensified her orgasm. His long middle finger pushed further in and tilted up.

Pressing on her g-spot, Pagan arched. She had shown him where her g-spot was as well.

A surge of aggression flooded her body. Pinching her nipples, he made sure it hurt her. She did not flinch. Pagan enjoyed 'giving and receiving' pain.

Delighted, Pagan rewarded him by reaching down, grabbing his penis. He stopped to enjoy the pleasure.

Slapping him across his face, he welted quickly. She had not given him permission to stop. It was not the first time she had slap him into submission.

In retaliation, he pushed hard up into her vagina.

Choking on her breath, she smiled at him, "Good boy."

His youthful body submerged on top of her body and in one smooth move, he grabbed the ropes that were tied to the bed, twisting them quickly around both her wrists. Submissive was a sexual 'turn on' for Pagan.

Plunging his penis into her vagina, she arched her back and held her breath. He knew how she liked it- hard. So hard, sometimes he thought he might tear her in half and still she asked for more.

Clasping one hand around her neck, he squeezed until she could not breathe. His other hand slid down over her waist, grabbing her right buttock, raising her bottom so he could enter her more deeply.

Biting her shoulder, he quickly tasted blood. He bit her again, this time ripping her flesh.

Pulling out of her before he ejaculated, he covered her stomach instead. She would be mad that he ejaculated without permission.

Wiggled out of the ropes, Pagan flipped him onto his back and mounted him.

He grinned at her.

She slapped the other side of his face with the back of her hand, "Don't fucking smile at me."

The other side of his face welted.

Scratching at his chest, picking up his skin in a clump, his blood bubbled up onto the surface. She licked his blood until it cupped her chin.

He grabbed her hips but Pagan slapped him again, "I'll tell you when you can touch me."

Obediently, he let go of her, placing both his hands smugly behind his head.

Looking into his eyes, she asked, "Tell me you want me."

He did.

"Tell me again."

"I want you, Pagan."

"Again!"

"I want you, Pagan."

Pagan felt the explosion propel up from her clitoris and through her head. Her ears deafened and all her senses numbed and then she felt it. The emptiness. It was always there.

It was time for Henry to go home.

Demeter

Tiptoeing across the hallway, through the lounge room and up a set of stairs and into another hallway, he entered his father's bedroom, but only Michelle slept in the king size bed.

Not sure if he should wake her, Demeter considered going to Deity's room and hopping into bed with her until the morning.

Sensing a dark figure beside the bed, Michelle sat up, turning the lamp on.

Groggy from being woken, she snapped at her stepson, "What are you doing out of bed?"

Sensing that Michelle was annoyed, Demeter wanted to return to his room but fear paralysed him.

His voice trembled, "He's back again, Michelle. He's in my room."

Michelle glanced at the alarm clock. It was 02:00. Why was John not home from work yet?

"For fuck sake," Michelle said under her breath. She could see that Demeter was genuinely frightened but she had only just drifted off to sleep and would be rising at 06:00.

Jumping out of bed, she threw her peach coloured chiffon dressing gown over her pyjamas and ushered Demeter to follow her back to his room.

Hesitantly, he followed her.

Turning each room's light on as she walked through the house, she considered ringing John. She loved Demeter but she was out of her league dealing with a mysterious dark figure.

Not having children of her own, she struggled at how best to deal with Demeter's wild imagination. John had certainly thrown her into the 'deep end of the pool' when he asked her to move in with them six months ago.

Wanting to hold Michelle's hand, Demeter shadowed closely behind her.

Secretly, he hoped that the man was still standing in the corner of his room so finally Michelle would believe him.

Michelle entered the downstairs hallway, flicking the light on, real or not, she was not about to walk through the house unprepared. She suddenly stopped at the Demeter's bedroom doorway.

Demeter comically ran into the back of her.

Had she not been apprehensive, she would have laughed.

Peering into his room, her eyes darted across the darkened area. All the bedroom corners were clear of any dark figures.

Grabbing Demeter's hand, she pulled him in front of her. He resisted moving forward.

"Can you see him, Demeter?"

Like a cautious emu, he pushed his head away from his body. Looking inside his room, he studied the darker spots. Relieved that they all appeared empty, he turned his light on and ran to his bed.

Michelle tucked him back into bed, "Would you like me to keep the light on?"

He nodded.

"Michelle, will you stay with me for a while?"

Accepting of her sleepless night, she nodded.

"Move over spunky. If I'm staying I might as well get comfy."

Demeter moved over allowing Michelle to squeeze onto the single bed. She lay on top of the covers while he snuggled in underneath them. Her head leaned on her arm and her feet hung over the edge. She could easily fall back to sleep.

He liked Michelle. She was very different to his mum but she seemed to make his dad very happy.

"Hey Demeter, tell me about the man?"

Demeter curled up, pulling the covers up above his nose. His eyes widened. Shaken up by the ghostly visitation, he glanced every few minutes across the room.

"I heard my name and woke up and the man was standing over there."

Poking his index finger out from the covers, he pointed to the corner opposite them.

"What does he do when he notices you are looking at him?"

Michelle noticed Demeter shiver as he thought about it. Regardless if it was a nightmare or something supernatural, Demeter was definitely frightened.

"He just stands there looking at me."

Demeter hid further down into the covers. Only the top of his eyes peered out from the safety of the bed covers. Except for his blue eyes, Demeter looked very similar to his father. His hair was darkening and he was starting to lose his childhood body chub. In a few years, Demeter would be a very handsome teenager. Deity, however, did not look like John or Pagan. Michelle had brought up her observation several times with John who had quickly changed the subject.

"Tell me what the man looks like again, Demeter!"

Pulling the covers down to his chin, Demeter's eyes darted across the room again, "He wears a long black cloak and a large hat, like what the olden day men used to wear."

Yawning, Michelle interrupted, "Top hat?"

"No!"

She guessed again, "Bowler hat?"

"I think so."

He drew the shape of the bowl hat with his index finger.

Michelle nodded.

"But he has no eyes but I know he is looking at me. And he's really tall."

Looking for a sensible explanation, Michelle interrupted him again, "Do you think you might have watched something like that on television?

Thinking about it for a while, he replied, "Don't know. Maybe."

"Does he look like a ghost?"

An adrenaline rush surged through Demeter's veins. Maybe Michelle was starting to believe him.

"No! He is solid black. I can't see through him?"

Michelle shook her head. Her eyes were closing. Several seconds later, she drifted off to sleep.

Demeter stared at the corner opposite him until he too drifted off to sleep.

Peony

Peony woke to Carl brushing his hands along the inside of her thigh. His hand was soft from obsessive moisturising of them and they slid easily under her flannelette nighty, resting in between her legs.

Cringing, she asked him to stop, "Carl! I'm trying to sleep."

Ignoring her, he grabbed at her underwear pulling them to the side.

Quietly responding, she moved further away from him, pushing his hand away, "Carl! I'm not in the mood."

Angry, Carl pounced on top of Peony, grabbing both her wrists with one hand, forcing them behind her head. The heaviness of his body pinned her underneath him and caved her chest in. With one hand, he removed his boxer shorts.

She did not struggle. This was not the first time he has used aggression during their sixteen years of marriage. Carl thought it was Peony's duty as his wife to submit to his sexual needs, and 'to keep the peace', she often unwillingly submitted to him. It never occurred to Peony to question it. She spent most of her time actively trying to avoid it by offering him another beer so he might pass out or encouraging him to spend more time with his mates.

Working in the Western Australia meant that their sexual encounters occurred less often, and this she was happy about.

Carl had always enjoyed porn, young female porn mostly. His fetish for shaven pussies in a school uniform repulsed her. During sex, he would make her say, "Oh Daddy, give it to me."

It was demoralising.

He often demanded that Peony watch porn with him and then act out the scene but since his new employment his sexual demands had worsened and at times, Peony had feared for her life. The bondage ropes were tightening and his desire to reduce her to tears intensifying.

Past terrifying altercations had taught her not to reject Carl sexually. He was quick to temper and enjoyed using cruelty to make her submissive. Complying with his sexual needs meant that it was over quickly, and any danger drastically reduced.

Pulling her underwear to the side again, he pushed his penis into her vagina.

Unlubricated, she swelled quickly.

Never having children and only ever having one sexual partner meant that her cervix had remained intact and her vagina entry small. Carl had great pleasure claiming that he had sovereignty over her 'pussy'.

On several occasions during their marriage, Peony had accidently orgasmed while riding a bike. Carl had only ever given her a headache.

For most of the time, she wished that Carl would look for sex elsewhere, but she would pity the woman Carl would have an affair with.

Wiggling on top of her, he buried his hawk looking face into her neck. Foaming saliva dribbled down into her hair and within a few minutes of him groaning, he ejaculated inside of her.

Hearing the woeful sound of Carl finishing was better than any orgasm. It meant it was over and over was great.

Rolling off her, he left her underwear lodged into the cress of her groin and a wet spot beneath her bottom. Chaffing from the underwear, she had bled a little.

Unsure of what to do, she turned over onto her side and closed her eyes.

The morning sun was just breaking through the bedroom curtains. Having to start the day with marital rape was not what she had wanted but it was what she was used to.

London
Kramer

Graciously accepting his new assignment, he simply nodded and left the room. Their glares warmed not only his back but his ego as he strutted out through the door.

Written instructions were to be picked up at the office on his way out.

Reading the print, he was amazed at how much the Crone Monarchy was willing to pay him.

Looking up from the paper, he winked at the secretary who shyly looked away.

Instructions- he is to fly to Australia by broomstick, so there would be no trace of him in the country. There, he is to spy on a group of Ancient Witches for any evidence that they were conspiring against the Crone Monarchy. If he finds any evidence, he is to kill them, leave no evidence and bring back their heads.

Startling the secretary with laughter, he imagined himself as Santa Claus carrying Witches heads instead of toys within a large blood stained sack.

The secretary asked him to leave the office.

Grudgingly, he did.

Meeting many Australian's on his travels through Europe, he had always wanted to visit Australia and now he was being paid to do it. His only annoyance was that he was leaving one winter to enter another but it would feel great to be back on a broom and fresh air on his face. Plus, he may have the opportunity to kill again. He was a Witch Hunter and paid by Witches to do it. Witches were clever like that. They never feared being hunted, so much so they capitalise on it.

Traditionally, Witches were only in Europe but they were being born all over the world now. It was a fucking disgrace.

"Witch convicts," he laughed as he left the building.

Witches were merely shells of their former glory- trapped within their own self-importance. They were arrogant to the point of foolishness.

In a large white envelope were the names, addresses and photographs of the Witches he was to survey. Flipping through the photographs, he froze. Running his thumb over Pagan's face, he recognised her name. As a powerful Ancient Witch she might sense that she is being watched? He would need to be very careful. These Witches were famous for being extremely cruel and loyal to each other.

No wonder Aggie was keen to have them surveyed. These Witches would be a serious threat to Aggie's Non-Ancient regime.

Pagan may prove difficult to kill but he suspected it would be fun trying.

He smirked, "They all have to sleep sometime."

Lifting his arms high above his head, the envelope dangling above his eyes, a surge of excitement lifted his spirit. He was keen to go home and pack.

CHAPTER 8

Inanna

The house was silent except for the occasional rustling of possums outside the bedroom window. It was still dark outside.

Inanna had slept the entire night, but now lay awake looking at the bedroom ceiling. Moving across the bed, she found comfort against Mark's body. Cuddling up to him, she instantly felt sleepy again.

Resisting sleep, she stared at Mark.

Snoring lightly, Mark was still in a deep slumber. Listening to the gurgling of his snore, she tried to envision a life without him, a life without the safety of his touch, his kind words and the compassion in his eyes. His friendship would be hard to replace by another.

She wished that she could stop 'time' and stay with him forever.

He was a handsome man; his healthy lifestyle and easy-going exterior helped him to age gracefully. His nicely shaped bald head highlighted his greying goatee – a brittle cluster of hair that warmed his chin while also tickling her chin when they kissed. The goatee suited him as did his bald head, her 'gangster' was missing his machine gun and violent disposition. A silent intruder, Mark's presence was always felt when he entered a room. He was a man who in stillness conquered sound and due to his education and rigorous travel expeditions, his ability to concur with almost every conversation left him well liked. Childless, he had welcomed an eight year old Morghana into his life as his own. They fought and loved as if he had produced the seed for her creation.

Inanna met him at a superannuation party. Giggling often about their unromantic introduction it was perhaps the most romantic moment of her life, actually every life. Both reaching for the same pen, his fingertips had brushed the top of her hand and a wave of exultation rushed through her body. Looking up at him, she was embarrassed and walked away. He had promptly sat next to her at the table and after several days of investigation had found her name, relationship status and phone number. Dating for two years, they had made the bold move of living together. It had been the right decision. They soon discovered that they were not only lovers but also best friends and their superannuation was also in bulk.

Wondering what time it was, Inanna looked at the alarm clock. It was time to rise and prepare for the day. She was looking forward to their family day. It would start with an Easter Hunt, Atlantic salmon and Greek salad for lunch, followed by a bottle of sparkling red wine, and to finish off their day, a walk to the beach or a game of chess, weather permitting of course.

Inanna slipped out of bed, entering the en-suite moments later. Turning the taps to the spa on, she poured a small quantity of rose aromatherapy oil into the steaming water. It quickly bubbled.

Slipping her nightie off and loosely tying her hair in a bun, she submerged her body into the spa. She welcomed the warmth. Once the water covered her breasts, she pressed the 'on' button. The spa took several seconds to start. The pressure from the vents instantly released tension from her back. She sat back into the warmth and solitude of the water. Life had never been so good.

Amelie

Re-lighting seven already half burned green candles, Amelie knelt in front of the wooden circular altar which faced north to symbolise stability and focus.

Her knees and hips ached. Rolling her eyes from the irony, she sat down on the floor enjoying the comfort of her padded bottom.

"Focus!"

Boring quickly of the ritual, she decided to have a cigarette instead. The ashtray sat alongside the silver chalice, bowl of salt, incense burner, a pentagram, a bell, altar oil, and a purple glass goblet that was filled with Chardonnay, an athame, a wand, a mirror and her book of shadows that was full of scribbles.

Rituals were really a waste of time, especially when all she was doing was going through the motions.

Grabbing the athame, she cleaned the dirt out from underneath her finger nails in anticipation of Pagan arriving soon.

Amelie looked forward to Samhain festivities, particularly this year because it was being held in Tasmania. Over two thousand Witches were expected to arrive over the next twenty four hours from all over Australia. The other bonus was that Maidens were not allowed to go to this festival. No pretentious children to get under her feet.

Her cold personality could not deny her excitement that both her sisters, Peony and Roberta, were joining her this year. Hopefully, Roberta would bring her Maltese husband Don and with a bit of luck, Peony would leave her 'fuckwit husband', at home.

"Yes! This weekend would be brilliant."

Amelie grabbed her goblet, "I'll drink to that."

Fay Ce'Line

Oscar and Fay Ce'Line's naked bodies knelt in front of the long rectangular alter that Oscar had made from old fence palings five years previously.

Wearing a large 'Green Man' mask that he had freshly covered in green foliage from his conifer bush that morning, Oscar felt as if he was also part of the ritual.

Fay Ce'Line wore a silver crescent crown over her crew-cut hair. It made her look 'fairy like' rather than a Witch and Oscar had teased her that she was offending the Fairies. Retaliating, she had punched him on the forearm.

They lit fourteen candles and the incense stick. The smoke floated straight into the air causing a ceiling cloud above them.

Two old broomsticks that Fay Ce'Line converted into ritual besoms lay behind their bottoms ready for when they swept the negativity from their home.

Oscar had used a boline- a knife shaped in a half moon to cut the garden flowers and Fay Ce'Line had tied them together with string, placing them into seven glass vases which were sat on the purple altar cloth. The sweet smelling aroma soon filled the room.

Large crystals; a Sunstone- raw, transparent and orange; a Variscite-opaque and green; a Sodalite- tumbled and mottled blue; and a Selenite- wand shaped translucent and white, accompanied the flowers.

A batch of 'Strega' bubbled in the cauldron. She would have to bottle the liquid before Pagan arrived to pick them up.

Giving thanks, they were grateful for everything in their lives, even the cancer. Promising to remain faithful to their path and to the Goddesses, they asked for guidance. Fay Ce'Line needed the Goddesses more than ever. She hoped that they had heard her prayers.

After the ceremony, Fay Ce'Line kissed Oscar on the check, "I'm especially grateful for my husband."

Winter was fast approaching and after the Samhain festival, Fay Ce'Line planned on cocooning within her home, concentrating on the twins and Oscar.

Standing up, her stomach twinged. Exiting the room quickly, she hoped Oscar had not noticed the pain on her face or the fear in her eyes.

He had seen both, but neither Fay Ce'Line nor Oscar noticed that the smoke from the incense stick had become erratic and broken.

Hensley

Camouflaged amongst the old Blackwood tree, Hensley hid in the rundown tree house. Wearing pyjamas mid-morning, memories of a happy childhood suddenly felt blemished.

Declining the offer to attend the Samhain festival, Hensley had not even waved 'goodbye' as her mother drove away in Pagan's Kombi van.

Now that she was a Witch she was welcomed to join them. In previous years, she had stayed with her grandparents on her father's side.

Ruby had been disappointed that Hensley had declined the offer but looked relieved to leave her unrecognisable daughter at home.

Wiping the tears from her eyes, Hensley wished that she was a Maiden again. Even the pain from her father's death had not prepared her for the heartache she felt now. Grief of her lost innocence, of people who had died in previous reincarnations and an uncertain future, swirled around inside of her head and sunk her chest. Grief was slightly more manageable than the knowledge of who she was! And who Ruby was! Although in another body, Ruby's energy was recognisable.

All the vile things Ruby and the Ancient Witches had done to her in previous reincarnations made her livid and now she was reincarnated with them. Why had the Goddesses placed her with them? What a cruel joke.

Holding a pair of silver scissors, she raised the scissors up slowly, snapping them open and shut. Cutting aimlessly, large chunks of hair fell upon the tree house floor. Blood dripped on her clothing.

Throwing the scissors across the floor, raged consumed her.

With one quick and deliberate slap, she smacked her cheeks so hard with her open hand that she instantly welted. She hit herself again.

Pagan

Pale blue, Pagan had named the Kombi 'Blue Bell'. The 1960's interior was furnished with jungle print curtains and a second hand kitchen sink, set into a dark green cabinet which separated the driver's seat to the back section. Two couch seats that flipped back to become a double bed made travelling stress-free for Pagan while comfortably seating six friends.

The Kombi hosted Amelie, Fay Ce'Line, Oscar and Ruby in a whirlwind of laughter and competing conversation. Stories were being embellished and exaggerated as the volume amplified.

Amelie who sat in the front passenger seat could barely hear Pagan's mobile phone ringing but managed to pull it out of Pagan's handbag before it rang out. She handed it to Pagan who while still driving, answered it.

"Hello."

It was Demeter.

Handing the mobile phone back to Amelie, Pagan switched the mobile phone to loud speaker.

"Mum, Deity is changing the clouds into animal shapes again and dad told her to stop it but she won't."

Pagan glanced out of the window at the cloudy blue sky; a large rabbit formation grabbed her attention.

"Tell Deity, that if she doesn't do what daddy tells her, I will ban her from jazz ballet for a whole month."

Demeter repeated what Pagan had just said to Deity, adding the always threatening, "Mum said…"

As the phone call ended, they erupted into fits of laughter. Laughter that hurt their stomach muscles and drowned their cheeks with tears.

Reaching into the glove box to pull out a tissue to wipe her eyes, Amelie found a hidden plastic bag under some papers. Opening the bag, she found freshly made cannabis joints. Eager to feel uninhibited again, Amelie lit one and passed it on to Pagan who took a large drag and then passed it onto Oscar. The sweet fresh smell of cannabis enveloped the Kombi rapidly enveloping their bodies and minds.

Keen to share a party mix of relaxation and hypertension, Oscar blew smoke into Fay Ce'Line's mouth.

They kissed.

Ruby sank solemnly into the back seat. The cannabis smoke only added to her anxiety.

Stoned or not, Pagan knew the road to the festival intimately and after forty minutes they had driven through Deloraine heading towards the Great Western Tiers and into Tasmanian's wilderness heritage area, Jackeys Marsh- an enchanted habitation where fairy-tale charm sweeps over the forest reserve like a thick morning fog. Long grassy paddocks protect the inhabitants while the blue-green native trees and silver coloured mountains surround the camp site in magnifying intimidation. The abundant greenery of the hills meets the neighbouring rainforest where the mossy grass feels like non-sticky marshmallow. Random sparse areas throughout the forest harbour lonely sunburned trees that persuade the conservationist to walk underneath the branches in humble euphoria.

A chrome coloured dome surrounding the festival site protects the Witches from the outside world. Invited human guests are privy to experience Witch rituals only to forget them when they exit. Only a few, like Oscar were unaffected by the amnesia spell.

The effect of the cannabis joint quietened them into a separatist miasma as they drove towards the entrance gates.

Large red and black stripped flags flapped angrily in the erratic wind and the haunting sound of an enormous wooden Aeolian harp placed at the entrance to clear negativity vibrated through the kombi.

Greeted by a hairless naked woman, covered head to toe in blue tattoos, Pagan opened the window while studying the tattoo artistry.

"How many bells, Witch?"

"Four, please!"

The tattooed woman grabbed four bells out of a rainbow coloured bag that hung over the barbed wire fence and handed them to Pagan and then ushered her to move on.

Entering the festival dome the Kombi slid on a wet patch of grass. Pagan gained control by slowing down. A long trail of cars piled up behind her reminding Pagan of a multi-coloured Rubik's snake.

Inside the dome the weather was a balmy thirty two degrees. The festival organisers controlled the weather inside the dome and although they attempted to keep the weather authentic, extremes were not encouraged.

Large flags- green, orange, purple and yellow marked entrance points around the festival and five large bonfires, purely for aesthetics, lit the parameters. Hundreds of tents were being put up and vehicles unpacked.

Witches were already drinking alcohol and starting up barbeques for lunch. Large communal cauldrons filled with alcoholic punch were placed around the festival area and had quickly become social expanses.

A large semi-trailer truck parked alongside the camping area, accommodated a large ensemble of young female adult musicians, playing European and Indian instruments: a nine piece tubular drum made from polyvinyl chloride piping, a fir top wooden balalaika, a sitar sounding acoustic Bazantar bass, an orange 1960's Swagerty ukulele, Ukrainian Bandura and a small flute made up the folk band.

Navigating with one hand on the steering wheel, Pagan rang her bell in the other.

Irritating the passengers, they begged her to stop.

Amelie jested, "Stop, you'll have horny men running at us and I know you could probably handle five tops. I however will need to be eased in."

There was only one man that Pagan was interested in giving her bell to, if he came. She suspected that he would after dreaming about him so often lately.

Parking the Kombi at the first available clearing, Pagan hopped out of the Kombi and inhaled the fresh air and even over the top of thousands of succulent aromas that filled the air, she could smell his Middle Eastern scent. She smiled, a childlike smile that puffed her cheeks out, and she felt excitement, childlike excitement that made her want to squeal, and jumped up and down. Finally, after all these years she would meet him again.

Peony

"No! I don't want a bell. Do I look like a Witch? Seriously, you should know the difference since you're working at the gate."

She did not wait for a reply but continued in a patronising manner, not at all concerned that she was holding the traffic up, "I'm a human and my sister, who is a Witch is waiting for me on the inside."

Peony ignored the look of pity from the tattooed woman and demanded one ticket. Paying for one ticket, she drove the silver Mitsubishi Magna sedan into the dome, frantically winding the window up as she entered. Once she felt secure inside the safety of the locked vehicle, Peony looked into the rear view mirror, scanning the crowd behind her for the tattooed woman. Once she spotted her, Peony verbally retaliated, "You're the freak Avatar, not me."

Overwhelmed by the magnitude of the strange faces and the congestion of vehicles entering the camping site, Peony soon caught up to the car in front of her and idled impatiently.

Her anxiety grew, "Couldn't they have come on their broom?"

She was the freak sideshow amongst this circus. In this crowd, she was nobody; the darkness between the stars. The feeling of worthlessness was not uncommon to her. She had lived an entire life of non-existence. The human middle sister lost within the wonderment of her Witch sisters, Amelie and Roberta.

Looking at the ticket, she wondered if Amelie would notice that Carl was not with her. She already knew the answer. Amelie hated him. She always had. If anything, Amelie would be relieved. Honestly, Peony was relieved as well. No husband to dictate every second of the day. Belittle her in front of her family and friends, and no embarrassment as Carl made sexual innuendos towards Pagan.

Pagan was that Witch that every woman wanted to be and every man wanted to fuck. Peony could never figure out why.

Not that she particularly cared what her family thought. She only tolerated them because of the small quantity of blood they shared. She only tolerated Carl to 'save face' in front of her family who had begged her not to marry him. Stubborn and proud, she slipped the wedding ring on. None of her family had been invited to the wedding.

Carl might be a 'cunt', but she liked him more than she liked her own family.

Parking the car in the first available spot, Peony fretfully exited the car, locking it before wandering into the crowd to search for Amelie. Luxurious costumes of feathers, umbrellas, top hats, masks and belly-dance wings, impaired her vision. Peony wore jeans, hiking boots and a white t-shirt.

Her anxiety was building.

'Pagan's Kombi is blue', Peony remembered.

Not being asked to travel with Amelie was not unusual. She was never asked to join them directly for any activity or event. She was peripheral.

Roberta, her younger sister had baulked at the last minute, messaging Peony as she drove out of Launceston onto the Highway. Apparently Roberta's husband Don had been occupied with his Club. Peony was left to spend her time with Amelie and Pagan.

The bond between Pagan and Amelie was undeniably secure, a friendship that was forged thousands of years ago. No one could compete with that.

Sitting down on a hay bale, Peony felt completely lost and the crowd was getting larger.

"Don't panic," she whispered underneath her breath.

Standing up onto the hay bale, she peered across the flamboyant crowd, spotting four blue Kombi's and all of them in different directions.

"Shit."

"Can I help you?"

Peering down at a man smiling up at her, Peony smiled back.

A pair of green eyes looked out from a mass of hair. A brown bushy beard hid most of his face. He wore a security jacket.

"Are you talking to me?"

"No offence, but you're the only person here looking lost."

It was unmistakable from his accent that he was Irish.

Jumping off the hay bale, Peony shrugged, "I can't find my sister's friend's Kombi."

Scratching his bushy beard, he responded, "Could you give me some information that might help me find the Kombi?"

After a brief description of Pagan's Kombi the Irishman pulled out a hand-held transceiver from his back trouser pocket and relayed the information. Then he looked at Peony and grinned, "We might as well sit down and wait."

Peony panicked. She was socially awkward. Superficial conversation with a stranger was challenging for her. Peony stared at the ground.

"Are you a Witch then?"

She shook her head.

He fiddled with his handheld transceiver, "I'm a backpacker."

Smiling politely, she sensed that he was trying to make eye contact but she focused on the bustle of the festival goers.

Sensing she was shy, he softened his voice, "I've been in Tassie for three months now. Nice place. Cold though!"

Peony laughed, turning to finally look at him, she stared at his nose instead of his eyes, "Is that why you grew the beard?"

He nodded, "It suits me. I'm thinking of keeping it."

Peony found herself touching his bristle beard. Tangling her finger around one of the curls, she tugged on it and laughed.

"Oops!"

Static from the hand-held transceiver ruined their moment. Pressing the red side button, he listened.

Assuring Peony by patting her leg, the Irishman spoke, "It seems your sister is east of us."

"How about I walk you to your sister, give me your car keys and when I come across your car, I can drive it over to you?"

Peony agreed.

Grabbing her hand, Peony felt a rush surge through her body.

"What is your name?" Peony asked. He may be the only friend she made over the festival weekend and knowing who she was talking to was a logical idea.

He squeezed her hand, "Liam. Yours?"

Peony hesitated. No-one had ever cared to ask her name before.

"Peony."

He nodded enthusiastically, "Like a Rose. It suits you."

Pagan

Pagan left the campsite in pursuit of an old friend.

The main area of the festival was called a Bizarre and it resembled a vibrant and culturally rich market area. Hundreds of paper lanterns hung from tall wooden poles which would be lit at night to help Witches shop and walk back to their camp sites after the entertainment had finished. Beside each pole sat a tub of paints and brushes encouraging Witches and their guests to decorate the poles. Ladders leaned against the poles for guests who were not afraid of heights to climb up the poles and continue painting. Witches used their broomsticks to reach the top. Already the poles were covered in snakes, rainbows and ancient symbols.

The conformity of the large rectangular and square tents was broken up by enormous multi-coloured tee pees that already housed workshops; meditation, yoga, new age spells, modern Witches/modern times forums, costume making, and 'hugging and laughing' appreciation. The list went on.

Some Witches had not wasted any time hunting-out the drug tents, swallowing pills immediately. Evidence of their altered state of consciousness, only enhanced the ambience of the Bizarre as they sat on mats conversing about the worlds troubles, or danced uninhibitedly along the Bizarre alleys.

Buskers had set up to gig in front of food tents; hurdy gurdys, violins, harps, accordions, foot drums, sitars and cow bells, blended together to form an erotic melody.

The smell of freshly prepared Tasmanian and foreign dishes made Pagan's mouth salivate. She stopped and bought a bottle of home-made brewed beer and a bowl of Labneth and hummus served with pita bread. The beer tasted foul but her Middle Eastern cuisine was sensational.

Determined to find the gypsy cart, she ignored the heckling from the shop owners. She knew the infamous gypsy cart would be parked close to the co-ordinators and volunteer campsite.

Spotting the sign 'VIP AREA', she changed her free-flowing walk into an unwavering stride. Pagan unlocked the gate that secured the VIP area and entered.

A bunch of hippies sat slumped around a firepot, soaking up the late afternoon sun and sipping red cask wine.

Pagan waved. The hippies enthusiastically waved back, calling out "Hola" and "Bonjour."

Pagan laughed, "G'day."

Walking behind the shower and toilet facilities, she spotted the gypsy cart.

It was splendid. Its large brown horseshoe shaped canopy was securely mounted onto a darker brown trailer. Golden engravings, decorated the exterior and a closer look revealed intricate carvings of the karma sutra. Amused, she ran her fingers along the contour of the engravings.

The four large wagon wheels buckled under the weight. The internal clutter was hidden by a heavy green coloured curtain at the entrance.

Finding nowhere to knock, Pagan climbed up the three steps and entered. Her friend Aquarius was levitating a metre off the ground and seemed to have fallen asleep.

Almost six foot and seven inches, Aquarius' doppelganger was Jesus with his soft pretty features and long unwashed and uncombed hair. Pagan had met Jesus on one occasion. He had been a little dramatic but a good sort of fellow.

Creeping slowly up behind Aquarius, she tackled him to the shag pile carpet that cushioned most of the impact.

Aquarius raged until he saw Pagan grinning down at him.

"Pagan, you gorgeous ninja, you took forty years off my life."

"Aquarius, as if you had forty years left anyway!"

When Pagan left the VIP area it was dark and with the help of the paper lanterns, she navigated her way back to the Bizarre, tripping occasionally due to the small holes and loose rocks.

Turning north east, passing a row of pop-up restaurants, she craved solitude before returning to the campsite. Minutes later, she stood on a small wooden bridge on the edge of the Bizarre. The sound of the running creek calmed her as she soaked in the night air. A sword swallower and contortionist performance, only amused her for a few minutes before she set off up the hill towards the allure of the Sitting Tree where she would hopefully find solace.

The Sitting Tree stood one hundred metres high. It contained so many secrets that it oozed honey coloured sap, that if you listened to, hissed stories from Ancient Tasmania.

It took forty two steps to walk around, which she did every time she visited Jackeys Marsh. Pagan found sitting on one of its large roots, caressing its mossing purple coat, relaxed her, and she was sure she could hear Gaia breathing inside of it.

The smell of the rainforest filled her lungs as she climbed higher but it was *his* scent that really took her breath away.

His scent was everywhere. Struggling to walk up the forest path quickly enough, his scent enticed her to move beyond her physical discomfort.

Finally, she reached the clearing.

Squinting, she could see him. The Sitting Tree's foliage hid him but his scent was unquestionably unique. His muscular body slumped against the Sitting Tree's base as if he had been waiting for her, as if he had known she was would be there.

Serendipity leaving her unprepared caused her stagnation. Insecurity made her stumble as she walked towards him.

He must be forty five now but he looked exactly the same to her. His very long dark hair was half tied up above his head and the rest fell down over his chest. He wore nothing but blue denim jeans. His feet were bare.

Ignoring her presence, she panicked that he might have been waiting for someone else. What if he had forgotten her? Surely not!

Composing herself, she approached him with eyes that searched for any sign of recognition from him.

He had watched her approach cautiously and wondered why she had hesitated. Pagan had been fierce when they met, surely life had not dulled her?

Kneeling down before him, her hands reached out to touch his face. His olive skin leathered underneath her touch. His pouty red lips and darkened eyes, were more potent than she had remembered. Grey hairs now glowed on his chest.

"It's been a long time, my friend," she smiled.

He placed his hands over hers. They were freezing cold.

"I've missed you, Little Witch."

His Israeli accent aroused her. She desperately wanted to kiss him but anxiety limited her. Slipping her hand into her loose trouser pocket, she pulled out the golden bell and rung it.

Tristan Dante smiled, graciously accepting the bell.

Amelie

The main festival event occurred on Saturday evening, but Friday night's opening ceremony was eagerly anticipated.

Huddled around the campsite, Amelie, Ruby and Peony sat dangerously close to the firepot, soaking in the heat. Pagan's absence was felt as the three of them struggled to find a common topic of discussion.

Pagan had always been a free-spirit, even at the inconvenience of others. A leader, she hated to be followed, despising the responsibility and the neediness of others.

"Where is Pagan?" Peony probed.

The question amused Amelie who was aware of Peony's disdain for Pagan.

"Don't fear, once the festivities begin, Pagan will be back. She would never miss a party."

Ruby interrupted, breaking from her solemn disposition, "Pagan is probably looking for someone to give her bell to before all the good ones are taken."

Snorting into her drink, Peony found amusement in Ruby's comment. Pagan certainly was a slut.

Lost in thought, Amelie wondered who she would give the bell to. It had been seven years since she had rung a ceremonial bell.

"I'm sure, I'll find cobwebs it's been that long."

Ruby laughed and then felt instantly guilty for her moment of happiness.

Sinking further down into the chair, Peony rolled her eyes, "I can't believe you are seriously going to ring your bell. What if you get an S.T.D?"

Witches were immune to human sexually transmitted diseases and Peony knew this, so her question had obviously been a snide verbal attack.

"Maybe, sister dear if you took the prunes out of your mouth and the lemon out from your vagina, you could get laid as well."

Peony shuffled uncomfortably on the seat. Eager to retaliate, she hesitated knowing that Amelie's comment held an element of truth.

Avoiding eye contact, Ruby wondered why Peony had come to the festival as she never enjoyed herself and her negativity impacted the entire group.

An awkward silence followed.

Focusing her attentions on the upbeat vibe of the surrounding campsites, Amelie soon recharged her energies, "I wonder why Roberta and Don didn't make it."

Peony's first instinct was to ignore Amelie's 'Let's change the subject' comment, pack up and head home, but going home to an empty house encouraged her to stay seated.

"All she wrote was that Don had club commitments."

Her brother-in-law, Don, was spending most of his spare time at the club lately and Amelie wondered if her sister's marriage was under some strain because of it.

Amelie shifted her attention to Ruby who had aged considerably over the last few weeks. Large black shadows as large as tea bags underneath her eyes, highlighted the dullness in her stare. Flaking skin indicated dehydration, most likely from drinking alcohol every night since Hensley's Witch Awakening. Some Maidens cope with their Witch Awakening and others do not. Being confronted with your past is terrifying without the added violation of the Witch Awakening ritual. Hensley had not coped and now she was at home alone to mull over the event. Not that Amelie cared for Hensley's well-being, but her instinct told her that Ruby should have stayed at home with her daughter.

A loud explosion from over the hilltop frightened the campsite occupants and everyone stood up to investigate. Relief followed when Aquarius' face was projected into the night sky, almost taking up one quarter of the dome ceiling. The crowd applauded with excitement. The opening ceremony was about to begin.

Aquarius' marine blue eyes sparkled as if he had just poured several drops of eye dilating liquid onto them. His dilated pupils were twice their usual size.

Amelie doubted Aquarius eyesight was anything but blurred. Aquarius would do anything to make an impact.

The projector screen expanded revealing Aquarius' attire; a black top hat, a long black eighteenth century double buttoned jacket and trousers to suit, accessorised with a black furry scarf and John Lennon glasses.

"Welcome horny Witches, execrable men and deplorable Bitches!"

Aquarius' voice ricocheted around the dome parameters. Holding both his hands above his head, he pointed towards the sky, "I declare the 2010 Samhain Festival officially opened."

Pulling his hands down like a football referee indicating a goal, Aquarius added with a wink, "Like your legs, Witches."

In unison, over four thousand pairs of feet stomped on the ground. The ground moved underneath them.

The next explosion lit up the sky as hundreds of performance Witches appeared dressed in all black attire, hovering for a few second before opening red coloured hand-held umbrellas which they positioned in front of their bodies as they slowly floated to the ground. The cluster of red umbrellas formed a new projector screen and images of the crowd, enticed more clapping. Witches waved at themselves as they saw their own faces highlighted on the red screen.

Two gigantic golden balls, fizzing like sparklers, bounced ten metres at a time towards the crowd. The crowd automatically reacted by hitting the two balls back up into the sky. They crossed the crowd at tremendous speed.

It was hard not to enjoy Aquarius's dramatics but Amelie questioned his motives. There was something about Aquarius that she did not trust but for tonight she would enjoy his antics.

The next morning, Amelie was feeling considerably healthy considering she had danced until 01:00 and drank copious amounts of alcohol. Persuading an unwilling Peony to party had been an exhausting task and Amelie had felt rather restricted by her sister's lack of momentum. At 22:00, she had eagerly encouraged Peony to retire to bed so she could finally enjoy herself. Subjected to instant karma, drumming had kept Amelie awake for most of the early morning. Peony had slept a sound eight hours.

"Someone should shoot those fucking drummers," she had snarled at 04:00.

It was time to worship the Sun God before he disappeared for winter. If there was one god Amelie happily worshiped was the god that promised warmth.

Since Gaia had fallen asleep, the Goddesses created masculine forms of themselves called Divinities to do the mundane activities, such as maintain the quality of the sun. They were 'workers' whose job it was to maintain the functionality of nature.

Amelie crawled out of the tent. Missing her comfy bed, her hips were already seizing up.

Naked bodies sat indiscriminately around the campsites. It did not take Amelie long to join them. Stripping nude and relaxing into a ritual state, the Sun Divinity instantly massaged her aching bones.

After one hour, Amelie had dressed and walked to the Bizarre. Today, she would shop, eat and drink and find some stupid fool to give her bell to.

Spoiling herself by buying a new dress to wear for the night's festivities, she left the first shop pleased with herself.

Purchasing a 'Strega' drink from Fay Ce'Line's tent, Amelie wandered along the Bizarre until she stumbled across a 'nude story telling' tent. The book being read was 'Alice in Wonderland' by Lewis Carroll.

Peering through the tent entrance, Amelie was not surprised to see the tent was full of men, women and Witches. Slipping through the tent entrance, she sat down on the carpet in the back row. The audience slumped over each other like lions in the hot afternoon sun, stroking and caressing the body next to them. The effects of an eventful night of partying had left everyone sluggish and uninhibited.

Attracting minimal attention, a couple gently fucked in the 'kneel and sit' position in the third row. Internalising their passion, they did not make a sound which only added to the sensuality of the room.

Sitting on a newly upholstered antique arm chair, the nude reader was an exceptionally beautiful and voluptuous woman, at least a size eighteen. The combination of her self-confidence, perfectly proportioned body (large hips that equalled her hefty breasts), naturally geisha coloured skin, long blond hair set in a 1940's wartime style, large sultry cat eyes, and the way she curled her lips around the spoken word, mesmerised the audience.

Lost in the pulse of the reader's heartbeat, Amelie ignored the person who sat down beside her.

After a few minutes, the stranger whispered into Amelie's ear, "Wow, she is beautiful."

Amelie pushed her hand up against his face, pushing him away.

Instantly moving closer to her, his musk-stick breath blew gentle on her cheek.

Raising her right eyebrow she faced the young man, "Now you're just pissing me off."

He looked like the character from Storm Boy with his bleached blonde hair and sun-bleached skin. His body was firm from his youth and his smile symbolic of a charmed existence.

Amelie held an unamused glare, "Ever heard of shade. You'll look like an old leather couch when you're older."

In confidence, he leaned in even closer, face to face and whispered, "I've been watching you. I would like you to give me your bell. I think a Witch like you, could make me feel closer to God."

Amelie held her composure and whispered back, "Firstly, I give you music points for quoting 'Nine Inch Nails', but you lose points for being 'creepy stalker guy'. Plus, there wouldn't be anything in it for me. There is a reason why young boys are for young girls."

Turning away from him, she sipped the 'strega'.

Waiting until she put the drink down, he grabbed her hand. Kissing the back of it, his lips tickled her skin as he spoke, "I think you'll change your mind because your mind knows I'm young but your body doesn't."

Amelie was mildly amused.

Pagan

Opening the antique jade jewellery box displaying a hidden empty compartment, Aquarius looked pleased with himself.

"It looks empty, Pagan, but if I pull this white piece of string, it unlocks."

Pulling the white string revealed six tiers that formed a triangle. The triangle shape tier consisted of an assortment of drugs.

Pagan browsed Aquarius's selection; Opium, LSD, Amphetamine, Cocaine, Ecstasy, and Cannabis in the top tier. The next tiers contained Heroin, Catnip, and Hallucinogens.

Pagan looked up at Aquarius condemningly. She was fearful of browsing the remaining four tiers.

Aquarius rolled his eyes, "Don't give me 'your body is a temple' look, Pagan. Hypocrisy doesn't suit you."

Studying the selection, Pagan decisively chose cocaine.

Using a silver spoon to spread out a small proportion of coke onto a tray, he produced a plastic card from a pouch and proceeded to thin out the cocaine. Once he was happy with the length and width of the two lines, he pulled out a one hundred dollar note from underneath his bed, rolled it up tightly into a cylinder and passed it to Pagan.

He winked, "Witches first."

Pagan blocked one nose and bent down, snorting the entire line in one inhale. Her eyes tingled.

Passing the note back to Aquarius, he also finished his line in one inhale but he automatically rubbed his nose and sniffed a few times.

"Come here, Pagan, I want to hug you. It's been too long."

Snuggling into Aquarius's arms, she rested her head on his shoulder.

Aquarius thought it was a good time to tell her some troubling information while she was feeling the effects of the cocaine. He pulled her in closer, wrapping his long skinny arms around her, "I've heard whispers of an underground Coven. I think they intend to cause havoc."

Unexpectedly, Pagan did not react.

Aquarius's voice dwindled, "They may attempt to kill you, Pagan."

Pagan's first thoughts were of Deity. Her own safety was not a concern. She had not experienced one reincarnation where her safety was not an issue.

"Here in Tasmania?"

He nodded.

"Are your resources reliable?"

He nodded again.

Pagan tugged on Aquarius's white seamless robe, "I'm at a festival Aquarius. They can kill me on a week day."

"I don't think you're taking this seriously enough."

Annoyed that he continued the conversation, Pagan moved away from Aquarius. She always become distant before she tempered.

Knowing better than to argue with Pagan, Aquarius stood up and left the cart. The best way to avoid the game was not to play it.

Angered by his ability to 'offload' information which had been weighing him down, only added to her disappointment, that he could then remove himself from the situation. She refused to absorb his negativity.

Grabbing the jade drug box, she flicked through the tiers again until she found the word 'Trip'. Pulling out one piece of paper, she placed it into her pocket. Noticing a little brown bottle hiding at the bottom of the box, she grabbed it out and read the label 'Alkyl Nitrite'.

She sat back. It had been a long time since she had seen this aphrodisiac inhalant. Alkyl Nitrite (also known as Poppers) had been used as a sexual enhancer by the gay scene and avant-garde enthusiasts.

Pagan shook the bottle and stared at the label again. It would give her a five minute rush, expand her senses, relax her muscles, decrease her blood-pressure and make her aggressively aroused.

She took the lid off and inhaled. Barely managing to put the lid back on before the dizziness hit, she lay down and enjoyed the intensity of the rush. Feeling anything but the truth was the best high.

Pagan

The sun vanished over the horizon to a silent apprehension. A Brown snake slithered past Pagan's leg, eager to find refuge in the bushes. Without hesitation, she grabbed the end of its body and tugged on it. Subordinately, the snake stilled. Several Witches sitting near Pagan, shuffled away, frightened more of Pagan than the snake. Ignoring them, she used her other hand to pick the snake up, to face it, "Hello beautiful."

The snake's forked tongue tickled her cheek. Pagan kissed it on the face and then gently placed it back down on the ground, watching it as it slithered away.

Over two thousand Witches, their adult families and friends sat on the grass.

Witches wore heavy polar fleece maroon ceremonial hooded cloaks, which failed to warm their heads and necks, from the evening chill. The cold did not dampen their anticipation.

Tightening the cloak around her torso, Pagan wished that she had brought thermal clothing with her.

Scanning the crowd for Dante, familiar faces acknowledged her by smiling or winking. On a second glance, Pagan wondered if any of the Witches from the underground Coven were there.

'Come and get me'.

Three gigantic bonfires were lit. Simultaneously, they erupted into balls of flames, dispersing a great amount of warmth.

The Witches would celebrate the 'Sexual Goddesses' tonight, starting with the ringing of the ceremonial Goddess Bell. The Goddess Bell was a natural 'upper,' transcending a cleansing vibration throughout their bodies, purging any illness or emotional negativity. It was this event that Peony had come for. The rest of the festival, she had simply tolerated so far.

Standing four metres high, the Goddess Bell was secured to a hard wooden fort that had been transported to the festival site on the back of a semi-trailer truck. It was a relatively modern metal Goddess Bell, cast by the West Asian Witches, less than one thousand years ago. Its age had given it a lime stained appearance. Its clapper a welcomed phallic symbol amongst female domination. The sound of the chime travelled for several kilometres, easily protruded the surrounding mountains that created a natural amphitheatre and the bush a natural fold back.

Two Witches from the organising committee stood anxiously beside the Goddess Bell waiting for the indication to start. A few more minutes passed before the ceremonial Witches grabbed the ropes and yanked. For five minutes, the chime of the Goddess Bell vibrated through their bodies. Pagan could feel her cells renewing.

Oscar leaned in towards Fay Ce'Line hoping to see signs of regeneration in her body.

Crossing her fingers, Peony lost herself within the rhythm of the chime. The power of the vibration almost knocked her over but she forced her body towards it. She was desperate for the Goddess Bell to heal her. A wave of anticipation rose as the Goddess Bell came to an end.

Eight Witches stood on either side of four taiko drums and with batons held high above their heads, they commenced playing.

Sitting in the middle of the crowd, Pagan could easily see a group of 'only' black haired performers enter the raised stage beside the fort. Fairy lights and round paper lanterns lit the stage as the performers walked on wearing only a coin belt that loosely hugged their hips, exposing a naked upper body. Some carried snakes that slithered aimlessly around their neck and shoulders while others carried ancient swords, positioning themselves into warrior poses.

Only Ancient Witches had lived in the warrior era. Only a myth to the rest of the crowd, who cheered and whistled.

Standing up, Pagan left the entertainment, choosing instead, to walk to the gig stage in the adjacent paddock where massive amps surrounded the stage giving it the impression it was built from large Lego blocks. A male DJ, warmed up, by playing his tracks to an empty dance area. Pagan knew the crowds would soon join them and he would immerse himself in the crowd's energy.

Before entering the dance area, Pagan swallowed the acid paper, instantly ushering the DJ to turn the music up.

He did.

Throwing the ceremonial cloak off, she laid it down on the damp grass. Slipping her shoes off, she threw them on top of the cloak. Closing her eyes, she concentrated on the music while she waited for the effect of the drug to 'kick in'.

Dancing seductively, the only person she wanted to seduce was herself. Soon the crowd danced around her and the grass became mud as hundreds of feet stomped rhythmically together. Hundreds of minds, in sync, to a single beat. A beat, that ignited every cell in their bodies, giving hope, giving purity and mostly giving them a single moment where rhythm outweighed thought.

Creepy Man

Watching as the Witch walked onto the congested dance floor, his body tensed and his heart raced. He had never felt such intense sexual arousal before.

This Witch had to be almost twice his age but there was something different about her than the other Witches. Hearing rumours that there would be several Royal Ancient Witches attending the festival, he was excited. He planned on fucking at least one of them.

Panicking as she disappeared into the cluster of movement of the dance floor, he jumped with the rhythm of the music to scan the top of the crowd.

Developing a fetish for Witches after his first sexual encounter with a Witch from Hobart, which had undoubtedly spoiled him, he was not going to deny himself the reality that sexual encounters *did* have a measure of importance.

Ordering a pork roast for lunch and beer at the pub several months earlier, he had noticed an attractive young woman sipping an apple cider.

Sitting alone at the bench seat in the corner of the room, she had smiled at him. Smiling without revealing her teeth had alarmed him initially. Already developing a fixation for nice teeth or a disdain for rotten ones, he wondered if she hid them for a reason. It would be a shame considering how sexy she was. He smiled back showing off his artificially whitened teeth.

The early afternoon sun had shone through the window, highlighting the vibrancy of her long straightened hair; dark red, artificially coloured fluoro-orange and ultra-blond streaks. Thick aqua blue mascara and matching eyeliner, outlined her penetrating electric green eyes. Her lips (painted with a baby pink coloured lipstick), pointy nose and cleft chin, made her one of the most beautiful women, he had ever seen.

Enticed by her sexuality, he foolishly approached her. Good or bad teeth, she was worth it.

As if she had predicted his approach, she sat back on the bench and smiled, showing a set of perfectly straight teeth.

"Can I sit here?"

Biting the side of her lip, she looked at him as if he was meat carved up for sale at the butchers.

"No! You may not."

Rejected, he flushed.

"But see that hotel over there?"

Turning on the seat, she pointed to the hotel across the road.

He nodded.

"After I finish this cider, I'm going over there to book a room for the afternoon and after you've eaten your lunch, you can join me."

Sculling the remaining cider, she stood up and left. Wearing a cute white and peach coloured 1950's frock, he noticed that she was not wearing any shoes.

Adrenaline pumped through his body as he ate the roast with such intensity, he felt the large pieces, even drowned in gravy, grasp for space in his chest.

Spending all afternoon in that hotel room, Sandra had revealed that she was a Witch.

Laughing at first, his face had paled when she showed him some Magick.

Disappearing into the darkness of the evening, he had not seen Sandra since, but finding Witches had now become an obsession. They were easy enough to find, standing out from anyone else in the room, asserting separatism and elitism, and they owned their sexuality.

Googling, he looked for evidence of their reality, hidden in conspiracy documents and in primary history sources, he was slowly putting all the information together of their existence. He read that Ancients Witches were something entirely different. Universal energy hummed within them, as if they were on a higher frequency. Non-Ancient Witches, at best, were only carbon copies, and even more exciting was the fact that there were specially chosen Ancient Witches to be Royal, which meant that they reigned over all the Witches. This information had been posted online by an eighty four year old man from a shire in Cornwall, England, who had discovered his great grandmother's diary who he claimed had been a Witch.

From that moment, he had to 'hook up' with a Royal Ancient Witch. The sexual activity might kill him but at least he would die happy.

Dancing deliberately in the centre of the dance area, he hoped that she would find him before the Bell ritual began.

The night before, he had stood on the outskirts of the dance floor watching her as she danced. Dancing, as if she could hear an extra beat in the music that the others Witches could not. Witches bowed their heads, scared to make eye-contact with her as she walked past them.

Embarrassed to admit it but he had followed her back to her campsite. Masturbating outside of her tent as she slept was something he was not proud of. He had been thankful the drums had drowned out his panting.

His penis hardened, tightening his board shorts. Just thinking about the Royal Ancient Witch made him horny. Appearing again only a few metres away, he stopped unable to look elsewhere else but at her. Eyes like a wild storm, Amelie stared him down.

He looked away, any confidence that he had that morning vanished.

Standing in front of him, her empowerment intimidated him.

He sensed that she was the type of Witch that never played games because she always won.

Amelie raised her right hand, opening her palm, "There you go, you little pervert."

The bell sat comfortably in the pit of her palm.

Automatically, he attempted to snatch it off her but she snapped her hand shut before he could grab it. Teasing him further, she placed her pointer finger over his eyes.

Obediently, he kept them closed.

Tensing, as she undid the buttons on his shorts, he desperately wanted to peek, but out of fear he kept his eyes tightly closed.

She walked away after tying the bell to his penis, leaving his board shorts around his ankles.

Fay Ce'Line

Entering the bush track, they diverted left, climbed over a fallen tree log and then headed straight up.

Using vague memory and the moonlight, Oscar led Fay Ce'Line through the eerie bush. Tangled tree branches occasionally smacked him in the face or the unseen rock tripped him up, but he made sure that Fay Ce'Line was safe.

"Do you need a rest, Fay?"

"I'm fine, Oscar. How about you watch where you're going rather than worrying about me."

Suspecting that she was lying, Oscar slowed down. Grabbing her icy cold hand, he squeezed it tightly, "Honey, let me know if you need to rest."

Working all day at the Bizarre, Fay Ce'Line was exhausted, even the Goddess Bell had not relieved any fatigue.

"Actually, I could do with a rest."

Stopping, Oscar reached his arms around Fay Ce'Line's waist, wrapping her up in his warm jacket. He felt her heart racing. Kissing the top of her head, he tasted Fay Ce'Line's own homemade shampoo; coconut milk, vitamin E oil, almond oil, and orange essential oil. It made him happy.

Resting her head on Oscar's chest, she looked down towards the energetic dance floor. Glad that they had decided to find a private place to rest, she was grateful that Oscar was not unhappy to leave the festivities for a while.

Unravelling herself from Oscar's embrace, she grabbed his nose with her thumb and forefinger, "Come on, let's keep walking," and dragged him along.

After a steep incline, they reached the creek.

Holding his hand out, Oscar helped Fay Ce'Line to cross the slippery pebble path before tackling it himself. His feet barely touched the first pebbles when he slipped, stepping his other foot into the icy water for balance.

Fay Ce'Line burst into a kid-like laughter with a snort or two to show her absolute delight in his misfortune.

Oscar splashed quickly out of the creek, "Bloody hell, that's freezing!"

She laughed louder.

Oscar bent down, scooping a cup full of creek water into his hand, splashing Fay Ce'Line.

Shrieking, she ran away from him.

Oscar chased her, only to scoop her up a few metres away. Picking her up, he threw her over his shoulder.

She yelped and then laughed again as she tried to make herself feel lighter to lessen the load on Oscar's work worn-out shoulder.

Wrapping his wet hand around her thigh, Oscar carried Fay Ce'Line for the rest of the way up the hill.

Enjoying Oscar's masculine expression of dominance, Fay Ce'Line spread her fingertips out, letting them run over the top of the foliage.

Finding a clearing around the bend, he placed Fay Ce'Line gently down onto the ground and collapsed beside her. The moisture quickly dampened their clothing.

"Now I'm tired, Fay."

"Time to star gaze, Baby!"

Thousands of stars glistened above them. Fay Ce'Line snuggled into his torso, slipping her cold feet in-between his, she released a long sigh. Not a sad sigh but a sigh that abandons the past for the present.

"Well! This is worth the cold," Oscar laughed.

"I never get bored looking at stars. No matter how many lives I live. They remind me of how insignificant we are."

The sound of the bass beat did not dampen the tranquillity of the natural habitat.

Oscar pulled open Fay Ce'Line's cloak, slipping his rough hand over her silky skin. She wore very little underneath.

"Gee Fay, you must be freezing."

Stroking his hair, she ignored his comment. She was already seduced by their environment. Nature had always been a natural aphrodisiac for her. It reminded her of Ancient times.

It had been at the Samhain that their twins had been conceived.

Fay Ce'Line had lost her sexual drive, preferring to concentrate on healing and preserving her energies while she was having treatment, but she had never stopped wanting her husband, just lacked the confidence and strength. Her self-identification had changed. She was unsure of who she was and what she had to offer.

"Oscar," Fay Ce'Line whispered, "Will you make love to me, gently?"

Turning his head to face her, he asked surprisingly, "Now?"

"Yes silly. Now!"

Peony

Peony sat alone at the campsite. Stragglers walking back to their tents politely said, "Hello" or smiled at her.

Everyone certainly seemed to be in a good mood.

One night of dancing had been enough for her and she was really impressed at the stamina of most Witches.

The constant thumping of the bass had given her a headache and the cheap red wine was not helping, however it had stained her lips and warmed her stomach.

Sitting on a cushioned plastic lounge chair, wearing a woollen beanie, gloves and Ugg boots, she felt rather toasty and happy with her decision to stay back at the campsite. The firepot warmed her legs.

The night sky was filled with a multitude of stars, hundreds of stars reaching out their points to touch the neighbouring star. Living in the city meant that she rarely saw the sky so beautiful.

"Evening, Miss Peony."

Only his Hi-Vis jacket illuminated in the dark but she knew who it was immediately.

Nervously, she asked him to join her.

Grabbing another spare plastic cup, she poured him some red wine. Her hand shook as she passed it to him.

Wearing thick gloves, he struggled to hold the cup, finally succumbing to holding it with both hands.

"Please, sit down, Liam."

He pulled the closest plastic chair alongside her and sat down.

"It's rowdy on the dance floor tonight. I'm not surprised you're hiding down here."

She laughed, "Closer to the red wine down here."

The fire lit up his face, highlighting his kind eyes. A rush of endorphins overwhelmed her.

'Why was he talking to her?'

"You're very brave to travel around the world, Liam. Have you been travelling for long?"

He told her of his adventures and she gazed at his face as he spoke of his journeys across the globe.

Underneath his beard was a younger man than what he appeared. He was twenty eight. He had looked thirty eight at least. He had no girlfriend, no commitments and would most likely travel for another five years backpacking throughout Europe into China, Japan, and India. He had followed some friends to Tasmania three months ago to work and now he was sitting with her on his journey of freedom and experience. He intended to travel north, eventually reaching Darwin by winter.

"I'm looking forward to the heat," he laughed.

"I doubt you will ever settle down, Liam. I hope you never 'stale' like the rest of us."

"I wouldn't call you 'staled', Peony. You're here aren't you?"

She avoided his statement, "Tell me about Ireland."

Peony noticed his eyes softened as he spoke of home.

"I miss my family of course. My sister has a couple of kids. I talk to them regularly on Skype."

"Are you close to your sister?"

He nodded his head, "Yeah. Very close. You're obviously close with your sisters?"

A sunken feeling in her chest dimmed her spirit, "I wouldn't say that. It's hard being the middle sister, especially when they are Witches and you're not. Let me put it this way. I didn't get my way a lot growing up."

Putting his empty glass on the ground, he asked, "So tell me your story."

He looked deeply into her gaze. Sensing she was a private person, he insisted, "Please."

Struggling to engage with him, she felt inadequate and stumbled over the larger details of her life, small details were not even an option for this conversation. She told many white lies.

Sensing her negativity, he chose not to ask too much of her, wondering instead who had hurt her so badly that she had completely shut herself down, even from a care-free stranger.

Looking at his mobile for the time, he stood up, "Regrettably, that was my break."

A wave of disappointment flooded over her, "Oh no! Already?"

"Stay beautiful, Peony. I might see you tomorrow?"

Standing up, she realised she was quite drunk and stumbled a little. She hugged him and was happily surprised that he welcomed her embrace. She felt him tickle her back with his fingers.

Pulling back, she distanced herself far enough away to look at his whole face, "Thank you, Liam."

"Why thank me?"

"Because you see me. Not many people do."

Screwing his nose up, he looked confused.

Realising she had got too heavy too quickly, she blushed from embarrassment, "Oh dear! I sound like such a loser."

Liam paused, "People see you, Peony. It's you that can't see yourself. It's a pity, cause it's a nice view. Turn the switch on. It's just a decision, not the end of the world to see where it might take you."

Watching Liam zigzag through the path of caravans, tents and small bonfires, she felt terribly alone. Standing amongst hundreds of Witches, she decided to go home.

Amelie

It was nearly midnight and Amelie felt the wave of anticipation and restlessness sweep over the dance floor.

The Goddess Bell rang again, indicating for those who were not participating in the Bell ritual to return to their tents and those who were given bells were to gather in a group on the dance floor, while the Witches obediently left to enter the bush.

In single file, the intoxicated Witches danced and frolicked along the Art Track to a large clearing on top of the hill.

Amelie was amused as some of the more excitable Witches fell into the bushes, only to burst into laughter and be pulled out. Other more promiscuous Witches kissed and fondled each other as they walked up the incline.

The atmosphere was erotic and capricious, a dangerous but alluring mix of elation.

Some of the Witches disposed of their clothes at the beginning, throwing them over the bushes to collect on their way back down, others removed their clothing on the incline.

Amelie chose to keep her cloak and undergarments on until she reached the top. There was no point being cold for no apparent reason. Non-Ancient Witches were so eager for instant gratification.

They gathered, squeezing into a tight pack into the small clearing.

Amelie could not see Fay Ce'Line and wondered if she and Oscar had already rung the bell.

As for Pagan, who would know where she was.

At the brow of the hill, four Goddess statues made from straw bales, lavender, white sage, cedar and imported Catuaba bark, stood thirty six metres high. Rich with sexual promiscuity, each pairs of large breasts fell upon four large pregnant stomachs. The statues were merely giant smudge sticks that would be lit, and the smoke used as a purifier to cleanse the Witch's energies and Magick.

The Cleansing ritual was an oxymoron. Cleansing before sexual intercourse was rather a useless requirement when the intent was to be unclean, odour wild and bodily juicy (mix that shit all up). Cleansing should happen after the event, if only in good will.

Amelie smirked. She was eager to ring her bell. That poor 'creepy' boy was about to have the ride of his life.

Sitting down on the mossy grass, Amelie removed her clothes, placing them beside her, only then did it occur to her that the clothes would smell of smoke afterwards. Being a smoker, she laughed at her own idiosyncrasies.

Without introduction the statues were lit, left to right. Smoke quickly enveloped the sitting Witches. Amelie inhaled the smoke as there was no point fighting the fumes. Panicking a little as her chest caved in, she inhaled again. Her throat tightened. She would symbolically die for a split second, release herself to the Goddesses and be reborn.

The area was quickly blanketed by smoke and only the sound of coughing alerted Amelie that she was not alone. Her eyes stung and air was quickly diminishing.

Someone squeezed Amelie's hand, probably a Witch feeling frightened and searching for safety. Ripping her hand away from the stranger, she snapped, "Get over it."

Amelie felt the familiar rush. It would subside quickly. Her body would accept its fate. It did now. The Goddesses appeared for a split second, long enough for Amelie to stick her middle finger up at them before she took the breath that brought her back to consciousness.

The smoke was clearing. It was time.

Pagan

Placing one hand on the trunk of the Sitting Tree, the moisture of the waterlogged bark reminded Pagan of past reincarnations.

A tree's strength comes from its age, knowledge that only 'time' can teach, alas the same could not be said for Witches.

Only a few hundred metres away, sat several hundred Witches experiencing a Cleansing ritual. The unnatural silence deafened her and the smell of smoke reeked up her nostrils. Glad to have forfeited the purification for the sake of her nostrils, she took a moment to settle her nerves. Dante was a mere man but he made her nervous. This was not a Witch characteristic.

Soon Pan, the Divinity of creatures and nature, who sprouted from the soil after Gaia fell into a deep sleep to protect his creators skin, would arrive, bringing with him a contagious sexual prowess that would possess the chosen ritual bell participants.

Pan would know that she was waiting at the Sitting Tree. Pan saw everything in nature. Nature was his kingdom and one he ruled over assiduously.

Straightening her dress, she sighed. The simple design of the dress contoured her body shape, highlighting her large hips, but still she felt inadequate. Especially imported, expressed post from Spain, she had bought it over the internet after working six extra shifts to pay for it, and already she had ripped it while walking up the Art Track. The orange-red Duchess satin underlay complimented the chiffon top layer and the lace that covered her shoulders. Finishing in a high turtle neck, she looked like an eighteenth century vampire. The bottom of the dress was also lace, but now it was covered in mud. She had wanted to be beautiful for him, and now, her dress was already ruined.

Hearing a twig break and several large thumps, Pagan panicked, only to see a wallaby bounce away into the thick undergrowth.

The sound of a flute enchanted her ears. Pan had arrived. Her heart raced and her eyes twinkled in the moonlight. Simultaneously, a chaotic orchestra of bells began, followed by movement.

Holding her hand high above her head, she animatedly yelled, "Come and get me, Pan."

Screams, followed by laughter, echoed over the hillside as an explosion of sexuality ambushed the recipients of Pan's Magick; growing horns of all shapes and sizes from their foreheads and a bushy mass of hair growth from their waist to the tips of their toes, they were released to hunt the Witches.

Pagan inhaled. She could smell him. Pan was racing up the hillside, through the bush to fornicate with her.

A strong gust of wind lifted her dress above her knees and she frantically pushed the fabric back down as she wanted to look perfect for him.

Like a surge of electricity, he arrived.

Her hair stood on its end.

Standing on the other side of the Sitting Tree, Dante teased her with his masculine sexuality. Pan's blood raged through Dante's body. The tip of his penis glistened around the tree and what a fine penis it was.

Pagan's stomach flipped from nervousness as his endorphins made her feel dizzy, but she sensed he was hesitating but why?

Peering around the Sitting Tree, Dante grinned back at her.

His long black curly hair hung down over his well-shaped chest and his large brown menacing eyes, took her breath away. Lust intoxicated her.

Twelve centimetre horns, thick half way, and liken to a pig's tail for the other half, poked out of his forehead. Pan's Magick had worked.

Dante undressed her with an intense stare, "Pretty frock, Little Witch. Pity it's coming off."

Walking towards her, she automatically stepped backwards. She wanted to play for a while, after all it was a game, and even if, it was one she wanted to lose.

Stepping cautiously around each other like two lions about to pounce on each other, their chemistry nurtured the other; a battle of will had begun.

Pagan felt alive again. Her old self purging into reality.

"Do you remember Dante what you said to me once, that if you couldn't catch me, you would set me free. Wanna play?"

A deep seeded growl moistened his lips.

She ran. Her bare feet swiftly galloped over the twigs and damp ground.

Closing her eyes, she embraced her Witch intuition. Instinctively knowing where she was going, she forged ahead without fear.

Dante had taught her how to channel her Witch abilities seventeen years ago and now, in irony, she was using it against him.

Closing his eyes, Dante became a predator. Pan's Magick surging through his body made him primal, eager to fornicate with her, be one with her, and own her. It was Pan's blood that made them more equal, after all, a Witch needs an equal.

Accelerating up the hill, Pagan could smell the creek, which from her estimate, was barely ten metres away. She would have to jump it. Dante would be disappointed if she gave up so easily and she was not about to disappoint him.

Reaching the creek, she leaped. Opening her eyes, she braced herself for the landing. Hovering for several metres, she landed clumsily onto the wet muddy creek edge. Slipping, she fell forwards landing on her hands and knees into the mud. Her dress caught under her knees.

Dante caught her.

Pagan retorted, "You're getting slow, old man."

Dante arrogantly responded, "I wanted you to feel like you had a chance."

Awkwardly, Dante flipped her dress up, exposing her bottom. He then, pulled her knickers down with one hand while wrapping her long hair into a knotted ponytail, forcing her head to bend backwards toward her shoulder blades.

Adrenaline surged through her body, "Fuck me, Dante!"

Before she even finished saying his name, he stopped.

Releasing his grip, he pulled her knickers back up. The elastic stung her waist. Standing up, he left Pagan on her hands and knees.

Pagan screamed from frustration, scaring a flock of birds that had not yet left for winter, now fleeing for safety rather than from routine.

She stood up, her body raging with disappointment. Gathering her dress up, she walked towards him slapping his cheek. His cheek immediately welted and burned. He withstood the pain gallantly.

"You don't do this to me, Dante, not to me. You've fucked every woman you've ever met, but I'm not good enough for you? A Witch isn't good enough for you? Do you know who I am...?" Her own words slapped her face and a sadness compared to heartbreak quietened her, "Who I was?"

He looked at her swaying like a snake about to bite him.

Dante responded honestly, "I'll never be yours, Pagan, with or without Pan's Magick."

Mud squished up through Pagan's toes and she swayed on the spot, "I'm under no illusion of what you have to offer me, Dante. No offence, I've been around for a long time. Love rarely comes into the equation. I just want you to fuck me. I mean, for fuck sake, you have Pan's blood raging inside of you and you can deny me?"

Confident of her sexuality and effect on men, she added, "I think it's you questioning yourself. I think you're scared you might love me, Mr Unavailable."

Dante bit his lip, "I am what I am, Pagan."

Ignoring him, she unzipped her dress, untied the corset and pulled down her knickers, throwing them into a pile. Standing naked in front of him, her vulnerability questionable, she offered herself to him, "Look at me, Dante!"

Dante looked at her womanly body.

"I'm not asking you to love me, Dante. All I'm asking for is this moment. Moments are all I have."

Softening her voice, she asked Dante to sit down.

Sitting down upon his hairy lap, she kissed his welted cheeks and drunk from his cut lip.

Pan's Magick raged in him and his senses caved into lust.

Lifting her torso, she placed her right nipple into his mouth. She pushed his head back kissing his forehead. The sweet taste of his sweat seduced her taste buds.

Grabbing at his long hair, she wrapped it fiercely around her hand and pulled, "How do you like it?"

Dante laughed.

Flipping her over onto her back, Dante spread her legs apart with his knees, lingering for a second before entering her vagina.

His hairy legs tickled her.

Arching, her breath shortened. Finally, after all these years, he was inside her.

Dante's breathe lengthened, as sparks of electricity pulsated throughout his body.

Lost in the moment, in time and space, he entered her, losing himself for a second inside of *his* 'Little Witch', and with each movement, he fell deeper into a fleshy trance.

Kissing her aggressively, he felt an urge to be gentle with her, to soften his movement.

Pagan opened her eyes looking into his. She placed her hand on his cheek, "I've wanted this for so long."

Looking away, he plunged his teeth into her bicep, ripping at her flesh, as if somehow, he needed to punish her for how he was feeling.

A good lover will make every woman feel as if he is in love with her, but somehow, perhaps because of Pan's Magick, he felt a great connection to Pagan and he felt unprotected, vulnerable and exposed.

Pagan winced from the pain, and her toes tingled.

Kissing him again, Pagan tasted her own blood. Pulsating aggression roared throughout her body.

He was about to ejaculate and she sensed it, which only increased Pagan's desire. Releasing her grip from him, she threw her head back and groaned. Her top lip trembled and her skin paled. The orgasm peaked and she ejaculated from her vagina, her juices soaking his hairy groin. The orgasm froze time for several seconds, and deep primal growl left her lips, and as if she was birthing her daughter, the energy released into the universe in one large explosion.

Climaxing, he ejaculated fiercely into her vagina. Hovering above her as if he was in pain, he collapsed as Pan's Magick released from his body.

Exhausted, he gathered his breath for several minutes as he was not as fit or virile as he had once been.

They both laid still for a few moments recording the elation into memory.

In one big heave, Pagan pushed him off so she could lie beside him, finally registering the coldness from the ground and the night air, and as if she had remembered a joke, she laughed.

"Why do you laugh, Little Witch?"

"I don't know. Just happy, I suppose."

Moving to lay on top of him, she kissed his lips again, savouring the moment, his flavour and his unique odour.

Belated desire, only increased her need to be with Dante, to kiss him, fuck him, or even, to just speak to him.

Had she meet Dante in a nightclub and had a one night stand, perhaps, she would have disposed of him, just like the others, as a source of amusement, a time waster? But she had waited seventeen years for this moment and her attraction to him was holding her back.

"There is something different about you, Dante. You're special. You're not like other men."

CHAPTER 9
Pagan

After roasting in the sun for three days and freezing for two icy nights, the Kombi started easily. Pagan sighed with relief.

Already suffering from the withdrawals of drugs and alcohol and the lack of sleep, the thought of packing and unpacking the Kombi depressed her. Also, the thought of returning to her mundane lifestyle positively reduced her to desolation.

The long windy road was congested. Pagan was relieved that there was little traffic on the highway once they passed Deloraine.

Sifting through Pagan's limited compact disc collection, Amelie snarled, "You really need to buy an iPod, Pagan. Stop living in the past."

Managing an annoyed nod, Pagan turned her attention back to the highway and Dante, who had simply vanished once the sun appeared.

Alanis Morissette's album 'Jagged Little Pill' played in the background as Pagan replayed their sexual encounter which had been amazing and something that she would like to repeat. They had 'missionary style' sex. Daggy 'missionary sex' but every cell in her body connected to his. She had never felt a connection like that with another person, other than her Soul-mate.

Amelie turned to the backseat to survey their sleepy companions. Fay Ce'Line was asleep on Oscar's shoulder. Shallow snores vibrated his shoulder.

Amelie smiled at Oscar who managed a half-hearted wink.

'At least Ruby was more relaxed', Amelie thought.

After forty five minutes, they drove into Devonport, merging left into East Side, Pagan made another two left turns entering into Waterloo Road.

Ruby lived on the edge of the city with farm land directly behind her. The home was country styled with the comforts of city living. Ruby had bought the house with her deceased husband's payout. The home represented a mixture of regret and new beginnings for Ruby. Except for the occasional lost dog visiting the backyard, Ruby lived there almost intruder free.

Pulling up to the kerb, the Kombi rattled as it idled. Knowing better than to drive down the steep drive-way, Pagan made sure that Ruby could easily step out onto the safety of the cement, avoiding the large dirt pot-holes that butted up against either side of the drive-way.

Gathering her bags, Ruby slipped out of the van. Eager to see Hensley and then head to bed for a few hours rest, she said goodbye abruptly.

Oscar, keen for home, slide the door shut while waving goodbye.

After a tight U-turn in the Kombi, Pagan wound her window down to say another goodbye to Ruby. The cold wind refreshed Pagan's face. She inhaled but before Pagan finished breathing in, she screamed.

Fay Ce'Line shuddered awake.

Yanking the handbrake on, Pagan jumped out of the Kombi and crossed the road.

"For fuck sake, Ruby. Stop!"

Oscar, Amelie and Fay Ce'Line sat uncomfortable in the van.

Reaching her hand out to Ruby, Pagan swung her around but it was too late.

The sound of the squeaking rope deafened Ruby.

Frozen, she stood staring at Hensley's dead body hanging from the tree house by a towing rope.

The smell of Hensley's decomposing body reeked up Pagan's nostrils, causing her to vomit, painting the cement drive-way with a 'drug and alcohol' composition of yellow, orange and black.

Pagan

A heavy late afternoon rainfall left the bush track sludgy.

Stepping out of the car, Pagan removed her shoes, throwing them onto the front passenger seat of the car. It made no sense to dirty a pair of clean shoes when she was only walking roughly one hundred metres into the bush.

Sitting in the car for an hour prior, the image of Hensley's corpse swinging from the rope had rotated through her thoughts many times.

Saturated from built-up emotion, Pagan feared that she was about to suffer from another bout of depression and this depressed her. She had a dam full of tears to release but found not a single tear to shed.

Relieved to see headlights winding through the entrance into the pool car park, she slid down into the seat hiding from Henry, who parked his very expensive four wheel drive vehicle that his 'mummy' had bought him for his birthday on the opposite side of the carpark.

He hopped out of the vehicle, pressing the lock button on the car's remote before the car door was closed.

Watching him walk into the bush alone made her feel guilty that she had hidden from him, but it was best that she always had the upper hand over Henry, as he was a young adult with a large ego and money to support it.

Following Henry five minutes later, she left the car unlocked and walked into the Don Reserve. It was a moonless night and the bush much darker than usual. Dry mud cushioned her footsteps and the occasional tree branch massaged her hardened soles. Steam rising from the warming ground hid her ankles and concealed the bush track. She appeared to be gliding effortlessly through the bush.

Among the trees, Pagan felt at home and politely, she said, "Hello" to Pan.

Heightened smell guided her to Henry, who stood anxiously in the clearing where they had met on several occasions before. His endorphins were already releasing.

Squinting, Pagan could barely see him but she confidently walked towards him.

Sensing his anticipation, she stopped a metre in front of him. He needed to remember boundaries.

No need for introductions, Pagan spoke, "Henry, I need you to not touch me, understood?"

Stupidly, he stepped towards Pagan, who stepped instantly backwards keeping a physical void between them, "I mean it, Henry. I can't explain it but I don't want you, but I just need you tonight. Do you get that?"

Confused, he bluffed his way through, "I'm at your mercy, Pagan."

Frustrated with his lack of understanding, she thought about returning to the car but knew she had to have an emotional release by not releasing an emotion at all.

"I need to fuck you but it's not 'you' I'm fucking."

Arrogantly, he replied, "Yeah, I get it."

"No! You don't get it."

Moving closer to him, she whispered into his ear, warming his neck with her breath. She would need to be cruel to him, "You're nothing but a piece of meat to me, Henry. You're just a vibrator with a pulse. Nothing about this is about you. Don't move, don't talk, don't touch and most importantly don't think! That shouldn't be so hard."

A little wounded by her unkind words, Henry nervously agreed.

Anxious to start, she removed his loose shorts and underwear over his sneakers. Leaving his jumper on, Pagan stepped backwards and stared at the young man. She was about to objectify an eighteen year old boy, a sexual tool for her own wretched needs, and he was enabling her to do it.

Passively, he followed her instructions by lying down on the cold grass with only his legs and groin area exposed, and his dignity disposed.

Already removing her underwear before she left home, Pagan lifted her cotton skirt above her knees. Lowering her vagina onto his hardening penis, she wiggled on top of him. Internally, she moistened, her body instantly responded to his seven inches.

Stiffening his body, he lifted his groin so he could enter her deeply.

Reaching out to touch her, she pushed his hands away.

Rejecting any possibility of intimacy, she grabbed his shorts and threw them over his face.

Moving her knees out in front of her, she now sat on him as if she was sitting upon a chair. Her toes gripped the grass as she moved unemotionally upon him. Wiping all thoughts of Dante from her mind, she moved jarringly on top of Henry.

His breathing hollowed.

Arching backwards, she placed her palms behind her on Henry's inner thighs. Fingernails pierced his skin but obediently Henry remained still.

The force of her aggression moved them along the grass.

He had never witnessed Pagan like this. It turned him on sexually to be treated like a sex object. Whatever had happened to her since he had seen her last, he was thankful for.

Pagan searched desperately for a reconnection with her inner self. Failing to find any part of her existence she was happy with, she physically rotated on Henry facing his feet.

Stupidly, his fingertips touched the back of her jumper.

"No!"

A wave of anger flooded her consciousness. Desperately wanting an out-of-body experience his touch infuriated her.

She let images of Dante enter her imagination. Instantly, a warm tingling sensation entered her chest. Responding quickly to the sexual rush, she pulled her jumper off exposing her naked upper body.

Sexually fit, Pagan accelerated her movement.

Henry was fatiguing underneath her but she ignored him and continued.

Struggling not to ejaculate, Henry concentrated on his year twelve mathematical equations that sat on his desk at home. His college math teacher would be proud of him. If he ejaculated, Pagan would kill him.

The sudden smell of decay interrupted Pagan mid movement.

She opened her eyes and scanned the clearing. She saw something moving in the bushes in front of her. Seconds later, a slow moving murky green glow floated through the trees but vanished before Pagan eyes could adjust to the image.

She jumped up preparing for the worst. Something supernatural was lurking in the bushes, watching them.

Seconds later, the murky green glow reappeared flying at tremendous speed towards her.

Pagan firmly pushed her palms out, protecting her body from the impact, a habit- wanting to release her Magick from her palms. The glowing murky green glow disappeared only inches from Pagan's hands.

Sniffing the air, she relaxed. The entity had gone and so had her orgasm.

Remembering Henry, she looked down at him. Dutifully, he had remained still, his shorts still covering his face and his penis still hard.

"For fucks sake, Henry, put your pants back on and go home."

PART TWO

London, 1976
Aggie

Aggie massaged her forehead. The effects of a hangover had set in.

Stepping off the Bakerloo Line, London, careful not to slip over in her new 'tie up' black knee high leather boots, Aggie entered the busy Oxford Circus underground station where she promised to set fire to it once she took care of other matters.

"Fucking congested tube!"

London had changed. No! The world had changed.

There were two Londons, parallel realities and Aggie moved in between them like a two-faced sniper.

Over the last decade, London witnessed strikes, blackouts and rotting garbage in conjunction with free love, self-exploration and daisy chains. Londoners were trapped within a juxtaposition of extremes and she rather liked it. Regardless if Londoners wore a 'peace sign' or a right-wing conservative flag, their underlying disposition was contempt.

London was also a melting pot of disease and artistic depression. Aggie predicted political upheavals over the next decade and she would use this to her advantage.

Walking along the streets of the East End, she moved quickly through the junction and into Oxford and Regent Street, which buzzed with large floppy hats, denim flares, floral dresses and afro styled hair.

Aggie shamelessly dressed to shock. Using an iron, her long, straightened, auburn hair hosted a heavy fringe that covered most of her short forehead. She wore thick black stockings under her denim shorts, a dark green velvet sweater and an additional long black coat, that kept her warm.

Men were mesmerised when she walked past them.

Aggie caught her reflection in a shop window and laughed, "So, they should be."

Strutting towards Berwick Street her intentions were to visit the market before work as she was in desperate need of fresh fruit and fabric. There would be plenty of hippy peddlers to help her out.

Passing the club, Marquee, where only twelve hours before she had partied, she felt hung-over again.

Her artist friend, Jamie had dragged her along to see a new punk band that he was obsessed with. Standing at the back of the room, Aggie had drunk alcohol excessively to cope with the chaotic atmosphere. The sound was louder, the crowd more aggressive and the band more political. After numerous glasses of 'scotch and dry', Aggie exited, leaving the punk vibe to the teenagers.

Aggie arrived at work a few minutes late. Slamming through the doors to the conference room, she had arrived to discover that an important meeting was taking place without her.

"Bollocks!"

She had worked too hard to be left out of the decision making. She would make them pay for their impatience one day soon.

Thirteen Ancient Crone Monarchs, known as the Highest Priestess and the Sisters of the Moon, quietened as she entered the room. Her new boots clunked on the new brown and yellow floor tiles which heightened the tension in the room.

She fantasised about blowing up this building as well.

Aggie sat next to the Highest Priestess whose disapproval twisted her upper lip towards her pointy nose, exposing her yellowing teeth.

Indignant to apologise, Aggie instead reached into her slouch bag, looking for a pen and paper. It took Aggie roughly fifty seconds to manoeuvre inside the bag which was full of purchases from the Berwick Market but it felt much longer in the silence of the room.

The Crones did not see her smirk as she prolonged her search on purpose. Finally, she sat up to face thirteen disapproving Ancient Crone Monarchs staring at her.

"Just die already," Aggie said under her breath.

Sensing there had just been an argument, Aggie decided to focus.

Processing quickly, Aggie paled as she realised the extent of their anguish.

The 'Soul-mates' had been reincarnated after a five hundred year void. This was serious. Named the Soul-mates because a leader of a magical group of men, fell inlove with a Maiden and after her death, he cursed her fate to his, forever in a karmic double-knot. Neither one was free of the other. It was a curse of eternal bondage.

Aggie grinned. 'What an awful predicament the Witch was in. Stuck with one man forever'.

The last time the Red Haired Leader had been reincarnated, he had been born Henry VIII of England. Anne Boleyn was his Soul-mate Witch and together they had ruled most dogmatically. Cutting ties with Rome had been the Witch's greatest achievement. Her reason- to break down male supremacy and incite a Witch uprising. Henry had quickly learned of her ambition and promptly removed her head, but he, unlike her, had no memory of their timeless love.

'How would his Soul-mate greet him this time?' Aggie wondered.

Aggie broke into a heated sweat, a sign of weakness that she hoped the Ancient Crone Monarchs had not seen. She felt odd, as if she had been told a joke but was under pressure to add her own punch line.

The Highest Priestess sat on the edge of her leather chair as if ready to pounce on the next disagreeable Ancient Crone Monarch, "Then we agree to order the death of the Soul-mates immediately?"

Ten of the monarchs placed their palms up, positioning them straight up towards the ceiling. Three hesitated.

Aggie rolled her eyes, 'Gutless'. Democracy was a waste of time.

And as if a cold shadow moved above Aggie, she had an epiphany. A wave of nausea bent her over the table.

'No! The child could not be? Surely not! What a fuck up'.

Aggie panicked. She knew who the Soul-mate Witch was.

The Ancient Crone Monarchs would surely kill the Soul-mates. It was not the first time Aggie had seen their brutality. Killing babies certainly did not keep them awake at night.

Aggie slid her hand across the table, resting it on her employer's wrinkly hand, "May I make an uneducated suggestion Highest Priestess and the Sisters of the Moon?"

The Highest Priestess agreed while the others voiced their disapproval.

Nervously, Aggie spoke, "The Soul-mates are of no danger to you or the Witch community until she is Awakened and he does not even know who he is or who she is. He lives in ignorance. We cannot condone killing Maidens your Highest Priestess as she has not yet committed a crime…well not this time around. There will be a public outcry. We need to remember the disharmony of recent times. Can you afford another rebellion? Enlightenment has given us knowledge. With knowledge comes power. Place surveillance on them. Let us study them, particularly her. It also gives us eighteen years to plan her downfall, perhaps we can finish her reign of terror forever."

She added, "He is nothing without her. Let us find a way to cage her as if she was merely your pet."

CHAPTER 11
Australia, 1980
Aislyn

She was broken; bones would heal and scars would conceal under makeup foundation but her heart would never mend.

Her twisted body was slumped up against the sliding wardrobe, and she was unable to turn her head in fear that her neck would break. The air around her body stung her nostrils (decaying aromas of stale tobacco and Sandalwood incense).

Here she was again, a scene too familiar and too heartbreaking to imagine but none-the-less it had become her reality since the birth of their last child, another Maiden. The birth of Pagan had burst forth such anger in Cain (her husband and her childhood friend), that she feared he would kill Pagan if she did not step in between them, luring his bitterness towards her instead of the Innocent child.

A Witch always protected her birth Maiden, even if the attacks, his tantrums, the outrage, left her near to death, and never did it occur to her to use her wand to fend him off, never occurred to her that she should leave this man who was now a stranger to her. Her duty to him had always been to her demise.

The silence drummed an earthy beat in her bleeding ears, and she threw up over her right shoulder; now a cocktail of blood, mashed skin and a torn apricot blouse. Tears fell down her face. Her twisted legs managed to support her bruised spine which would straighten again after a trip to the osteopath but she feared that her fingers would never be elegant and long again.

The foetus within her belly would have surely died from the massive blows but she had prepared herself for this moment as they came so regularly that she could almost predict his eruptions.

She missed her husband who was unrecognisable to her, a stranger who shared her house but nothing else. It had been a long time since she had heard a kind word spoken from him. Even as she sat coated in blood, she knew she would stay loyal to their love, regardless of any emotional and physical risk he put her through; it was her duty as his wife.

She saw his pain, she felt his despair, and in those moments, she forgave him, as she always did, as she always had. Forgave him for his faults. He had always been a strong man physically but his heart was wounded and weak, his morals blurred and his sexual desire unstable, but she had and did love him, for all his faults. He had been her only true love.

But the loss of another child weighed heavily upon her. It had been a boy. She had sensed it. She had seen it, in a vision, another vision- another useless vision. They came so infrequently now. She had heard the cry of a baby boy while she was hanging the washing out, and knew another life grew inside of her. Instantly her spine had bent a little, knowing that soon he would hit the child out of her and she would suffer another loss of a child, aborted due to hate.

Out of guilt that day, she had checked that Pagan still played safely in the back yard. Pagan was the most peaceful child, easily hurt, and unloved.

Aislyn closed her swollen eyes and rested. It would take a few days of hiding from the outside world before she would begin to heal physically.

Emotionally, she would never heal. When would this nightmare end?

Hearing the door squeak but too exhausted to react to it, her thoughts drifted in and out of consciousness. She did not hear the little four year old walking into the bedroom.

Standing in front of her mother, the four year old Maiden holding tightly to a Barbie Doll, looked at her.

Rocking back and forth, she whispered, "Mummy."

Aislyn did not reply.

The little girl ran out of the bedroom and tiptoed across the hallway. The sound of her father snoring on the couch scared her and she moved twice as fast. Crawling into bed with her sister, Inanna, she hid under the sheets.

Inanna pulled her little sister closer, wrapping her arms around her.

Inanna had blocked her ears when the fighting began and was now relieved it had finished.

Refusing to cry, Pagan had listened to every word yelled, recording it to memory, adding her own hatred to every word.

1985
Pagan

Hidden underneath the single bed, protected by a beige valance, Pagan felt safe cocooned in her linen cubby house.

Disappearing for hours in hidden dwellings, Pagan preferred to be alone; ignoring calls from her family to interact with them or invitations from the kids in the street to play four square, hopscotch or chasings, so she was annoyed when she heard heavy footsteps invading her asylum.

Two knees landed on the olive green coiled carpet and then Inanna's face poked through the valance, "Tea time."

Pagan replied indignantly, "I'm not hungry."

Reaching under the valance, Inanna tugged on Pagan's leg, "I don't care if you starve, but Mum said now!"

Wriggling her way out from underneath the valance, Pagan ran down the hallway. Opportunity urged Pagan to push her older sister in the back as she ran past. The shove hurt Inanna who retaliated by slamming her into the wall and pinching Pagan's bicep.

Pagan yelped, pushing Inanna off, "Knick off, Inny!"

The age gap between the sisters was eight years. The continuous strain of their home life caused sibling tension and loveless vapours that seeped from their pores. Their sisterly love had turned into bitter rivalry, where once Inanna had been Pagan's protector, she was now her blood enemy and happily so. It seemed innate that they should dislike each other.

Sitting at the dining table, Pagan snubbed her family, preferring to interact with her thoughts instead.

The room was well lit but a coat of cigarette smoke covered the room making it difficult for her to appreciate the late evening sunbeams that radiated through the large window.

Aislyn carried two plates at a time to the dining table. Making three trips, she remained loyal to the patriarchal hierarchy, feeding Cain and their son Norman first. Inanna and Pagan next and as usual Aislyn sat down at the table last.

Steaming roast pork and mashed potatoes accompanied with baked potatoes, bribed Pagan's stomach to growl and her nose to explode from stimulation. All the vegetables were overcooked but she chewed into the meal enthusiastically.

The evidence of a dysfunctional marriage had aged Aislyn and as she ate her meal, heavy lines and scars on her face were plainly evident in the evening light.

Cain, her father, began to eat.

Pagan studied him. The mere sight of him chewing his pork, his fork scrapping along his teeth while he guzzled down his long neck beer made her feel physically sick. He was already drunk and would probably choke on his un-chewed meat again. A scene that now infuriated Pagan where once she had felt pity for him.

Rarely speaking to Pagan, he only grumbled at Aislyn's request to discipline the boisterous child which only exasperated their already toxic father-daughter relationship. As far as Pagan was concerned she had no father, he was merely a man that lived in the same house as she did, and something that she would rectify once she turned eighteen.

Clutching her knife and fork, Pagan ignored her hands turning white.

Aislyn noticed the contempt in her daughter's eyes as she stared at her father. There was so much that her daughter did not know and was far too young to find out. While cutting the umbilical cord, Cain had begged Aislyn to keep

Pagan's fate from her until she had been Awakened. Somewhere in his tortured soul, he had wanted to protect her, if only for a second.

Sitting Inanna down at age five, she had taken the news of being born a Maiden badly. Like most young girls, she had wanted to be a princess not a Witch and she had worn the news like a mouldy tiara.

With the news of a little sister, potentially another Maiden, Inanna had been excited that she would have her own confidant to share her deepest secrets with, but it soon become apparent that when Pagan was born, her father's kindness and tenderness had vanished and Inanna would never forgive Pagan for that. Inanna had been 'daddy's little girl' but now she was 'no-one's, little girl'. She had lost her father to alcohol and her mother to another Maiden.

Pagan stared across at the span of deadpan faces she called 'Family'.

Norman, her brother, sat quietly throughout the duration of the meal, only stopping occasionally to chew his fingernails. Seven years older than Pagan and one year younger than Inanna, he rarely spoke to anyone, not even Pagan, although she saw him as her only friend in the house. They shared a mutual disdain for Inanna and Cain which brought about a fabricated loyalty based on mutual hatred rather than an intimate bond. Loyalties were scarce in the house, so Pagan took what was on offer without question.

Her mother was too busy trapped within her own thoughts to be loyal to anyone, not even to herself.

Caged, they were all caged.

Swallowing her last mouthful, Pagan was asked to help Inanna wash up the dishes. Rolling her eyes in protest, she swung the tea towels around the kitchen while the sink filled up with hot water. Holding back the temptation to whip Inanna with the tea towel, she watched as Inanna pulled her long golden hair up into a floppy bun without the aid of any hairbands. Envious, Pagan tried to pull her knotty hair up, only for it to look like a birds nest and fall out.

Inanna was stunning with pale skin and golden hair, complimented by cherry red lips and large almond shaped eyes.

Norman had inherited his mother's looks which made him look vastly different to his sisters. Pagan thought that Norman had received the best looks of all.

An ugly child, Pagan had dull dopey eyes, knotty black hair and chalky white lips, naturally tanned freckled skin and a long skinny body. If she was to cut her hair off, she could easily be mistaken for a boy.

Finishing the dishes, Pagan exited the house entering the quiet street.

Latrobe was a quiet town comparable to a retirement village but it was the only place she had ever known and within those uncultured streets was a community spirit seldom experienced elsewhere else, she assumed. She appreciated the stability of the community; it helped to lessen her family's instability.

Running for two street blocks, Pagan found herself puffing at the gates of a prestigious red brick federation home. Surrounding the residence was a four metre high hedge, which the local kids climb, playing amongst its sturdy green conifer leaves.

Waving at the moving curtain, Pagan waited for her friend, Thomas to join her before scaling the hedge.

Throwing his jacket on and sneaking out the front door, Thomas joined her moments later, quickly climbing the hedge in case his father saw him.

Thomas was a pretty boy with straight blonde hair that hung down to his shoulders, hair that his father made him wash twice a day. It shone and never dared tangle. Standing at five foot nine inches, he was taller than most twelve year old boys and awkward because of it. Growing up in many foreign countries, Thomas struggled to assimilate to the dullness of Tasmanian life, preferring Malaysia or Croatia.

Had Pagan not met Thomas on the monkey bars at school the previous year, she would not have had one friend her entire life. It was loneliness that brought them together, an exile by their peers and a general subconscious feeling that they did not belong in 1985, let alone in this town. An unspoken bond had been made after Pagan pricked her finger pressing it against Thomas's already bleeding finger- a pact that they both intended to stay loyal to.

"We are blood family, forever."

Settling into the hedge, Thomas unzipped his jacket, pulling out a Walkman and handed it to Pagan, "Have a listen. I've made you a mix tape."

Pagan wiggled into a stable seated position on the conifer branch before placing the headphones over her ears.

Thomas pressed play.

A surge of rock tones, electronic percussion, synthesiser and a deep beat from the drum machine, jolted Pagan's imagination.

She grinned, "Who is this?"

Thomas pressed the stop button so she could hear him, "Wild Boys' by Duran Duran. I taped it off the radio last night. I had to be careful that father didn't hear me. He doesn't like me listening to commercial radio."

"Thanks Thomas, this is cool."

Thomas blushed.

Pressing the start button, she closed her eyes to fully immerse herself into the sound.

Thomas enjoyed watching her moonlit face sway from side to side to the beat. He wanted to hold her hand but fear persuaded him otherwise.

They both relaxed into the moment.

By the time Thomas felt the cold hand wrap around his ankle, he was already being pulled out of the hedge. Landing onto the footpath with a thud,

Thomas aimlessly hit out at who ever had hold of him. Laughter confirmed his
fear. It was Carl, his own personal bully who conveniently lived on the same street
as him and terrorised him whenever he ventured out of his front gates.

Lost in lyric, Pagan felt the hedge shake. Opening her eyes, she saw Carl.

Slipping out of the hedge her feet searched for the footpath. Once
secured, she spotted Carl pulling Thomas along the footpath. His trousers had
slipped underneath his bottom so that his bare bum was exposed, the gravelly
footpath tore his buttocks apart.

Carl was fourteen and much taller than Pagan. The height difference did
not stop Pagan running at him. Using her entire body to knock him over onto the
grass and without hesitation, she punched Carl on the side of the head, like she had
seen her father punch her mother.

"That's enough, Pagan!"

Thomas's father had appeared from the driveway to pull Pagan off Carl.
Her feet dangled in the air but she still kicked wildly at Carl.

Jumping to his feet, Carl scuffled along the footpath and as he passed
Thomas, who still sat on the ground, he managed one last taunt before he ran
home, "I'm gonna get you, pretty boy!"

Thomas's father silently wandered back inside the gates, too angry to utter
a word, leaving both Thomas and Pagan to comfort each other.

Pagan looked at Thomas, who still sat on the ground.

Kindly, she ignored his tears, "He's a jerk, Thomas. Don't worry about
him!"

"You better go, Pagan, I'll be right," Thomas's voice had hardened.

She understood that Thomas wanted to be alone but she hesitated. She
wanted to protect Thomas but she knew he was trying to avoid the embarrassment
of standing up and pulling gravel from his bottom.

As she ran off down the street, she imagined that his bottom would be
rather scratched and bloody. She promised herself that she would make Carl pay
for his bullying, one day.

Thomas climbed into the hedge to fetch his Walkman. He found the
headphones tangled and the tape still playing, and hidden from the world,
he belittled himself for letting a girl protect him.

Carl

Carl had run for a while before slowing down into a slouched walk.

Picking up a rock, he hooked it left, it bounced across the top of the
corrugated galvanised steel roof of his neighbour's home, coming to rest in the
bush near the shed.

Loud music vibrated down the street. He recognised the band. It was, 'Fleetwood Mac'.

Carl spat on the ground. It was his mother playing her vinyls, which meant that she was drunk. Looking up at the stars, he hoped that she had 'passed out' already.

Jumping the metal fence and walking across the overgrown lawn, he entered his home through the back screen door, locking it behind him.

Grabbing a packet of chips from the bottom of the kitchen shelf and a large bottle of fizzy cordial from the fridge, he headed to his bedroom, glancing into the lounge room as he walked past. His mother was asleep on the couch. Three bottles of Stones Mac and an empty packet of cigarettes sat on the floor beside her.

Entering his bedroom, he switched the light on.

Placing the food and drink on the bedside table, Carl kicked his desert boots off which thumped against the door, and then he threw his jeans and flannel shirt onto the piles of dirty clothes already on the floor in the middle of his room.

Wiping the grimy mirror, he turned his head so he could look at where Pagan had hit him.

He smiled, she was feisty. The egg shaped wound was hidden underneath his mullet haircut which meant his mother would not notice it in the morning. If she did, she would clout him again for being in another fight.

Pressing play on his cassette player, he lay down on the unmade bed. Cold Chisel's song 'Khe Sanh' muffled out his mum's music.

Carl looked around his room. It smelled and its apricot painted walls made him angry. Several holes in the walls were covered up with Van Halen, AC&DC, Motley Crew, Megadeth and Rush, posters. Not that anyone really cared. His mum was not really the domestic type or a motherly type for that matter, so she rarely entered his room. She had no idea that mould coated his windows.

Wide awake, he drank another mouthful of fizzy cordial and opened the packet of chips, shovelling them into his mouth.

Bored, he grabbed his jeans off the floor, pulling a box of matches out of the back pocket. Igniting a match, he burned the hairs on his legs. His short blonde hairs shrivelled, melting into black stumps.

Still bored, he spotted a fly on his wall. After some concentration, he caught it and ripped off its wings.

Pagan

"Come quick. Dad's really drunk," Inanna whispered as she pulled Pagan along the street towards their home.

Pagan followed her, hesitating with each step, afraid at what they were walking towards, wanting to return to the hedge.

Scared Inanna's voice quivered as she spoke, "Pagan, you need to climb in our bedroom window and stay in our bedroom. Don't be a hero tonight. Just looking at you makes dad worse. He hates you so much."

Inanna gave Pagan a lift up, her hands dirtied from the mud off her sister's shoes.

As Pagan pulled her body through the bedroom window, she scratched her stomach on the window latch, a scar that would remain with her for the rest of her life. Hovering for a moment as if she was a human scale, Pagan slid down onto Inanna's bed and quickly jumped underneath the doona cover.

Kicking her shoes off, she stained the sheets with muddy footprints.

Inanna climbed through the window only moments later, pulling the doona up over their heads. The darkness underneath the doona helped to increase their hearing.

Pagan lay still, listening to her parents fighting, a sound that she had heard hundreds of times; the same arguments, the same insults, the same tone and the same results. Nothing ever changed. Why did her neighbours never come to help them? Why did no one ever call the police? Why did two people who hated each other so much stay together? If this was marriage or love, then Pagan promised herself that she would never do either.

The arguing stopped. Pagan's ears were on high alert. Someone was walking down the hallway.

Inanna sat up to push the doona off them and as if in a trance, Inanna started rocking from stress, "Please, don't come into our room. Please, don't come into our room."

Pagan leaped out of the bed, her toes bracing the carpet as she readied herself to run at Cain.

The door slowly opened. The creaking of the door lasted an eternity.

"It's me," Aislyn said, walking quickly to the bed to sit with Inanna. Wrapping her arms around her eldest daughter, she was not surprised that Inanna's body was shaking uncontrollably.

Reaching out to Pagan, her daughter refused her comfort. Her baby daughter was alert and ready for whatever would happen next. Pagan was always a warrior in such moments.

There were more footsteps and then the house was unnervingly quite.

Pagan flinched as she heard Norman, her brother's voice.

'What was Norman doing? Why was he confronting a man three times his age and twice as big as him? He had never confronted him before, always preferring to disappear to a mates place for the night, returning after Cain had left for work the next morning'.

Then they heard Cain roar and then more thumps, then silence.

When Cain was in a rage, his eyes would widen and the blue iris would become the most radiant blue colour- beauty amongst the ugly, and his bottom lip would curl up. Lost in a nightmare only privy to him, it was if he was fighting demons that no-one else could see.

Without thought, Pagan ran out of the bedroom and down the hall, "Norman!"

She had to protect her brother- her only friend in the house.

Opening the lounge room door, Pagan saw Norman. His body was rigid. His eyes fixed on his drunken father.

Cain took a swing at Norman, hitting him on the side of the head.

Norman closed his eyes as if he was internalising the pain. Reopening them, he urged his father to hit him again.

Cain danced to a wicked tune as he prepared himself for another punch.

"Hit back you weak cunt," Cain taunted his only son, as if he heard his own mother saying it to him but now he was in power, he was the torturer not the tortured.

Cain hit Norman in the stomach and a second blow to his cheek. Norman bent from reflex but refused to react. He stood back up, spitting blood out into his palm.

"Hit him back, Norman," Pagan screamed.

Aislyn covered Inanna's ears. The sound of her daughter's sobs shattered her heart but she could not find the strength to go to the other children, to protect Norman or Pagan. She was a weakling.

Cain yelled at Norman, "Get the fuck out of my house, get the fuck out and don't ever come back!"

Norman remained composed as blood trickled out of his left nostril.

Cain walked back over to Norman and spat in his face, "You're not my son. You're nobody's son." Once again, Cain could hear his own mother saying those words to him as a child, a life time ago.

Norman swayed. His body was in shock and his mind in turmoil. A million thoughts spun around in his mind, he could finally leave this 'hell hole'. Free himself from this life. Surely, living on the street was better than this?

He looked at his little sister and managed a grimace, as if he was translating a secret code she did not understand.

Pagan screamed as her heart broke, "Norman no! Norman, don't go, please Norman."

Norman left.

Pagan wild from heartache attacked her father, biting him on the leg.

Cain tugged at her hair until she let go and then walked off to his bedroom where minutes later he was asleep.

The females in the house cuddled into one bed and cried.

1990
Pagan

Pagan watched as several utility vehicles drove past her house, slowed down and parked on the nature strip next door.

Placing the breakfast bowl on the coffee table, Pagan watched as three young virile men jumped out of the utility and proceeded to open the locked gate to the vacant house. Excitement grew as she realised that the new neighbours had arrived.

A 'Sold' sign had been placed on the realty advertisement two weeks prior and she had waited anxiously to see her new neighbours.

Fearful that they would be the next victims to be exposed to her family's toxicity, she hoped that they would be active in their protests to live in a quiet neighbourhood, asserting their displeasure of late night arguing.

A small black car parked next to the kerb.

Cain shook his head, "Ha! A Porsche 944 and in this neighbourhood too."

Pagan distanced herself from Cain by stepping closer to the curtains.

She pulled the blinds up so she could have a better look at the driver of the lush car. A young woman stepped out of the Porsche. A short red dress showed off the young woman's muscly thighs and small delicate ankles. Her straight short black hair sharply contoured her delicate neck, giving her an air of sophistication.

Pagan felt instantly inferior.

"She doesn't look old enough to own a car like that, she's barely twenty," Cain asserted.

The woman lit a cigarette while she surveyed her new surroundings. With a flick of her hand, she ordered the men to unpack the utilities. They obeyed. Unexpectedly, she turned towards Pagan as if she had known she was there all the time.

Pagan jumped back, dropping to the floor.

Looking up at Cain, Pagan noticed that he had paled. Glaring back at the woman for a several seconds, he walked off.

Her heart was racing when she stood back up. Peering out through the blinds again, her eyes darted from the front lawn to the Porsche. She had obviously entered her new home.

Another car pulled up beside the kerb, parking directly behind the Porsche. Two more unusual looking women jumped out of the car. One woman looked similar to the first woman. The third woman was plain and her movements were awkward, as if she wanted a car to lose control and hit her. Their ages were so close, Pagan wondered if they were triplets.

Pagan tilted her head, who were these women and why would they move to Latrobe?

Excited, she ran to Thomas's to tell him about the mysterious women that had moved next door. Thomas sat engrossed in his PC game, remaining focused on the monitor, even after Pagan slumped down beside him.

Pulling the chair up even closer, she actively invaded his personal space, promptly telling him all about the new female neighbours, delving into exaggerated detail.

Eyes darting across the computer screen, he still ignored her.

Reaching out, Pagan turned the power switch off to his monitor.

"Hey! What did you do that for?"

Pagan smirked, "Well, listen to me."

Thomas sat back stiffly, "Well, maybe the world doesn't revolve around you, Pagan?"

Offended, Pagan remained silent while she selected her options of retaliation.

Thomas had distanced himself from her over the last six months and although she had brought up the awkwardness, he had remained adamant that nothing had changed. Broaching the subject with her mother, she had responded steadfastly that it was most likely due to male hormones.

"They use the 'hormone' attack with us to externalise blame, but men have hormones as well, but never talk about it, not that I would use it against them as an excuse for their behaviours," Aislyn had snarled.

Thomas interrupted, "Look Pagan. Dad is taking me on holiday again."

Pagan sat up as the pit of her stomach twisted. In one moment her happiness had turned to despair. Thomas was her only friend.

"When and for how long?"

Anticipating a tantrum, he inhaled, "For one year. We leave on Monday."

Pagan stood up, pacing around his immaculate bedroom. Her blood heated but she felt cold, "One fucking year? Where's he taking you this time and what's so fucking important that he has to go for one fucking year?"

Crossing his arms in defence, Thomas replied, "It doesn't matter Pagan, does it? Plus, I'm not sure where we're going. I just do as I'm told."

Pagan stood up, "Well, it matters to me!"

Sadness turning into rage, she walked to the door. Slamming the door shut, she sarcastically told Thomas to, "Have fun on your holiday."

Flicking the monitor back on, he released a nervous laugh. It had always amused him when he witnessed one of Pagan's explosive moments. She really was predictable.

CHAPTER 12
Pagan

With Thomas gone, Norman vanishing and Inanna now moved out, Pagan found herself fastened to the chair in front of her lounge room window surveying the mysterious neighbours for hours each day. It had become an obsession.

They rarely left the house in the daylight, limiting their interactions with the locals, preferring to spend most nights hosting noisy parties for an abundance of out-of-town visitors, usually 'wrapping it up' at sunrise.

The irony amused Pagan, who thought it was karma that their music drowned out her parent's arguing, and infuriated Cain on nights he passed out early, only to wake to the thumping of the bass.

She wondered if God (if there was one), had organised the strange neighbours to move in next door, because he too, could hear Cain and Aislyn arguing in heaven. Not that Pagan registered the arguing anymore. Somehow, her brain had learned to 'shut it out'.

What intrigued Pagan was how the guests were getting to these parties. There were never any extra cars, buses, motorbikes or pushbikes to transport them and they seemed to simply disappear the next morning.

One night, she had jumped the side fence and crept up to the window. Luckily, there had been a slight gap in the curtain and she could easily see inside. There appeared to be hundreds of people squeezed into the small living area. Strange looking people who all danced as if someone had used a remote control and pressed half speed.

On several occasions, Pagan had caught the eldest woman staring at her as she walked to school in the mornings. Too scared to make eye contact, Pagan stared at the footpath as she walked past.

Witnessing a group of Jehovah Witnesses walking up to their front door one morning at 09:00; suitcases, pamphlets and children in tow, only to leave stumbling over themselves as they scrambled out the gate, only increased Pagan's interest in them.

"What strange women you are."

Her mother asked, "Talking to yourself again, Pagan?"

Pagan nodded, "Well, I don't have anyone else to talk to."

Handing Pagan her lunch, Aislyn stared out the window, "I hope you're not thinking of bonding with those weirdos next door. They are rather scandalous; the whole town is talking about them."

Pagan snarled, "Talking behind their backs you mean?"

Aislyn ignored her daughter's sarcasm, "It's too nice a day to be locked inside. After you've finished your lunch you should go outside and play."

"Mum, I'm fourteen. I don't play."

Aislyn walked towards the kitchen, "Well, do something productive then, like homework."

"How about you get a life," Pagan said underneath her breath, missing the irony of her own pathetic life.

If Pagan was honest, she enjoyed watching the neighbours as they offered an alternative lifestyle compared to her mundane existence and a liberation that she had not known existed. She promised herself that when she left home that she would be just like them.

Turning to look at her mother who was already fussing over the dishes, Pagan already knew that the latter was not an option.

Ten hours later, another argument penetrated the walls of her bedroom.

Pagan stared at the mess of papers and books spread out over her bed and wondered if she should just retire for the night to wake in the morning to finish her essay.

Aislyn and Cain's voice suddenly increased in volume as they entered the hallway.

Rolling her eyes, Pagan anticipated that Aislyn was leaving Cain again and was heading towards her bedroom to pack, but surprisingly, Aislyn slammed through Pagan's door, snapping it shut behind her.

Within seconds, Cain attempted to open the door. The door ajar, a struggle between her parents began. Aislyn's only advantage was Cain's intoxication which made him weaker.

Pagan was wild with rage, how dare they invade her space, they had the entire house to fight in.

Cain quickly fatigued and with the last amount of energy, he smashed his fist through the door, only to return to the lounge room to pass out. Aislyn had screamed as Cain's fist missed her face by only a few inches but she held fast on her side of the door.

Pagan was furious.

"Pack your bags, we're leaving," Aislyn scream desperately.

Wanting to escape from this life, Pagan had always wanted to leave but not to take her mother with her, and in that moment of potential escape, Pagan strangely felt a loyalty to the only home she had ever known.

Aislyn repeated herself, this time a growl exited her throat, "Pagan, quickly. Start packing."

Pagan jumped off her bed and ran at her mother and without warning, she slapped her mother across the face, "You make me sick."

Bursting into tears, Aislyn collapsed onto the floor.

A rage burned inside Pagan, "When are you going to stop this bullshit? You do this every week. You're pathetic. Do you think he cares? He knows you'll return tomorrow. You're too weak to survive on your own. You're too weak to be a mother!"

As if a cold wind entered the room, reality smacked Pagan in the face and she fled from the house. Running fitfully down the street, adrenaline and guilt, led the way. Fear navigated her to the Church where her parents had married and where now she collapsed onto the cold stone steps.

Gulping for air, Pagan considered running, running away for good, but where would she go? How would she survive? What about school? Could she find Norman? Would Inanna take her sister in?

Erratic thoughts buzzing around inside of her head was made worse by the silence of the town. It was as if the whole world was asleep. She felt very alone.

Curling up on the step, sheltered by the church's alcove entrance, sleep soon quietened her thoughts.

Waking an hour later, memories of the evening flooded her thoughts, only now, the regret tormented her.

"Pagan?"

Pagan stood up, panicked because the voice come from somewhere inside of her brain.

Bravely, she stepped out of the alcove and into the church's carpark expecting a man to be standing there, but Pagan was surprised to see only the stillness of the night.

"Who said that?"

Was she losing her mind? She had definitely heard a man's voice.

"I wouldn't listen to him if I was you. God tends to be a little dramatic at times like this and you can never really tell if it's him or the Darkness. Both enjoy a joke," said Pagan's mysterious female neighbour.

Pagan

Slinking one body length behind her night-time savour, they journeyed quickly through the township. Their ears acutely responsive to their surroundings; haunting cow cries from dairy paddocks only a kilometre behind them, truck engines juddering through their gears at the highway roundabout, and municipal dogs alerting their slumbering owners with 'rubber-spine barking,' that danger lingered nearby. Suddenly the town was alive with noise whereas only moments earlier the world had been silent.

Pagan swallowed her anxious breath, only as far down as the bottom of her rib cage. She took another half-breath to fill the void.

Questioning the sudden appearance of this woman at the church and her Mary Magdalene hospitality, Pagan's thoughts fought an uncouthly scepticism while she attempted to settle on a rational resolution, finally deciding that she had no other choice but to follow this woman and trust her.

Aislyn had warned her daughter against ignoring 'gut feelings'. A feeling that was at this time highly suspicious of this woman; a woman who in particular her mother had warned her about. Pagan wondered if her mother's fears were warranted.

Using peripheral vision, she stared at this woman. After some thought, Pagan concluded that her mother was most likely jealous of her.

Honouring a controlled sexual competence and mental astuteness, emotional stiffness, an unsympathetic chin and a reedy stare that reached into your brain to steal veiled thoughts, she was the scariest woman Pagan had ever met and the most intriguing.

Her mother, who frequently 'switched off' Madonna's sexually progressive music film clips because she believed they pushed back 'women's Liberation' by fifty years, amused Pagan, who harshly measured the distribution of liberation between the two women- Madonna versing her mother, easily favouring the American pop singer. Her mother had no idea about women's liberation.

The neighbour who Pagan had been stalking for months and now, ironically, was the person who came to Pagan's rescue, introduced herself as Amelie. Not offering an explanation to how she had found Pagan or why, Amelie kindly offered refuge for the night.

Baulking at first while her intuition quarrelled with curiosity, Pagan finally agreed to stay with Amelie, mainly due to a chill that had settled into her bones, and there was 'no way' she was going home until the next morning when Cain had left for work. It would be hard enough facing her mother let alone him as well.

"The full moon does strange things to people. Makes them do things that they normally wouldn't," Amelie had calmly stated.

Pagan had not noticed the moon until Amelie mentioned it. The moon glistened to the right of them. Commanding and beautiful. The full moon had guided Pagan to the Church and without pride or ego the moon had not asked for gratification. A flawless night, Pagan predicted a vanilla twilight followed by a severe frost in the morning.

For the majority of the walk, Amelie remained silent, only the sound of her high heels clacking on the road and the squeak of her leather trousers rubbing together at the top of her thighs made her existence real.

Pagan snuck another look at Amelie. She looked grand wearing a large fur coat.

Pagan shivered from envy. Maybe next time she ran away she would wear appropriate clothing.

Catching Pagan staring at her coat, Amelie laughed, "Don't worry. It's not real. I know how much you would hate that."

'What a strange thing to say', Pagan thought.

Amelie had spoken several times in the last fifteen minutes as if she was familiar with Pagan's character. Had Amelie been stalking her as well?

Relieved and scared, Pagan entered Amelie's home. The smell of patchouli instantly consumed her nostrils while the wood heater warmed her skin.

Grabbing Pagan's hand, Amelie led her through the drunken visitors to the hallway, another turn and they were in Amelie's bedroom. Amelie shut the door to block some of the sound out.

Drawing breath, Pagan felt a wave of euphoria.

"Welcome to my boudoir."

Three walls were painted 'blood clot' red while the fourth had been turned into a wardrobe but without any doors. Pagan had never seen so many clothes of all tastes and fabrics squashed into a claustrophobic manifestation. Running her fingertips along the fabric, Pagan's hands experienced a sensory delight; silk, sequin, cashmere, woollen knit, and tweed.

"You must be rich to afford all these clothes?"

Ignoring Pagan's bluntness, Amelie pulled out an orange angora cardigan and passed it to her, "Here, put this on."

Pagan obeyed, instantly feeling warmer as she pulled it over her head. She sensed Amelie was annoyed that she had not unbuttoned the cardigan instead.

Amelie pointed at the bed, "Please sit!"

Obediently, Pagan sank into the waterbed mattress. The bed took up most of the space in the bedroom. Made from hardwood, the four corners of the bed supported cane pillars that looked like string toffees that had been thrown to the opposite corner of the bed creating a web cathedral pattern. Pagan had never seen a bed like it before.

Two bedside lamps sat on either side of the bed, just close enough to the bed for Amelie to stretch her hand out and turn them on. Pagan was in awe of the lamps; four brass coiled snakes twisting up towards the ceiling. Twisted light bulbs were positioned in the snake's mouths.

Inquisitively, Pagan touched one of the lamps at its base, switching it on. She jumped from surprise.

"They're exquisite aren't they? I had them especially made after I turned eighteen. They remind me of a good friend. Someone I haven't seen for long time but she'll be back with me one day but until then these gorgeous lamps will remind me of her."

"Why snakes though? Snakes are terrible things."

Lost somewhere in an intimate memory, only privy to Amelia, Pagan witnessed for the first time compassion in her neighbour's eyes.

"Anyway!"

Amelie continued, "Yes, I am wealthy, not that it will last forever. A twist of fate saw my family lose almost all of its possessions but my mother was savvy enough to stash some of it away before 'they' confiscated it."

"Who confiscated it?"

"It's a boring story really and we have a party to attend to."

There were at least fifty people lounging around the house, lazing on the couch, kissing against the wall, playing Backgammon at the coffee table, playing strip poker on the floor (where they all appeared to be losing) and a group of people lying on bean bags in a sitting circle, touching palms as if they were transporting information from one person to another like the game Chinese Whispers.

Leaning against the wall, waiting for Amelie to return, Pagan curiously studied the guests. They all had a certain knowing about them that unnerved Pagan, as if they understood a riddle that Pagan was yet to hear.

A man only dressed in baby blue corduroy overalls and with hair liken to straw, danced over to the stereo system turning the techno music up. The progressive beat of the music hyped a few of the guests, who jumped up from their seats and proceeded to dance haphazardly around the lounge room.

Fortunately, Pagan did not recognise any of the guests in Amelie's home, and found a certain fetish staring at them. A feeling of awe consumed her. Selfishly, she was pleased that none of them knew her, as she did not want anyone 'titter-tattering' back to her parents. But their complete refutation of her existence made her feel invisible and unimportant, especially since she desperately wanted to fit in for the evening.

Much to Pagan's relief, Amelie appeared from the hallway and pushed her into the kitchen where she fixed an alcoholic cocktail, one for herself and one for her under-age guest. Slopping the green concoction over the kitchen counter, she ignored the mess and handed Pagan her glass, "Drink! This will warm you up."

The drink burned Pagan's throat and she felt drunk even before the liquid reached her stomach.

"I made it strong so your toes will sweat. We don't want you catching a cold after sleeping in the elements this evening."

Pagan suddenly felt homeless.

Braver this time, Pagan took another larger gulp. The alcohol felt as if it had burst into flames when it reached her chest. Bubbling like lava in her stomach, she thought she would combust only to be found in the morning as smoking ashes.

"Now stick out your tongue and let me pop some 'happy acid' on it. This stuff will blow your mind."

Obediently, she pushed her tongue out as far as she could.

Amelie placed a small piece of paper onto her bile coated tongue, "Now let it dissolve. Just go with it. I'm here, so you're safe and I promise it will take you to your subconscious quicker than any shrink sweetheart. Let's see what you've learned this lifetime."

It tasted bitter, metallic even.

Pagan clenched her teeth.

Dizzy, she closed her eyes only to open them again as she felt unstable. The dimensions of Amelie's face changed before her, shrinking and moving unnaturally like a Picasso painting in a washing machine cycle.

Heart racing and an overload of sensory surplus, Pagan grabbed Amelie's hand and squeezed, "How long does this last?"

"Let go, Pagan. Don't fight it. Enjoy the ride. Somethings you can't control, honey. Just flow!"

Closing her eyes again, Pagan concentrated on the voices in the kitchen and dining room, an orchestra of conversation rolled like the tide; ebb and flow, making her nauseated.

She opened her eyes, 'I don't like it. I want it to stop!"

Amelie leaned in, almost until their cheeks kissed, "Make what stop, Pagan?"

"This life, I don't like it."

1993
Pagan

Aimlessly wandering through the Devonport mall, Pagan walked from one clothes shop to the next on a lethargic whim to pass the time and decrease her wardrobe space.

The icy wind from Cradle Mountain cursed the city and stung Pagan's already flushed cheeks. Pulling her pale pink beanie further down over her forehead and tightening her scarf, she reprimanded herself for wearing a long but thin skirt, even though her knee-high socks were woollen and her cherry red Doc Martin shoes were cold resistant and weather hardy.

Her purse contained a ten dollar note and after one hour of shopping, Pagan was losing hope of making a purchase with it.

Exiting the mall and turning right, Pagan decided she would rent a video instead with her money, after all the weather summoned complete submission indoors.

Bracing herself for the blistery weather, she threw the video into her school bag. Walking out of the video shop with Bram stoker's 'Dracula', she was pleased to be going home.

A business sign rocking 'back and forth' on its hinges grabbed Pagan's attention as she walked towards the bus top. It read 'Second Hand Books'.

She looked at her watch. She still had twenty minutes before the bus was due.

Pagan felt a rush of exhilaration.

Dodging the traffic, she crossed, careful not to slip as she entered the busy street. Looking left, right and left again, she ran across the road, slipping as she jumped over the kerb onto the slippery footpath outside the shop. She laughed from embarrassment.

Bursting into the basement shop, eager to find a unique gift for Thomas, she sneezed from the dust.

A voice, somewhere from behind the thousands of books said, "Bless you!"

"Um, thank you."

Pagan's eyes adjusted. The small shop was packed with thousands of books of all sizes and widths, jammed into books shelves while the excess was piled onto the floor; piles of books, in clusters of five or six reaching the high ceiling. There was barely any room for her to walk through the maze of books.

'Where to start?'

She dropped her school bag at her side, leaving it near the front door and walked over to the closest pile of books. Squatting down to read the titles, she laughed when her knees creaked.

There was no obvious alphabetical system, nor any system she could recognise. Strangely her eyes glazed over making it difficult for her to read the book titles. Her fingertips helped as she ran them underneath the leather bind.

"Wow, these books are old," she said underneath her breath.

Pagan blinked several times as she read, 'Wollstonecraft, Mary'. The author's name was familiar. Slipping her fingers carefully around the brown leather, she dusted it off. Smelling the pages, a wave of nostalgia swept over her. Books reminded her of Thomas and the special time that they spent together in the hedges. It seemed like a life time ago.

She read the title again 'A Vindication of the Rights of Woman'.

'What did 'Vindication' mean?' She wondered.

Flipping the cover over, she bit her bottom lip as she read more. The book had been published in 1792 by a woman in England.

Had Thomas read her this book? It seemed so familiar.

Tempting fate, she flipped open a random page and read…

'THAT *woman is naturally weak, or degraded by a concurrence of circumstances, is, I think, clear. But this position I shall simply contrast with a conclusion, which I have frequently heard fall from sensible men in favour of an aristocracy: that the mass of mankind cannot be anything, or the obsequious slaves, who patiently allow themselves to be penned up, would feel their own consequence, and spurn their chains. Men, they further observe, submit everywhere to oppression, when they have only to lift up their heads to throw off the yoke; yet, instead of asserting their birthright, they quietly lick the dust, and say, let us eat and drink, for tomorrow we die. Women, I argue from analogy, are degraded by the same propensity to enjoy the present moment; and, at last, despise the freedom which they have not sufficient virtue to struggle to attain. But I must be more explicit."*

Pagan read the same paragraph several times. The words were written in English but were foreign to her because of the era they were written but oddly familiar at the same time.

A male voice broke her concentration, "All books are fifty percent off this week."

Pagan slammed the book shut, "Excuse me!"

Taken back by the young man standing in front of her, Pagan drew breath, as if it was the first breath she had ever inhaled. A breath that tingled her toes and fluttered her stomach. A breath that was indeed the most relaxing breath, she had ever taken.

Her eyes focused on him. Tingling all over, the sight of him made her gasp. She had this overwhelming feeling to run into his arms.

Stepping backwards instead, she knocked a pile of books over which landed on the floor, creating an obstacle behind her, limiting her escape.

She blushed.

"All books are fifty percent off this week," he repeated, but this time with a smirk.

Pagan looked at the book for a price tag. She had enough money to purchase the book. Fumbled in her pockets, she pulled out the remainder of her spending money.

He would need to give her change.

Following him through the labyrinth of books to the counter at the back of the shop, Pagan handed him the five dollar note. Still blushing, he made her nervous; a worthy nervousness.

Pagan knew him from somewhere but could not place him.

Smelling of Brut cologne, wearing old grey trousers and a red velvet jacket, purchased probably from a 'second hand' shop, a baby face that reminded her of a freshly groomed gangster with a resilient posture, Pagan felt an eccentric safety with the stranger.

Aesthetically, he was pleasing to Pagan; his ash blond hair that curled softly around his tanned face, and his exceptionally long eye lashes that highlighted his vivid green eyes made her hormones rage. She suddenly felt very insecure in her own attractiveness.

"Here is your change."

Placing the change and the book into a white plastic bag with a receipt, he forcibly handed it over the counter to her.

She thanked him and then lingered and then she thanked him again but this time attempted to leave the shop, only managing to move backwards a few steps.

Flipping around eventually, she marched out of the labyrinth of books, jumping the book obstacle only to slip on a book.

He followed her through the shop.

Realising only after a few steps that she had forgotten to buy Thomas a book, she smiled, it would be a good excuse to return to the bookshop.

Flinging the shop door open, the wind howled along the street and in through the shop door blowing her hair up and off her face.

Placing the book in her school bag, she swung it over her shoulder. She lingered again.

"I have a movie," she splattered out.

Red-faced and awkward, he accepted Pagan's invitation as she stood firm in the bookshop doorway.

Confidently, she had organised her first ever date.

"Ok! Friday night at seven pm!"

Scribbling on a scrap piece of paper from her pocket with a broken pencil that she found at the bottom of her school bag, she handed it to him. Her double jointed elbow firm with intent was left to defend for itself as her hand shook, revealing the fake shield.

Her hand tingled as their skin touched, "Here is my address and phone number," then she tilted her head pulling her hair back exposing the delicacy of her neck, "I'm looking forward to Friday."

Amelie had taught her the art of gentle persuasion and bogus buoyancy-"You see honey, everyone wears a mask. Choose your mask carefully because one day you will be your mask. Self-illusion is powerful darling, don't underestimate it."

Heading to the bus stop, Pagan could not contain her excitement. Her footsteps floated and her cheek bones heightened to where her eyes squinted. She felt absolute happiness.

Pagan

Rogan sat on the lumpy three seat chocolate brown embossed leather couch. His legs stretched out, his long and muscular feet rested on the ottoman, giving him the appearance that he was relaxed while his lifted shoulders and crossed arms suggested the opposite.

The smell of his cheap cologne intoxicated the seventeen year old, who sat only a 'bums' width away from him in the dimly lit room. A tension of desire and fear, consumed her.

With Cain and Aislyn gone for the evening, Pagan had the house to herself until 23:00. It was 20:30. It was the first time that Pagan had ever invited a male over to her home. If in fact, he thought it was a date, she was unsure.

On purpose, she had kept it secret from her parents that a 'boy' was coming over for the evening.

She had never felt so scared in her entire life. Tonight there was not a mask that could save her from the anxiety that she felt and in the dim light of the lounge room she had no option but to present the truth to him.

A bowl of microwave popcorn and two cups of lime green fizzy cordial sat on the table. Neither refreshments had been touched.

Struggling to converse with him, Pagan wished that he would make the effort to communicate with her, instead of using his eyes to speak. Liken to a darting champion, he aimed, throwing his gaze towards the target, her. She could not handle one more intimidating stare from him in fear she would faint.

From insecurity, Pagan's eyes darted around his face.

The only three men in her life were her father, Norman and Thomas and none of them had taught her about men, or if anything, only how 'closed off' they are.

Pagan had only learned the negative aspects of love, and so in that moment of lust, she struggled with her desire to please Rogan. It never occurred to her to please herself as well, she was her mother's daughter, even though it pained her to believe it.

Pagan brought her attentions back to the movie. The movie's dark connotations enticed Pagan to move noticeably closer to Rogan. When their elbows touched, her chest flushed and she felt as if she had just bathed in tabasco sauce.

The plot of the movie explored a love that far surpassed one lifetime. 'A love' between a man who became a beastly entity, and a woman, both trapped within a state of unhappiness until they found each other. 'A love' that created catastrophe to anyone who tried to hinder it.

'How romantic', Pagan thought.

Her peripheral vision was working overtime, checking every few seconds at Rogan's physical attributes; muscular hands and prominent veins the pulsed along his forearm.

'Kiss me already' her body screamed.

Her skin was on fire and her heart was beating so fast she was sure that Rogan would notice her chest heaving.

Pagan grabbed her cordial and sculled it. The glass fumbled as she clumsily placed it back on the coffee table.

"Can you please, 'stop' the movie for a second, Pagan?"

Grabbing the remote, she pressed 'pause' and unbeknown to her, she touched his knee cap, "Is everything ok?"

Screwing his face up, "Can we just chat for while? I'm struggling to concentrate."

Sensing his rejection, Pagan shuffled away from him on the couch.

Her gums dried and she suddenly felt an overwhelming sensation that she was about to experience her first heartbreak before they had even kissed.

"How is the book going?"

Pagan screwed her face up, "Book?"

"Yes, the book from the shop," his eyes refused to look anywhere else but at her.

Wiggling on the couch, she attempted to settle into their conversation, "I've read a few pages but I am struggling with the content. I know this is weird but I feel like I've read it before but I can't remember when. Strange, hey?"

Lifting his feet off the ottoman, he swung himself around to face her, his feet now buried underneath his thighs, "Can I say something really weird as well?"

Without waiting for her response, he continued, "I feel like I know you. Like, really know you. Like forever."

Grabbing the bowl of popcorn, she shoved a large handful into her mouth, awkwardly munching in an animated manner. She had felt the same, her body had burned the moment she saw him but how was she to respond to him?

Nodding, her mouth too full to reply, she urged him to continue by circling her hand in a fast forward motion.

His eyes searched for acceptance as if he too was scared of rejection, "A knowing! I've never felt like this before. I know I'm only nineteen but it feels really intense when I'm near you. I feel a humming between us."

The conversation had suddenly become serious. Pagan crunched and swallowed the popcorn.

"Can I kiss you, Pagan?"

Nervously smiling with eyes as wide as saucepans, she shook her head in approval, unaware that mushed popcorn unattractively coated her teeth.

'Put the mask on before you lose yourself to him', she repeated in her mind.

He leaned in.

Pagan froze; she had never kissed anyone before.

He pulled her chin closer to his. His lips touched hers.

Her body quivered as a rush so intense consumed her body and she felt dizzy. In one kiss, she became addicted to him.

London
Aggie

"Of course, I felt it you fucking moron. I don't pay you to ask me questions. Now organise the Crone Monarchs to get their fat arses down here right now!"

Slamming the phone down on the office table, it rolled landing near the pens.

Aggie screamed; a shriek so vile that her personal assistant who was returning from the toilet hurried back to her office. It was going to be a bad day.

Slumping into the office chair, Aggie kicked off her black high heels. Hurtling the first shoe at the wall, it bounced off the plaster, landing like a rock skimming across the water onto the carpet. Not satisfied, Aggie threw the second shoe which pierced the plaster, lodging itself firmly into the wall.

Aggie's black humour unconfined released a crazy cackle. Tears from laughing formed watery paths down her puffy cheeks, smudging her heavy eye make-up.

Decisively, Aggie reached into her handbag pulling out a small mirror in a vain attempt to feel attractive. For whom, she was not sure.

Arms stretched out, Aggie's eyes struggled to focus on her senior face.

"Old hag, Aggie," she said, as she wiped away the smudged eyeliner from underneath her sagging eyes with a tissue she had wet by spitting on it. Pulling a lipstick out of her tailored suit pocket, she sloppily painted it on her dry lips. Her pale wrinkly face needed the colour.

"I look like a clown!"

Aggie dropped the mirror into her handbag. She heard it crack.

Feeling a headache developing, she rubbed her forehead with her palm. The ache simply moved to the back of her head.

"Pfft!"

Regretting a decision that she had manipulated seventeen years earlier, Aggie now had to deal with the Soul-mates for the first time, by herself and without previous knowledge of them. She knew that this day might happen but she was disappointed that someone who she trusted and had paid well, had let her down, perhaps betrayed her on purpose. She would deal with them later. Their job had been easy; make sure the Soul-mates are at all times separated before the Witch Awakening.

"If only I had the Ancient Doctrine."

Enjoying most of her reign as Supreme Femineity there had only been the odd Ancient Witch uprising to deal with, but otherwise it had been a relatively easy transition. Queen Lizzy and all her public servants had welcomed Aggie and the newly chosen Non-Ancient Crone Monarchy without raising one judgemental eye.

Of course had they objected, it would have been hypocritical, and Aggie would have enjoyed pointing that fact out to 'Her Majesty?'

Aggie sat back on her office chair rubbing her aching feet.

"I do look forward to meeting you, oh powerful one. The powerful, Pagan."

Playing out several different scenarios in her head, she finally settled for what felt right. It was time to collect the wretched Maiden. It was nearly time for her Awakening and it was safer to have her supervised properly by Witches, she could trust, rather than those who she could obviously not trust in Tasmania.

Aggie cackled, "And won't it go off with a rip!"

Opening the top drawer of the office table, Aggie dragged all the contents of the drawer out, sprawling it across the table top. Squinting, she found her personal phonebook and flipped through the pages until she reached the letter 'D'.

"Uh ha, there you are. Now where did that fucking phone go?"

Aggie's patience was waning as she dialled the international number.

Australia
Amelie

Amelie butted out her cigarette into the ashtray, annoyed because she had just lit it. She had been expecting a phone call and had hesitated lighting up, but then once she did, the phone rang.

Sitting down on the chair, she answered, "Hello."

Not surprised to hear a female voice, she praised herself for her excellent intuition.

"Yes, I've been expecting a phone call from you."

Crossing her legs, Amelie doodled on the pad next to the phone in an attempt to channel some of the rising wrath towards the Witch who had rung her.

Now was not the time to be emotionally explosive; she had to think clearly.

"No! I had nothing to do with them meeting and I'm very upset that you would even assume that, and then to have the gumption to accuse me of that, knowing how much I love her and that she is the High Priestess of my Coven, I have an undying loyalty to her which is more than I can say for you."

Tapping the pen on her thigh, Amelie's internal rage was bubbling. How dare a Non-Ancient Witch speak to her as if they were equals? They were not equals.

"Can we focus? I have a feeling they have already sent someone to collect her. They would be petrified that she will regain her Magick before they can get to her first. We don't have long, so panicking won't help."

Placing the pen down with her right hand, Amelie flipped open the cigarette packet pulling out a cigarette. Placing it into the left side of her mouth, she grabbed the lighter and lit the cigarette while the voice on the other side of the phone battered her with more apprehensive babble.

"Don't swing your sword my way. I've been 'Awakened' for five years. There is only so much I can do in a world I have no power in," Amelie snapped.

Resentment had settled in her throat.

The voice retreated slightly, now was the time for Amelie to take precedence over the conversation, "There is no point worrying about how they met. We need to make sure we swing the pendulum our way. Aggie thinks she is clever but she isn't that clever."

Amelie took an exaggerated drag of the cigarette, "We both know that there is a way for Pagan to gain her Magick prior to her Awakening. They fear it, why don't we do it? Once Awakened, she will be too powerful for them to curtail."

The voice became fearful.

"Oh, you've had a vision. Your visions don't really help much, do they?"

Amelie rolled her eyes in repugnance and waited impatiently for the voice to calm down before she spoke again, "I understand that you love her and you fear what will happen afterwards. I doubt they will kill her in fear it will cause another uprising. I love her too but we are dealing with something larger than love. Pagan should be sitting on the Thirteenth Throne with me beside her. Not that bitch."

The voice interrupted, angering Amelie, "I don't give a fuck what Aggie and the Monarchs will do to me if they hear me. No one has hacked my phone. I am fucking Royalty and I always will be, and you, my dear, are a Non-Ancient and would be wise to remember that when you speak to me."

Amelie took another drag of the cigarette, "Look! We encourage their bond; make it look like Pagan encouraged it."

The voice compliantly agreed.

"How can we fail? We have the Goddesses on our side."

Tired of the conversation, Amelie slammed the phone down.

Aislyn heard the phone disconnect but she continued the conversation as if Amelie was still on the other end, but now she said what she was really thinking.

"Amelie you are so conceited by ego and pride, you foolish Witch. What if the Goddesses are not on your side? I may not be an Ancient Witch but I've lived long enough to know how unreliable dogma is, and my vision told me you will fail. She will be travelling soon to meet Aggie and I have seen Pagan die."

Aislyn wondered if she should contact the Crone Monarchy and hand Pagan over to them peacefully. Make a deal? Save her daughter from potential death. Surely, they would use her to make a political statement which meant that Pagan was about to experience the worst fate imaginable. Perhaps, they would spare Pagan the foreboding misery that was surely planned for her if they saw that she was compliant to their plight, after all her own mother is a Non-Ancient.

Pagan was an Innocent until Awakened, it would be political suicide to have her killed before she gained her Magick. They would not want to upset the Goddesses, although they seemed to have fallen into a slumber, sleeping next to their mother, Gaia.

An expectant nervous laughter escaped Aislyn's mouth, Aggie had spent the last seventeen years making sure the Soul-mate's paths never crossed and she had failed, and they had met in a bookshop, of all places. Maybe the Goddesses were very much awake.

Pagan

Pagan sat in the passenger seat beside Rogan, who drove like an 'old' man.

Determined that they reach their destination safely, he had driven ten kilometres under the speed limit.

The world was a better place the moment their lips had meet and Rogan wanted to preserve and protect his happiness, as if it was a crystal ball, perfectly shaped and capable of seeing into the future.

Pagan had never felt so attentive. Suddenly details mattered. The way sunlight entered a room though a window leaving ghostly shadows on the walls. The way a person walked; hunched and slow, or fast and wispy. And the way a child licked an icy pole and how their eyes squeezed together to combat the ice headache. It all mattered. For the first time in her life, Pagan's thoughts stayed firmly within the present.

The spring weather channelled hope and clarity. Fresh regrowth burst from the bare trees- a welcomed comfort for the returning birds. Lawns were being mowed for the first time in months, and children filled the open grassy spaces and the fast flowing rivers just outside of town.

Packing a picnic basket in the kitchen an hour earlier; watermelon, green grapes, brie cheese, pepper crackers and one bottle of Pinot Noir wine, that she had pinched from Amelie's cabinet the night before, and a knitted rug stolen from her mother's private collection, she suddenly realised how much effort she was putting into another person. She had never been so unselfish in her whole life and it felt good.

Exiting Railton, a town known for its front yard topiary sparingly scattered along its main road, and for its once thriving railway industry, now entertained an intimate quiet community that tourists overlooked on their way to Cradle Mountain, Pagan's nerves increased.

Rogan focused as he prepared himself for the sharp right turn into a gravel road. Swerving around several wide bends, he saw the 'Forest Walk' signage and slowed down to enter the forest area.

The sunshine quickly hid behind the intimidating trees.

Stoodley Plantation Forest was an array of mystical habitation: Tasmanian Blue Gum, Western Red Cedar, Radiata Pine and natural forest which accompanied the exotic Robinea plant and Douglas Fir.

Pagan felt a wave of euphoria. She was about to lose her virginity in this forest, a forest that she had chosen simply because it was only a short driving distance from home.

Pulling the hand break on, Rogan peered out into the forest, "It's really scary out here. Are you sure this is where you want us to do this?"

Pagan's eyes darted across the landscape, "Absolutely one hundred percent."

Planting of the Radiata Pine in the 1980's produced an unnatural foreboding, a darkness that circulated the pruned trees; enticing and frightening. The tree's spiky growth and additional egg shape cones darkened the area, allowing only a sprinkle of kaleidoscopic sunlight through the branches. The bark shimmered like silver glitter, and the dark brown soil produced limited groundcover. Fallen logs produced a wealth of places for small forest creatures to live.

Rogan smirked. He was about to have sex with the girl, he could see himself spending the rest of his life with. His parents had voiced their concerns that he was too serious about this girl and that it was affecting his common-sense but looking at her, he was sure that she was the woman he wanted to marry. When Pagan turned twenty, he was going to propose to her, he was sure of it.

Jumping out of the car, he ran around to the passenger side, opening the door for her, "After you, Miss Pagan."

"Well, thank you, Mr Rogan," she giggled.

After grabbing the picnic basket from the car boot, they walked together down the spacious forest track. Their hands moulded into one, her right hand inside of his left.

Settling on a spot, they scanned the area. It was as if nature had made a room just for them. Colours: greens, browns and amber, created abstract forest art and a grassy bed for them to lie on.

Pagan felt a natural connection to the trees. Spending limited time outside, she wondered why she felt a strong chemistry to an unfamiliar bushy landscape. The smell of bark and fresh air calmed her nerves.

Suddenly, she realised she had missed out on a childhood that she would have cherished, lost for hours exploring hidden cubby houses or tree tops but instead, she had sulked around inside a home she hated.

Opening the picnic basket, she grabbed out the knitted rug, shaking it until it naturally smoothed out, placing it over the grassy patch, spiky leaves and pine cones.

Without acknowledging the irony that she was turning into her mother, Pagan poured Rogan a glass of wine handing it to him first. After all, it was only polite to serve your guest first.

Pagan took a large sip from her own glass.

"You know Pagan, you're underage?"

Pagan laughed loudly, scaring a flock of newly arrived birds to fly away.

Since meeting Amelie, she had tried almost every drug and alcohol beverage that Amelie could buy in the small island state. How smugglers managed to fly drugs into the state always concerned Pagan but she had learned not to ask questions and just flow with it. Amelie was not about to tell Pagan that Witches trafficked the narcotics in via broomstick.

A glass of wine was not going to harm her now.

"Cheers," they twanged their glasses together and sipped.

Rogan placed his glass down and grabbed her chin, "Pagan, I'm so crazy about you."

He kissed her, lingering in the flavours.

Trembling, he remove her skirt and knickers, catching them on her knee caps and then again, once he reached her ankles. Relieved to finally have part of her body naked, he looked at her pubic hair; dark and curly.

He took his t-shirt off.

She removed Rogan's jeans and then his silky boxer shorts, placing them on top of her clothes, and then she removed her tank top and bra. Worried about her appearance, she pulled her stomach in. She wanted to look her best for him.

Kneeling in front of him, naked and vulnerable, the sunlight highlighting her innocence, she felt a strange empowerment as if she finally understood the power she possessed and how to will it upon others. She wanted nothing more than to please him.

Bending in, she kissed him gentle on his lips. She kissed him harder only to smack her teeth into his.

"I'm so sorry. I'm nervous," she blushed.

Once they composed themselves, she kissed him again while running her fingertips across his hairless chest, observing the dip between each chest pectoral.

An urge to dominate him gushed through her body. Considering, she was a virgin, she followed her strange sexual instinct; an instinct that seemed familiar to her somehow.

Pushing him down onto his back, she kissed his chest, stopping to suck his nipple, but as if she was suddenly possessed by another person, she bit him. Pagan's vagina swelled as the taste of his blood coated her tongue.

Looking up at him through her hair, she noticed that his eyes had lightened in colour and his lips had thinned. His penis had hardened underneath her stomach. He had liked the pain as well.

She sat up.

Reaching out, she gently stroked his hair away from his forehead, "I love you."

He reached out massaging her hardened breasts.

She grabbed his hand from her breast, placing it in between her legs, forcing his hand to cup her thigh.

Impatient, she lay down motioning him to lie on top of her.

He struggled to find her vaginal opening but after some persistence, he slowly entered her.

Pagan felt a rip. She held her breath to cope with the pain.

"Am I hurting you?"

"No!"

Her breath shallowed, "Keep going."

Rogan hesitated but started again slowly. Floundering around inside of her, he was unsure of what he was doing. A virgin as well, he struggled between satisfying his own needs while sufficiently satisfying her, but in time, he found a rhythm that both of them enjoyed. Relaxing into the pace, he noticed Pagan's vagina was producing much needed lubrication.

Rogan's lips smothered hers while his blonde hair restricted her from seeing the lush habitat.

Feeling dizzy, she panicked.

Suddenly, she felt sick.

Focusing on how amazing it felt to have Rogan's penis inside of her, tricked the nausea for only a few more minutes before her entire body burned as if it was on fire.

As if possessed, her head turned to the side and her eyes disappeared into darkness.

She heard the cheers of an enthusiastic crowd as if she was at a football game. The rise and fall of their voices signified that Pagan was entering an event she should be fearful of and then as if she had entered a dream state, a new world presented itself.

A crazed crowd stood behind a drum line of soldiers.

A man whose shoes were covered in mud, grabbed Pagan by her hair, throwing her from a large wooden cart into a short line up. Her long frock hooked underneath her black boots and she stumbled for a few steps before gaining her composure.

She soon realised, she was in a line-up with several other scruffy looking men and women.

Feeling a wave of recognition, a deja vu sensation that she had done this before, she settled into her dream state. Was she indeed sleeping, she was not sure.

A lady with a mouth full of black teeth, and hair so uncombed that large clumps of dust had settled in it, spat at Pagan, the saliva landing on her cheek.

Wiping it quickly off, Pagan smiled at the woman, "Tell your daughters of me."

'Why had she said that in a French accent?'

Lost somewhere between reality and fiction, both worlds seemed completely plausible to Pagan, as if one foot was trapped in the past and the other in the present but her natural instinct was to jump with both feet into the future.

Huddling closely to the people in front of her, she felt a man of shorter stature grope her breast as he pressed up behind her, his hand slipping over her shoulder, ripping her already dirty and torn dress.

A soldier hit the man in the head with his musket.

The prisoner screamed and let go. Cowering behind her the smell of his urine soaked trousers reeked up her noise and she fought the urge to vomit.

Wide and joyous, hundreds of pairs of eyes glared at her, all enjoying her anguish, some she recognised while the others she did not.

The adrenaline-pumped spectators, all cheered and waved their banners while the next three prisoners' heads were cut from their bodies by the guillotine's blade.

She was next.

One set of eyes, stared solemnly, a silence among the noise; tears falling down her pale cheeks; she managed a wink and half smile, a goodbye. It was Amelie in another woman's body.

Pagan shrugged her shoulders in reply, not a goodbye but a 'here we go again'.

Amelie would miss her but Pagan felt nothing but hope as she walked towards the scaffold.

She had achieved what she had set out to do, to write a book, a diary for her to read in the next life. But for now, it was time for her to lose her head again. And it had been a pretty head and a delicate neck.

Her hair had greyed quickly during the male driven trial but as she walked towards her death, she sent a prayer to her only son.

She knew that she would not live for a long time, she never did. Why would she have thought any differently this time, particularly in a time of war, a war she had chosen over the her duty?

She mounted the scaffold, her heels clanking on the sturdy wooden steps as she pompously took the stage. Pride calming her nerves, she smiled at the crowd, a crowd that hated her... for now.

Breathing in the view, the crowd fell silent as she said goodbye to the late afternoon sun, its warmth massaging her face.

Life was indeed beautiful.

Hands grasping at her neck, Pagan bolted upright, throwing Rogan onto the rug.

Relieved that she was still alive, she sobbed.

Confused, Rogan violently reacted by hitting the ground with his fist.

CHAPTER 13
Pagan

The carpet tickled her bare feet as she tiptoed across the bedroom floor. The rusted latch was difficult to open but with a little more friction, Pagan flipped it up and pushed the bedroom window open. Fresh air stung her face.

Ears alert, she listened. The evening was stone quiet but she was sure she heard a noise.

Cautiously, she peered out into the darkness. Slowly moving towards the window, she was fearful that a hand might come through the window gap and grab her. Someone was out there. Her senses were alerting her of danger but why?

Then she smelt a foreign odour. A digestive pong. A male with unclean teeth and unwashed hair. It was an unpleasant odour; a mixture of unfamiliar spices and food, seeping out of the pores of his skin.

Latching the window back up, she raced back to the bed and sat down.

Heart thundering, she considered alerting her mother that someone was lurking outside but she was still angry with her mother.

"Stupid bitch!"

Aislyn had forbidden Pagan from spending any more time with Rogan until she was eighteen, which was months away.

After a huge quarrel, Aislyn had grounded Pagan, confining her to the house until she learned boundaries and some respect for authority.

Pagan had stubbornly locked herself in her bedroom in protest, refusing to speak to either parent. After five days, the solitary confinement was waning on her righteousness.

There had not been one morning or afternoon that Rogan had not stood outside the house, just so he could see a glimpse of his girlfriend.

Aislyn quickly intersected any potential contact by standing at the front gate, threatening to call the police if either teenager made a scene.

Wishing Thomas was back from holiday, Pagan grabbed a school book from her bedside table, rubbing her thumbs over the hard cover for comfort. Thomas would know what to do.

Thomas's father never seemed to work but they always managed extended and exuberant 'getaways' each year. After the last holiday, Thomas had changed his name to Aquarius, demanding that she would refer to him as that or nothing else. Pagan hated the name, promising herself that she would never refer to him as Aquarius, ever. He would always be 'her' Thomas.

Unexpectedly, the door opened and a frantic Aislyn entered, "Pagan, we have to get you out of here! They're coming."

Jumping up off the bed, Pagan asked, "Who is coming?"

"No time, get dressed!"

"Mum, who's coming and how come you know someone is coming?"

Aislyn grabbed Pagan's jumper from the floor, "Sometimes, I just know things. I see things before they happen. Throw this on and put some shoes on."

Confused, Pagan obeyed.

The fear in her mother's eyes was enough proof that something was terribly wrong and now was not the time to argue.

Fumbling with her jumper, she then struggled to untie the shoe laces. Finally, she squeezed her feet into the shoes with them tied up. She was relieved that she had not changed into her nightie.

Finally dressed, Aislyn grabbed Pagan burying her fingernails into Pagan's shoulders, pushing her down the hallway to the front door.

"You run, Pagan. Run to a church. Get inside. Don't stop. Don't look behind you. Just run."

It was too late, Pagan smelt him the moment they reached the front door, but Aislyn persisted by pushing Pagan through the scarcely opened front door and straight into him.

Pagan screamed as her body bounced off a dark shadow standing in front of them. She stepped back into her mother's arms.

Smug, the stranger bowed. His long dark curls fell over his face, "Shalom, Pagan."

Aislyn stepped in front of Pagan, hiding her daughter behind her back. Through closed teeth, she asked, "Who are you?"

Pagan smelt her father. Turning quickly to see his reaction, she was disappointed to see he was composed, almost enjoying the entertainment.

The stranger stepped forward with his palms facing out. His smile curled, "I am just the Bounty. I am not here to hurt her, simply to transport her to London."

Aislyn retaliated. Stepping towards the stranger, her motherly instincts masked her fear, "I want your name."

Searching for an escape, Pagan's muscles tightened. She would have to make a run for it.

"My name is Tristan Dante. I have come to collect your daughter on the orders from the Crone Monarchy."

Aislyn's top lip quivered, "Well, you can't fucking have her. I've seen what she does to her."

Pagan felt her lungs expand, her heart increase and pupils dilate. With tunneled-vision, she searched for a path around the Bounty where he might not catch her. She could push Aislyn into the Bounty, run and jump the fence. The nearest church was two blocks away. She could make it.

Cain noticed his daughter's body language. Sensing she was about to run, he wrapped one arm around his daughter's waist and the other hand clasped her chin.

Pagan tried to bite him but he increased the pressure on her chin, almost crushing her teeth. She continued to struggle but he suspected that she would.

"Enough," Cain's voice echoed down the street, "Aggie wants the child. It's time."

Aislyn flung around to face her husband, "Don't you fucking say her name. Don't you say her name to me!"

Pagan had never seen her mother react with such raw command. Then, unexpectedly, Aislyn fell to her knees, defeated. That, Pagan had seen hundreds of times.

Cain loosened his grip, pushing Pagan towards the Bounty, "She's yours."

Free from his grip, Pagan swung her fist at her father.

Cain felt the wind from the punch breeze past his face.

"She's spirited like her mother. Watch her," Cain warned Dante.

Without helping his wife up or saying goodbye to his daughter, Cain slammed the door shut.

The security light went out, leaving Pagan no choice but to surrender to this stranger who called himself a 'Bounty'.

He put his hand out to her, holding it in mid-air. His hands were soft, square, and olive, "Little Witch, it's time to take flight."

"What?"

Ignoring her, his gaze penetrated her conscious, "Please take my hand, Little Witch. I won't hurt you."

Studying his face in the moonlight, he was definitely foreign. Foreign people were untrustworthy. He must have travelled a long distance to collect her.

He had a gentle face; bushy eye-brows, dark brown eyes, large red lips and hair that reached his waist and an aura that oozed compassion. But foreign people could not be trusted.

"Come, we have quite a journey."

Like a caged lion, she cautiously grabbed his hand.

Her mother's wailing faded as she walked down the path with him.

"Where are you taking me?"

He laughed, "To your destiny"

CHAPTER 14
Pagan

One hundred metres above the ground, Pagan clung to Dante's leather jacket with a death grip. Her hands were white and numb, not only from the cold air but from fear of falling off the broomstick and plummeting to her death, supplying her with brute strength to stay balanced on the thin wood.

Her feet entwined with Dante's feet, gave her little comfort but she was thankful that he had acknowledged that she was frightened and allowed her feet to stay there.

The icy cold air and his long curly hair, whipped her face, giving her a smashing headache. She was grateful that Dante had given her a pair of sunglasses to wear. At least her eyes were protected from the harsh air.

Snot ran down her nose and into her mouth causing her to gag.

Dante leaned back, stretching his shoulder and then his arm out. He tapped her thigh with his hand, offering reassurance, "Half way there, Little Witch. Sleep. I promise, you won't fall."

Tapping her leg again, he chuckled, "And if you do I'll catch you. There is a pretty large bounty on your neck, Little Witch."

"You're not a Bounty if you're contracted to collect me. You're just a delivery boy."

He laughed. He would need to watch this Maiden.

Closing her eyes for the duration of the journey, she only opened them when she felt the air pressure change. Flying for what seemed like hours, they had flown over Bass Strait, then a watery explosion alerted her they had reached the mainland of Australia. Looking down it seemed the whole world was asleep.

Quickly the lights from the cities and towns vanished as they flew over the Australian desert. The desert's warmth enticed her to sleep. Nestling closer to him, she buried her head into his broad back. Several minutes later, she drifted into an altered sleep.

The broomstick tilted.

Alarmed, she woke. Her eyes fought for a few seconds until they closed again.

She dreamed of Rogan.

"Wake up."

She heard his voice in the distance but she was happy in her dream.

"Wake up, Little Witch, we are about to land."

Blinking awake, the glare from the morning sun stung her eyes. The morning sky was a haze of plum, purple and gold, accenting a white sandy beach.

Dropping sharply, Pagan desperately grabbed onto Dante's leather jacket, strangling him with it.

The broomstick vibrated. Her feet desperately tried to wrap around his, as fear consumed her.

The lower they flew, the broom sped up.

Only metres from the ground, the wind ruffled up her already knotted hair, twisting it angrily around her face.

"You must start running with your feet before we land and keep running until we stop. Understand?"

"No! I don't understand," she yelled.

"Run, Little Witch, run!"

His feet touched the sand. Running, his calves took most of the impact while his large thighs controlled the broomstick at the same time.

Pagan's legs were too stiff to move. She clung onto him out of desperation.

Closing her eyes as they landed on the beach, she opened them to see that they had made a long and deep skid mark in the sand.

Once stationary, Pagan toppled off the broomstick due to her legs seizing and were unable to support her. She landed onto the warm sand with a thud, an aching pain ripped through her body, crippling her as she lay on the beach.

Sticking the broomstick into the sand, Dante stood above her. Stretching his arms out, he offered his hand to her. He was tired but still capable of carrying her to the safety of shelter.

Screaming as the feeling in her legs came back, she felt a lovely warm sensation in the lower half of her body as she urinated in her trousers.

Dante pulled her shoes off, flinging them up the beach. Her toes were red from the cold. Awkwardly, he gently rubbed them until her toes warmed up.

"The sun is very hot here. You will soon be warm."

She panicked as she was unable to defend herself due to shock. Lying catatonic on the beach, she had to submit to Dante's flippant sovereignty over her body. She was too tired to fight and he had not hurt her... yet.

He then unzipped her urine soaked trousers pulling them down to her ankles. Slipping them over her ankles, he opted to leave her wet knickers on.

Lifting Pagan's limp body up into his arms, Dante carried her up the beach, lying her down in front of a beach hut.

The sand burned her skin but she dug her heels into the sand to stabilise herself regardless of the potential burning.

"Rest. Wiggle your toes. When you are ready, you can sleep in the hut but first you must eat."

Pagan looked up at the beach hut. She would need to walk eight steps to reach the door of the small pentagon shaped building which at best was a cubby house. She wondered if she would ever make it considering the numbness in her legs.

"I will organise some food. We fly again tonight. You will need your strength."

Patting her on the top of her head, she pulled her head away from him. She was nobody's trained dog.

Watching as he disappeared into the jungle behind the beach, she considered escaping, rolling, if she had to.

The elongated beach appeared isolated. Behind it, a vast jungle butted up against rolling mountains, that seemed to reach the sky.

Pagan was fearful that her legs would not carry her far and if they did, she might not survive any potential dangers that the new environment offered, and Dante would surely recapture her, and perhaps, even punish her for attempting to escape. Should she risk it? Perhaps, where he was taking her was not that bad? And surely, he would expect her to at least try to escape? She wondered if he would be disappointed if she did not attempt an escape. Perhaps, he was testing her right now?

Movement in the jungle, alarmed her. Forcing her stiff neck to twist to the side, Pagan spotted a long slimy green tail in the long grass just behind her.

'Snake'.

Heart racing, she frantically wiggled her toes.

Searching for Dante, she was relieved to see him walking back along the beach and even more relieved to see the snake slither off in the other direction.

A woman, middle-aged with delicate youthful olive skin, had joined Dante. She was no taller than five foot. A white and yellow frangipani flower tucked neatly behind her right ear, complemented her long straight black hair, large oval brown eyes and perfect white teeth. She wore an orange sarong and plain beige t-shirt. Her toe nails were painted brightly.

Pagan suddenly felt safer that a woman had joined them, even if she was embarrassed that she was wearing urine soaked knickers in front of a stranger.

Carrying a straw tray on her head and placing it down on the sand in front of Pagan, her stomach twisted from hunger pains. Several bowls of food, water and orange juice accompanied a small leaf container that was filled with colourful flower petals and rice.

Sitting down beside Pagan, sand flicking over her sarong, the woman placed her hand on Pagan's forehead, "No good, Dante, this child is exhausted."

"Yes Rosa, she needs sleep, water and food. I am on a schedule, so she will need to be strong as well. I can't keep the Monarchs waiting."

"Help me to sit her up, so I can feed her, Dante."

Placing both hands underneath Pagan's shoulder blades, he pulled her up, resting her against his chest as he sat behind her.

Scooping a spoonful of food from the bowl, Rosa placed it inside Pagan's mouth. She munched down. The flavour exploded in her mouth, overwhelming her taste buds.

Pagan ate the sweetened black rice until she felt sick. It had tasted like her mother's rice pudding. The meal, saddened and comforted her. The orange juice made her nauseous and after several mouthfuls, she opted for the water instead.

Dante and Rosa were very familiar, speaking at length, sometimes in English and then at other times in Rosa's language, Indonesian.

'Did Dante always bring the people he collected to this woman?'

'They must be more than good friends', Pagan thought, as she watched how intimate their body language was. There is something about two people trying to hide their affection that always seemed to amplify it.

As Rosa prepared to leave, Dante wrapped his arms around her. Their embrace lingered. His large physique enveloped her tiny structure and Pagan feared he would break Rosa, accidently. Rubbing his hand along her back, Pagan decided that they must be lovers or accomplices.

Rosa turned back to Pagan, "I wish you well. Take care of her, Dante. This one is a mere child."

Dante shrugged his shoulder, "I'm not paid to care, Rosa."

With a double pat on Dante's shoulders, Rosa collected the straw tray and walked off along the beach.

Once again, she was alone with the Bounty.

"You have colour in your cheeks again. I'm sure you can walk now to the hut," Dante assured her and then he walked off, leaving her alone to fend for herself.

Warm and full of food, Pagan slowly stood up. Wobbling, she stumbled towards the hut. Her heavy legs took each step cautiously. Holding onto the rail, she looked up at the door. She was relieved that she would soon be sleeping in a bed.

Testing the door, it stuck. Pushing it the remainder of the way, she struggled to close it behind her. She did not have the strength for obstacles, not even the easily overcome.

The room was basic; a double bed and a large white mosquito net that hung from the ceiling to cover it. The floor was covered in dark green tiles and a cockroach scampered along it as if scared by *her* presence.

Too tired to close the window shutters, she still appreciated how beautifully decorated the window was before falling into bed. Pulling the mosquito netting around her, she knotted the ties together and slept.

Bolting upright in bed, Pagan's lips stuck together from dried saliva and her head hurt. She needed water.

What the hell made that noise? Something has woken her up. She heard it again.

"What is that?"

Untying the mosquito net, she peered out. Her eyes darted around the hut for whatever creature made that strange noise.

Hiding in the crack of the hut's ceiling, a gecko stared down at her, annoyed that she invaded his home.

Relieved Pagan laughed.

The gecko was harmless, unlike the mosquitoes that had swarmed the bed. Luckily, the netting had protected her from their fury.

Kicking the damp sheets off her legs, she enjoyed the fresh air. She was excited to have her strength back. Stepping onto the heated tiles, she tiptoed to the door, struggling to open it again.

"They really need to fix this door," she cursed.

A pile of clothing neatly folded, most likely by Rosa, sat outside the door.

Excitedly, Pagan grabbed the pile of clothes and walked back inside. Yanking her dried smelly knickers, t-shirt and jumper, off, she slipped into the loose yellow pants and white singlet top. Both smelt of 'Ylang Ylang' oil.

Exiting the hut, she sat on the top step, observing the pink and blue pastel sunset; she must have slept all day? The sunset illuminated the sparkling ocean.

Squinting, Pagan realised that Dante was swimming amongst the waves. He was diving underneath the water, only to pop back up several metres away.

Flicking his wet hair off his face, Pagan realised Dante needed to shave due to a hairy shadow that had grown over his triangular jaw line. For an old man, he was very fit.

Pagan wondered who he was. She had never met anyone like him before.

The wash from the waves made a fizzing sound, and Pagan suddenly felt very homesick.

Standing up to ignore her heartache, she suddenly realised she could escape. Looking along the beach for a jungle track, adrenaline surged through her body. Once inside the jungle she could easily disappear. There must be people around somewhere who could help her. Surely, the police would fly her home to Australia.

"Your eyes give away too much, Little Witch," Dante stood in front of her, the ocean still popping over his naked body.

She straightened up, righteously glaring at him, "It was worth a try."

He swaggered towards her, his nakedness making her nervous.

Lowering her eyes, she concentrated on the sand that was stuck to the bottom of his feet.

"Come. I have more food."

Sitting in silence they ate cold fried chicken and freshly made salad-another meal made by Rosa. The mosquitoes feasted on her skin.

Offering her a beer, Pagan sculled the entire bottle, burping the gas back up.

Dressed in jeans and a polo top, Dante laughed at her as he tore another piece of chicken from the bone with the back of his teeth.

It repulsed Pagan who voiced her disapproval, "Didn't your mother teach you how to eat properly?"

"My mother's taught me many things, Little Witch."

The alcohol made her confident, "I have a name, Old Man."

The right side of his mouth turned up in a half smile. Ignoring her, he passed a bottle of water to her, holding it out as a reminder that he had the power not her, "As do I."

Angrily, Pagan grabbed the bottle of water, unscrewed the lid and sculled it. Screwing the lid back on, she calmed, "Thank you...Dante."

"You give me less trouble when you are exhausted."

The sun suddenly disappeared over the horizon and a chill arrived.

Dante stood up, walking over to a large suitcase left by Rosa, he pulled out a bunch of warm clothes; thick woollen socks, two fleecy jumpers, long black boots which were too large for Pagan's feet, beanies for their heads and an extra jacket and gloves for Pagan.

Dante put his long leather jacket back on.

Rosa had also packed a bag of fruit and water for their journey.

Picking up the broomstick, Dante held out his other hand to Pagan, "Ready to fly, Little Witch?"

"Why do you keep calling me a, Little Witch?"

He studied her, the moonlight now illuminating his hauntingly dark eyes, "Do you not know that you are a Maiden?"

Pagan answered swiftly, "I suddenly feel like I don't know who I am at all."

CHAPTER 15
Pagan

Dust blustered around them.

Pagan frantically mimicked a running action as they touched down on a dirt road in the middle of a hectic city. Strangely, although the road was buzzing with people, they managed to not to be seen, or knock anyone over.

Her legs instantly cramped. Pagan slipped off the broomstick landing onto her bottom. Stretching her legs out and wiggling her toes, she remained seated until the tingling subsided.

"You definitely need to work on your dismount."

Unimpressed with Dante's revelation, she rolled her eyes.

During their flight, Dante had chatted with Pagan enthusiastically, pointing out numerous locations to her. Unlike the night before, the landscape was lit up with thousands of flickering lights as they flew over cities, roads and homes, swooping occasionally lower so that Pagan could take in the sites of the countries they were flying over. Surprisingly, she found herself enjoying the ride and with the sunrise, they had quietened into a lazy friendship, enjoying the colour and hue of a new day.

"Welcome to India, darling," a woman screeched at Dante.

The English woman pranced over to Dante, hugging him tightly against her bony body, "I've missed you, you gorgeous man."

Dante responded by kissing her hard on her thin lips.

Ignoring Dante's catch up antics, Pagan looked along the street. A sensory surplus wedded to a scene of heart-breaking deficiency, overwhelmed her. She angered that Dante and his new mistress, were oblivious to it, choosing artificial human interaction over human rights.

Compacted with exhaustion, Pagan closed her eyes to cope with the scenery. Wiping the heavy teardrops from her cheeks, she sensed that while India appeared spiritual and unlimited, she sensed that a garish corporal system, wilfully hid in the shadows, only metres from where flatfooted children played in the garbage.

The smell of garbage made her gag.

Pagan turned to face the house. The house was four storeys high, with three balconies that overlooked the city, which seemed extravagant by anyone's measure, especially since every other house in the congested street was made from mismatched tin.

"Oh and aren't you divine, Missy. Come here, so I can look at you."

Standing as if she was on trial, the English woman pinched and tugged at Pagan's skin as if sizing Pagan up for a skin graft.

Squeezing Pagan's cheeks together, the English woman kissed Pagan.

Pagan screwed her face up. The woman tasted of paprika and coriander.

"Oi girl, sort our guest out. I want Dante to myself for a while," the woman ordered her servant.

Escorted into the house by the servant girl, who was roughly the same age, Pagan suddenly became overwhelmed by the lavish furnishings.

The hallway was well lit with black candelabras and the carpet looked as if I was made from pure gold flakes. The candle light flickered on the dark red stone wall providing brief entertainment with a free shadow show.

She had seen more of the world than she could have imagined. When she saw Rogan again, she would have a wealth of tales to tell him.

Arriving moments later at a five inch thick wooden door, the servant girl unlocked it and ushered Pagan into the room, only to lock it again once she was inside. For a brief moment, Pagan had forgotten that she was a prisoner. Standing alone, inside a windowless room in the middle of the house, she felt very vulnerable. She was not free to enjoy her new surroundings, nor however, was it wise for her to do so.

Searching for a light switch, Pagan resigned herself to the fact that, the only light she was blessed with, was from two large circular candles that sat on the floor in the corner of the room.

"Lucky, I don't want to set fire to the place."

Sitting on the single sized bed, Pagan struggled with fatigue.

The only other items in the room were a large engraved wardrobe, and a bath tub that had already been filled with hot water.

Walking towards the bath tub, she ran her fingers along the reddish charcoal cast iron exterior and then along the white porcelain interior. She flicked the hot water, the heat stung her fingers.

Smelly, she was eager to freshen up.

Slipping her clothes off, she kicked them across the room, almost setting fire to them with the candles.

Placing one foot into the hot water to test it, she submerged her entire body into the tub, surrendering to the heat her body released its tension. Lathering up the soap, she scrubbed her skin until it looked like ice-cream. Smelling of green tea and jasmine, Pagan then washed her hair with shampoo and conditioner. Dust and wind, had left her hair knotted and unmanageable.

Once clean, she relaxed. Her toes played with the opening of the cold water tap, turning it on and then off while her thoughts travelled uneasily over the last couple of days.

At first, she had been scared of Dante but now she was sure he would not hurt her. He wanted to hand her over unharmed to the woman, Aggie so he could collect his full payment.

"You're just a glorified postman, Dante."

Pagan sat up splashing water over the edge of the bath tub. Were *they* cleaning her up for a reason?

Pagan

The sound of music alerted Pagan that she had to dress quickly for dinner.

Pagan pulled out a yellow outfit; crop-top, skirt and sari, which was complimented with an abundance of silver and blue beads for her to choose from.

The servant girl had pointed to the wardrobe only moments before. Her speech sounded like a robot, in a failed attempt to mimic her boss, "Madam Audrey has asked you to wear the yellow," and then she had left the room.

Struggling to put the items of clothing on, Pagan got hopelessly tangled. Taking the garments off, she started again. The crop-top barely covering her small breasts and her stomach now tastelessly exposed, left her grateful that the temperature was still somewhere between 'bloody hot' and boiling.

"This would be easier if I had a mirror," Pagan whined.

Pulling the long skirt up, she tied the string into a basic knot around her waist. The weight of the skirt felt uncomfortable but she was happy that the skirt covered her legs to the ankles. Her inner thighs were black from bruises, acquired from flying on a broomstick.

"Hmmm is this a sarong or Sari?"

Holding the fabric out, Pagan could not decide whether she wanted to wear it or not, eventually deciding to throw it onto the bed.

The door unlocked and Audrey walked in.

Wearing a slinky sleeveless black dress that unflatteringly clung to her bony figure, she stopped mid-step and clasped her hands together, "Don't you have promiscuous shoulders? Men must just love your clavicles?"

Pagan shrugged her shoulders, confused.

"Now. Some make-up to rosy those cheeks up. You're awfully pale, Missy."

Crossing her arms, Pagan insisted, "I don't wear make-up."

Laughing as if she was reacting to a joke, Audrey giggled back, "Oh darling, you're pretty but not that pretty."

Insulted, Pagan continued to protest until Audrey, out of frustration, gave in by throwing a contour kit across the floor. Multiples of glittering brown makeup formed a pasty abstract, highlighting that Audrey preferred to be in control. And as if the 'adult tantrum' had not occurred, Audrey softly smiled, "Come! Our guests have arrived and they are eager to meet you."

Freaked, Pagan stood still, unable to move, the fear of the unknown paralysed her. Memories of Amelie advising Pagan to 'just flow' flooded her consciousness.

Audrey extended her arm out, "Come, Miss Pagan, dinner is being served."

Escorted back down the hallway and then up four flights of stairs, they entered a room on the rooftop. The roof was supported by twelve boundary posts and four internal pillars. The lights of the city twinkled within the blackness of the night while the aroma of dinner masked the garbage scent.

Several servants holding onto large pleated silk fans stood around the dining table waiting for instructions, while a musician played a sitar in the corner, his eyes fixed on the floor, as if he had been instructed not to look at the guests. What Pagan had not realised is that he had no eyes to look at them with.

Four smartly dressed guests sat at a large dining table but Pagan fixed her eyes upon Dante.

Wearing olive green four quarter trousers, that revealed his hairy muscular calves and an unbuttoned white linen shirt that exposed his hairy chest, Pagan felt seduced.

Men in Australia never wore garments like the men in India. There was something sensual about the soft fabric and how it fell over their genitalia, that made Pagan's heart race.

Guilty of staring at Dante for too long, she sent Rogan a mental apology for her unfaithfulness.

In turn, Dante sat at the end of the table, ignoring Pagan's entrance, as if she was invisible to him. His hair was pulled back into a ponytail and in a flirtatious manner, she pulled it as she walked past him.

"Brushed your teeth, Old Man?"

Dante managed a grin, keeping the cleanliness of his teeth a secret.

Clapping her hands three times, Audrey energetically introduced Pagan once she had reached her seat at the table.

Pagan awkwardly smiled.

Sitting down on a firm pillow, Audrey wiggled several times until her bony bottom found some comfort.

Then unexpectedly, Audrey hopped back up and ran around the table to the man who sat beside Pagan, who was so fat that he took up two chairs. If someone stuck a pin into his skin, Pagan was sure he could fill up an Olympic size swimming pool from the amount of water that his body was holding onto. He was a human dam.

"This is my dear friend, Alexander. We call him Fat Alex."

Audrey patted Fat Alex on his bald head. Pagan swore she saw water ooze from the pores of his skin.

"Don't stay stationary for too long Pagan, Fat Alex might eat you," she teased.

Strangely everyone laughed at Audrey's rudeness, except for Dante who munched on a carrot stick.

Pagan grimaced at Fat Alex, who licked his lips as he stared at her.

Alarmed, that they may have been an element of truth about Audrey's warning that he might eat her, she shuffled her chair back, creating a further four inch gap between them.

"Next we have Fat Alex's wives."

Audrey stood between the identical twin sisters, resting a palm on each on a shoulder, she spoke, "Thelma and Wiz, please welcome Pagan. Pagan is from Ozzstralia."

Prominent white gums, bucked teeth and feeble chins disabled both sisters with a speech impediment.

Pagan swallowed down her amusement as they sprayed the table with their saliva, covering the freshly cooked papadums.

Surprisingly, Audrey politely ignored the saliva that soaked the dough and continued around the table, stopping at the last guest who was so old, Pagan was not sure he was even alive.

"And this handsome gentleman is Monsieur Jehrome. He's a French artiste, Pagan. The best I know. So much so, I can't afford any of his blasted paintings and he's too stingy to let me have one as a gift."

Monsieur Jehrome body shook wildly, so much so, that Pagan was not entirely sure if he was laughing or having a seizure.

The table rich in exotic food, and smelling of organic spices, tantalised Pagan's nose. The bread was puffier than any bread she had ever seen and she watched as the guests started breaking the bread up, dipping it into an assortment of white and green dips and then shoving it into their mouths. Mimicking them, she hoped they would ignore her inexperience of Indian cuisine which soon became apparent once the food touched her lips. Burning lips and steaming eyes, Pagan quickly poured a glass of water, which only added to the heat.

Dante politely poured her a glass of milk and handed it to her. It took several minutes for the tears to dry up.

The conversation was worldly; their lavish gestures and outspoken comments made Pagan feel inferior and she was glad that they seemed to have forgotten that she too sat at the table. Her comfort was short lived as Fat Alex shuffled in his chairs around to face Pagan, his mothball breath washing over her face, putting her off the meal.

"Tell me about Australia."

She hesitated, as she was unsure of what to say.

Dante sensing her confusion intervened, "I think you'll find Fat Alex, Tasmania, the island state in Australia where she is from, is very similar to England. However the trees are very different and the people are backward."

Pagan flared her nose in protest.

Thelma piped up, spraying the table with more saliva, "After all, they all came from convicts, settlers and natives. A melting pot of bits and pieces really, so of course they're backwards, poor little retards."

Wiz giggled, as she agreed with her sister's biases.

As if suddenly full of life, Monsieur Jehrome spoke, "Certainly a table of insults and prejudices tonight and as much as it amuses me, I must return to my room!"

Fumbling to grab his eagle top walking stick, Monsieur Jehrome slowly stood up, "My memories are noisy tonight and I fear only returning to the solitude of my room will quiet them."

Audrey jumped up from her seat and proceeded to help Monsieur Jehrome steady himself.

Unexpectedly, he walked in the opposite direction to the door, heading towards Pagan instead. Grabbing her nose, his dry course hands sanding her youthful skin pretended to pull her nose off, capturing it in between his pointer finger and thumb.

Pagan laughed, as his warmth radiated from him to her.

Drawing in a deep breath that almost knocked him over, Monsieur Jehrome seemed haunted by a memory he could not shake, "Aggie, can't kill what she can't find. Fais de beaux reves, my girl."

Unable to straighten his torso, Monsieur Jehrome hunched. Frail, he shuffled out of the room, leaving the guests reflective, solemn and confused.

"So Audrey tells me that you're heading to the Monarchy? Been a naughty girl, I heard?"

Pagan turned to face Wiz, unsure if she was asking a question or making a statement. She chose not to reply.

"I'm afraid she has no idea of who she is or what lies in front of her," Dante interrupted.

Gasps echoed around the room.

Audrey shrieked, "That's ghastly news, Dante! How could you take an Innocent to the Monarchy and not have her prepared?"

Wiz answered, "I think you'll find Audrey that there will be no mercy for this Maiden, regardless if she is prepared or not. Ignorance is bliss, after all, and I think, they have every right to want to contain her before she is Awakened."

Fat Alex picked up his knife, twisting it around his fingers before diving it into a piece of lamb, "And the history books warn us what she is capable of."

Pagan flushed as the room suddenly become hotter. She poured herself another glass of milk which she spilt down her chin.

"Well, Fat Alex," Audrey snapped back, "For tonight this Maiden is my guest and we will show her some common decency. You and your wives can take at least one night off from your blatant bigotry."

Thelma raised her voice, "Audrey, you better hope that she returns the same decency towards you once she is Awakened."

"I doubt once she is Awakened, mere me, will cross her mind at all. Those who have crossed us, steal the most amount of memory, I've found. So if I'm charming, I will never be thought of again."

Audrey's eyes darted to Dante for reassurance.

Sitting back on his chair, Dante stared at Pagan, lost in thought, he hesitated before speaking, "What I've found is when you're powerful it's best to assume that everyone is your enemy, especially those closest to you for they know how best to destroy you. The powerful have many friends, many, many, friends. It's in the closeness that we are vulnerable. The dilemma is not who is your friend and who is your foe but, which friend is a greater threat. I am under no illusion that Pagan, Awakened or not, is more powerful than I, so it's best to treat her as an enemy, Audrey, even if she offers friendship. You will save her the guilt later on when she must turn on you to achieve what she must achieve. There is only loyalty when there is payoff."

Fat Alex laughed, "Oh Dante, I do like you, you see everything as a pay check. Let's call each other friends."

Turning back to look at Pagan, his face hardened, "So enjoy your innocence, Little Witch and remember you have no friends in this world, especially those closest to you. Everyone will turn on you in the end. It's what Witches and humans do."

Struggling to hold back tears, Pagan looked up towards the ceiling.

Blinking wildly, she told herself that Dante was wrong. She did have friends and she was not a wicked person like they think she is. She was a teenage girl from Tasmania.

"Well…aren't you… just cheery, Dante, remind me to not ask for your opinion again."

Audrey stood up, grabbing another bottle of wine from the table. Filling her guests' glasses, she made a toast, "To a good meal. Please drink, a lot."

She then filled her own glass up to the brim, sculled it and then filled it up again.

"Grab another bottle of Cab Sav from the cellar, actually grab four more," she barked at the servant.

Audrey plopped herself into the chair, slouching down defeated that the evening was not going as well as she had planned.

Lost in thought, Audrey spoke, "Well, I think you are all dreadfully unkind. I couldn't possibly hand her over to the Crone Monarchy without preparing her in some way."

Grinning, she turned to Dante, "And don't think you're not helping me, Dante."

Dante choked on his food but politely lifted his glass to salute Audrey.

Several hours later, drunk and full of food, the guests left and Pagan hoped that she would never meet any of them again.

Watching as Dante disappeared into Audrey's bedroom, Pagan noted how much women seemed to like Dante.

Before closing her eyes, she wondered if Dante liked them. He seemed to be just going through the motions. Was having sex with Audrey a tactic? A pay cheque? Making her vulnerable to him? Surely, Audrey was not naive to his advances.

Pagan smiled as she decided Audrey knew what Dante was doing, manipulating, but it was Dante who was blind to her tactics.

Who would have thought 'a touch' could mean so much and so little.

Pagan

The next morning suffering from heat exhaustion, Pagan sat down beside Audrey, "It's hot!"

Cheeks flushed while shivering from an internal cold, the ground added more stress to her immune system by burning her bottom.

Her vision blurred, while black spots sprinkled over her eyesight, "I feel faint."

The street outside of Audrey's home was manic. Cows roamed freely, hoards of pedestrians erratically walked around the cows, motorbikes zig-zagged around the people and the cars 'gave way' to no one. It was chaos, one massive ball of knotted wool, that no one could be bothered untangling, but somehow, it worked.

A taxi driver nudged his car through the madness, honking his horn from habit rather than a reaction to the congestion, carelessly driving over a massive pot-hole and dodging a stubborn cow and a few inattentive children, who ran out in front of the vehicle; all seemed very normal to him.

The sound irritated Pagan, who wondered why at night the city was as quiet as it was except for the non-stop honking of car horns. Where did all the people go?

"It's so hot!"

Audrey raised one eyebrow, "For a Maiden, you sure do whinge a lot."

'I'm not a Maiden," Pagan hissed at Audrey.

Too hot to continue arguing, Pagan searched for shade, finding shelter underneath a line of clothes that hung from a fraying rope outside a shanty. Three house lengths along the street, she lay down. There was no way she was attempting to cross the street. Old buildings barely holding their own weight, supported newer buildings, that had been haphazardly built on top. It was dangerous just to stand in this city.

Pagan questioned if she should seek refuge elsewhere or just move back out into the direct sunlight.

Decisively, Pagan walked towards Audrey again opting for the safety of someone familiar, even if she did not like them, than the possibility of being run over by a stranger who would leave her for dead.

Sitting down beside Audrey, she sensed Audrey was enjoying watching the heat and environment stress her.

Conditioned to the heat, Audrey sat fanning herself on a lounge chair that had been assembled fifteen minutes prior by the servant girl, who now stood behind Audrey, unprotected from the sun.

Wearing a blue riding helmet to shade her from the sun's rays, Audrey's hair was pulled back so tightly into a bun that it stretched her wrinkles out making her look five years younger. The black tailored suit reflected the sun but not the dust.

Elbow length leather gloves, gripped a short black whip, which Audrey swung in the air every few minutes as if she was playing with a sword. Pagan thought her attire was a strange choice, considering she had not seen a horse or a stable anywhere to warrant it.

Three servants followed by Dante emerged from the front door.

Dante wearing his usual casual apparel; bare feet, blue jeans and a plain black T-shirt. He leaned against the external cement wall. His face was hidden by a mane of endless black locks, his eyes swollen from a lack of sleep.

Jumping up from the lounge chair, Audrey swung the whip in the air making a figure eight, "Nice of you to grace us with your presence, Dante. It's almost lunch time."

Insensitive to Audrey's sarcasm, he flicked his hair off his face, "And I see you're using the whip you used on me last night. I hope you've cleaned it."

'Yuck', Pagan thought as she swallowed down a mouthful of bile.

She noticed that the servants were also struggling to control their reaction to Dante's comment.

"Well, let's hope Pagan reacts to the whip as well as you do."

Suddenly alert, Pagan jumped up, "What?"

Audrey giggled, "Oh relax, darling. It's for your own good."

Pagan turned to Dante, desperate for him to intervene. Dante reacted by pulling his hair up into a bun on the top of his head, securing it with a head band.

"Relax, Pagan. Think of it as a game. We just want to test how well you are guided by your instincts. So when I say run, I want you to run down the street, lose yourself in the crowd and return to us."

"But I'll die out there."

It was Audrey who now requested encouragement from Dante, "Dramatic little thing isn't she, Dante? When I say run, I suggest you run, Pagan, don't get all precious. The youth today. All whinge, whinge, whinge and no action."

Before Pagan could ask why, Audrey screeched, "Run."

Unsure of what to do, Pagan hovered on the same spot as if she was about to serve in a game of tennis.

"Can I at least have some water first?" She begged trying to postpone the run.

Audrey snapped the whip down on Pagan's back, "I said, run!"

Pagan screamed with pain, jumping on the spot to disperse the sting. She noticed Dante smirking. Pagan angered.

Audrey took her riding helmet off so that Pagan could see the honesty in her eyes and her pleasure, "Pagan, you need to trust us. Just run. It's for your own good."

Pagan screamed, "Well, stop hitting me!"

Audrey calmly replied, "Well Pagan, I'm simply enjoying it too much to stop. So this time when I say 'run' please have the decency to run, we don't have all day, especially since Dante has slept most of it."

Dante now in fits of laughter, walked towards them, intimidating Pagan into submission.

Pagan looked around. Everyone seemed oblivious to Audrey's treatment of her.

Externalising her frustration towards Dante, she snarled, "Fuck you!"

Audrey brought the whip down onto Pagan's left buttock, "Language."

"You crazy, bitch!"

Audrey reacted by whipping her on her right buttock.

Wincing from the agony, Pagan ran without warning into the street, dodging and weaving through the madness, cursing the obstacles in her way. Suffering from the limitations of her exhausted disposition, she slowed into a fast walk. Turning a corner, she was overwhelmed by the abundance of people who surrounded her.

Dizzy and scared, she stopped fearful that she was going to faint.

Without warning Dante rugby tackled her from behind, smashing her into the ground. Flipping several times, they both came to rest in a tangled mass of arms and legs.

Gasping for air, Dante helped her up.

Once standing, she brushed the dust from her body, "You nearly killed me, Dante!"

"Oh didn't Audrey tell you I would chase you?"

It took Pagan the entire walk back to Audrey to remove all the gravel from her knees and chin.

"And run!"

Pagan ran faster this time knowing that Dante would be chasing her. This time, she turned the opposite corner, diving straight into the back of an opened ended truck, frightening the chickens that scattered to the front of the truck. Some of the liberated chickens took the opportunity to jump off the sides, running off down the street, only to meet their fate under a motorcycle wheel.

Dante tagged her shoulder, "Gotcha."

Fed up already, Pagan jumped off the truck, "I hate you."

After five more attempts, Audrey's enthusiasm lessened. Her once boisterous command had reduced to a mere whisper, "Run."

This time, Pagan sat straight down onto her bottom, "Oops, you got me Dante. Can we have lunch now?"

Dante, squatting down in front of her, his eyes connected with her pupils, "I will let you go home, Little Witch, if I can't catch you."

"You promise?"

Dante tucked her hair behind her ears, "Of course, I promise."

Pagan bounced up, "Ok! Let's do this!"

Audrey did not hesitate with one large twist of her waist, the whip snapped Pagan's bottom and she screamed, "Run."

Adrenaline surging, Pagan sprinted. She felt lighter as if she had discarded half her body mass. Jumping over the potholes, she navigated herself around the cars, people, and animals with ease, focusing only on the finish line. The crowd moved out of her way as if they sensed she was approaching before her physical body reached them.

Smelling Dante, she estimated that he was just behind her, a few metres at most. Increasing her speed, she felt the euphoria 'kick in' and any previous exhaustion disappeared along with the dizziness. The gift of home was too great of an incentive to not channel all of her energy into winning, after all, she was in control of the path she was running, so how could she lose?

Compared to the sneakers Audrey had lent Pagan, Dante's bare feet were cutting up and he was losing traction on the unforgiving ground.

She could smell Dante, he was right behind her. It was time to liven things up before she ran back to Audrey.

"See you later, Old Man."

Closing her eyes, she imagined Amelie and Rogan encouraging her from the side line.

Turn right at the second turn off.

She did.

A donkey blocked most of the lane. Running underneath it, it kicked, making an obstacle for Dante who had almost tagged her.

Pagan was now a few metres in front of him.

Turn right!

She did.

If she turned right at the next two streets she would complete a full square back to Audrey.

No, turn left.

She turned left entering a main street. Frantically pushing people out of her way, she headed towards a green door on the right. Running inside the building the shop keeper dropped a bundle of clothes onto the floor.

"Sorry," she screamed.

Running through a maze of corridors, she eventually opened a door that led directly back out onto the road she had started the race on.

Audrey stood, waving her whip only two hundred metres away.

Fatiguing, her legs were burning and her chest felt as if it was about to cave in. She still managed to gather speed.

Fifty metres to go.

She could no longer smell Dante.

Her excitement grew as she committed herself to winning. She was going home.

Throwing her body over the make-shift line, she slid over the markers only stopping once she reached Audrey's heels.

Pagan had won. She was going home but then she felt a tightening around her ankle. Peering back over her left shoulder, she saw that Dante was also on the ground behind her, holding her ankle, which lay before the finish line.

Pagan hit the ground with her fists, "No!"

Audrey squealed with delight, "Oh, I wish we could whip all children."

Dante shook his head disapprovingly, "No Audrey. Not right now."

Pagan

Mounting the broomstick, Pagan wrapped her arms loosely around Dante's waist. She could hardly stomach the thought of touching him, but right then, he was the only person in her life.

Blood blisters and chafe in her groin area hurt as her thighs straddled the broom, but the physical pain was bearable compared to a depression that had set in.

Heavy chest, and ideas of suicide, plagued her thoughts. She dabbled with the idea of letting go of Dante and plummeting to her death. At least, she would be controlling her destiny rather than a woman, a Crone named, Aggie, and Dante would not receive his bounty payment.

Depression was not unfamiliar to her, it was a comfort. It was perfect numbness, beautiful and dependable. It was the happiness in a time of feeling trapped in a situation she could not escape from. She could move through life when numb. She could stare at death, lips separated and welcome it.

Flying for a very long time in silence, tears rolled down Pagan's cheeks, soaking Dante's leather jacket. The wind scooped the tears up, showering the landscape below them.

Dante ignored the sobbing. He knew that she would feel stronger once she had a good cry. Once broken, she would be better mentally and emotionally prepared for her uncertain future but only if she was prepared to leave the past behind her.

What Pagan did not know was Dante was preparing her for whatever Aggie had planned. Aggie was fearless and cruel and Pagan would suffer more than any other Witch in herstory. She would need to be strong to withstand the torture.

Dante angered, Aislyn had not prepared her daughter for Aggie's wrath and now the responsibility lay with him, and the Little Witch hated him for it.

Before they left India, Dante had cupped her chin, "I'm taking you to visit a good friend. Lucinda will cheer you up. She cheers the whole goddam world up."

Drifting into a nightmarish sleep, Rogan called out to Pagan but she could not find him within a vastness of corridors.

Distressed, she woke herself up.

Stopping several times to sleep, eat, and stretch their legs, Pagan refused to speak to Dante, preferring her own thoughts over speech.

"This time when we fly, I will not stop until we reach our destination. You need to prepare yourself, Little Witch, for the long trip."

Her lips faced Dante while her eyes remained lost in another direction.

She spoke, "When I was thirteen, I visited a new friend after school. I think it was on a Friday, I suppose the details don't matter. Excited that I had actually made a new friend, I remember skipping to her house. The friendship lasted that afternoon. I was such a loser. In the backyard three dogs were kept in cages. Running up to them they barked and tried to bite me. You see Dante, the dogs were hunting dogs, trained to kill, loyal to the hunt. Unlike pets, these dogs had never been patted or shown any kindness of any sort and I feared them, even hated them. I even kicked their cage, angry because they tried to bite me when all I offered them was a pat."

Suddenly looking at Dante, she softened, "I have a lot of growing up to do, don't I, Dante?"

A thousand responses haunted Dante and all of them risky. He responded with wisdom, "Be careful that you don't cage yourself in with those thoughts of yours, Little Witch."

At day break, they had reached their destination.

Her feet systematically and in sync with Dante's, helped him slow the broomstick down, and effortlessly they landed.

Pagan stiffly dismounted, walking around encouraging blood to circulate. Within minutes, she had regained her composure, ecstatic that she was conquering the dreaded dismount.

The sun was peering over the horizon, presenting a barren rocky landscape.

"Where are we exactly?"

"Spain. Lucinda will be here to pick us up shortly."

"Wow, I can't believe we are in Spain. I've always wanted to visit here."

Pagan shivered, Spain was close to England. This would be her last stop before she met Aggie.

Dante pointed towards a cloud of dust that followed a rickety aqua coloured truck, "Look! Our ride is here."

Within minutes the truck squealed to a stop. The smell of burning oil poisoned Pagan's nostrils, as a voluminous and far-fetched beauty struggled to open the truck door, but once she did her walnut eyes greeted them.

Pagan gasped, Lucinda was the most beautiful woman she had ever seen. Instantly wanting to hate her, Pagan was spellbound by her beauty.

Wearing denim shorts that scissor cut at her bum cheeks and a baby blue t-shirt, Pagan could see her nipples through the fabric. Like Pagan, she was not wearing a bra.

It was not surprising that Dante wanted to visit Lucinda with such urgency.

Her black hair, speckled with grey highlights, hung wildly down to her hefty bottom. Swaying like a cat prancing in between its master's legs, she walked towards Dante.

He embraced Lucinda, lifting her off the ground.

She re-paid him with a slap across the face, "Dante, you leave me for far too long! Your life Dante is all hola and despedidas."

Then she smiled, "But I am always pleased to see you."

Dante smiled at Lucinda, "Hola!"

Pagan laughed at Dante's corniness.

Lucinda turned to Pagan, "Ah! Dante you bring me gifts. You are too kind. Come girl! You must rest."

Then she turned swiftly back to Dante, cupping his groin in her palm, "And you Dante must come straight to my bed."

Lucinda drove erratically.

Out of fear, Pagan gripped the dashboard while Dante gripped Lucinda's thigh.

The torn leather seat covers poked into Pagan's back.

Dante had thrown the broomstick into the back of the truck, Pagan had kept her eyes fixed on it. How quickly she had bonded with her new form of transport. At that stage, Pagan would have opted to have flown to Lucinda's home than run the risk of dying from Lucinda crashing the truck.

Dust poured out behind the truck and finally after twenty minutes of Pagan praying for survival, Lucinda parked the truck outside of a salmon coloured, two storey high, villa.

Peeling her white fingers off the dashboard, Pagan noticed Dante's hand remained firmly on Lucinda's thigh. A wave of jealously washed over her but who she was jealous of she was unsure.

The villa looked insignificant against the vast barren landscape, hosted by a cloudless dull blue sky, distant smoky mountains, stark trees, corn yellow grass and sandy coloured soil, and although the house was splendidly rustic; flaking pillars, chipped render and a rusting roof, it looked as if it could crumble from a gust of wind.

Pagan exhaled, she had survived Lucinda's driving. Surely, she would survive the house?

Lucinda walked Pagan immediately to her room for a nap, "Sleep my beautiful. We shall have a party tonight."

Pagan had become accustomed to sleeping during the day, although today she was keen to explore the surrounding environment that encompassed the house. Dante would not notice if she disappeared for a few hours now that he had Lucinda to occupy him. Her heart sunk as she thought of Rogan.

Naked, she pulled the sheet over her. Snuggling into the lumpy mattress, she fantasised about making love to Rogan and after a few minutes, she slept.

The heat from the late afternoon sun woke her up.

Dante's life may be all 'hellos and goodbyes', but her life was now 'sunrises and sunsets'.

Slipping out of bed, she threw a sheer, white, dressing gown on that had previously decorated a white, painted rustic, chair.

Sneaking down the spiral staircase, her plan was to raid the kitchen for food and water before she explored the Spanish landscape. Resigning to her status of kidnapped, ironically, she did not even think about escaping. Half way down the staircase, a board creaked. Stopping, she held her breath. Listening, she heard the sound of rhythmic thumping coming from a room downstairs. Pagan panicked. She must be near Lucinda's bedroom.

Heavy grunting coached her to investigate.

Reaching the bottom of the staircase, Pagan peaked around the corner and into a room adjacent to where she stood.

Sheer, white, curtains swayed elegantly from the breeze. A bulky bed positioned in the middle of the room appeared tiny in the open space. The ceiling was laced with purple fabric that hung like bubble wrap.

Lucinda straddled Dante. Moving slowly on top of him, her long hair tickled her fleshy back. Bending down to kiss Dante, Lucinda's large round breasts covered his face and he drank from her dark brown nipples. Sitting back up, Dante, almost out of habit, clasped her hips. His chest had tightened and his calves clenched to take the tension. Only an occasional grunt or exhilarated breath, escaped from their lips, and although Lucinda barely moved on top of Dante, they both were lost in a moment of erotica.

Pagan was startled by how aroused she was. Ashamed, she looked away.

A few more steps and she was safe in the kitchen. Closing the kitchen door behind her, she opened the pantry and quietly feasted on its contents.

Pagan

Pagan stuck her index finger into the melting wax. Wax from an assortment of burning candles, that sat clustered on the battered wooden kitchen table, making an oddly formed sculpture which the house guest happily added to, pouring the red, blue and white hot wax over the dried wax, forming a technicoloured river over the existing wax mound.

Dressed in a pair of Lucinda's cotton shorts; pink polka dots on cream and a plain pink singlet top, the evening welcomed a cooler temperature and with it a respite from heat stroke acquired in India.

A dull distant rumble, warned them that a thunderstorm approached and several minutes later fork lightning lit up the night sky in a melodramatic supremacy.

"The goddesses are angry tonight," Lucinda jested, as she prepared the evening's sangria; two bottles of cheap red wine, freshly squeezed lemon juice, a ripe peach, a cored and cut apple, a thinly sliced lime, two and half cups of brandy, a small bottle of soda and eight large spoonful's of sugar, mixed and poured over fourteen pieces of cubed ice that covered the bottom of a large three litre jug.

"Now we must wait until the sangria chills before we can drink it."

Pagan studied Lucinda as she rolled an almost perfect cylinder joint; rice paper with a mixture of marijuana, tobacco and an unfamiliar spice, with no filter.

Lighting it, she handed it to Dante first.

Playfully, Lucinda skipped over to Pagan sitting on her lap, "Tonight, my girlfriend Francesca is coming over to meet you."

Passing the joint back to Lucinda, Dante grinned. Tonight, he would sleep with both Francesca and Lucinda.

Taking a drag of the joint, Lucinda blew the smoke into Pagan's face, "She is looking forward to meeting her first Witch."

Lucinda grabbed Pagan's hand holding it firmly in between her palms, "I told her that you have soulless eyes and a nose that is so long it pokes me in the face when I speak to you and warts not only on your nose but on your chin as well and whiskers that cover your neck. I don't know if she will be disappointed or happy, that you are simply orgasmic."

Pagan blushed.

Inhaling again, Lucinda handed the joint to Pagan.

Potent, Pagan felt the effects immediately. Taking another drag, the smoke swirled and confined, only to release and relax on the exhale.

After a journey of extremities, Pagan appreciated the recreation Lucinda's hospitality offered her and it also reminded her of Amelie, who she was missing terribly.

Suddenly the ugly kitchen; the scratched cobalt blue cupboards, black and white splashback and greying floor tiles, seemed more attractive, another effect of the marijuana.

"Am I a Witch, Lucinda? You see they keep saying that I'm a Witch and to be honest, I don't know what that means."

Pagan took another drag and answered her own question, "I'm not a Witch or Maiden or anything else. I'm nobody."

Dante stole the joint away from Pagan. Inhaling the persuasive mix his eyes reddened, "I think you'll need to prepare yourself for the truth, Little Witch. We have stresses in our life, it is how easily we bend that makes us strong."

Lucinda took the joint from Dante. Spiritedly shaking her head, she charmed even Pagan with her childlike mannerisms, "Don't worry her with such troubles, Dante. You can be such a party pooper."

Francesca arrived at 19:00 with a chocolate mousse for dessert. Placing one hand behind Lucinda's head, Francesca kissed her girlfriend while the other hand caressed her breast.

Walking over to Dante, Francesca passionately kissed him.

Pagan stiffened from awkwardness as Francesca approached her next. Frigid, Pagan politely held her hand out.

A very tall woman, Francesca's feet and hands were almost twice as big as Dante's and she was handsome rather than attractive, with short spiky blond hair and a rectangular face. She was the type of woman who would win an arm wrestle before it had even begun, but ironically her extra-large smile tempered her giant figure and Pagan instantly warmed to her.

Francesca kissed Pagan's hand, "I've been so excited all day that I've almost wet myself twice."

Dante quickly interrupted, "Pagan would know all about that."

Self-conscious, Pagan glared at Dante. Worried that he would embarrass her in front of Francesca by telling her the story of her 'pissing her pants', she quickly changed the subject, "I would say the sangria is ready to drink, Lucinda."

Skipping dinner and deciding that it was time to sample the sangria and the chocolate mousse, they moved upstairs to the balcony, where they could enjoy the evening. Any threat of a thunderstorm was short lived and within half an hour the stars glistened above them.

Lucinda placed the jug of sangria and the large bowl of chocolate mousse onto the small round outdoor table. Running back inside, she returned half a minute later carrying four jarra sized beer glasses and four large spoons on a tray and an acoustic guitar. Handing a glass and a spoon to each guest, she urged them to drink and eat. The guitar, she carefully placed beside Dante for later.

"Feast my friends. We are a long time dead, so let's live for now, with sangria to warm our tummies and dessert to seduce our tastebuds."

After they finished the bowl of chocolate mousse, Lucinda with a chocolate smile, grabbed the guitar, "Play for us, Dante, we love it when you do. What about 'Recuerdos de la Alhambra?' An oldie but one of my favourites."

Dante pulled his long black curls back into a loose pony tail; tossing his head, he flicked the pony tail off his shoulders. His physical preparation reminded Pagan of a stallion flicking his mane from his eyes, before galloping across to a fresh paddock in a burst of adrenaline-fuelled liberty.

Picking up the acoustic guitar, his fingers slid along the six nylon strings as if he was reuniting with the instrument, seducing it with his fingertips and praying that it would also return his affections. Tuning it, he cursed a few times and Pagan could not help but enjoy his frustration.

Lucinda and Francesca waited for a few minutes before deciding to dance. With blood shot eyes and drunken playfulness, they swirled and waltzed around the crumbling balcony to the sound of silence. Uncaged by socialisation their love projected from their grip; bodies touching, they seemed to still struggle with separation. They would be happiest inside of the other's skin.

Pagan decided the need to connect completely to another person only intensified the separation. Perhaps, it was the completely independent person who felt the most connected to those around them and the world?

Satisfied with the tuning, Dante played.

Pagan envied Francesca's and Lucinda's ability to dance in front of people and for a brief moment while Dante played the guitar, the Spanish heat seduced her aching bones, the fresh air tickled her face and all thoughts of the past 'paused', and she succumb to a moment of happiness.

Shyly glued to the chair, Pagan studied Dante. The Bounty was an aloof-unknown to her. Unsure, if he was a friend or an enemy, even after he declared she was his enemy, she reminded herself not to trust him, even if she liked him at times but she could not deny that she was intrigued by her Israeli captor.

Head facing down, eyes closed, forehead muscles enlarged, and shoulders squared, Dante appeared to be lost within the instrument, passionate and disturbed, by whatever haunted him. His rigid complexity intensified through the contrast of his right and left hand. One deformed and grotesque, whilst the other agile and quick. It sounded as if two extra guitars and a piano accompanied him.

The music made her feel as if she was floating.

After he stopped playing, Pagan noticed he was crying, tears that were ignored by Lucinda and Francesca who cuddled on the outdoor sofa committed to their intimacy.

Pagan wondered why he was crying. Why that song meant so much to him. Perhaps, she did not know Dante at all.

"Lucinda, have you always been a lesbian?"

Startled, both women looked at each other and laughed but replied to their new friend, the Witch.

"The world is full of labels, Pagan. Don't place us in your judgemental box. We see people for their energies and personalities," Lucinda stated.

Francesca lifted her glass, "To good energies."

Dante took both Lucinda and Francesca to bed that night, while Pagan listened from the bottom of the staircase. The world seemed more colourful with people like Dante, Lucinda and Francesca in it.

These people petrified her.

Pagan

Lucinda hesitated; it seemed unkind to wake Pagan up when she looked so serenely asleep, curled up under a mass of crocheted blankets.

Lucinda had always wanted a daughter.

Pagan's long black hair scrunched up into a knotted halo, and her freckly skin, rosy from the cold morning air, pinched her cheeks. Pagan was certainly going to be a stunning Witch when Awakened.

Lucinda gently tickled Pagan's eyelids, "Wake up, beautiful. You have a lot to get through today."

Pagan brushed Lucinda's hand away from her face, but once fully awake, she smiled at Lucinda, who stood naked in front of her.

"Wash outside underneath the garden shower, Pagan, while I wake Francesca and Dante and prepare something for us to eat. There is a towel hanging over the door."

Hungover from four glasses of sangria, Pagan looked forward to a cold shower. Swinging the towel over her shoulder, she wandered down stairs and out the front door, around the house and into a court area. The shower head fitted into a large wall. Orange and purple tiles formed a checkerboard pattern while a wild leafy climber softened the harshness.

Undressing, she threw the shorts and singlet top towards a shrub near the towel. The early morning sun instantly burned her skin. Turning the tap on, she jumped back to avoid the splashing water, which remained lukewarm. Stepping underneath the shower, Pagan held her breath, allowing the stream of water to engulf her entire face. Tension released from her facial muscles. Turning, she allowed the water to massage her back. Feeling dizzy from dehydration, she sat down on the grass and enjoyed the water sprinkling over her whole body.

Wrapping the towel around her torso, she walked back to her room.

Dante, still slumbered in Lucinda's bed. His cheeks were squashed against his hand and he was cocooned in a white sheet. His feet poked out at the bottom, hanging over the edge.

Pagan wondered how all three of them had fitted comfortably into one bed.

Dressing in a pair of Lucinda's overall's and a white t-shirt, which had been left on the bed, Pagan strolled casually down stairs to the kitchen. Lucinda and Francesca sat at the table.

"Good morning."

Both women enthusiastically greeted Pagan, "Buenos Dias."

Lucinda poured her a black coffee and made her several pieces of toast with jam, while Francesca sacrificed her own comfort by offering Pagan her chair, opting to sit on the kitchen bench top instead.

"I should be kidnapped more often," Pagan teased.

Finishing the last mouthful of her toast and swallowing it down with the coffee, Francesca jumped down from the bench top, placing her cup and plate into the sink, "I'm leaving for work now."

Staring at Pagan her eyes saddened, "I am afraid this may be the last time we see each other Pagan. Once you are Awakened you will be too majestic to worry yourself with us…little people. Promise me, you will not forget us however, for we will not forget you."

Embracing in a farewell hug, Pagan permitted Francesca to kiss her goodbye on the lips. Strangely, the peck seemed natural and Pagan wondered why more people did not adopt a more intimate gesture of friendship.

Washing up the dishes, Pagan's thoughts drifted to home.

Unsure of the time zones, she wondered what Rogan would be doing. Questions flooded her imagination; had he forgotten her, did he still love her and would he still want her when she returned, if she returned? Only time would tell. Pagan realised 'only time' knew all the answers.

Waiting outside at Lucinda's request, Pagan enjoyed the morning sun by lying down in a star position to watch the clouds float past her. She wondered if those same clouds would reach Tasmania within a week?

Dante joined her wearing only pyjama bottoms.

Taxing signs of tiredness; large black rings under his eyes and a permanent frown had aged his face, which Pagan thought were justified, considering Lucinda's and Francesca's libido and stamina.

"Not really a morning person are you, Dante?"

He ignored her cheery sarcasm, "Get up, Little Witch. You have much to learn today."

Lucinda rushed out the front door carrying two swords, one in each hand, "Dante! Dante I've found them."

Standing up, Pagan's angered as she realised she was being tested again, "How many times must I tell you? I'm not a Witch! These tests are stupid, Dante. I failed the one in India. I'm going to fail this one."

Lucinda shook her head in disbelief, "Giving up before you've even tried Pagan? Attitude like that, well of course that's why you failed in India. We say what we create."

Handing Pagan the smaller silver sword with an engraved bronze cat as a handle, Lucinda smiled, "You like?"

Pagan had never seen a real sword before, let alone held one. Running her finger along the edge it took several seconds for the cut to bleed. She sucked her finger until the bleeding stopped.

"Think of this as fun, Pagan. It doesn't matter if you fail then does it? Your aim is to learn not win."

Swinging the sword aimlessly around her body, she apprehensively agreed, "So what exactly am I meant to do with this?"

Dante grabbed the other sword. Lifting it above his head, he pointed it at Pagan, "Hit me with it."

"Oh Lucinda you're right. This does sound fun."

Lucinda burst into laughter.

"But I also get to hit you, Little Witch," Dante rejoiced.

Pagan dropped the sword stepping backwards, "No way, am I duelling you."

Dante's patience was short and he was quick to temper, "Useless bitch! What kind of Witch are you? I have one day, one day, to prepare you! I am nothing compared to Aggie."

She retaliated, "Firstly, not a Witch and secondly, is there a manual I should read first, called 'dealing with cranky, old men?'"

Dante yelled back "Yes actually, it's called 'I'm a stupid Witch, volume one."

Pagan screamed back, "Well, I'm sure you've fucked enough of them to have written it yourself?"

Lucinda heckled safely from the side line, "Oh no, Pagan, Dante doesn't fuck Witches, only humans."

"Is that because they don't fuck the 'help' Dante?" Pagan stirred.

Furious, Dante lifted the sword above his head and charged at Pagan.

Screaming, Pagan frantically ran for her sword, wrapping her hand around the handle, but not before, Dante brought down his sword, piercing the ground only inches from her hand.

She squealed.

Lucinda giggled. Enjoying the entertainment, she crouched down burying her bare feet into the ground.

Picking the sword up, Pagan used the sword like a cricket bat, knocking Dante's sword out of his hands. It skidded along the ground, resting two metres away from both of them.

Pointing the sword at his hairy chest, Pagan snarled, "You're dead, Postman."

Dante nodded, "Well done, Little Witch."

Picking up his sword, he held it out straight in front of him. Stable on his feet, his strength came from his hips, "Come here and copy me."

Walking cautiously towards him, her sword held out in front of her. Struggling to hold it up for long, her upper arms burned from the heaviness of the weapon. Wishing she had a shield to protect herself, she bounced, preparing to flee not fight.

Their swords crossed, Dante held firm, while the other shook.

Dante tapped the end of her sword, "Here is weakness."

Sliding the sword down the blade towards Pagan's hand, he tapped again, "And here is strength. Understand?"

Pagan nodded.

"Be a sword, Pagan. Know your strengths and weaknesses."

Without hesitation, Dante knocked her sword to the side; lunging at her, his blade missing her neck by a few inches.

She screamed, mostly from relief but also from frustration.

"Never assume because there are rules that your opponent is polite enough to abide by them. I've never meet a Witch that followed any rules or...promises!"

Pagan snapped at Lucinda, "I thought you said this was going to be fun."

Lucinda clapped her hands, "It's fun for me, Pagan."

Reset, she prepared herself for his lunge.

Scared, she attacked him first, attempting to knock him off his feet, her sword missed his legs, slicing the air instead.

Dante easily blocked her attack by simply moving sideways.

She leapt at him with her eyes closed, guard down, he pushed her backwards with his hand, "Eyes open. You want to see your opponent die, your intuition will only get you so far."

Eyes opened, she attacked Dante before he had time to prepare his defence; the end of the sword nicked his chest. Blood clotted in his chest hair.

The smell of blood reached her nostrils, "Dante, your blood smells funny."

He ignored her comment, "Concentrate! I am about to swing at you, you need to block me."

Without warning, he swung his sword in an infinite symbol, walking slowly towards her, her eyes rapidly blinked with each swing.

Panicking, she deflected his sword, knocking it from side to side, in a haphazard attempt of survival.

Annoyed, she slid to the side; swinging the blade at Dante's head, the breeze of the sword cooled his ear.

Laughing, she boasted, "You fight like a Viking, Old Man."

Lucinda stood up, "How do you know that Pagan? Did you have a memory?"

Fatiguing, Pagan sat down on the ground, "I don't know why I said that."

"Get up, Little Witch, no time to rest."

"Don't worry, Pagan. He's enjoying it because he knows that once you are Awakened, he won't be able to beat you."

Dante flicked Lucinda an unamused glare.

Blocking his attacks and continually falling over, Dante was impressed that she continued to stand back up and face him.

"Your core muscles are slack and your balance needs work. Why did your mother not teach you to sword fight?"

Puffing she replied, "I think you'll find killing people is illegal, Dante, and to be honest, I think my mum taught me all the wrong things."

Pagan's eyes stared at the sky and then back to Dante, "Why do you blame my mum for everything? Surely, my drunken arse dad, gets some of the blame?"

"Your mother is a Witch, so therefore she out ranks your human father."

"Out ranks? So if my mum wasn't a Witch, but a female human, he would out rank her?"

"Yes!"

"I really hate you right now."

Placing one hand on his hip, Dante's face hardened, "I'm going to kill you. This time you are fighting for your life. I don't need Aggie's money and I can dispose of your body here. No one will know what happened to you."

He licked his lip, "I would like to slice that pretty head from your body."

Pagan silenced as Dante's body stiffened and his eyes squinted.

A surge of heat rushed through her body when she realised Dante was serious. She wanted to run but she knew Dante would catch her. She would need to fight. She was not prepared to die, not now. Plus, if his theory was correct, she out ranked him.

She taunted him, "Well, I'm going to cut that pretty hair off before I kill you."

Pagan repeatedly launched at Dante who deflected her approach easily.

Lucinda jumped up and down, enjoying the spectacle.

She forced Dante backwards several times, only for him to manoeuvre around her to gain the dominant position. Her confidence was decreasing. Her only hope was if Dante tired. Planning to tire him out, she danced around the ground covering a larger area of Lucinda's lawn.

She tired.

Provoking him, she screamed, "Come on, Dante! Kill me. I dare you."

He swung his sword above his head, aiming for her neck, he brought the sword down, his goal to chop her head off.

Reacting, Pagan blocked the blade. The sound of impact twanged and hurt her ears.

Mustering all her strength, she pushed it back up. In one move, she swung her body around in a three hundred and sixty degree circle. The blade missed Dante's legs, but in his attempt to move out of the way, he lost his balance toppling to the ground.

Swiftly, she placed one leg on his throat and placed the sword only centimetres from his temple.

Lucinda ran towards Pagan, "No, he was just playing with you!"

Dante struggled to breath. He knew he had gone too far. The Witch was releasing.

Dizzy, Pagan's eyes rolled back inside her head and she collapsed. The sword slid, cutting a portion of Dante's hair off.

Unconcerned with Dante, Lucinda dropped to the ground, "Pagan, wake up."

Shacking Pagan, Lucinda screamed, "Dante, what's wrong with her?"

CHAPTER 16
Dante

Lucinda pleaded with Dante, "Please take her to your mother. She will fix her. She is so sick, Dante. You can't take her like this to the Monarchy. Remember the contract, Dante?"

His mother would scold him severely for meddling, but Lucinda was right, he could not risk flying her to the Crone Monarchy like this. He was not even sure that she was well enough to fly.

Unable to make a decision, he waited another hour to monitor her symptoms but she worsened. Her temperature increased to thirty nine degrees and her body fell limp, only for her temperature to drop and her entire body to shake uncontrollably.

"Her pulse is weakening, Dante!"

Acknowledging the fear in Lucinda's eyes, he anxiously agreed. The safest option was to fly her to his mother, where she could be treated, for what illness, he was not sure.

It meant that Pagan's delivery would be pushed backed a few days but considering her health it was the only option.

Wrapping Pagan up in a blanket, he picked up her feverish body and carried her to the broomstick. Her arms and legs dangled in rag doll fashion.

Concerned she might faint again, Dante positioned Pagan on his lap.

Chest to chest, she straddled him, legs bound to his waist and her head leaning against his shoulder. He pulled the blanket tightly around her, hoping that his body warmth and the blanket would keep her warm.

Lucinda tied a rope around both of them, securing Pagan to Dante. She then blew on Pagan's cheeks until she was somewhat coherent, before speaking to her, "You must not die, Pagan. You hear me? When you are better, Dante will bring you back here before he takes you to that nasty Crone, Aggie and I will see your beautiful smile again."

Kissing Dante goodbye, Lucinda watched as they flew off into the mid afternoon sun. Running along with them for a few metres, she watched as the Magick kicked in and they vanished from sight. Unbeknown to her, Pagan watched Lucinda until her Spanish friend was just a black speck on a yellow landscape.

The sun soon retired to the moon.

Checking her pulse, Dante sped up.

Moaning, Pagan woke, vomiting over the blanket and Dante's shoulder. Luckily the majority sprayed out into the night sky. Lumps of fermented fruit and chocolate bile fell into the Mediterranean Sea. Her head flopped to the side as she fell back into an exhausted inactivity.

"I deserved that, Little Witch."

In the early hours of the morning as the sun was yawning, the purple and gold lights of Tel Aviv welcomed him home. The broomstick vibrated as he flew over the land. A large community garden, a busy highway and a few skyscrapers and he would be flying down the narrow streets of his neighbourhood, Neve Tzedek, finally stopping at the back door of a low-rise peach rendered home.

Having received a phone call earlier from a hysterical Lucinda, Meira angrily paced the floor, waiting for her son to arrive with one half of the Soul-mates.

Landing at the back door, his feet barely touched the ground, when Meira ran out of the back door, slapping him across the face, "Idiot son. What have you done?"

More concerned for Pagan's welfare, Dante ignored his mother.

Untying the rope, he dismounted carrying Pagan immediately inside the house and down the hallway to his childhood bedroom, where he laid her, limp and icy cold body, on the single mattress bed.

Pushing Dante out of her way, Meira placed her palm on Pagan's forehead.

Grabbing Dante's chin, her eyes burned from fury, "She is not yours to play games with Dante. This Maiden is dying, now go and fetch me my herbs and crystals from the cabinet while I ring the Coven."

Dante panicked. Death was not an option.

Rushing, Meira accidently dialled the wrong phone number, calling random strangers who she quickly slammed the phone down on. Breathing deeply, she settled her nerves. Dialling the correct phone numbers, she reached eleven members of her coven, one she did not call.

Since Aggie had righteously crowned herself Supreme Femineity, she had enforced a law that made it illegal for thirteen Witches to gather as a Coven. In laymen's terms, Aggie had stripped the Coven of its full Magickal power. Without thirteen Witches, the Coven was redundant.

Travelling from all directions across Tel Aviv and Jaffa, the eleven Ancient Crones arrived within hours, cloaked and flustered. With emergency ointments and spell books in their carry bags, they poked and jabbed their non-responsive patient while deciding which treatment was best. Finally, they agreed that it was too dangerous to use Ancient methods, opting for the safer option: intention and Meira's first aid kit.

Requesting Dante to leave the room, he was shoved out into the hallway with only his guilt to keep him company. Showering and eating, he waited three hours before his mother opened the bedroom door. Twelve fatigued Crones exited.

Meira looked at her son, "Go to her. We have tried our best."

Hesitating, Dante lingered at the bedroom door, afraid of what he might find once he entered.

The bedroom was lit up with an assortment of coloured candles. The floor was covered in fresh herbs, a sea salt pentagram symbol that had been sprinkling around the single bed, and an ancient symbol that was painted on the wall directly behind the bedhead.

Hastening to Pagan's side, he was shocked by how pale she was; if in deed she was even breathing.

Sitting down on the mattress beside her, he pushed her sweat-drenched hair from her sticky forehead. Picking up the towel that was left on the floor by the Coven, he gently patted it across her face. New beads of sweat reappeared moments later.

Dante had never noticed how perfect, Little Witch's side profile was; high cheek bones, long forehead and a wobbly chin.

"You will grow up to be an intensely stunning, Little Witch."

Pausing, as if he was stung in the chest by a bee, he fretted, "If you make it?"

Pulling the blanket back, he was surprised that the Coven had undressed her. The candle light flickered across her body. A pool of sweat gathered in her belly button.

Scanning her naked body, he was overcome with grief. She was perfect in her youth.

Crawling into the bed beside her, he wrapped her tiny body up into his. They slept.

Dante

"Ima, please come sit with me. I've made you a coffee."

Meira dropped the dog brush onto the ground, frightening not only Lily, the Canaan dog, but herself.

"Dante, I am still angry with you!"

"Please, Ima, please I am your son. I am only here for a few days. Join me. Plus, you spend too much of your time on that bitch. You forget that you need human interaction."

Sitting down, her hips stiffened and it took her three wiggles before finding comfort on the balcony chair, "I trust Lily, which is more than I can say for humans."

Dante gazed at the house across the street, where a 'once loved' creeper, seeded in a small basket that overhung the balcony, was now left to grow wild, covering most of the external front wall. The front door was almost lost behind its foliage.

"Humans just need guidance, Ima."

"As does my son," she chuckled, sipping a large mouthful of coffee. The effect of the caffeine kicked in immediately, making her feel giddy and through a drug induced high, she forgave her son for bringing danger to her doorstep.

Dante studied his mother. Elderly, she could still fight a lion and win, however her pride left her lonely and her past encouraged a self-eluding protection from human intimacy.

"Ima, you should be growing old with someone. Someone special. You live in a young city; a city of young ideas and fresh emotions. Why not warm your body beside someone at night?"

"I could say the same for you, Dante, but I forget that you warm your body most nights."

Reaching her hand out, she patted Dante on the hand, "I've known great love, Dante, this life time it was with your father and in the next, ha, I can only imagine."

"I just worry about you. I am gone so often."

Indignant, Meira stood up, "I've lived many lives without you, Dante. Don't patronise me with your antics. Remember, it was I, who changed your diaper."

Taking another sip of her coffee, she ran her fingers down Dante's face, eventually tugging on his hair, "Now go and check on that Maiden. She is healing quickly and should be ready to fly soon."

Closing his eyes, Dante absorbed the sun's warmth. His eyelids burned.

Probing his thoughts, he defiantly replied, "I don't want to deliver her to Aggie."

Meira gasped, "You must take her to them as soon as you can, Dante, and you must never speak a word of her being here, we used a Reflective spell but they might already know that she has been ill."

Tongue-tied and depressed, Dante sipped his coffee.

"Tell me you don't care for this Maiden? She will never be yours Dante. She is a Soul-mate and once Awakened there will be blood and I'll be damned if I'll allow your blood to be spilled for Witch stupidity. If you don't deliver this Maiden, Aggie will label you a traitor and sentence you to death. Dante, her fate has nothing to do with you! Your part in this situation is to deliver her."

Dante refused to interact in the conversation. His only act of insubordination was his silence.

"Dante, you don't even know this Maiden. She doesn't even know herself yet. You are trying to fill a void son but not with this Maiden. Find another."

"I'll never find, another."

Sitting back down, Meira called Lily, who obediently sat at her owner's feet. Stroking Lily's thick creamy coat, Meira lightened, "Perhaps, you are right,

Dante, maybe I do need to see more of the city. It grows and changes so fast I can't keep up."

The balcony door creaked. Surprised, they turned to see Pagan standing at the door. Pale and shaking, she still managed to smile.

"I think it's time for me to go now."

Dante sadly turned and looked at the creeper across the street.

CHAPTER 17
Pagan

"Adios Pagan," Lucinda squealed.

Lucinda's face expressed both melancholy and cheerfulness, making Pagan feel uneasy, however she waved goodbye enthusiastically.

Holding onto Dante's waist, Pagan snuggled into his leather jacket. Her feet entwined around his ankles and her head rested on his shoulder blade. His scent, once making her feel unwell, now soothed her like a baby blanket. It would be the last time she would fly with her Bounty and weirdly, she missed him already.

Deliberately flying over the Eiffel Tower in Paris, France, circling it several times, Pagan giggled, forgetting for a moment that Dante was delivering her to Aggie.

She had seen, like a bird, the world from above; its depths, valleys, cities, textures, smells, sunrises and sunsets. Although scared of what she was flying into, she was mentally ready to face this woman called, Aggie.

The journey had challenged her, broke her and made her stronger and along the way, she had laughed. Laughed so hard she thought her stomach would burst and cried so much she thought her eyes would pop straight out of her head. Aggie had brought her happiness and sadness already, what more could she do?

Once they reached the English Channel, Pagan pulled out a blindfold from Dante's jacket pocket, previously put in there with an explanation as to why. Tying it around her head, her eyes fought the restriction.

Aggie had instructed Dante to keep the Crone Monarchy location a secret and in fear of putting Dante in danger, she did as he asked. Blindfolded, she sensed Dante was baulking as he approached.

Smelling his endorphins increasing and his body stiffen, she squeezed his upper thigh, encouraging him to finish the journey. She was resigned to her fate. Like an exam, she just wanted it over.

Feeling the broomstick tilt, Pagan braced herself for a blindfolded landing. Ten minutes later, they landed.

Pulling the blindfold off and poking it back into Dante's jacket, she jumped off the broomstick. The street was covered in thick fog. It was just how she had imagined London to be; Dirty, grey and foggy. She loved it.

"And to think you've brought me to a church."

"It's a cathedral, Little Witch."

At first, she released a giggle which quickly evolved into a frenzied cackle.

Dante waited until her moment of hysteria was over. Amused by her reaction, he wondered if he should comfort her. Her mania soon turned to a silent reflection.

"It is the strangest thing, Dante, I feel like I've been here before. Do you believe in Déjà vu? It's like a distant dream."

"When you are Awakened, you will remember everything, Little Witch. I will become very small, as you remember millennium."

"How sad, Dante. How sad that someone who is so big to me, who kidnapped me and forced me on a journey, would become so small. I don't believe it."

Pagan turned to Dante, a cold shiver fell through her body. She finally realised why he never called her by her name. A person, who has no name, is only an object. He was protecting his own feelings by objectifying her. In his mind, he was dropping off a parcel.

Dante unbuttoned three buttons of his shirt, removing a dull grey necklace from around his neck. A round amulet dangled from it. Silver, a large moon shaped amethyst sat in the middle surrounded by symbols. Pagan had not noticed him wearing it. He must have just put it on for their last journey, Pagan decided.

Dante placed the necklace over Pagan's head. The amulet dangled in between her breasts.

"This was my father's gift to my mother. She gave it to me and now, I'm giving it to you. It's a Moon Guard. It will protect you."

Before Pagan could thank Dante, he knocked on the large Cathedral doors, "Delivery!"

Mounting the broomstick, Dante vanished into the fog. Without a word, he left her, alone.

Rubbing her finger over the amulet, she decided to hide it under her jumper.

Movement behind the door made her jump. The handle turned clockwise. Fear suffocated her. It took a few blinks for her eyes to adjust, "Thomas!"

Throwing her arms around him, a mixture of joy and relief, reduced her to tears. Innocently, it took her a while to acknowledge that Thomas had not returned her affection.

Stepping backwards, she looked at Thomas. It was if all the unanswered questions of her childhood smashed her into adulthood.

She slapped his cheek, "You backstabbing, prick!"

Not content, she slapped him again. Still, he did not react. Her aggression no longer affected him.

Licking the blood from his cut lip, he calmly spoke, "The Crone Monarchy want to see you now, Pagan. You are four days late."

"Backstabbing cunt."

"Charming," he replied matter-of-factly.

Thomas led Pagan through the Cathedral. The holy ambience was overwhelming and the irony was not lost on her. Limited moonlight shone through the decorated glass windows, giving an empowering sense of cosmos. Modern lighting features lit the walkway, and large renaissance paintings of Jesus and his mother, the Virgin Mary hung intimidatingly on the white walls.

Walking in silence, Pagan followed Thomas through a maze of rooms until they reached a downward spiral staircase. Was Thomas taking her to an underground train station? After walking down the stairwell, they reached a metal locked door. Thomas produced a set of keys from his trousers, unlocking the door.

"No one will ever find you down here," Thomas threatened.

Entering a round tiled tunnel, the air was stifling hot and she struggled to breathe.

Thomas ignored her discomfort.

Next, they entered a large hall. Standing ten metres high and thirty metres long, the glossy white tile floor and starch white walls and ceiling, exaggerated the room's actual size, but even still, Pagan wondered how a room of this size could be underground and not have it collapse under its own weight.

"What is this room?"

Thomas retorted, "Heaven."

Shocked, Pagan scanned the room again.

"You're so gullible," he snarled, enjoying his power.

Stopping at an old mahogany door, Thomas knocked twice. The door opened instantly and to Pagan's surprise Thomas' father greeted her by wrapping his arms around her.

"I can't believe, I've just flown across the world to be greeted by you, Mr Crabtree."

Slouching against the opposite wall, Thomas limited his eye contact with Pagan, preferring to stare at the floor.

Pagan stared at him, eager for him to show any sign of weakness or guilt. He disappointed her.

Mr Crabtree held Pagan's hand, occasionally rubbing his thumb over her knuckles to reassure her. It only added to her anxiety.

"Pagan, you are about to be presented to the Crone Monarchy. It would be wise not to antagonise them. It's in your best interest to be agreeable."

Three loud thuds from inside the Crone Monarchy's room indicated they were ready. For the first time in her life, she could smell her own fear.

Pagan

The aroma of sandalwood and jasmine drifted around the small circular room, mind-altering Pagan into a heightened reality.

Black walls, contrasted the blood red carpet, while laser lights flickered onto the walls, changing from red, blue and white every few flashes, forming ghostly images.

Hundreds of large twisting tree roots completed the ceiling. The roots looked as if they were breathing, and bugs buzzed within them.

Why anyone would want to sit in this room, baffled Pagan.

Thrones positioned against the wall, formed a thirteen digit clock. Stiffly, Pagan stood between the numbers six and seven.

The thrones were decorated with hundreds of sparkling stones; emeralds, bloodstones, jades, opals, pearls, onyx, sapphires, ruby, diamonds and agates. Each throne could feed the entire population of a third world country. This angered Pagan.

Blushing, Pagan realised that all the women in the room were naked.

Determined to be strong, she refused to drop her gaze.

Breasts that appeared to have an independent sovereignty of their own; heavy and sagging, as if they yearned for someone to hold them; firm and erect, as if they were a lone soldier searching for their regiment; skinful piles of malnutrition; and, or, beanbags- joyous and playful, ready for adventure. And nipples; fierce or bleak; tanned, flushed or pale, judging, pointing, and speaking: paranoid and rude.

Counting eleven women (Crones), Pagan wondered if another two would join them as two thrones were empty. Ten of the women were very old; leathered and worn out, except for one woman who seemed at least twenty years younger than the rest. Pagan wondered if she was Aggie as she also sat upon a very polished golden throne.

What they did all have in common was a small smudged blue tattoo of a triangle, without a bottom line, likened to an arrowhead, pointing towards the ceiling, hidden in various places on their bodies. Looking at the tattoos made the women wiggle uncomfortably on their seats, except for Aggie who sat firmly upon her throne.

Turning to face Aggie, they locked eyes.

Pagan refused to break the stare, even daring to walk towards her sitting opponent. Estimating that Aggie was barely five foot tall, Pagan felt empowered.

"Yes Maiden, keep walking towards me."

Now that Pagan had been summoned to walk to Aggie, her bravery quickly dispersed.

"Hurry," Aggie commanded in a low tone.

Another five steps found Pagan in arms reach of Aggie, who smelt familiar.

The other women were not humble in their curiosity as their eyes scaled all of her body, diminishing any self-worth Pagan had.

Reaching out, Aggie ran her hands through Pagan's hair, tugging it to pull her closer. Leaning in, she sniffed Pagan's hair. Satisfied, she let her go.

Aggie sat back on her throne, readjusting her petite bottom.

The wiggling had exposed her plump genital area. Pagan strategically ignored the view, focusing on Aggie's badly painted red lips instead.

"I hope you've enjoyed your journey from Australia? I'm sure Dante would have looked after all your needs. Not all of them, I hope."

Several of the women sniggered. Pagan knew that they were referring to Dante's sexual exploits. Defensive of Dante, Pagan frowned.

Aggie waited until the sniggers stopped before she commenced speaking again, "I have brought you to London because I believe it is in my best interest to have you Awakened here, where I can control it."

Pagan replied, "I don't know what an Awakening is."

An eruption of laughter echoed around the room. Pagan covered her ears until they stopped.

Aggie continued, "How rude of me, Pagan, I haven't introduced you to my Crone Monarchy."

Sensing sarcasm in her voice, Pagan wondered if Aggie actually liked, let alone respected any of the other women sitting in the room.

"Crone meaning *old* Witch?" Pagan asked naively.

Displeased, Aggie curled her lip, "Crone as *wise* Witch. I suggest you remain quiet until I have finished introducing them to you."

Pagan glanced around the room. Each Crone looked as if she wanted to tear the flesh from Pagan's bones.

Unaware that she did not have a choice in the first place, Pagan submissively agreed by nodding her head.

"I am the Supreme Femineity and these are my disciples."

Brushing her fringe back from her forehead, Aggie turned left, "This is Handrel."

Handrel sat on the white throne with the word 'Psychic' engraved at the top. Short white hair, shaping a strong firm face, she looked more like a man than a Crone, and someone who would prefer to be playing golf than sitting in an underground cave.

"Next is, Titania."

Titania sat on the bloodstone red throne with the word 'Life Force' engraved in it. She reminded Pagan of Margaret Thatcher with her perfectly rolled hair. Unlike the other Crones, she wore heavy make-up and an upside down smile.

"Helia, next."

Sitting on the baby pink throne with the word 'Love'. Helia wore a scarf wrapped on her head but her heavily wrinkled face made her unlikable.

Pagan studied the word 'love' and strangely she thought of Dante.

Unconsciously, Pagan lifted her hand to touch the amulet through her jumper.

"Seated next to Helia, is Rosamond."

On the burnt orange throne which was engraved with the word 'Communication' sat a very tall slender Crone with long white dreadlocks, piled on top of her head. With hand on chin, she browsed Pagan as if she was selecting a book from the library.

Bored already, Aggie snapped, "Llona!"

Llona sat with one leg swinging over the arm of the throne, exposing her shaven pubic hair area. On the peat brown throne the word engraved was 'Protection'. Agitated, Llona looked like a Crone who would punch you in the face just to relieve some of the aggression she held in her body.

"Loreena."

Loreena sat crossed legged, and although she was the same age as the other Crones, she had soft unwrinkled skin and delicate silver earrings that hung from tiny ears. Pagan instantly gravitated to this Crone, especially as she sat on a canary yellow throne, engraved with the word 'Mind'. Yellow was Pagan's favourite colour.

"Next is, Morag."

Morag reminded Pagan of a horse or someone who preferred to spend time with animals, because animals are easily controlled unlike humans. She had small pocky breasts and a 'six pack' stomach. Morag sat on a moss green throne with the word 'Prosperity and Fertility' engraved on it. Morag certainly did not look like the motherly type.

Pagan thought the Crones were poorly matched to their thrones. Probably a ploy by the Supreme Femineity to weaken the competition by keeping them in chaos? Surely, an organisation would run better if everyone was suited to their positions?

Next, Aggie introduced Maeva who was so elderly that her body jumped randomly. Pagan was relieved that she was not paired up to play the board game 'Operation' with Maeva which requires a still hand. Slumped in the cobalt blue throne with the word 'Healing' engraved on it, Pagan though she was in desperate need of some.

"Number nine is, Siobhon."

Pagan acknowledged that Aggie had referred to her disciple as a number.

Siobhon sat on the vibrant purple throne with the word 'Strength' engraved on it. Siobhon looked like a secretary stereotype, wearing thick reading glasses and a permanent squint from administration work. She moved on her chair nervously.

"Last is, Eveline."

Rotund, Eveline's fat stomach hung over the sides of her Black throne, reminding Pagan of Fat Alex in India. The word 'Death' engraved on it. Pagan shuddered.

The Bronze throne was empty with the word 'Worship' engraved on it.

Aggie raised her voice, pointing at the empty throne next to her, "And this throne is also empty as a reminder to me to never to trust anyone."

'Wow, everyone has trust issues', Pagan thought.

Erupting into laughter, Aggie added, "Goddess knows, we can't even trust ourselves."

Pagan stared at the silver throne with the word 'Betrayal' newly engraved on it and wondered what word they had erased to have replaced it with such a vengeful word.

Aggie sat back on her throne, "It's fitting that you should end up living on the continent that you helped conquer. I love the irony of reincarnation and karma. Proves the Goddesses have a sense of humour."

Pagan remembered the vision of her dying on a platform, losing her head and seeing it fall into a bucket of blood before a soldier pulled it out to hold it up for the entire crowd to see, a crowd that cheered and clapped with joy.

She remembered Rogan.

The room suddenly felt excessively hot and Pagan collapsed.

Aggie raised one eyebrow, "Oh dear, we have a fainter, and I was just getting started."

CHAPTER 18
Pagan

Her hand instantly reached for her neck. The pain travelled from her right shoulder to the top of her head. Her eyes were stuck together from dried gunk and after several failed attempts, Pagan finally forced her eyes open.

She was in a dimly lit room, laying on a large king sized bed. Her head rested uncomfortably on the pillows. The bedspread was dark purple and the stiff sheets had been starched white as if they were used often for such bed rest.

Art equipment; easels, paint brushes, paint tins, half started canvases and rolls of paper accompanied by hundreds of books monopolised the circular room.

Hundreds of acrylic paintings and faded charcoal drawings covered the walls as if a 'lovesick' teenager had plastered their teen idol on their bedroom wall, despite her parent's disapproval.

Further study of the paintings revealed that only one man was the subject of the artist's obsession, a muse!

The ceiling was made up of glass panels- a window ceiling showing a snippet of the night sky, through dense tree branches and leaves.

Pagan panicked. There were no doors or windows.

Pulling herself up slowly, her hand automatically cupped the back of her head where she discovered a dried blood clot packed with a concoction of herbs.

A glass of water sat on the bedside table. Taking a sip, she swirled the stale water around in her mouth, spitting it back into the glass, just in case, it was poisoned.

Gently laying her head back on the pillow, she fell asleep holding onto the amulet, which still hung around her neck.

When she woke again, for a moment, Pagan forgot where she was.

Comforted by the sunlight shining down on her face and the branches from the tree tops scratching the glass ceiling, she could have happily gone back to sleep.

She bolted up. Pushing the doona cover off her and pulling up a ghastly black nightie to her waist, she checked the bruises on her inner thighs. The bruises were still prominent but were now a mottled pink and mustard colour rather than the dark purple they had been when Dante dropped her off. She calculated that she must have slept for a few days.

Looking around the room, Pagan concluded that there was definitely no entrance into the room and therefore no escape.

She shuffled to the edge of the bed. Her legs were weak and it took a few steps before she stabilised.

"Get back into bed, Maiden. You need to rest."

Snapping her head to the side, Pagan was confronted by a woman with a Scottish accent, standing only metres away from her. The woman quickly tucked Pagan back into bed and then produced a large bowl of pea and ham soup and a cup of hot, Milo, on a tray.

"We ordered the Milo for you especially. All the way from Australia you know?"

Hungry, Pagan hesitated.

"I'll assure you, Maiden, that I will not harm you. It's my duty to make sure you are healthy for your Witch Awakening."

Pagan studied her with caution, "Are you a Witch?"

"Yes. Well no. I'm a Crone."

"Then how can I trust you?"

The voluptuous Crone looked up towards the ceiling as she thought about her response. Her delicate hands, curled her artificially bright red hair.

"Well, I suppose you can trust me as much as you can trust."

Pagan screwed her face up, confused.

"You can't break trust. Someone can break loyalty, but trust isn't broken. You can decide to trust fully, even if they do not change their behaviour or refuse to say sorry. Understand?"

Pagan shook her head. She had no idea what the Crone meant?

"When is a Witch considered a Crone?"

"I suppose when a Witch feels wise, or old. You feel it- the transition. Of course there is menopause but it's more than that. A deepening of mind over matter. It's freedom. A letting go."

"Sounds like heaven."

"No! Heaven is not freedom. It's very judgemental up there."

Pagan released a surprised giggle that pulled on her drying wound.

"Eat," the Crone demanded.

Famished, she ushered to the Crone to place the tray on her lap. Picking up the spoon, she snuck another look at the Crone before plunging into the bowl of soup. Within minutes, she had finished the soup and drunk the Milo.

The Crone grabbed the bowl and cup, placing them on the bedside table.

"Now. Time for a wash," she said excitedly, producing a bucket from underneath the bed.

Frigid, Pagan replied, "I think, I am more than capable of washing myself."

"I've been washing you for the past three days. One more time won't hurt, will it? Now I'll just go and grab some hot water."

"Why don't you just use your wand to fill the bucket, since you're a Crone?"

Raising her hand to her forehead the Crone flushed, "You sure know how to insult, don't you. I'm an Ancient! We don't use wands."

Indignantly, Pagan crossed her arm, "Oh really. That's just an excuse."

The Crone winked at Pagan.

Placing the bucket on the bed, palm down, she swirled her hand in a clockwise circle until the bucket filled up with warm soapy water.

"It's all about intent," she winked.

Dumbfounded, Pagan placed a finger into the water. It burnt, "Holy shit, that's cool! Hot, oh you know what I mean."

"Ha! And I wasn't even showing off. Of Course, it's nothing like what you can do."

Surprised and proud, Pagan smiled, "Really?"

"Absolutely."

"What is your name?"

"Jaide."

"Am I an Ancient, is this why I'm hated?"

"Hate is such a strong word. I could sit here and explain but once you're Awakened you will remember. How about you enjoy your Innocence? You won't be Innocent for long."

Flooded with memories of *this* life, Pagan sighed, "I don't feel innocent."

Pagan

The cool breeze massaged her face. She felt free.

Laughter howled above the town.

Flying above the roof tops, peering into stranger's homes through their curtains, her voyeuristic tendencies were fulfilled.

She responded by wrapping her arms tightly around Dante's waist and diving her nose into his long hair.

Nude, she wrapped her legs around his. Her breasts pressed against his broad back.

Dante reached back, rubbing his large square hand over her thigh. His rough palm made its way slowly towards her wet vagina.

She grabbed his hand, placing it between her legs, "I want you, Dante."

Kissing his neck, she tasted his spicy skin on her lips.

Gently, she started to grind her groin against his back. Back and forth, she rubbed her clitoris onto his hand until her vagina tingled and pulsed.

Sucking on his neck, the bitter taste of his blood ran down the back of her throat.

Turning his head, Dante kissed her. Mouth to mouth, they found each other.

Free to be together, Dante stroked her hair, "I miss you, Little Witch."

Pagan could feel his lips on her lips, his hips on her hips and his hands on her hands. It felt so real that she thought Dante was really in the room with her.

Fluctuating between a lucid dream and wide-awake, she pleaded to go back to sleep in case he disappeared.

"You feel so good, Dante! Please. I want you."

Pulling him closer, she opened her legs, willing him to enter her. Running her fingers down his back, his soft skin bristled as if it was blistering from an intense heat.

Inhaling, he smelt metallic.

Fearful that he was disappearing, she kissed him harder, "Don't leave me."

His sweet taste turned bitter.

Opening her eyes, she shuddered.

Paralysed with fear, she tried to scream but it covered her mouth. An entity pinned her down. Its long fingernails piercing her skin. Her blood bubbled.

Wide eyed, Pagan struggled underneath it. Its vile breath discharged from his large toothless mouth, blanketing her face. An elongated jaw rubbed against her chin as the monster kissed her.

She closed her eyes.

This isn't real. This isn't real. This is a dream. This is a dream. Wake up. Wake up. Wake up.

The monsters long toe nails hooked her skin while its knees bruised her thighs.

Out of desperation, she grabbed at its hair to only discover it was bald.

Fiercely, she punched at its head, and screamed, "Noooooo!"

It stopped, as if it had suddenly woken from a trance.

Too frightened to open her eyes, she was surprised to hear the monster whisper, "Sorry," before it vanished.

Pagan

Alarmed, Jaide sat down on the edge of the bed. Twirling her hair while in deep thought, she considered what she should do next.

Unsatisfied with Pagan's answers, she questioned her further, "But why did it just stop?"

Pagan shrugged, "It just stopped and disappeared as if it somehow it knew what it was doing was wrong. I could feel it pull away as if it was horrified by what it was doing. It didn't have a face but it did. It felt like melted wax. It's hard to explain."

It sounded like the Darkness.

Jaide had arrived to find Pagan fast asleep in the morning, wrapped up in the doona cover, her head hidden underneath the covers.

"Thank goodness it's you, Jaide. I've had the craziest dream."

While eating breakfast, Pagan animatedly told Jaide about the monster that had pinned her down, strategically leaving out the details of the sexual assault and that she had fantasised about Dante prior.

Looking intently into Pagan's eyes, Jaide's concerns deepened. Suspecting the Maiden was skimming over parts, she decided to leave her for a while to contemplate what to do for the best.

"It is odd. I suspect it was just a bad dream. They can feel very real sometimes. Especially after the emotional trauma you've experienced the last few months. Your mind is probably just playing tricks on you."

Collecting the empty breakfast bowl and mug, Jaide patted Pagan on the top of her head. Moments later, she vanished through the wall.

Pagan waited a few minutes before jumping out of bed to examine the area that Jaide disappeared through. It was a solid wall.

Frustrated, she scaled the bookshelf closest to her. It was sturdy and would easily support her weight.

Climbing up five shelves, she had reached the top. Pushing on the glass ceiling with one hand while holding the bookshelf with the other the ceiling did not budge.

"Shit!"

She pushed on it again, still nothing. Climbing up another shelf, Pagan squashed her face against the glass and peered out. All she could see were tree branches and thick leaves of all variety. Was she in a forest or a large garden?

"Do you really think you can escape from this room?"

Nearly toppling off the bookshelf, she scurried down. Standing upright, she crossed her arms and frowned, "What do you want, Thom-arse?"

Smug, Thomas sat on the bed. He straightened out the doona cover, "You will refer to me as, Aquarius or not refer to me at all."

Pagan fought the urge to punch him in the face. He had betrayed her, lied to her and now he was dictating how she was to refer to him. He still looked like her best friend, the boy she had protected from Carl's bullying only years earlier. His hair still long and silky, thick glasses still a prominent feature on his delicate face but now he was much taller, standing at least six foot and five inches and seemed older. His face had paled and dark purple rings highlighted his comatose eyes.

Aquarius took a long patronising inhale, "I've heard you had a visitor last night."

Pagan angered, now Jaide had betrayed her. Gossip certainly travelled fast.

"It was a dream," she bluntly stated.

"Quite a vivid one, I hear. Would you like to tell me about this dream?"

"No!"

Aquarius sat back a little on the bed, searching for another angle to tackle her stubbornness. He knew that Pagan would be difficult, she always was. He decided on emotional manipulation, "Look Pagan, this is my job. I've been training for this position my whole life, not a choice. The job requires me to perform tasks that I don't necessarily want to do. It doesn't change my feelings for you and to be honest, what we think visited you last night is more dangerous than any Witch."

Using his new name as ammunition, Pagan quickly interrupted his speech, "Get fucked, Aquarius!"

She leaned in closer to him, "You smell of bullshit."

She laughed, "Get fucked, Aquarius. Has a nice ring to it."

Bored with her attitude, Aquarius retorted, "Short version, Pagan, the Crone Monarchy have a Protection spell on this room and someone managed to get 'in and out' without detection. This is a major concern. We can't risk you escaping. The Crone Monarchy has decided to move your Witch Awakening to tonight."

Pagan laughed, "You mean the 'Supreme Femineity' decided."

Aquarius grinned, "Regardless who decided. It's tonight."

Aquarius stood up, "You'll need that spirited personality of yours to survive it. Oh and by the way," pulling a book out from his back pocket, he threw it on the bed, "Happy early birthday! All the time, I spent educating you on books, you were already an author."

Pagan read the authors name, 'Olympe de Gouges'.

Aquarius smirked, "A good book. You should be proud. The advantage of being a famous and dangerous Witch means everyone but you knows who you are, well before, your Witch Awakening."

"Huh!"

"You wrote that. Looks like you've 'always' been a feisty, Witch."

Mr Baker

His secretary rescheduled his clients' appointments at short notice. It had been messy but she managed to juggle his busy schedule with limited fuss. He would buy her a pretty frock or something shiny in appreciation for her ability to handle high stress situations.

By mid-morning, he had picked up his own dry-cleaning- a novelty, collected the parcel that had been especially sent to him personally by Aggie, organised a chauffeur to have him picked up at noon, and booked a hotel room; the one he always used.

The receptionist from the hotel recognised his voice, "Same room, Mr Baker?"

He had to admit that the phone call had pleased him. The hotel staff always treated him well. Money assured that!

The Witch Awakening had been rescheduled for tonight, two weeks early. It had cost five hundred thousand pounds upfront in booking fees and another five hundred thousand pounds prior to the ceremony. Refunds were not offered. Customer service guaranteed. He had transferred the remainder of the money promptly ten minutes after the phone call. This Maiden must be exceptional to cost ten times more than any other.

His penis hardened. Organised rape made him so fucking horny.

Placing the leather box on his office table, he opened it. A black cloak was neatly folded inside and a red mask sat beside it. He ran his hand over the fabric, the softness aroused his soft skin. A note sat on top. It read, "Kind Regards."

Pulling the full face mask out, he positioned it over his face. Tying the two pieces of ribbon behind his head, his eyes stared out of the small holes. Facing the mirror, his heartbeat increased and his pupils dilated, "I can't wait to hear you scream, Maiden. I'm going to tear you apart."

Pagan

Carrying a long standing mirror, Jaide placed it against the wall. Balancing it in the circular room took some manipulation but she was stubborn and found a way.

Politely asking Pagan to undress, she handed her a scarlet crushed velvet ceremonial gown that the Supreme Femineity had chosen personally for her.

Undressing, Pagan threw her clothes disrespectfully onto the floor.

Ignoring the eye roll from Jaide, she walked to the mirror. Standing naked in front of the mirror, she glanced over her body. Her body had changed. Her hips were widening and her breast had grown a full cup size. She was growing up and quickly. The bruises on the inside of her thighs were nearly gone as were the memories of her home. She had changed both internally and externally. Life would not be the same again.

Whatever Aggie had planned, she was ready for.

"Put the gown on, Pagan. Can't have you catching a cold?"

Feeling comfortable in her nudity, except for the amulet that decorated her cleavage, Pagan attributed her new found esteem to Lucinda.

'We are who we meet,' Pagan decided.

She stared at the gown, why could they not simply buy clothing from a normal shop rather than the medieval shop?

"Oh Jaide, it's hideous."

The gown buttoned at the front as if it was a dressing gown.

Once buttoned, Pagan suddenly felt very nervous.

"Is the Witch Awakening like a party?"

Jaide stiffened, "Not really."

Using a fine tooth comb, Jaide brushed Pagan's long black hair, lastly brushing the scraggly pieces off her face, "Can't have a beautiful, Maiden, like you hiding behind that hair of yours, can we?"

Pagan had never thought of herself as beautiful. She certainly had never been told she was beautiful, accept from Lucinda. She liked that Lucinda encouraged other women to feel beautiful. She had always been a stick-figure with a long face, a face that kids from school had called a 'horse face' while taunting her on the school bus.

Suddenly remembering that their time was limited, Pagan turned to Jaide, "Who is the man in the paintings?"

Jaide stopped to look at the paintings, "Not sure, Love. Do you recognise him?"

Pagan walked over to the charcoal drawing of him on the aisle, "No. I don't know this man. The artist was certainly obsessed with him."

"It's best to concentrate on the present, I find. Now Maiden, march on over to the bed and eat the roast I made for you."

Pagan turned to Jaide, "I'm sorry, but I don't feel like eating. I'm too nervous."

It was Jaide's turn to smile, "I thought you might say that, so I've brought you some wine instead. An early birthday drink."

Pagan would turn eighteen in two weeks but she hankered for the warm buzz of alcohol on her lips.

Sitting on the bed, Jaide opened up a leather flask, handing it to Pagan. The wine tasted woody.

"Merlot?"

Jaide frowned, a facial declaration that she had betrayed Pagan, "Yes, with a sprinkle of sleeping herbs."

Feeling a heaviness creep through her body, Pagan collapsed on the bed, asleep.

Hidden amongst the mass foliage of garden that surrounded the room, a van idled outside. The driver hopped out of the front seat of the van and walked over to the oak tree, unzipped his trouser and urinated, outlining a figure eight for amusement. Zipping his trousers back up, he walked to the back of the van, opening up the double doors.

He was tired of night shift. He wanted a normal job with normal hours and to work for normal people. A job, he could tell his mates about at his local pub, but no, he had to work for a bunch of Witches.

Remorseful, Jaide wrapped the sleeping Maiden up into a blanket and with a twist of her hand, Magickally lifted Pagan into the air. Placing her palms underneath her torso, they left the building through the wall.

Hearing the usual thud of a Witch landing behind him, the driver greeted her, "Evening, Jaide."

"Help me put her onto the bed, Sam!"

He stepped up into the back of the van to help Jaide position the prisoner.

As far as he was concerned, 'Witches business was Witches business'.

He had been instructed to take 'extra care' with this Maiden but he intended to treat the prisoner the same as he had treated the other prisoners. If they wanted extra care they could pay for it.

Tightening the straps across the prisoner's torso, he gave an additional tug, pinching her skin through the gown and blanket. Pleased with his interpretation of 'extra care', he jumped out of the van allowing Jaide to step up into the back.

Jaide peered back at Sam, "Sam!"

"Yes."

"You're an arsehole."

Sam stopped and with only the effort of a half-smile, he replied, "Well, I guess that makes two of us."

Aggie had also given Jaide instructions to stay with the Maiden at all times during the journey. It was not wise to disobey Aggie.

Slamming the doors shut, she sat down on a stool beside Pagan and laughed, however as the engine started up, Jaide's anxiety increased.

From the safety of the van, Jaide unbuttoned Pagan's gown, only a few top buttons were needed to look at the neckless. Jaide had discovered the amulet the first night she had undressed Pagan. Pagan had not attempted to hide it from her and out of respect, she had not questioned her about it.

Jaide touched it with her bony index finger. The amethyst set inside it pulsed at a high frequency. The symbols engraved on it were not Witch symbols.

It was fear of the unknown that Jaide could not find the strength to remove it from Pagan's neck.

Who had given her the amulet? It was for protection, that Jaide was sure of. The Maiden would need all the help she could get.

"From one Ancient Witch to another. I wish you the best, Pagan."

In the beginning, distribution of power did not exist in Witch culture. Over centuries, greed and ego produced a hierarchal Witch society, and after the War, Ancient Witches became monsters to cope with the breakdown of their culture.

Pagan was much older than Jaide in the timeline and was now suffering for the atrocities she had committed in past reincarnations, even before Awakened. Witches certainly did hold grudges.

Jaide thought about her recent past. No-one, how righteous, was free from their past. None of them had chosen retribution, it had chosen them.

Mr Baker

His chauffeur had picked him up precisely at noon. The car rolled along until it stopped directly in front of him. The Chauffeur had quickly exited the driver's seat, putting the car in park and then pulling the handbrake on. Then slipped around the vehicle until he opened the back door for his employer.

Thanking the chauffeur, he slipped into the back seat. He was instantly impressed with the state of the car. The leather seats had been cleaned and additional pillows placed on the seat for his comfort. He would reward his chauffer with a bonus sum of money in his next pay.

Travelling for several hours until they reached the hotel, he poured himself several scotches to relax and ate a variety of fresh fruit. He would need his strength.

Arriving in the village, he was glad to stretch his legs. The chauffeur carried his luggage to the front desk.

"Take the rest of the day off. Spend tonight with your family and be back here promptly at noon tomorrow."

"Yes Sir."

The hotel was humble but the employees were always discrete, never asking him what brought him to their village so often.

The receptionist smiled, "Mr Baker, we have your room ready with complementary scotch and the kitchen has made Green Thai curry, just as you like it."

He winked at her, showering her with male endorphins that made her feel dizzy, "You spoil me."

She blushed, "Well, you are one of our favourite guests, Mr Baker. Would you like me to organise someone to carry your bags to your room?"

"Actually, I'm feeling very energetic today. I will carry my own luggage, thank you."

Walking up two flights of stairs, he entered the hallway. Swaggering to door, he opened it with a key. Walking in, he placed his luggage on the bed and untied his scarf. Clammy, he decided on a shower to freshen up. Masturbating furiously in the shower, he was annoyed to be interrupted by room service.

"Your curry is ready, Sir."

Sam

Sam slid out from the front of the van and opened the back double doors, "We're here."

Untying the straps from around Pagan's torso, he scooped Pagan up into his arms, tossing her up over his right shoulder. It was only for her youth that she flopped over him without causing injury.

The ceremonial gown exposed Pagan's thighs.

Jaide quickly pulled it down, scorning the driver for his brazen behaviour, "Have some respect, Sam."

Jaide watched anxiously as Sam walked up the grassy hillside to the tower, slowing down the further he went until exhaustion fatigued him.

The tower was a ruin now, a modest host chosen specifically for Witch Awakenings because of its connection with the past, and its isolation. The tower had once been Pagan's home in the twelfth century. She had been happy in the tower. It had been a place of happiness, dancing and singing, a mass ceremonial building, now- a torture chamber.

The twenty metre high tower would eventually crumble, becoming rubble, dust and then be forgotten but until then it was a place of organised rape; rape that fetched an ample profit for the Crone Monarchy who cashed in on the fact that their Magick only co-exists with their sexuality.

The ceiling collapsing ten years earlier, allowed the quarter-moon to shine down into the centre of the tower, lighting up the large black raw obsidian altar where Pagan would be laid, tied down, while the Crone Monarchy sat from a partition at the top and watched.

Lanterns lit the other areas.

The driver entered the tower. The old wooden door hung from three rusty hinges.

Pagan moaned, as he knocked her head into the door frame.

Laying her down on the altar, he was relieved that she had not woken.

The altar was positioned in the middle of a large pentagram. When he had first started with the company the pentagram use to scare him. Quickly shuffling into the tower, he would exit as swiftly as he could but now he hardly noticed it.

He secured Pagan to the altar. At the top of the pentagram point, he positioned her head, placing her hands towards the outer top points. Then he latched her wrists via the rope to the bolts. He double checked the rope ties.

He hated his job but he had a mortgage to pay.

Satisfied, he relaxed, "This bitch ain't moving."

Pagan

She woke. The moon illuminated the youthfulness of her seventeen year old body, a body that she was still yet to explore but eager to. Flying across the world had expanded her consciousness. A consciousness that was now keen to discover its own physical host as well as its surroundings.

A slight breeze lifted her gown, a gentle reminder that she was outside, unprotected by a glass ceiling, a ceiling that she had become accustomed to.

As Amelie had told her, "Just flow."

Pagan intended to do just that. The last few month had proven that Amelie's wisdom worked.

"Flow."

She was in a ruin of some sort, a castle perhaps, where aggressively growing ivy claimed sovereignty over the stone wall.

Remembering the amulet, she attempted to pull her hand down to hold it. A rope burnt her wrist instantly, tightening around her bony wrists. Both wrists were tied with rope, rope that was attached to a bolt. She wiggled her wrists but the ropes only tightened causing a hot pain that quickly numbed if she stayed still.

Elevated on a hard surface, she surmised that she had been placed on a rock boulder or altar. Wiggling her toes and then her knees, she felt a strange sensation as if she was completely relaxed from the sleeping herbs but anxious to defend herself from whatever Aggie and the Crone Monarchy had planned for her.

Slowly, her body started to tingle as if every cell in her body was igniting from a foreign heat.

Dante's word resonated with her, "Trust your instincts."

His annoying tests in India and Spain had taught her to trust her instincts, but Pagan still questioned the legitimacy of Dante's teachings.

Was the trained robot inside of her really capable of disobeying the remote? Living outside of the parameters of her creation? Do certain people tap into sealed compartments of the brain that other people skip over, for whatever reason? How many hidden compartments did she have, and can the compartments only be opened from experience and other people? Did she have any control over which doors were opened or was that purely controlled by the society in which she lived? Did people only open in others what they recognise in themselves? How many realities could she have? How many had she missed? Drugs had altered her states of consciousness but was that a compartment opened or a fantasy? Was there a script writer in her head, editing every few minutes to cope with what she was seeing? If she was to marry Rogan would he only ever open one door for her while another million remain closed?

Pagan's trapped physical body, tied and bound to a man-made rope had suddenly opened her mind to a million possibilities and potentials her mind could explore, all because she had only one path now. A path that stole all other paths.

"I will not die tonight. I've come too far to die now! I have too much to experience," she screamed into the night air.

Was she a sacrifice?

She wiggled her wrists again, "Help me. Somebody help me!"

Her voice was alien to her; hoarse and deep. The effects of the sleeping herbs, she suspected.

Jaide winced as Pagan's pleas rolled down the hill like a rock.

Sam ignored Pagan's appeals for help, continuing to eat his cold fish and chips as if he was spending a leisurely day at the seaside.

Scanning the night sky in search for any glimpses of the Crone Monarchy, Jaide looked back at the tower. How had she come to help the Non-Ancients in torturing an Ancient Witch? The Goddesses would surely punish her for the portrayal.

Somewhere in Pagan's subconscious she recognised this place. A memory so wrapped up in docile nodes that she could not retrieve them but her heart recognised the building. Perhaps, this would be to her advantage? Everyone kept telling her that she would remember things after the Witch Awakening. That must be a good thing? It must mean that she would survive.

A little voice in her gut told her that she would not survive. She told that voice to 'shut up'.

The only positive was that she would die in a place where her heart told her that she was home. How could a place on the opposite side of the world feel more homely than where she grew up?

Something moved in the night sky. The glow from the lantern made it hard for Pagan to focus but she sensed that the Crone Monarchy was arriving via their broomsticks.

Why were they so personally invested in her? She was just a girl from Tasmania, an island at the end of the world.

Eleven Witches landed on a partition high above her. Their aging bodies suffering from the uncomfortableness of their broomsticks.

Aggie lead the Crone Monarchy; Handrel, Titania, Helia, Rosamond, LLona, Loreena, Morag, Maeva, Siobhon, and Eveline. Their awkward dismount was evident that they preferred to travel in luxurious motorcars rather than on the stiffness of a Magickal wooden stick. A cliché they would be happy to stamp out.

Wearing different coloured cloaks; peat to dark chocolate brown, burnt orange to blood red, and aubergine to Tokyo purple, and a black rope that tied around their waists, they looked pompous in their ceremonial attire. Another cliché, they could do without.

Jaide had seen the Crone Monarchy enter the tower, only to switch the car radio on, turning the volume up as loud as it would go.

"You won't kill me, Aggie. I won't let you," Pagan bellowed.

The Crone Monarchy ignored her profanities, instead taking their cloaks off and placing them over their broomsticks which leaned against the stone wall.

Once again the Crone Monarchy was united in nudity, a feature that no longer disturbed Pagan.

The Crone Monarchy linked hands, looping a half circle around the tower partition. Their chants echoed down the hill, oblivious to Jaide and Sam who were listening to the nightly news.

The air temperature suddenly dropped and the wind arrived, irritated and threatening, lisping over Pagan in a satanic stutter.

Pagan's eyes darted from one Crone to another who had started to sway in unison. As if in a trance, they seemed to be summoning someone or something.

The chanting became louder and more venomous. They seemed to be calling for an entity to join them using a foreign language; a language that she suddenly understood.

Mr Baker

A Witch driving a black 'stretch' limousine parked outside the hotel. Instructed to not use her horn, she looked for Mr Baker, smiling at him when their eyes meet.

Waiting in the foyer, he stepped outside into the refreshing breeze. Slipping into the backseat, he immediately undressed. He placed his clothes on the seat beside him, neatly folded and in order and preference to how he would dress later once he was back inside the limousine. From bottom to top; jacket, trousers, shirt, and singlet, he was pleased that he was organised and controlled in his manner.

Even as a child, he had been the 'master of his destiny'. His parents had surrendered their parental control over to him at an early age. Money and power were handed to him in a nappy while they focused on their world, checking in occasionally to see how worldly their son had become. The word 'no' rarely uttered to him by his nannies had taught him one thing- that he was in control and women knew their place.

Opening the leather box, he pulled the black cloak out and then the red mask. He suspected the other eight men would be doing the same thing as they drove from their residences.

This virgin Witch was quite a commodity, nine million pounds in fact, once totalled. She must have immense Magick to warrant such a high fee.

221

Jo Green

Participating in over eight Witch Awakenings, he had become accustomed to the manifestation of Magick reuniting with its owner. It was a 'high' like no other, but perhaps tonight, he would witness something else? Perhaps, he would witness one million pounds worth of climax?

He swung the cloak around his shoulder as if he was gallantly preparing to rescue a persecuted Maiden from herself. Tying the buttons together, he pulled the rest of the material around his naked body. The fabric tickled his skin. Then as if he was now free to do as he pleased, he positioned the mask over his face. Now, he was the face of 'all men' but unlike them, he was in a position to get away with it.

The limousine pulled up half an hour later at the bottom of the hill. The mere sight of the tower excited him, visual porn for the measured pervert.

In a quiet single-file line, he hiked up the slippery hillside with the other eight men; nine the perfect number for the power of three. The perfect balanced number for casting spells. He wondered how powerful a spell would be cast if all thirteen Crones were there.

In their ignorance, the Crone Monarchs were enlightening him to the sacred teachings of Witchcraft, and he had a diary filled with what he had learned.

He pulled the hood of the cloak over his head. Now, he was no one, but somehow, everyone.

Pagan

Pagan knew straightaway that the masked men were going to rape her, all nine of them. Screaming and kicking did little to rattle them as they seemed unaffected by her theatrics, if not aroused by them.

Pagan screamed again, a primal plea as if she was summoning a voice unbeknown to her; a stronger and wiser voice, a fearful and innate voice. She knew her cries were unheard by anyone who would help her and that any attempt to escape was futile, but she had to try.

Forming a semi-circle around her, their cloaked bodies stood only a body's length away from her. Their dilated pupils were already raping her as if she was a ripe peach ready to pick from the tree.

"Silence," Aggie roared from the partition.

The Crone Monarchs halted mid chant, gathering their composure as if they too were unaware of what was happening next.

Chest thumping, Pagan could smell the endorphins from the nine men. They were eager to start.

Pagan repeated, 'I can handle rape' like a vinyl record waiting to be turned over.

One of the masked men walked towards her. She kicked at him but he dodged her, moving to the side of her instead. His hand reached across her chest to

222

unbutton the ceremonial gown. His breath smelt of curry and his poised hand slid underneath the gown as if he wanted a moment with her to himself, away from the watchful eyes of the Crone Monarchy and the other eight men. His heartbeat was slower than the other men and Pagan suspected he thought he was the alpha male of the pack.

Loathing while calculating, he was a dangerous mixture of precision, thought and emotional remoteness. He wanted to taste virgin, feel her hymen rip, and take away the innocence that she had been born with. Implant a nightmare where he plays the main character.

Pagan spat at him. The saliva landed on his cloak.

Grinning from amusement, he leaned in, "Virgin Witch is feisty. I'm going to tear you in half!"

She now hated the word, 'feisty'.

Throwing her gown to either side of her body, he spotted the amulet.

Pagan panicked, humping her torso away from him.

He looked up at the Crone Monarchy who hung over the banister as if they were watching a footy game. He looked back at the Maiden, who wildly tugged at the blood filled ropes. Decisively, he snapped the amulet from around her neck, throwing it aimlessly into the air. It landed on the dirt metres away from them. There were to be no reminders that this virgin Witch was anything but a sexual device for his misogynistic desires. He had paid a lot of money to have his fantasies fulfilled.

Stroking her hair as if he was a father saying goodnight to his daughter, he leaned in. His lips almost touching her earlobe, "Rest virgin, you'll need your energy for me."

He walked back joining the other cloaked men.

Aggie leaned over the banister to stare at the exposed Maiden. She had waited impatiently for seventeen years for this moment. Tonight Aggie would become the most powerful Witch that had ever been reincarnated.

Closed mouth, Aggie commanded, "Begin!"

Pagan shuddered. Lifting her head up, she eyeballed Aggie who was unaffected by the aggressive stare.

The same cloaked man approached her again, walking this time up the stairs to the top of the boulder. He dodged her direct kicks, easily grabbing both her ankles, forcing them back towards her waist. Eager to conquer the virgin, he opened his cloak, showing her a fit physique and a large erect penis.

Pagan tried to fight him off by attacking him with her knees. Bucking and twisting, Pagan also verbally attacked him. Her words were lost in the silence of the night while her anger only fed his grotesque need to dominate.

He felt like a predator, a conqueror, even if this wild animal was physically tied to her fate, it fed his natural masculine instinct to rape the weaker sex.

Before he broke her virginal seal, he wanted to watch her bleed first. Swinging his hand back, he viciously smacked her across the face with the back of his hand. He heard her nose break on impact. Her blood sprayed across his face.

Blackness. After a few seconds, Pagan woke back up. The pain was indescribable. She could feel her own blood dripping from her nose and into her mouth.

He pushed her knees further down until they almost touched the altar, "Open up, virgin!"

Blood and tears filled Pagan's eardrums; the sound of deep water soaked her hearing.

She looked back up at Aggie who clutched the partitioned banister, "I'm going to kill you!"

Rigid and dry, her vagina ripped apart as he entered her. Clutching her hands and holding her breath, she prayed that she would survive. Pressing down on top of her, he consciously rammed his penis deep inside of her.

Refusing to scream, she bit down on her lip.

In one movement, he lifted his closed fist, upper-cutting her chin with the bottom of his palm.

Her teeth pierce through her lip. The taste of her own flesh made her gag, "Do it again, fucker. Is that the best you can do?"

He hit her again, breaking her cheek.

Blood ran down her throat, choking her.

Releasing some of his grip, Pagan slipped her right knee up, smacking him in the face. The mild impact enraged him.

"Hold her knees down," he screamed to the other men. He was losing his cool with his prey. Obediently, two men held her knees down.

She felt a tear in her groin and her hip pop as her knees made contact with the altar. It felt like they had torn her right leg from her torso. She threw up from the pain. The acid from her vomit burnt her eyes.

He entered her again. His first few movements were not rhythmic but instead they were slow as if was computing a horrifying realisation. Her hymen had already been broken.

"You stupid, fucking whore!"

Raging, he punched Pagan continuously in the face. Each closed fist smashing her youthful face until she looked like scrambled eggs.

Deafening all those who stood near her, Pagan's screams, a fearful cry released from her body, tortured all those who heard it until she feel silent.

He kept hitting her.

Jaide had heard Pagan screaming. Sobbing, she had covered her ears as the screams continued.

Sam hid a single tear, from Jaide.

The cloaked men let her ankles go, fearful that he had killed her. They hardly ever used violence to rape the Maidens, restriction and brute force but not malicious violence to inflict bodily harm. The Maidens often fainted while their memories reunited but never from physical violence.

Aggie and the Crone Monarchs seemed to enjoy his display of perverse bondage.

Pagan's eyes opened. Choking on a river of blood and flesh, she hyperventilated. Convulsing, her body went into shock.

"You ruined one hole, Maiden, now I'm going to ruin the other."

He entered her up the rectum. It took force to get his entire penis into the tight hole but he wanted to teach her a lesson.

Possessed by an innate need to live, Pagan screamed. Silence followed.

Pressing down on her shoulders, he tore at her breast with his teeth, ripping flesh from her body as if she was a chicken leg. Then, he wrapped his hands around her neck, wringing it as if it was a wet towel.

"You're going to beg me to kill you, Whore!"

Purple from a lack of oxygen, she gave up. He had won, she wanted to die. She wanted the pain to stop and there were another eight men ready to rape her, even if one of them was vomiting from the sight of her torture, she was sure he would regain his composure and fuck her corpse.

Climaxing into her arse, he made sure every drop of his semen filled her up. He owned every part of her now, inside and out. Finished, he released his grip from around her neck and ushered for the next cloaked man to start.

The next man cowered. The vile torture of her body was too much and any sexual desire he had previously had disappeared. Looking at her broken body repulsed him. Rape was one thing but he had nearly killed her and the Crone Monarchy had let him do it. Was this what they had paid extra money for? A murder? And where was her Magick? It had usually arrived.

Pagan lay in a pool of her own blood. The ropes had cut through to her bone, displaying her veins. Her left lung was punctured where he had pressed down on her chest and her hip was dislocated. It was a scene that even the hardened ambulance worker would have been affected by and it was accomplished by one man.

Pagan glazed over. A bright light shone above her. She took a short breath, the pain was unbearable. She closed her swollen eyes.

In the distance, she could hear a voice, it was Dante as if in shadow, hovering above her.

She took another shallow breath, the pain now numb, distant and foreboding.

She heard Dante again, whispering, repeating, and pleading. A shadow floated above her body. She reached out to it. Dante had come to take her home but in shadow form.

Her body was cooling. Her heart beat slowing down until finally she took her last breath. Mid breath, she died.

Jaide

The van rocked from side to side as a gust of wind tore down the hillside. Jaide felt her stomach knot, something was not right.

Turning the music off, she wound the window down and listened. A cold wind whipped her face. There was malice in the air.

Troubled, Jaide snapped at Sam, "Get out, something isn't right."

Falling clumsily out of the van, he joined Jaide at the back of the van who was standing intently, studying the night sky. The wind gushed and the moon disappeared behind the fast moving clouds. Darkness crossed the sky at a rapid pace and the air had thinned.

Even Sam sensed something bad was happening.

"She can't die before the Awakening, Sam. If she's not dead already?"

Concerned with his own safety, Sam questioned Jaide, "What the hell is happening?"

The roaring wind deafened them.

Jaide struggled to reply as the wind slapped her face, stealing the oxygen that she required.

She turned towards the van, pulling hair off her face, "It's a Quickening."

"A what?"

"A Quickening!"

Sam moved in closer to Jaide, "What the hell is a Quickening?"

Wind howled past Jaide, lifting her black dress up. Frightened, she shook her head, "No time to explain."

She pointed at the van, "Can you drive the van up the hill?"

He shook his head. The intensity of the weather threatened her chances of getting to Pagan quickly.

Looking up at the tower, she could see that Aggie was in the grips of summoning Pagan's Magick. If Pagan died before her Awakening the Magick would be in transit, limbo, uncontrolled and susceptible to foreign powers. Pagan was not only an Ancient Witch but she had become the most powerful. Her Magick far surpassed any other Witch.

Jaide could see Aggie standing on top of the tower and suddenly Aggie's motives became clear.

"Clever bitch!"

Jaide grabbed her dress, lifting it above her knees, and scaled up the hill. She would stop Aggie, even if it killed her, even if, it meant betraying the Crone Monarchy.

Mr Baker

Retreating towards the safety of the stone wall, he was tempted to take his mask off as it was hampering his peripheral vision. He needed full sight to comprehend what he was witnessing. He looked at the other eight men who were also running for shelter from the unexpected uninhabited weather and from the threatening anarchy.

He looked at the entrance. Was his one million pounds worth dying for?

Cocooning amongst the heaviness of the ivy, he hoped it would camouflaged him from the coming danger.

The dead whore's Magick had not arrived but he anticipated it was on its way.

The Crone Monarchy had changed the usual Awakening ritual for a reason. Now he understood why he had paid so much more for the Maiden. He was a just a pawn, and they expected that he would die tonight.

Aggie had read from an old script, the weather had angered and now the eleven Crone Monarchs had danced themselves into a frenzy; contagious rhythm of an unknown choreography. Ataxic shrills, arms stretched up towards the night sky as if something unlimited and powerful was coming. Blood curdling cries, howled from their mouths as they summoned the whore's Magick and it was coming.

The eleven Crone Monarchs chanted in unison, "Goddess of Fire, Niran, we summon thee, release the Magick, set her free."

Accustomed to seeing Magick arrive as an animal totem; unicorns, wolves, hawks, cats, dogs, and leopards, he shook with fear as her Magick arrived as a horrendously large serpent; whipping and coiling around itself.

A large serpent of fire, it slithered over the top of the stone wall of the tower. Its large tongue rolled out several metres in front of it to guide its way. It was at least thirty metres long and two metres in circumference.

The serpent roared, releasing a ball of fire which turned the tower into a furnace.

Not registering that he had suffered second degree burns to his legs, he was happy to still be alive as he watched two of the cloaked men burnt to charcoal.

"Goddess of Water, Nimue, we summon thee, release the Magick, set her free."

A larger serpent with green scales and gills arrived, smashing through the tower's wall. Stone and debris became flying missiles.

Opening its mouth, it picked up one of the cloaked men with its fangs, shaking him wildly, breaking his back before swallowing him whole.

The two serpents coiled fiercely around each other.

"Goddess of Air, Nephele, we summon thee, release the Magick, set her free."

Petrified, his eyes darted around the tower. The storm had intensified but he spotted something easily flying towards them. It was another serpent, gliding through the lightening and fast moving clouds.

Soaring at tremendous speed it reached the tower quickly. Metallic blue in colour it had four large bat wings and a dragon's head. Opening its mouth, it revealed two large fangs.

Hissing, the sound pierced his ears until one eardrum burst.

The Crone Monarchs ignored the serpents and continued to chant and dance, "Goddess of Earth, Nepthys, we summon thee, release the Magick, set her free."

He felt the ground shudder. Another serpent was coming up through the ground. Surely, the tower could not possibly withstand the movement? The black serpent cracked through the ground, spraying dirt across the tower.

He watched as one of the cloaked men attempted to flee, only to be hit backwards by the black serpent's tail. His body smashed into the tower's stone wall, crushing his skull on impact.

The Black Serpent opened its mouth and ate him.

Jaide

Lightning bolts followed by thunder, echoed along the countryside, whipping and slapping Jaide's face as her tired body struggled to make it the top of the hill, her age, and the weather slowing her down.

Jaide cursed, "Why didn't I bring my broom?"

Not really sure that the broomstick could handle such terrorising winds it was probably best that she was on foot. Absolute determination helped her to push through the pain threshold, even when her shoes slipped on the damp grass, and her chest felt like it was about to collapse, she kept moving forward. Placing one burning leg in front of the other, she scaled the hill.

Pagan's Magick was trapped in a Quickening and it was unhappy inside the void, searching desperately to reconnect with its host. Unconstrained Magick was dangerous for humanity as it caused electrical surges that quickened up time. It also destroyed anything it came in contact with.

Jaide anticipated that Aggie would try to absorb Pagan's Magick into her own body. It had never been attempted before; a Non-Ancient had never wanted total power before either. It was one more step along her chosen path.

Could a Witch absorb two amounts of Magick into her body? Jaide was not sure but Aggie was obstinate and narcissistic and would gamble with the chances, even if it destroyed her. But Aggie was not a gambling sort and chances were she knew she would achieve her goal.

Pagan would need to die for her plan to succeed, and only out of desperation would Magick attach itself to a foreign host.

Magick was a Witch's core, a second soul, her essence and it would not easily absorb into another Witch. There would be two cores in one body; they simply could not survive together. Jaide feared that Aggie had found a way that they might.

The sound of the air serpent deafened her.

Stumbling on the gravel at the tower's entrance, she fell landing on her hands and knees. Looking up, she scanned the scene. Several cloaked men had been killed while the other men cowered underneath the ivy.

Aggie and the Crone Monarchy were lost somewhere between trance state and euphoria.

Pagan's Magick was desperately circling her body, trying to enter.

Frustrated, the serpents were attacking each other, biting and whipping each other as if they were rivals.

Jaide ran to Pagan. Dodging the serpents, she placed her hands on Pagan's chest. Her body was already cooling. She was indeed dead. Her gown was soaked in her own blood and her beautiful face a fleshy mash of torture.

"Fucking Monsters," she screamed.

No one heard her over the storm and the Crone Monarchs were deep in chants.

The Serpents whipped past her, fire, water, air and earth attempting to balance by joining their host.

Jaide looked back up at Aggie who now floated several metres above the ground, a Magick trick she had taught herself as a child 'apparently'. Their father had called it a 'party trick', which Jaide could only imagine had added to Aggie's thirst for male attention.

Jaide did not remember her father, too young to recollect a single memory. Aggie spoke highly of him which suggested Aggie had not always hated men.

Aggie had enough power for one Crone. She was not worthy of Pagan's Magick.

Jaide closed her eyes. She would need to summon forbidden Witchcraft to save Pagan's life. Magick forbidden by Aggie twenty years earlier.

Crows were flying towards Pagan.

Jaide decided to summon Ancient 'healing' Magick to bring Pagan back from death before the Goddesses collected her.

Mr Baker

Tripping and tangling himself up in the ivy made his escape difficult. His palms bled from the harshness of the stone but he was determined to live. He clung firmly to the tower wall, moving slowly towards the exit.

The serpents were agitated, hissing loudly while swinging their tails violently around the tower, smashing large holes in the stone wall.

The Crone Monarchy continued to chant, although the partition they stood on was falling away.

Aggie was somehow floating.

He angered, "Witches, can fucking fly without their brooms?" This was something, he did not know.

Spotting something shiny underneath the dirt, he remembered he had ripped the Whore's necklace off. Hope at last. It might protect him.

Dropping to the ground, he crawled towards the necklace. Dodging a flying serpent tail, he recoiled back to the safety of the ivy with the necklace safety in his hand. The amulet buzzed in his palm.

Lightning flashed across the sky, highlighting an additional Witch standing at the boulder where the dead Whore laid.

The Serpents looped around her as if they were protecting her.

He had seen her before. Usually on the partition with the other Crone Monarchs. Was it possible, she was here to save the dead Whore?

The Witch placed her palms together. Yelling, she was summoning something or someone. The sound of the serpent's wings flapping only metres away made it hard for him to hear what she was saying.

'She must be mad', he thought. The serpents will kill her, that's if Aggie did not get to her first.

The Witch separated her palms, a glowing orb of light spun in between her palms. It looked like an x-ray of a large orange fruit, fizzing and sparkling. He had never witnessed Aggie or the Crone Monarchy produce Magick with their palms. She had to be an Ancient? Although, he assumed all the Crone Monarchs were Non-Ancients.

The serpents hissed as they prepared to enter their host's body. Their large serpent bodies thrashed around the tower, knocking another hole in the stone wall.

The Witch placed the glowing ball onto the dead Whore's head. Her body shook wildly.

The serpents reacted immediately flying directly at the dead Whore's stomach.

The Whore woke, but her tied wrists kept her attached to the boulder as electricity soared through her body. Her feet lifted straight up into the air, her body arched and her head unnaturally twisted backwards towards her shoulder blades.

Pagan released a haunting shriek of pain that echoed around the tower as if a hundred tortured souls screeched an eternity of grief and agony.

The Crone Monarchy woke from their trance as the weather calmed.

Aggie opened her eyes, releasing a high pitched scream.

Spotting Jaide, they mounted their brooms. Landing on the ground, they immediately dismounted and gathered around Jaide.

Aggie jumped from the partition and as if she was floating landed carefully on the ground.

She ran at Jaide. Grabbing her half-sister's neck, she sharply snapped it, almost tearing her skull from her spine. The glowing light disappeared as her dead body hit the ground.

Aggie

Jaide's body hit the ground. Aggie felt both sadness and bitterness as her half-sister's head landed on her own right shoulder, snapped like a carrot. She had killed Jaide and now her dead body lay in front of her. Her delicate wrist flopped over Aggie's foot, an image that she instantly regretted but Jaide had betrayed her and Jaide had understood the consequences. Aggie would not take responsibility for her death.

Pagan's body fell down onto the altar. Her broken body was unhealed but now her Magick surged through her veins and her heart was beating again.

Pagan was now Awakened and dangerous.

Panicking, Aggie devised a new plan. She could not lose, not now, she had come too far. She had to retrieve Pagan's Magick before she broke free from the ropes. No one would want a 'Reign of Terror' again, which is all Pagan had brought the Witch community in past reincarnations.

Aggie yelled at the Crone Monarchs, "Hold the bitch down with the Adstringo spell."

Without wands the Crone Monarchs would have to use group Magick (if only they were a full Coven).

Latching hands, they formed an uncomfortable circle around Pagan's broken body, kicking Jaide's body out of the way.

"Contringo, Contrixi, Constrictum!"

Mummifying her, a transparent white light twining around Pagan's legs travelled along her body until it reached her head.

Jo Green

Aggie stuck her long and sharpened thumb nail through the white mist and into Pagan's stomach, slicing her skin from her pubic hair to the top of her solar plexus.

Cutting a pentagram shape into her stomach, Pagan screamed and twisted but it did not stop Aggie who was determined to steal her Magick.

Using the same thumb nail, Aggie cut open her own forearm, dripping her own blood over Pagan's stomach. Pagan's blood bubbled as the two become one.

The pentagram ignited and a small flame sizzled.

The night sky calmed to an eerie quietness and the moon reappeared from behind the clouds.

"Chant louder, I want the Goddesses to hear this. It's time they realized, I am the one in power now. Not them!"

"Potentiae Artis Magicae Carruo," Aggie yelled.

The pentagram burst into high flames almost burning Aggie's eyebrows.

Pagan screamed in agony as her stomach turned to ash. The smell of burning flesh unsettled the Crone Monarchy who struggled to keep chanting.

"Louder you fools! Louder! It's time she burned from the inside!"

Stumbling backwards the Crone Monarchs feared for their own lives.

Handel who had died by fire several times shook from fright. Hands slippery from sweat, she considered breaking the circle. It was only from fear of Aggie that she remained loyal to the moment and Aggie's insanity.

"Potentiae Artis Magicae Carruo," Aggie screamed again.

In one large motion, she sliced open her own stomach. Aggie's eyes rolled back inside her head, "Potentiae Artis Magicae Carruo!"

An endless stream of Magick realised from Pagan's stomach.

Four serpents coiled around each other like a chain, lifting Aggie into the air. Aggie glowed, her body alight with sparks and electrical surges.

Finally her body consumed all of Pagan's Magick and she dropped to the ground, triumphant.

CHAPTER 19
Aquarius

The news of his mother's death reached his ears the next morning. Quietly excusing himself from the chamber where he was speaking with the foreign minister about a potential internship, Aquarius had headed straight to the bathroom to wash cold water over his face.

Pagan had survived her Witch Awakening and was being treated for her injuries, and Aggie no longer feared her. A Witch without her Magick was a human, at best.

Aggie had stormed into the toilet demanding that he, "Fix Pagan up and send the bitch home. She is not a threat to me anymore!"

The Supreme Femineity had not even stopped to offer her condolences or to see how he was coping. She had known him since he was an infant and yet she could not muster up a drop of kindness.

He had tried to contact Dante but the notorious Bounty had disappeared, so he organised for Pagan to fly home via an aeroplane in several months.

Her injuries would take an extensive period of time to heal, her emotional scars even longer. Aquarius hoped they would never heal.

Pagan was now the first Witch in herstory to have had her Magick pilfered. It seemed unwise however to refer to her as a Maiden as any experience like the one she had survived qualified her for the title of Witch and her memories had returned before her Magick had been burned from her stomach.

Aggie had survived the dual Magick in her body. How she had learned to do that without the Ancient Doctrine was a mystery. It was like she was an encyclopaedia of information.

Sitting alone in his parent's sitting room that night, the ticking of the clock was his only distraction, the silence a bleak reminder of his loss. His father had initially collapsed when he heard the news. It took three Witches to carry him to the taxi. Crying until he slept, he fell asleep on top of his blankets in bed, calling out Jaide's name once he reached dream state.

Aquarius' parents had been happily married for many years. Warranted, they had spent a lot of time apart but their love never wavered. Time or distance were no barrier.

It was the first time Aquarius had ever experienced lament. It was a kind of conscious numbing mixed with acute heartache so concentrated it caved his chest in and fragmented his thoughts. He never wanted to experience this feeling again. How long it would last, he did not know.

He had suspected that Pagan might not have survived the Witch Awakening and he had prepared himself for that, knowing her as intimately had heavied his conscience, even though he had not wanted to admit it.

Warranted, Pagan's injuries were life-threatening but she had survived and would most likely mend quickly, unlike his mother whose body was now inside a coffin made from pine straw, grasses and her totem Magick animal hair, and her energy already greeted by the Goddesses.

Why had she protected Pagan? Why did she disobey the Crone Monarchy and her half-sister for the sake of cruel and vindictive Soul-mate who had only ever brought grief for the Witches in the past? Is the alliance between Ancients so strong that they would die for each other and betray those they love? The 'us and them' so concreted in loyalty that shared blood was less than?

"Reincarnation must be a comfort to you, Witches, regardless of the mess you leave behind."

Resentment consumed him. Aquarius accepted that he would never know the truth. The truth would be partial at best, manipulated by those who possess power and retold in a manner that suited the Crone Monarchy's agenda.

"How the world rotates on lies," he muttered.

Aquarius decided that he would immediately terminate his employment with the Crone Monarchy. He doubted that they would trust his alliance now his mother had betrayed them, even though he would never make the same mistake as his mother. He would never think so little of himself that he would die for another.

His mother had already forfeited her own family's normality to survey Pagan's upbringing, separating the family for years at a time. Jaide had sacrificed her husband and her only son, out of loyalty to the Supreme Femineity and the Crone Monarchy and in return she had killed her. How was any of this fair? Jaide's obsession for Pagan's safety had ultimately led to his mother being labelled a martyr.

Staring at a family portrait that hung on the wall above the fireplace. The heat from the fire had bent the plastic frame and melted the corners of the photograph. It had been taken one year ago when Aquarius had been initiated into the Sacred Coven of Devoted Men, who were loyal to the Supreme Femineity and the Reign of the Non-Ancient. It had been the proudest moment of his life, ever since he could remember his life purpose was to monitor Pagan, befriend her and report back to his mother. He had been dutiful to his aunty Aggie, and thought that it had also been a sense of pride to his mother. He now wondered if he had known his mother at all.

No job, no mother and no foreseeable future, Pagan and Aggie had taken everything from him. Weighing up his emotions, he was not sure who he hated more.

Bent over from anguish, his hands covered his face. One entire body surely could not withstand the amount of bitterness he felt.

Aggie

Agitated and clenching her fists, Aggie marched around the room.

"What is the point of having Magick if I can't control it? You're a bloody Ancient you should know these things? Tell me everything you know!"

Kate sat stiffly on the chair. Vulnerable, she hoped diplomacy would save her during the consultation. Although none of the situation was her fault, she sensed that she was about to pay for the Supreme Femineity's inability to control Pagan's Magick.

The tension in the room was already unbearable. Shuffling the chair back a few inches to distance herself from Aggie, Kate contemplated how she would handle her employer's fury without insulting her in the process.

"An Ancient's Magick cannot be tamed your Supreme Femineity. It's like a wild animal, fierce and unpredictable. Only through loyalty to its host, a host that created it, can it be controlled. It's a negotiation, a contract, a life time partnership so to speak. One cannot over-rule the other. Nor can another host domesticate it."

Walking directly towards Kate, Aggie bent down, "So, are you telling me that I will never control the Magick?"

"I don't mean to be condescending but its Pagan's Magick. It is only loyal to her."

Aggie stood up, internal rage overpowering her, "But how has her Magick increased? It must be fluid?"

Struggling with pride, Kate, an Ancient, contemplated attacking the Supreme Femineity, after all, she had no right to steal an Ancient's Magick and she also had no loyalty to the wannabe who called herself 'Supreme'. A pizza topping?

Dying at the hands of an imposter would surely make her a martyr, like Jaide, perhaps even evoke an uprising.

Aggie had no right to exist in any other form but what her birth-right suggested. She was a Non-Ancient. Her Magick was poison. Mixing of two breeds, Ancient Witches and the Red Haired Men, had not made them twice as powerful but degenerated them. Non-Ancients were the shit underneath an Ancient's shoes. They were only reminders of the destruction the Red Haired Men had brought to the 'pure' Witches. The Ancients should have used democide on the Non-Ancients when they had the chance to. If they had, she would not be submitting to a Lay Ruler. A Non-Ancient's Magick was restricted to a Wand, evidence that they were 'less than'. If only Aggie's pride could accept her limitations.

"As Pagan advanced so did her Magick. As I said, they are the same. One is nothing without the other."

Hiding the happiness she felt, Kate continued, "The Magick you have…borrowed… is dormant without Pagan. Sure enough you might accidentally trigger the Magick but you will never command it."

Aggie sat at her desk.

Lost in thought, she forgot Kate was in the room. How come Jaide had never told her this? The thought of Jaide twisted her gut.

"There are no problems just solutions, Kate. I haven't come this far to hit a brick wall. I need the Ancient Doctrine. I'm sure it will have the answers. No offence but I don't trust any breathing Ancient. You're all full of disdain for variation. Loyal to a Golden Age that never existed."

Angering, Kate tried to conceal her contempt. Aggie had no right to the book and she was not about to help her find it. Someone had known of Aggie's plans to dominate, and they had hidden the Ancient Doctrine just before her reign began. Kate assumed someone had betrayed Aggie, someone close to her, perhaps a friend. Wondering how deeply that must have hurt, Kate hoped it still kept her awake at night.

"Find me someone to hunt down the Ancient Doctrine. They can travel to the ends of the earth for it. Are there any disciples graduating from the Sacred Coven of Devoted Men who would be competent to do this?"

Kate smiled, "There is one. His name is Kramer. From the beginning of his course, he showed great potential for cruelty and persuasion."

Straightening up, Aggie let delight resurrect her enthusiasm. Her eyes danced to a waltz named 'Bingo'.

"Is he loyal to me?"

"No! He is loyal to no-one, except money.

Aggie laughed, "Then, he's perfect!"

Although, she suspected the conversation had ended, Kate hovered.

Every ounce of her Being needed to know the truth but fear of the truth kept her lips stuck together.

Aggie asked, "Is there anything else, Kate?"

"You cast the spell without a wand."

Leaning back on her chair, Aggie grinned, "Yes, that is correct, Kate. It seems the Non-Ancients are evolving. Remember, it's all about intent."

Mr Baker

He had ordered a virgin, preferably a brunette, ideally a girl with long black hair, tanned skin with freckles and blue eyes. Her physical size was optional but she had to be prepared to role play and cost was not an issue.

Charles the Butler answered the door, and promptly escorted the girl through the large inner city London home until they reached the master bedroom. Once reaching the bedroom door, Charles panicked that he might not have enough bleach to clean up the mess afterwards.

He had wanted to leave earlier than usual as his sister was celebrating her thirtieth birthday at a new restaurant in Camden but considering his employer's mood after the botched Witch Awakening, he feared he might be in for an 'all-nighter'.

Knocking until he heard a reply, Charles opened the bedroom door. Then asked the girl politely to enter.

Brazen the teenager walked into the bedroom. Stopping at the end of the large kind size bed, she smiled at the man.

Charles deadlocked the bedroom door from the outside. The smell of detergent wafted up his nose.

Painted white, the entire bedroom was decorated in white furniture with over fifty down lights in the ceiling highlighting its starkness. The room looked more like a laboratory than a bedroom. The bed sheets looked as if they would snap in half if she was to lie down on them. An iron gate also painted white, made an unusual bedhead and unlike everything else in the room it at least had some character. Closer inspection revealed that some of the white paint on the bedhead had been rubbed back to the metal. Large knobs, also painted white had been meticulously nailed into the wall. Hanging from each knob was a display of ropes all tied in specialised knots.

"Boy Scout?"

He laughed, "Yes. Something like that. I like the Constrictor Knot personally, but I have been partial to the Zip Snare."

Ogling the girl, he was disappointed that she was easily three dress sizes larger than the Whore but she had most of the traits he had requested.

"Do you like knots?"

She shrugged her shoulders, "Haven't really thought about it I s'pose."

Composed, he was amused by the girl's innocence, "How old are you?"

Pulling her hair to one side, she pouted, "I'm fourteen."

He nodded, "And what is your name?"

"Laura."

"It is a pleasure to meet you, Laura."

He wondered how a fourteen year old girl ended up working for an escort company.

"Did the agency tell you what I want from you?"

"Yeah! Kind of."

Turned off by her common speech, he wished he had asked for an intelligent girl, book smart rather than street wise. He supposed it did not really matter, they all scream the same in the end.

Laura was keen to start. The Madam had instructed her to obey all of his instructions as Mr Baker was a special client who paid well and was loyal to the business.

"If he likes you, you can make a lot of money."

"What are you going to do with me?"

"Well Laura, I want to play a game."

His voice lowered, "Do you like to play games, Laura?"

She nodded enthusiastically, eager to please her first client, "Yes, Mr. I'm ready for anything."

"The first thing I want you to do is to take your clothes off."

She rushed, unbuttoning her blouse and slipping off her bra. She threw both clothes items onto the bed.

He quickly flicked the two pieces of clothing onto the floor.

She was sure, she saw him turn his nose up at them, as if they were contaminated with bacteria.

Blushing from embarrassment, she slipped her mini skirt off and white panties to her ankles, stepping out of them. She waited for reassurance but he gave her nothing.

"I had hoped you would be taller and slender but you will do."

Walking over to Laura, he placed his cold hands on her shoulders, "I have a special gift for you. Do you like presents, Laura?"

"Yes."

From his trouser pocket, he produced Pagan's amulet.

Laura's eyes widened as he presented it to her. Without hesitating, she pulled her hair up so he could clip the necklace around her neck.

"Now Laura, I want you to pretend you are another virgin, named Pagan. Can you do that?"

"My name is, Pagan."

Pleased, he squeezed her hand, "Good girl."

Unzipping his trousers, he pushed her head down.

Following his cue, she dropped down onto her knees. The escorts had taught her only the week before how to give a 'head job' using a banana. It had been fun and afterwards they had made banana split with it. Larger than a banana, she feared that she would not be able to fit his entire penis into her mouth.

Breathing deeply, she opened her mouth, managing to fit half of his penis inside. Pulling back, she worked up enough saliva to spit on his knob, giving him a quick hand job until she braved a second attempt.

Obviously a patient man, he waited until she gained her composure before he asked her to start again.

'He had requested a virgin. If he wanted an escort who knew what she was doing surely he would have asked for that?'

Her throat dried again. Only fitting in a portion of his penis, she bluffed her way through with tongue tricks that the escorts had also taught her.

"Take it all, Pagan!"

Forcing her closed throat over his penis, his pubes tickled her forehead.

"Deeper, Pagan."

Gagging, her eyes wept. She felt the vomit leave her stomach but he held her head so she could not release her grip.

Hardening, his penis ejaculated into her mouth as she vomited. She choked, as vomit came out her nose.

Calmly, he walked over to a toolbox that sat beside the bed. Pulling out a cloth, he wiped the bodily fluids off his limp penis.

Shaking and humiliated, Laura remained on her knees.

"Do you know how to fight for your life, Pagan?"

Confused, Laura remained silent.

"It's where I rape you, cut you up, smash your pretty face in and then you die. Are you ready to play?"

CHAPTER 20
Australia, 2002
Pagan

John offered handy hints on arranging the clothes and accessories to minimise the space. Reducing Pagan's clothes by half, he threw what he thought she would not need back onto the bed, "Put them back into the drawers can you, sweetheart."

"Honey, I really appreciate what you're trying to do here but if it's ok, I would like to pack my own suitcase in the future!"

John rolled his eyes, "I'm only trying to help, Pagan. Honestly, you don't need half of what you pack."

Fuming as she watched John repack her suitcase, meticulously arranging her clothes and toiletries in chronological order, her anxiety increased.

"Sometimes, John. I just want to stab you in between the eyeballs."

He laughed, unsuspecting that she had fantasised about knocking him onto his arse several times in the last minute.

Trying to appreciate her partner of six years obsession with 'order' was not easy for Pagan who saw his 'helping' trait as 'controlling'.

Zipping the suitcase up, John instructed her on which roads and turns she should drive to reach the destination the most efficiently.

The conversation was interrupted as a loud crash travelled down the hallway into their bedroom. Demeter had rammed his toy truck into his bedroom wall, gauging a large hole in the plaster.

John cursed under his breath, "Frickin oath, that kid has no respect!"

Placing her hand on John's shoulder, she asked, "Are you going to be ok with him for the whole weekend. You can always call my mum for help."

"I'm more than capable of looking after our son for a few days. I'm not the one who can't pack a suitcase."

Nodding, she picked up the suitcase. Pagan was fully committed to her mundane existence, safe and secure in its predictability but she was keen to 'get away' for a long weekend, away from John and the toddler, away from the boredom.

Ignoring the guilt, she kissed John, "Goodbye."

They had met at a mutual friend's party. She had instantly disliked him, finding him arrogant and aloof.

He had pursued her with gallant conviction.

Grudgingly, she accepted his offer of a date with a certain amount of unease. After months of romantic persuasion, she gave in to his advances, after all, he was safe and she was in desperate need of benign intimacy. The irony was, that once he had captured a small part of her heart, he had become complacent and comfortable; sex replaced with early to bed and early to rise, especially after Demeter was born.

Their relationship was not built on passion but it was reassuring and to Pagan's surprise, they had become good friends, discussing everything as if they were best friends. He was the safety in a world that she felt unsafe in. What they lacked was laughter but what they cherished in each other was honesty and companionship.

Financially secure, they were happy to plod along void of extremes. Up until now.

Demeter ran towards his mother as she walked into his bedroom. A beautiful looking child; round face, a dimple on each cheek and blues eyes that flickered liked a wood heater on a winter's night.

But unfortunately his physical attributes did no match his personality. Bad-tempered, he would erupt into rages that frightened even Pagan; more than a toddler tantrum, Demeter possessed a repressed anger that internally tormented him.

Pregnant, she had been bitter, still holding onto the trauma of her Witch Awakening. A son filled the void of where her Magick should have been. She feared that she had genetically cursed him with her own internal rage.

The doctors had told them it was his diet, only to change their minds months later, writing out a prescription for Ritalin.

Pagan had politely told them to, "Fuck off," while reducing sugar from his diet.

Picking Demeter up (determined to hug the anger out of him), he instantly snuggled into his mother's warm body, "Be a good boy for Daddy this weekend, won't you?"

Holding him tightly, she struggled to release her grip, "Mummy loves you, so much."

Pagan turned to John who was standing stiffly in the door frame, looking at the hole in the plaster, "I love you too!"

Several minutes later, she was driving along the highway.

It was going to take three hours to reach the beach house. One hour along the Bass Highway towards Launceston, one hour towards Hobart where she planned to stop at the petrol station to fill the car up and grab a coffee, and the last hour would consist of turning off at the Conara Junction and driving towards the East Coast.

Guilt overwhelmed her during the first hour of the trip. Waves of anxiety were followed by an emotional numbing and then a rush of excitement that kept her sweating hands on the steering wheel.

Turning the music up, she hoped that the lyrics might quieten her mental state.

Inundated with road works, she waited at each road block, questioning if the road works were a sign that she should turn around and go home?

Pagan clenched her jaw so tightly that her gums bled, another sign that she was stressed.

Pulling into the petrol station, Pagan filled the car tank up, and then ordered a coffee. The petrol station was busy with people heading home after their working week or heading somewhere other than here. It was a place of necessary transition.

The woman made Pagan's coffee.

Attempting to hide her fury that 'quick was not quick enough', Pagan pulled out her mobile phone to check the time. It was also a symbolic gesture to tell the woman to 'hurry up!' At this rate it was going to be dark before she reached her destination and since she was unsure of where she was going, now, she wished she had been more organised. She imagined John shaking his head disapprovingly.

She quickly sent a text, "At Perth getting coffee. xx"

The coffee calmed her nerves while adding to her excitement, only to smother her happy thoughts with morality again.

Several more times, she thought about turning the car around and driving home but a persuasive voice inside her head urged her on.

Committed to John for six years this would be her first act of betrayal.

They had a child together, a home, and a life but the further she drove away from Devonport the more alive she felt. It was exhilarating to feel a much needed mixture of anticipation, excitement, fear and naughtiness.

It had been a long time since she had driven alone in a car without her son in the back seat, diapers to be changed or toddler-level communication.

Freedom felt like a drug, experimental and conscious shifting.

The last half an hour, Pagan found her thoughts drifting to *this* reincarnation; their first kiss, first belly laugh, and to their heated ending.

A sharp pain crossed her chest.

She turned the music off as she entered St Mary's Pass. The winding of the mountain road assimilated her life in an ironic parody. Dusk dulled the view but the vision of the sea overwhelmed her as she exited the mountain. The East Coast of Tasmania was truly magnificent.

She would be at the beach house in less than ten minutes and new anxieties tormented her now. It had been eight years since they had seen each other. He had children now, a wife, and an existence separate from her.

The internet had reconnected them. They had shared many photographs over several months and endless love letters via email but to finally meet up with him in the physical world was truly petrifying to her.

The ocean was velvet blue and guided her safely to the beach house.

Relieved to have found the driveway, she pulled in and parked behind several large Wattle Trees that hid the car in dense foliage. Scared, she sat in the car for several minutes.

Opening up the mobile, she typed, 'I'm here. Zone it!'

Several minutes later, she received a text, 'Done'.

The weekend was about to begin. She could be making the worst mistake of her life but she was prepared for the consequences.

Gulping down the doubts, she exited the car and grabbed her suitcase from the boot. Throwing her suitcase on the ground, she unzipped it and messed her clothes up. John had no authority here.

The driveway was steep but she reached the front door quickly.

Hearing movement, she sniffed. Her acute sense of smell was the only Magick that Aggie had not stolen from her. He smelt divine and he was nervous, probably as nervous as she was.

The door was the only thing separating them. She knocked once and then shimmied on the spot while she waited. The door opened and there he was, handsome as ever.

Stepping into his arms, he accepted her advances. He shook as if he had just experienced a trauma.

Pagan pulled away to look at him, "Rogan, you're all grown up."

Rogan mimicked her laughter, "I am. And you are still beautiful."

"Smooth Rogan, smooth!"

As he escorted her into the house, throwing the suitcase into his bedroom, she looked around the beach house. Quaint, its charm lay somewhere in between its modernising of an old home and its airy seaside subtitles.

Nervously, he poured a glass of Merlot wine, clumsily handing it to Pagan before filling his half drunken glass back up.

Tapping their glasses together, they both took a large sip.

The tension between them was unbearable. They were, after all, strangers. Strangers who once had been lovers, lovers who had never stopped longing for each other. A Soul-mate connection, where only one knew for sure while the other had only need listen to his heart to find the answer.

"Are you warm enough? There is plenty of fire wood."

Pagan nodded and took another sip of her wine. Without food in her stomach, she felt immediately intoxicated.

"I've made dinner. It should be ready in about twenty minutes," he said, as if he had read her mind.

Pagan was impressed at how much effort he had gone to (but they all do in the beginning).

The last few months, they had fantasised about this moment but in reality it was proving difficult.

Slipping her shoes off, she threw them onto the chair across from them. Then she took her jumper off, throwing it over the top of her shoes.

Rogan sensed that she was easing into her new environment and this pleased him. He took a large gulp of wine and placed it on the coffee table. Scooting along the couch alongside Pagan, he grabbed her glass of wine, placing it beside his glass on the coffee table.

She turned towards him; her body language accepting of his advances.

Touching her chin, he lingered, fearful to kiss her. His wife's face flashed before him.

She leaned in, their noses touched, "I love you. I've always loved you!"

Their chests pounded in unison.

Running her hand through his sandy coloured hair, she pulled him even closer.

Cheek to cheek, their lips were only a breath apart.

Rogan's right hand groped at her breast. It was if they were teenagers again, lost in the simplicity of a kiss, a touch, a look.

She kissed him; slowly, hard, sloppy, and tight.

Eager to be inside of her, Rogan undressed her. Once nude, he placed her onto her back. Grabbing her face, his eyes, piercing her with an intense glaze, he entered her, fucking her hard.

Gasping, her nails scratched his back.

Within minutes, they fell off the couch but neither one wanted to reset. Slipping, their bodies thumped onto the floor.

Lost in the moment, Pagan did not feel the floorboards rub the skin away from her spine, or the heat from the wood heater warming the top of her head.

She grabbed his bottom, "Fuck me, harder!"

The sound of a smashing glass broke the intensity.

Frustrated, Rogan hopped up. Red wine and broken glass covered the floor beside them. They had obviously kicked the coffee table.

Pagan sat back up on the couch, thankful for the break as her sexual fitness was lacking.

Patting the couch seat, she giggled, "Come here, Rogan."

Shattered glass and red wine massaged the soles of his feet as he walked towards her. He sat down.

Pagan straddled him so she could feel every part of his penis inside of her. It never occurred to her to feel conscious about her body. She had gained weight; her nipples were breastfeed large, stretchmarks on her stomach, chubby inner thighs and a floppy belly, only made her feel more womanly. She was not that innocent seventeen year old anymore, she was so much more.

Not kissing, their foreheads connected instead, making a third eye thread, every cell connected as they had become one.

Pagan closed her eyes, sensing that he was looking at her, only increased the eroticism. The longing that she had missed since they were together was present: his unconditional love for her, his unwavering lust, his lust equalling hers. It was safe to be a sexual person with him. He empowered her. He always had.

Her hips danced on top of him; she smelt his hair, tasted his breath and touched his skin. Senses quietening and intensified, warming, she orgasmed.

Listening to her moaning, he ejaculated.

They forgot they were unprotected and that he was potent as his semen filled her up.

The moment ceased and reality quickly returned, "I shouldn't have let you cum in me."

He kissed her nose and then anxiously pulled away, "Oh shit, Dinner!"

Pagan

Wrapped up in a red and orange crocheted blanket that Pagan had pulled off the couch; her hair tangled and her makeup smudged, she sat up on the kitchen bench eating 'two minute' noodles.

Rogan fluffed around pressing random buttons on the coffee machine.

Their burnt dinner sizzled on the kitchen sink and another bottle of red wine sat beside it.

"Seriously, don't worry about the coffee, just make some instant coffee, when did you become so snobby? Coffee is coffee!"

"Coffee is not all coffee. Instant is instant for a reason. Plus, I want to spoil you. I've got a few years of catching up to do."

"Just looking at your naked body is spoiling me."

Blushing, he laughed, "You're great for my ego. You know what's weird but we have a 'naked' relationship. It feels so right when I'm with you, as if secrets and superficiality don't have a place to reside."

She felt guilt drop like a penny from her chest to her stomach. There were secrets between them, many.

The sound of the waves crashing on the beach only a hundred metres away from them gave Rogan an idea, "Eat up. I'll grab a blanket. We can drink the bottle of wine on the beach. The coffee can wait."

Pagan loved the idea. Scurrying around the house collecting their clothes from the lounge room, they dressed haphazardly, clothes inside out or twisted up in other garments.

Grabbing two coffee mugs from the pantry, Pagan spotted a dusty tape recorder hidden behind the cereal. Battery operated, she pushed the 'eject' button.

"Rogan, it has a cassette of the Kinks in it. I'm taking this with us."

Winking, he grabbed the bottle of red wine.

"I'm going to fuck you on the beach."

"Yes! Yes you are," she laughed.

A small torch led the way across the pebbled road, through a native reserve and onto the cold sand.

Pagan held onto Rogan's woolly jumper, occasionally tripping over tree limbs and clumps of grass. Turning the torch off, the waning moon and the stars helped guide them to a secluded part of the beach.

The tide was low but the sound of the waves weaving and cutting-up the sand deafened them. The beach seemed to travel in either direction for eternity.

In a district of about thirty residences, they felt very alone. Lights from the homes hidden behind the trees gave them a sense that they were isolated from humanity. They had always preferred to be in each other's company, only when they added societal elements did their relationship fail, every time.

Rogan kissed Pagan before spreading out the blanket for them to sit on.

Memories flooding back for both of them. They snuggled beside each other while the sea breeze tickled their intoxicated bodies.

It was if they had never been apart.

Taking the lid off the wine bottle, Pagan took a swig, "Oh, I was so excited about finding the tape recorder, I forgot the mugs."

Remembering that they had smashed the wine glasses, she added, "We might need to use plastic glasses for the rest of the weekend."

Rogan laughed, "I'll be pulling glass out of my foot for months. Totally worth it though."

A wave crashed heavily on the beach, "Gee, you wouldn't want to swim here."

Rogan agreed, "The guy that owns the beach house surfs here. Crazy hey?"

"Let's play the Kinks."

Fumbling in the dark, she pressed play. The sixties band instantly lightened the mood.

"I was so unlucky to have missed the sixties. It would have been groovy."

Rogan put his arm around her, "I can't really imagine you as a hippy."

He reconsidered, "Actually, yes I can. You would have been an activist for sure."

They drank from the bottle again.

"There is nothing really to fight for anymore," Rogan contemplated.

Pagan replied, "Boredom, the mundane and apathetic, that's worth fighting against. How many wars have been started purely from boredom with religion the excuse?"

Squeezing her, Rogan understood what she meant. He too had felt his soul shrivelling up the last few years. His wife was a rebound after being dumped by Pagan.

Returning from England, Pagan had changed, she had darkened, distanced herself. The end of their relationship had broken him. It had been easier to hold anyone than to spend each night in bed alone thinking of Pagan. He loved his wife but he had never been in-love with her, not how he loved Pagan. He was jeopardising his family, friends, his finances, his future, stability, just to hold her. He wondered how many men were married to the wrong women due to loneliness or circumstance.

Pagan jumped up, "Hop up, let's dance!"

Locking hands, she pulled him up.

Brushing the sand away from his body, the sound of the music and the red wine freed his mind from any inhibition.

They danced frivolously on the beach.

Rogan swung Pagan around in a clumsy waltz, laughing when they stumbled several times, "One two three, one two three, it shouldn't be so fucking hard, should it?"

"You had plenty of rhythm an hour ago."

Rogan laughed.

Pagan pulled away from Rogan, raising her hands above her head, dancing whimsically on her own, "I don't think in the sixties people were waltzing anyway Rogan. Love, freedom, and revolution, baby!"

Collapsing on the blanket, Rogan drank more red wine and watched the 'love of his life' dance around him.

"I'm so fucking happy right now! I don't want this night to ever end," he laughed and then he remembered the spliff he had made them.

Pulling foil out of his pocket, he showed Pagan, "Look what I have. I had to visit a pretty dodgy character to get this."

"Be sure to give me his name."

Pulling out a lighter, he lit it. Taking a drag, he laid down to stare at the stars.

Pagan collapsed beside him.

Rogan passed it to her, "I haven't had a smoke in five years but I thought we should relive our teenage years this weekend."

Inhaling, Pagan coughed, "John hates drugs, of all kinds. Aspirin! He loves Aspirin."

She took another drag and passed it back to Rogan, "I shouldn't bag John out. He's a good bloke."

"The worlds full of good blokes, Pagan, you need more than that. You need an equal."

Pagan thought about that comment. There was only one man that equalled her and that was Dante.

Rogan took another drag, swirling the smoke around in his mouth. He turned his head towards Pagan. She willingly opened her mouth as he swirled the smoke through her teeth.

"I've really missed you."

Snuggling into his torso, Pagan paled from the effect of the marijuana.

Rogan brushed her cold cheek, "What are we going to do once the weekend ends?"

Pagan pale, "I think, I'm going to throw up."

Pagan

Turning the ignition on, Pagan felt a mixture of sorrow and bliss. Their weekend together had been everything she had hoped for. Their goodbye hug had lasted for far too long and pulling away from the safety of his arms, almost tore her apart. What had alarmed her the most, was how many times, Dante had entered her thoughts.

It was only the love for her son that finally gave her the strength to re-pack the suitcase, walk down the driveway and sit in the car.

Boredom was three hours away.

Pulling out the mobile phone, she sent a text, 'Finished'.

Endless golden valleys and train tracks kept her visually awake during the first hour until she reached the Midland Highway. Perth's cascading river was the next landscape to drag her thoughts unkindly back into the present.

Entering Perth, she was annoyed at how hectic the town was. Vehicles travelling from the North West Coast, Hobart or to Launceston all merging at the same junction.

Pagan drove through the junction into the main street, slowing down to twenty kilometres as she looked for the chemist, finally parking across the road from it. She sat and watched people enter and exit the busy chemist for ten minutes.

Her hand found the door handle but could not open it.

They had performed unsafe sex all weekend. She had to buy the 'Morning After' pill, swallow the abortion tablet and abort the Witch they may have made. She had to protect Rogan. She had to protect herself.

Turning the key in the ignition, she indicated and drove off instead.

An hour and fifteen minutes later, Pagan opened the back door to her home. John had left it unlocked so she would not struggle with the key lock. Always thoughtful, always controlling.

The house was dark but she knew her way through the house.

Dropping the suitcase just inside the door, she slipped off her shoes and tiptoed through the house so not to wake Demeter.

Pagan found John sitting in the lounge room. The room was lit with several candles and patchouli incense was burning.

John had waited for several hours in anticipation of her arrival.

Pagan made her way over to him, throwing several pillows at his feet, she sat down, laying her head on his lap.

Gently stroking her hair and massaging her behind her ears, he calmly asked. "Did you do it?"

Pagan found only the strength to nod as tears merged and rolled down her face.

John took a bottomless breath, "Now, let's hope for a daughter. I've always wanted to meet Queen Elizabeth the First."

Pagan

She sat in the car.

The pregnancy test had been positive. She had known only several weeks after her lustful weekend with Rogan that she had fallen pregnant. Her breasts had filled, her stomach had tightened and the nausea struck her in the early morning, continuing all day.

She looked over at the brown bag that wiggled on the passenger seat and sighed.

Rogan would be joining her soon. She had to remain strong. Stick to the plan.

Rogan's foetus grew inside of her. It would be a daughter, a full born Witch. The same Witch that they always made together, an energy that only existed because of their Soul-mate status. The Witch would be born strong, empowered and commanding. She would also be unaffected by Aggie's power and her savage vengeful supremacy.

Aggie might have stolen Pagan's Magick but she could not steal her daughter's.

The Witch would be born with both Witch Magick and Red Haired Men's Magic. She was indestructible.

Pagan already felt her daughter's Magick humming deep within her womb. She missed her own Magick. She was lost without it.

Amelie, Fay Ce'Line and Aislyn had placed a Reflection spell over the beach house. The spell was only a precautionary procedure. When Aggie violently stole Pagan's Magick it ironically broke her ability to track Pagan. The irony amused Pagan but she was not about to jeopardise her daughter's life with illusions of security.

Rogan drove into the Stoodley Forest carpark.

She had suggested that they should revisit that disastrous day when she tried to lose her virginity to him. She wondered how different her life would have been, had her Magick, Awakened, that day.

He jumped at the chance to see her and to be inside of her again.

The weekend he had spent with Pagan released a need in him that he had previously buried deep. He knew that Pagan was the woman he wanted to spend the rest of his life with. He was prepared to divorce his wife. The kids would adapt. They would love Pagan as much as he loves her. His desire for Pagan was like an addiction. He always needed more.

He bounced out of his car, elated to be in her presence again.

Grabbing the brown bag, she jumped out of her car and joined him. She tucked the brown bag neatly away behind her back.

"Lunch and wine," she added.

They walked off into the Forest Reserve.

Caressing and cuddling on the incline into the valley, they walked further in this time; down to the first main dirt road, turned right and then left. Pagan wanted to be near the creek. It would be private there.

The Forest was enchanted with impenetrable foliage, birds flying above them, and the sound of water running in the distance.

They reached the creek. The sound of the water trickling relaxed them. The lush moss grew on the wet rocks.

Pagan pushed Rogan down onto a log, "Sit!"

She smiled devilishly at him, her head bent toward her left shoulder, revealing her long neck. Her lengthy black hair hung down over her chest.

Rogan hardened, the mere sight of her made him horny.

Pagan opened up the brown bag, pulling out a small brown bottle, "It's a gift from Amelie."

She handed it to Rogan. He looked at it, "What is it?"

"It's called Poppers. You inhale it up your nose and it gives you a sexual rush for about three minutes. Amelie said, 'it's amazing'."

Rogan felt a jolt of rejection, "Don't I make you horny, enough?"

Pagan laughed, "Yes, silly. But I want to try everything with you. I thought that every time we catch up that we could try something new. Keep the boredom at bay."

Pagan glared at him and took a large breath, "We don't have long, so you will need to sniff it now."

Appreciating Pagan's deviate personality, he agreed, "Yeah ok."

He twisted the bottle open and took a small sniff.

"Inhale it up both nostrils. Inhale as much as you can, apparently it relaxes you and when I kiss you it will feel amazing."

Obediently, he did, the left nostril followed by the right. She watched as the liquid evaporated immediately up into his nostrils. He dazed and then it 'kicked' in.

"Wow. This is amazing. Fuck Pagan, you need to try this!"

Pagan wasted no time grabbing the brown bag, flipping it up, and shaking four Tiger Snakes onto Rogan's lap. All four Tiger Snakes obeyed their mistress and attacked Rogan. Flattening out, they all raised their heads, showing off their yellow belly, striking Rogan repeatedly.

Rogan frantically swung and kicked at the Tiger Snakes which only made them angrier. The Tiger Snakes bit him again.

The look of betrayal from Rogan's terrified eyes would haunt Pagan for eternity.

Rogan flung one Tiger Snake off, falling off the log onto his back, the other three circled on top of him.

"Stop," Pagan commanded.

The Tiger Snakes slithered off Rogan's body, fleeing into the dense bush.

Pagan jumped on top of Rogan, smothering his mouth with her hand while the other hand held his nostrils shut.

"This is for having my head removed. A Witch *never* forgets!"

Struggling for several minutes, he stopped moving beneath her. The love for their unborn daughter motivated her to keep a firm grip on him until she knew for sure he was dead. Eventually, she laid his dead body down on the moist ground. Lying on top of him, she sobbed.

"That was payback. Next life, we can start again, afresh."

She cradled his warm body in her arms.

Silently howling, she rocked. Holding his head up against her head, she kissed his dry lips.

"I'm so sorry Rogan, but karma is karma," she wailed.

PART THREE

Australia- June 2010
Pagan

Pagan finished assembling the Kombi's bench seat into a fold-out bed. Making the bed, she threw a pale pink fitted sheet over the thin mattress. Two fluffy pillows recently purchased on sale, and a doona pinched from her own bed, concluded any effort she was prepared to commit to.

Sliding the Kombi door shut, she double checked the door handle and walked around the front, hopping into the driver's seat.

The Kombi was ideal for an overnight sleepover and she was keen to turn the ignition on and join her friends for a gathering that was 'way overdue'.

Roberta and her husband Don had invited her, Amelie, Ruby and Fay Ce'Line for a night of 'shits and giggles' at their farmhouse in Sprent.

Pagan had happily agreed. An evening surrounded by Coven Witches who knew her intimately, although she had mastered the skill of masquerade, was a relief.

It was a short drive to the district of Sprent, roughly twenty minutes, through winding roads into a valley, a country road which eventually paralleled a healthy pumpkin patch and then a sharp turn into an overgrown paddock that housed a farmhouse built in the convict era.

The sandstone exterior was unkempt, lending an appearance of abandonment and hostility. The forward-facing windows were covered up with old fence palings, hiding a home that once entered, sparkled a soulful warmth.

The interior had been gutted. Cedar wooden panels on the walls and polished cement floors replaced the plaster and rotting floorboards. The ground floor consisted of: a make-shift highly glossed kitchen, a bathroom partitioned by a curved blue stone wall, a combined dining and sitting room with 'bikie' memorabilia just to add a subtle beefy oddity against a backdrop of wispy female gratitude. The second level consisted of a mezzanine floor that harboured gypsy style décor, clothes thrown around the room and hundreds of scarves tied to the mezzanine banister.

The farmhouse, although small in structure was rich with home-spun thankfulness for all things simple. It was impossible not to feel completely tranquil once you entered their abode and instantly homesick once you departed.

Pagan grabbed from the passenger seat a previously prepared platter; watermelon, green grapes, brie cheese and dried biscuits, off the passenger seat, plus a knitted cardigan, her favourite broomstick, a bottle of half-drunk scotch and a large bottle of dry ginger.

Bumping the Kombi door shut with her right knee, she strolled carefully to the back door. Entering through the kitchen, she leaned her broomstick against the internal wall and then unburdened the platter and bottles onto the congested kitchen bench. She excitedly waved at her friends who lounged in the sitting room.

Greeted with squeals of delight from the Witches, Don welcomed Pagan by wrapping his hairy hefty arms around her shoulders.

Nestling into his rotund stomach, she buried her face into his soft chest. It was comforting to be hugged by a man who loved her, only as a friend, without wanting more from her.

Roberta's husband, Don was the president of a motorcycle group. It was a private part of his life that he kept to himself, even from Roberta. It was safer that way for all of them. He was also the man who tidied up their messes, asked no questions and finished the jobs off under the protection of the moon and a motorcycle helmet.

Pagan's memory flickered back to Rogan. Don had quickly squashed any rumours of 'foul play' regarding his death. The forest had been swept clean of any evidence and the whole sordid ordeal forgotten about, except in the back of Pagan's consciousness where the image of Rogan's dead body plagued her still.

Being born from Sicilian parents, Don was quick to temper but even faster to calm down. Not a man to hold a grudge, he was known to knock a man clean off his seat while ordering the same man a beer several minutes later. His stout physique and large round face harboured a pancho villa moustache and infinite brown eyes. His generous disposition complimented his passionate nature, making him an ideal husband for a Witch. He was a bad boy with a swollen heart and Roberta had loved him by the time she threw her leg over the seat of his motorbike.

Pagan pushed Don away, "Don, I don't know how you don't break Roberta?"

Don

Don grabbed his car keys off the phonebook that sat on top of the cluttered kitchen bench. Double checking that his mobile phone and wallet were still in his trouser pocket, he finally said goodbye to the Witches. He was not about to join them in a night of partying when he had business to take care.

Shoving his feet into a pair of white sneakers, left followed by the right, he shuffled out of the backdoor towards his 2008 white Utility.

Unlocking the door, he squeezed his rotund body into the seat. He had already lost his breath.

The leather seat, cushioned his bottom as he shuffled through his collection of CDs that were spread out across the passenger seat. His selection consisted of Aussie rock: Dragon, The Easybeats, Australian Crawl, Ol 55, Choirboys and Killing Heidi made six. Inserting all six CDs into his CD player, he turned the volume up. He was almost deaf in his left ear and he appreciated his good quality speakers.

Driving along the dirt road, dust churned behind his utility making a dark puffy cloud. Annoyed that his vehicle was now dirty from the dust, he verbally reminded himself to seal the driveway before the next winter.

Turning onto the road, Don drove only a few hundred metres before reducing his speed. Slipping down each gear until he reached first, he accelerated a sharp right turn onto a bush road, opposite his property, and then another right turn into a pine tree reserve where he slowly drove down a dirt track until he reached an intimate clearing. The pot holes made his drive unpleasant. He scolded himself for lowering his utility.

Two easily spotted men, wearing dry weather motorbike clothes hovered nearby. Wandering purposefully along the fence line of the reserve, their view was directly in front of Don's home.

Both men looked relieved to see their President arrive to swap shifts since they had been there since 06:00 that morning.

Pulling on the handbrake and idling beside the men, Don pressed the window button down to speak to them.

"Seen anything?"

The larger of the two men shrugged his shoulders, "Nah Don, nothing suspicious. Just a few kids running around the reserve but that's it."

Don felt some relief, "Thanks guys, you have no idea how much this means to me," and he meant it.

Twirling his moustache with his thumb and index finger, Don smiled, "Call into the pub on your way home. Have a couple of beers on me. Tell 'em to put it on my tab."

Both men thanked him, mounted their motorbikes and rode off, leaving Don alone in a pine tree reserve that was already darkening as the sun set in the west.

It took half a minute before the rumble of the motorbikes faded.

Reversing his vehicle, he parked where he had a clearer vision of his home.

A half-wit snitch had nervously repeated information about an underground radical Non- Ancient Witch faction, whose harmful intent of eradicating all Ancient Witches was only months away from a full scale attack. They wanted to finish off what the Supreme Femineity had started thirty years earlier, but this time without mercy.

Don snorted, "Probably armchair extremists, sitting behind a keyboard with broomsticks stuck up their arses."

Regardless, he had to take the rumour seriously, just in case. He would never forgive himself if he let something terrible happen to Roberta. Roberta was in possible danger and so were the rest of her Coven, a Coven that existed of only five members this reincarnation. He always wondered why the other eight Coven members were still with the Goddesses. Perhaps, it was Pagan's vulnerability that gave rise to such calculating opposition rather than Aggie's sovereignty?

He would be damned if he would allow something to happen on his shift. "No one hurts my wife," Don said underneath his breath.

Surveying his surrounding landscape, he hoped that his intuition would alert him to anything unusual. It was probably a bad option to have notorious Ancients all bundled into one home considering the rebellious atmosphere but at least they could help protect each other if anything was to happen.

Leaning over, feeling the top button of his trousers pop open, he opened an esky container that sat on the floor, grabbing a bourbon can.

Flicking the lid, he sculled half of the can in three gulps and then burped.

Next, he opened a packet of snake lollies that were hidden in the glove box away from Roberta's sweet tooth. Sucking on a blue snake first and then a yellow snake, he stared at the lolly for a moment before sucking on it.

Remembering Rogan, Don shuddered, "Poor bastard!"

Caleb

Caleb was stuck on a spiky twig. Tugging on his robe, he tore a hole in the fabric. Wearing a robe was definitely trickier than he had first thought, especially when walking through dense bush. Next time they planned on summoning Satan, he would put the robe on once they were set up.

Squishing into the sludge, his sneakers were covered in a mixture of wet and drying mud while buzzies stuck to the laces of his shoes. His mum was not going to be happy when she saw the state of his new shoes.

Spending one hour after school clogging his mother's en-suite, the three boys applied white face paint, black lipstick and heavy black eyeliner. Satisfied with their first attempt to look gothic, they rode on their bikes for one hour, quickly suffering from exhaustion as they peddled through the valley. Finally, stashing their bikes at the edge of the pine tree reserve.

Underneath their cloaks they wore skin tight skater pants, black t-shirts and multi-coloured thermal tops to keep warm. Unsure what to wear for Satan's appearance, the boys felt happy with their attire.

Walking along a man-made track, they stumbled across a clearing; five by five square foot glade, surrounded by fully grown pine trees. Yahooing, as they kicked around the fallen pine cones, they prepared a large circular space for their sacred circle.

He wanted to be organised before sunset. He had brought a large torch but doubted the batteries had been fully charged.

Caleb had carried a backpack that contained ten red candles, ten black candles, a bag of chicken bones left over from a Sunday chicken roast, a bundle of virgin hair that he had stolen from his sister's hairbrush earlier that day, a voodoo spell kit that he had purchased online with his mum's credit card, and a spell to summon 'Satan' that he had found during math class in third period at high school. He had jotted down the spell onto his school note pad in large printed letters so it would be easier for him to read it aloud in dim light.

The youngest of the boys, Smithy, a sickly looking teenager who sadly inherited his mum's rabbit facial features, carefully placed a shoebox on the ground. The sound of a healthy mouse scampering around inside of the cardboard only amused the three boys who looked forward to cutting the rodent's head off.

Clayton, a type of boy who hugged grandmothers purely so they would spoil him with yummy treats like cake, coconut biscuits and jam tarts, headed off in search of firewood. Accident prone, Clayton could hear his mother warning him, 'Clayton for god's sake, don't touch anything'. Moments later, he pierced his skin with a large splinter from a piece of wood he had wrestled with before carrying it back to the sacred circle. He decided to keep the splinter to himself to avoid any ridicule.

The full moon would rise in a few hours.

Caleb scanned the area again as he wanted everything to be perfect.

Satan worshipping, was the only activity in his life that kept him from suiciding or killing the boys from school who tormented him every day in class.

Perhaps Satan may ask him to sacrifice a heterosexual. Caleb could only hope.

Tasmania was still homophobic, yet it hid underneath a façade of political correctness. He sensed what people thought of him, saw the flicker of judgement in their eyes before they disguised their disgust with politeness. They seemed to thrive on liberal exploration while stabbing the queer population in the back with a conservative knife.

Bogans outnumbered any other subgroup in Devonport. Walking the streets, he had to be on high alert after being bashed three times already in the last twelve months, twice at school and once walking home from a friend's home.

Taking a deep breath, he clenched his fists as anger surged through his veins.

"Satan, has to show up tonight."

Amelie

Another drink was poured, the music turned up to compete with the flamboyant conversation and old stories challenged the catch-up ones.

After her fourth chardonnay, Amelie divulged that she had started dating a doctor from the hospital. The reaction was positive as the Witches shrieked with excitement, demanding to be told more, particularly graphic details of their assumed passionate love affair.

Amelie had always been a passionate lover, her standards were high and her favourite catch-phrase, "Oh, I'm sorry, it's not all about you," had crippled the most self-assured male sexual companion.

Pagan felt a jab of jealousy. Her best friend had found someone, maybe? Again!

She had enjoyed having Amelie's affections to herself. They had been best of friends for centuries. It was rare to find members of a Coven so loyal to each other. Men had come and gone but their loyalty to one another had been unwavering.

Lighting up a cigarette, Amelie leaned back on her chair, crossing her legs, pointing her toes towards the ceiling and with great illustration, she spoke of how they had met and how he romanced her into their first date.

"Living as long as we have," she jested, "And I don't need to tell any one of you Witches just how old we are."

She cackled and then continued, "And we are really fucking old. Sometimes, and I say sometimes, a Witch needs a fuck. A really good, 'oh my Goddess' I just wet the bed kind of fuck! And they don't come along very often."

Fay Ce'Line jumped up from the sofa to re-fill everyone's glass, "I'll drink to that, Amelie."

Amelie composed herself, "But seriously, just when I thought I would never met another sensational fuck, it's like he just fell out of the sky and right into my vagina."

Ruby who had been sitting quietly decided to speak, "Thank goodness, someone is getting some action. I can't remember the last time I had a man touch me."

The atmosphere thickened.

Amelie sneered, "Who invited her?"

Ruby solemnly continued, "It would be nice just to have someone to curl up with at night. I'm tired, tired of starting our lives over, falling in love only to lose them, and especially tired of fighting a karmic battle that we have lost before we have even started. I don't want to be reincarnated anymore. I just want to sleep. Sleep forever."

Fay Ce'Line jumped up out of her chair to envelope Ruby, "Oh Ruby, I know it must be hard, losing your husband and then a child. It never gets easier losing the people we love but this is just some sort of depression happening. It will get easier, you know this. We would miss you so much if you were not reincarnated."

Fighting the urge to agree with Ruby, Pagan shuffled away. She too wanted to 'hop off' the karmic rollercoaster, reset, and do things differently from the beginning. It had not mattered how much she changed the way she viewed the world, broadened her expectations, and chose new paths, she always died prematurely by the sword, as she would this life. When and by whom was the variable? Perhaps, she should take her own head? That would surely unbalance karma and the Goddesses control over her life?

Ruby's sobbing filled the room.

Unable to stand the tension, Pagan fumbled through her knitted jacket pocket until she pulled out a cookie that she had wrapped up in foil earlier that day.

"Look, what I have!"

Fay Ce'Line

Fay Ce'Line ushered Pagan, Amelie, Ruby and Roberta outside onto the front veranda. The veranda flexed from their combined weight.

She needed the late afternoon sun on her face before it disappeared for the evening. Her body was aching and she had an unexplained chill in her bones.

Pagan buttoned up her knitted cardigan as she exited the farmhouse. The weather had quickly settled into autumn.

Once everyone was comfortable, Pagan snapped the cookie into quarters passing them around. She already anticipated Amelie would say no to an altered state of consciousness, remaining loyal to her glass of Chardonnay.

For the last ten years, Amelie's longing for experimental drugs had waned as Pagan's increased. The more Pagan's life seemed out of control and mundane, the more she craved an altered state.

Usually avoiding marijuana cookies due to their effects being unpredictable, Fay Ce'Line grabbed a quarter, eating it straight away.

"Potent as usual, Pagan," Fay Ce'Line grinned.

Pagan had used her favourite recipe; cannabis butter, brown sugar, vanilla essence, flour, baking soda, salt, water and a sprinkle of pecan nuts and chocolate chips.

Fay Ce'Line felt a placebo effect almost immediately, giggling over random topics, she faded out of the conversation within minutes to follow a prism of colours into her subconscious. Soon laughter echoed off into the distance as her mind floated elsewhere.

Roberta sat on the porch, her legs dangling over the edge, she looked like a child, "Ok Witches, what's better now compared to previous lives?"

Pagan responded first, "The drugs!"

"Hot showers. Electricity," Ruby said, abnormally louder than what was necessary.

Amelie pounced in with her answer, "Vibrators, batteries, electric blankets and in that order."

They all cackled until their stomachs hurt.

Roberta thought for a while, "For me, it's the music."

Nodding, they all agreed

Amelie asked, "Best decade then?"

Pagan piped up, "Not sure if I can 'lock in' a decade but 1985 was an awesome year for pop music. It was almost as good as 1785. Now that was a ripper of a year."

They howled with laughter again.

Roberta asked, "Best band or singer?"

"Neil Diamond," Ruby yelled.

Pagan disapprovingly asked, "Really Ruby? And why are you shouting?"

Ruby threw Pagan an unamused glance. In retaliation to Pagan's critical judgement, she replied, "Pagan, what's your favourite band, Smartarse?"

Pagan thought back over her most recent life. Closing her eyes, she travelled backwards in time to compose the soundtrack of her life, "Alanis Morisette, Nirvana, Nine Inch Nails, Tea Party, LCD Soundsystem and Muse and heaps more. So much music and not enough time."

She immediately questioned the irony of her comment as time was abundant to them.

Roberta interrupted, "Beatles, Led Zeppelin, Queen, and the Stones."

They all agreed.

Fay Ce'Line sat up from her trance, "Pumpkins!"

Amelie screwed her face up, "Seriously, Fay Ce'Line, I have never heard you listening to the 'Smashing Pumpkins'."

Fay Ce'Line smirked, "No I mean, let's go smash those pumpkins over there," pointing to the pumpkin patch across the road.

"No more drugs for you," Pagan laughed.

Fay Ce'Line stood up, jumped off the veranda and marched off across the paddock.

Amelie shuddered. Her tolerance level had reached its peak, "Fuck! She really is going to smash those pumpkins."

Don

"What the fuck?"

Don had witnessed some messed up shit but this scene was indescribable.

Placing his second can of alcohol into the drink bay, he shuffled out of his vehicle to get a better look.

Don howled with laughter, "They must be fucking wasted?"

He had watched Fay Ce'Line bolt from the veranda, cross the road and enter his neighbour's pumpkin patch. A bolt of electricity burst from Fay Ce'Line's palms, blowing up several large pumpkins. Seeds, pulp and skin sprayed five metres into the air.

Fay Ce'Line was joined by Ruby and Roberta who also took aim and joined in on Fay Ce'Line's fun. A shower of misty orange and green flakes clouded the sky as the three Witches blew up a mass of pumpkins.

Don controlled his laughter only long enough to grab his mobile phone out of his pocket and press record. A sea of orange hue as high as twenty metres fell down over them, covering them in pips and half fried pumpkins.

Amelie yelled from the safety of the road for them to stop. They ignored her.

Running as if she was holding a sword, Pagan hit a pumpkin with a rake that she had grabbed from Don's vegetable garden. The rake stuck in one of the pumpkins, angering Pagan who kicked at the pumpkin, only to slip on some mashed pumpkin and landing on her back.

Don had never witnessed the Witches produce Magick from their palms before, he understood that Ancients could, unlike Non-Ancients, but he had, until that moment, only ever heard about it in past tense.

It was the funniest scene he had ever watched and he had never seen the Witches so happy. Cackling until tears flooded their cheeks. Turning on each other in a whimsical pumpkin war: orange missiles skimming the ground, exploding, covering the enemy. It only took several moments for the three Witches to attack the weakest, Pagan, who ran from the pumpkin patch hovering behind Amelie, who was now wearing most of the smashed pumpkins on her new clothes.

She was not amused!

Eventually, they suffered exhaustion and wandering back to his farmhouse, only to collapse on the veranda.

How was he going to explain this to his neighbour? They had just destroyed half his crop.

Caleb

A blue haze filtered through the pine trees. Hauntingly beautiful, the tree branches formed an eerie earthy abstract formation above them. The starlight emitted though the density of the tree tops, a solace amongst the harsh green foliage where shadows hid creatures they were unaware of.

Caleb, Smithy and Clayton drew very little warmth from the fire; a fire that was only moments from blowing out, delving them into the dark again. The fire positioned directly in the middle of the upside down pentagram, marked their centre point. Position was important. Twenty candles strategically placed on the outer circle, ironically produced more heat than the fire.

Caleb shivered. It was a cold night.

Looking at his mates, he studied the flickering firelight that crossed their faces, casting grotesque masks upon them.

Waiting impatiently, they were keen for the full moon to appear through the tops of the trees and shine down on their sacred circle. Once the full moon was above them they would start.

Anticipation had made them agitated and snappy, so they had decided to remain silent until it was time.

The mouse slept in the shoebox unaware of its fate and the materials required to summon Satan sat beside the shoe box.

Smithy's head snapped sideways, "Hey, check that out!"

Caleb and Clayton turned. The hairs on the back of their necks stood up as a thick black mist hugged the ground, floating quickly towards them. It appeared to know where it was heading.

Staring at the black mist, Caleb detected it was breathing.

Squatting down to greet the entity, he waved his hand through the knee-high mist. Its dew soaked his skin and smelt rank. Caleb rubbed his hands on his cloak and waved his hand through the mist again, this time the moisture burned his skin, it was acidic.

Smelling his hand, he worried the pong would seep into his pores and the toxicity poison his blood.

Smithy shuffled uncomfortably on the spot as the mist reached him, an Irish jig in movement his dance motivated by panic, was neither joyous nor voluntary.

Clayton wandered backwards until it glided by him. His heart pounded as he spotted a pair of eyes looking at him in the mist.

Watching intently as the mist disappeared, Caleb smiled. Satan would join them tonight.

Coven

Fay Ce'Line lay on the single fold-out bed, snoring loudly which made it difficult for the Witches to converse. Surprised at how quickly Fay Ce'Line fatigued, Pagan wondered if it was due to the chemotherapy.

Amelie sat with her knees bent up on the sofa with Roberta's head resting upon it. Stroking her baby sister's hair, Amelie admired the thickness of it. They had both inherited the same hair; black and wiry, a common feature in each reincarnation.

Amelie wished that she had the same bond with their other sister, Peony, but Peony had made it very clear that she had no desire to improve their relationship. At least, they only had one reincarnation to put up with her sulkiness.

Ruby and Pagan sat at the table, picking at the food platter and finishing off the Sambuca.

"One, two, three. Go!"

Throwing the Sambuca shot down their mouths, it burned. Tears rolled down their cheeks and their stomachs heated up.

"Let's drink to the rest of the Coven that was not reincarnated beside us. To the Coven, wherever the fuck you may be."

"We are going to regret these shots in the morning," Ruby anticipated.

Pagan rolled her eyes, "Well, we only live once… Sort of."

Laughing until they both felt guilty for their moment of happiness, they quietened, only the sound of the Hermle oak grandfather clock ticking, and the low hum of the generator entertained their gloomy thoughts.

Tearing at the label on the Sambuca bottle, rolling it up and then flicking it across the table, Pagan's drunken thoughts wandered and feelings that Pagan controlled most of the time when sober, now darkened her spirits.

"I think about Rogan, you know, all the time. Every time, I look at my daughter, she reminds me of him. Ruby, she looks so much like her father. The guilt is eating me up."

Exaggerated in her drunken state, Ruby placed her hand on Pagan's face, "I'm hearing you, Pagan. I miss Graeme all the time as well, and I just can't even bring myself to say my own daughter's name."

Angering, Amelie snarled, "Shut up, Pagan. What's done is done. You can't change the past. Lucky for you when you're both reincarnated again, Rogan won't remember you murdered him, so just get on with your life. You did what you had to do to protect Deity, and you know what, payback *is* a bitch. Henry VIII was a total wanker. And he'll be born the same boring twat he always is, so don't worry."

Pagan sat back on her seat. The depression suffocated her.

Pouring the last of the Sambuca into the shot glasses, Ruby badly estimated the size of the shot glasses, spilling some of the Sambuca over the edge, creating a pool of white liquid on the table.

"None of us live without regret, Pagan, not even Amelie."

Ruby gave Amelie a cheeky wink.

"All of us have committed monstrous acts of cruelty and most likely will again. It's what we are. It's what we do. We're Witches; bitches, with a capital W!"

Roberta sat up, "I don't think that's a fair comment, Ruby. We weren't always like that. Life has made us cruel. We were warriors once, not murderers."

Pagan snarled, "What's the difference!"

Pointing at Fay Ce'Line, Roberta giggled, "Example! Fay Ce'Line hasn't poisoned anyone on purpose for over two reincarnations. There was that one accident but that doesn't count. All I am saying is that we are evolving."

"Oh little sister, you always see the good in everyone but I agree with Ruby, we are basically horrendous Beings. We have become what we were destined to be. Like humans we are innately cruel, and let's not forget how many cruel things we have actually taken pleasure in. None of us are without debauchery."

Pagan felt a wave of nausea as the mixture of scotch, marijuana and Sambuca fought for sovereignty in her stomach, "I need to go to bed. I feel sick."

Standing up, she stumbled towards the back door.

Amelie, Roberta and Ruby watched Pagan fall out the back door as she headed towards the Kombi.

Pulling out the sofa bed to make a double bed for both Ruby and Amelie, Roberta offered them extra blankets. They eagerly accepted the extra warmth.

Turning the lights off in the kitchen and lounge room, Roberta skipped up the stairs to her own bed where she slipped underneath the covers and wondered where Don was?

Don

Don struggled to stay awake. Rubbing his eyes until they reddened and were tender to touch, his vision blurred.

His lower back ached. Leaning forward, he repositioning himself on the seat and stretched his neck but it did not help.

Checking his mobile phone again, he sighed as it was only 23:50.

The cold welcomed itself into the utility like a nosy neighbour, making the last hour almost unbearable, so much so, his nipples erected. All he wanted was to sneak back into the farmhouse and join his wife in bed.

The lights had been turned out, but he thought it would be safer to wait another fifteen minutes so they would not suspect him of spying on them.

Turning the music off (as his anxiety preferred the silence), he contemplated opening another bourbon can. Four empty cans already sat in the back of the utility trailer with the empty packet of lollies.

"Maybe not."

His blood pressure was already elevated and drinking alcohol only made it worse.

Needing to 'take a piss', Don exited the vehicle.

Seeking relief in a bushier area, Don unzipped his pants and steamed up the rocks in front of him. Completing a figure eight on the rock, he was pleased that he still had control over some bodily functions.

Staring off into the distance, he admired the darkened landscape.

Roberta had wanted to live in the country. He had wanted to buy a house on the coastline. Easily falling in love with the gently sloping hills and the seasonal transitions that changed the landscape every few months, he was glad his strong-willed wife had 'stood her ground' and persuaded him with her girly smile and tender disposition to move to the country.

It was difficult for him to say 'no' to his wife at any time, especially when she had her 'mind set' on something.

His peripheral vision spotted something in the distance, a flickering amber light, likened to an exotic belly dancer.

"What the?"

Zipping his jeans up, he headed back to his vehicle to grab a long black waterproof jacket and his unregistered semi-automatic rifle. He thought of ringing the lads at the club but chose not to waste more of their time. His men were already being asked to do more than what was expected of them.

"Probably some kids hiding out?"

Treading as softly as his large structure could on unstable ground, he struggled to manage a safe passage through the pine trees. The pine trees were denser and he needed to use his peripheral vision to guide him. He stumbled a few times but managed to stay upright. Cursing underneath his breath, he fantasised about wrapping his arms around Roberta and enjoying the warmth of their bed, instead of tracing across a darkened pine tree reserve in search of 'god knows what'.

Stepping on a twig it snapped. Frozen, Don held his breath. Waiting a few minutes to ensure he had not been noticed, he walked only a few more steps before his foot hit a log. Sliding his hand along the moss, he estimated it was a large fallen log at least twenty metres long and a metre round.

"Shit!"

He felt his blood pressure rising.

Lifting his right leg over the log, the rifle positioned above his head, Don cradled the log as if he was riding it. Swinging the other leg over the log, he praised himself for how easy it had been, but then the ground gave way and Don slid onto his bottom, down a four metre gully, landing spread-eagled on his back soaked in the mud. Twigs were stuck in his hair, and one shoe rolled down, lost in the shrubbery.

Fuming, Don silently cussed.

Deciding in his moment of anger that he would shoot whoever it was at the fire, now for fun.

Caleb

Finally the full moon shone down and midnight was only a few minutes away.

Caleb felt the anticipation welling up in his concave chest.

Placing their hoods over their heads, only the teenager's faces were recognisable.

Caleb grabbed the shoebox, yanking the alerted mouse out. He held it tightly around its stomach. Its failed attempt to escape from Caleb's grip, tired the mouse quickly. The sharpened stainless steel army knife glimmered in the light. Flattened out by the weight of Caleb's hand against the shoebox, Caleb hacked its head off. Taking longer than he had predicted, its neck cushioned the blade causing the eyes of the mouse to pop out before he cut through its bones. The squeals of pain echoed through the trees. The mouse's blood gave Caleb an adrenaline rush and he decided that next time he would use a cat, and a bigger and sharper knife.

Smithy and Clayton looked away, repulsed by the cruelty, both struggled with their morality.

Disappointed with their lack of enjoyment, Caleb stood up. Dripping the mouse's blood over his fingers, he rejoiced in the sacrifice.

Turning to Smithy first, he painted an upside down cross on his forehead. Obediently Clayton offered his forehead to Caleb before painting his own.

Emotionally cold, Caleb then threw the mouse's body and head into the fire. The fire sparked and hissed as it roasted the rodent's remains.

Caleb spoke, "Lord Lucifer, our gracious father, we come here tonight as your children of Darkness. We follow the path of carnal knowledge. We are your humble servants. Do with us as you will."

Caleb directed his speech at Smithy, "Do you claim yourself a Satanist?"

Smithy enthusiastically nodded.

Pressing his army knife into Smithy's right palm, he cut a three centimetre long incision in it, followed by the left palm. It took several seconds before the blood reached the skin's surface.

Turning right towards Clayton, Caleb repeated the ritual, "Do you claim yourself a Satanist?"

Hesitating, Clayton scanned the circumference of the circle. He sensed something supernatural was already watching them. Instinct to pull his hand back only aggravated the situation.

Bad-tempered, Caleb grabbed Clayton's fingers so he could not flinch and sliced his palm open. The pain felt like a thousand bee stings as Caleb dug the army knife in deeply. Clayton closed his eyes as Caleb cut his other hand.

Lastly, Caleb performed the ritual on himself. Digging the army knife, the ripping of his skin gave him relief. Partial to cutting, he found self-harming an effective tool for releasing his anxieties.

Caleb believed he was a child of Satan. His long term plan was to eventually offer human sacrifices to his Father. Perhaps, Clayton and Smithy, if he had to prove his loyalty.

Pressing their palms together; left hand to right hand forming a human triangle around the fire, the heat from the fire warmed their legs.

Caleb closed his eyes and chanted, "Hail Satan, our lord, I pray, I plead to thee, you are the truth, the one true God, we ask that you manifest before us."

Smithy joined the second chorus followed by Clayton for the third, in rehearsals Caleb had been adamant that they could not 'screw up'.

By the fourth chorus a gust of wind whipped past them.

Raising his voice, Caleb's mood elevated by the intensity, "Hail Satan, our Lord, I pray, I plead, to thee, you are the truth, the one true God, we ask that you manifest before us."

Caleb's heart was racing. Finally, he would be powerful, and finally, he would have Satan to help him revenge everyone who had ever bullied him, or got in his way, or made him feel 'less than'.

The boys raised their hands, "Hail Satan, our lord, I pray, I plead to thee, you are the truth, the one true God, we ask that you manifest before us."

Hearing ruffling in the bush, Clayton opened one eye and scanned the area. Silhouetted by the moonlight, something was limping towards them. It was enormous, standing at least two metres tall, with two large horns protruding from its head. It held a huge pitchfork or something.

Clayton froze with fear. Subconsciously, he never really thought that they would, or could, conjure Satan, and now they were going to die.

Satan raised his pitchfork above his head and let out a forceful command, "Get the fuck out of here!"

Cowardly, Smithy jumped backwards, fumbling over his feet. He fled into the safety of the darkness.

After drenching his skater pants in urine, Clayton followed Smithy.

Caleb knelt down, "Lord Lucifer, you've come."

Satan aimed the pitchfork and shot at him, the bullet impacting the ground only centimetres away from where Caleb knelt.

Caleb realising that it was not Satan but a madman instead, began pleading for his life.

Another bullet skimmed past him and without hesitation, he ran off, through the pine trees, screaming.

Pagan

Stepping through the Kombi door and up onto the metal floor, drunk, Pagan slipped, twisted, and fell onto the bed on her back. Fully clothed, she slept in an alcohol induced semi-coma.

With the Kombi door left opened, the intoxication kept her warm from the evening chill as she lay snoring on top of the bed. Emotionally and physically exhausted, her dreams gave her little reprieve, fast-forwarded like a video on double time, her heartbeat quickened as she found no consolation in her fantasy world.

An angry grey mist swirled underneath the van, lifting it up slightly, rocking it 'side to side'. Glad that it had finally found her, it peered into the van. Swaying, a three headed cobra with dark crimson eyes stared at the Witch in her slumber. Its foul smelling breath blanketed Pagan's body.

As if she had found an old friend, Pagan felt a wave of tranquillity floating over her, a knowing; a surge of love heating her entire body. A voice from the past called her name.

Smiling, she reached out to touch him, her fingers desperately clenching at the mist.

Inhaling, he smelt good, her heart raced, he was home. He had finally returned to her. The rush of euphoria elevated her spirits and she giggled in her sleep.

"Pagan," the cobra hissed.

The saliva from its fangs dropped into her eardrum, forming a deafening pool that over-spilled, running down her neck.

Opening her eyes, attentive somewhere between a lucid sleep and consciousness, she sat up.

Only inches off the bed, the mist ambushed her, transforming from a cobra into a small red devilish creature with red scaly claws that pinned her shoulders to the bed, bruising her instantly. Small bubbles of blood outlined the scratches. Sitting on Pagan's torso the weight of the creature caved her chest in, while a second pair of hands wrapped around her neck, strangling her.

Petrified, she tried to breathe. Paralysed, her eyes stared at the creature. She tried to scream but her jaw locked from fear.

It was trying to force itself inside of her; frantically burrowing into her stomach like a cat's back feet kicking.

Tears rolled down her face as she realised what was attacking her and what it was attempting to do. As if a best friend had betrayed her, her heart broke.

The Kombi shook from the ferocity of the attack.

The sound of gun fire, deafened her.

The creature squealed from pain as the bullet entered its body. Releasing its grip, it fled from the van, like a wounded animal, knocking Don backwards onto the ground.

Once again, Don lay spread-eagled on his back gripping the rifle.

Touching her neck, Pagan's skin stung and she coughed, wildly.

Reaching them first, bare feet and only a long t-shirt to cover her body, Ruby frantically yelled at Don, "What the hell happened Don?"

Amelie, dressed in a silky dressing gown arrived shortly after, jumping immediately into the back of the Kombi, finding Pagan still gasping for air. Relieved that Don had not shot her, she cradled Pagan, placing her head into her bosom.

Roberta and Fay Ce'Line still half asleep joined the group half a minute later.

Roberta helped Don stand up, automatically brushing the twigs out of his hair, "Baby, what happened?"

"I don't know what I just saw, but it ain't human. It nearly fucking killed Pagan."

Shaking from shock, Pagan sat up. Mascara stained her cheeks.

Hoarse, the pain of pronouncing made her stutter, "It was my brother, Norman. But he's different. He reeks of the Darkness. The smell is undeniable. It's something you never forget. He was trying to burrow into my torso."

Roberta yelled, "Why would he do that?"

Pagan collapsed onto the bed. Disbelief that Norman her brother, who she had not seen since she was a child, had returned as the Darkness. But why? She rested her palms over her face.

'Fuck! The Darkness is back. And this time, they would surely lose the war'.

CHAPTER 22
Inanna

It had been a crazy idea to slide the king size mattress from the spare room and up two sets of staircases. Inanna and Mark had giggled liked naughty children.

Morghana slammed her door shut. Unamused by their sudden stupidity, particularly on *her* level of the house, she turned the speakers up on the IPod to drown-out her, mum and stepdad's laughter.

Plopping the firm mattress onto the carpet in the study, Mark rearranged the furniture to accommodate for it, while Inanna went to the linen cupboard to grab a fitted silk sheet. On the way back, she grabbed the doona and four pillows from their bed, which she threw onto the naked mattress.

Grinning at Mark, she suddenly remembered the wine and galloped back down the hallway and into the kitchen where she grabbed the chilled Sauvignon Blanc and two crystal glasses.

Waiting for Inanna, Mark fitted the sheet onto the mattress and sat down ready for her return.

Unscrewing the cork from the bottle, Inanna took a swig of the white wine, spilling it down her chest. Uninhibited, Inanna ignored the spillage and drank some more.

Pouring Mark's wine into his glass, she walked back to the study where she found Mark laying on the mattress. She slammed the study door shut and locked it.

Handing the glass to him, she placed her empty glass on the desk after deciding to continue drinking from the bottle.

"Cheers, Mark."

"Cheers, Inny," Mark said, tapping his crystal glass onto the half-finished bottle.

They drank.

Snuggling into Mark's warmth, Inanna grabbed Mark's hand and wrapped it up into her own. It had been a long time since they had done something spontaneous together. Warranted it was fairly subdued deciding to sleep in the office so that she could be close to Mark as he worked through an 'all-nighter' but it was as spur-of-the-moment as the couple got.

Mark appreciated that Inanna was giving up her cosy bed to sleep on a mattress on the floor, just so she could support him through the night.

Finishing his drink, he placed the glass on the carpet and stood up.

Disappointed, Inanna complained, "Oh honey, don't start yet."

Bent over the desk, he pressed play on his iTunes list. Nina Simone sultry smooth blues voice forced the silence into the room into submission.

"Inny! I spent all morning putting this playlist together. So you better dance."

"How could I say 'no' to Nina? My hands are tied."

Mark teased as he pulled her up into his arms, "Not yet, Inny."

Swirling her around, he turned her away from him so he could run his hand around her waist.

Finding each other's gaze, they lingered.

Mark procrastinated before he kissed her. His lips hovered above her lips as if he was waiting for her to give him permission. She gave him permission by lifting his t-shirt over his head and throwing it over the computer screen.

Lips touching, he groped her breasts, cupping her as if it was the first time he had ever touched her. Tugging on her dress, he lifted it up over her shoulders, throwing it aimlessly across the study. It landed on the filing cabinet.

Staring at Inanna in the darkened room, lit up only by the computer monitor and an old lamp, Mark was overwhelmed by her essence.

"You are so beautiful, Inny."

Inanna untied his trouser zipper and pulled them down. He easily slipped out of them, kicking them to the side.

Rubbing his penis, she replied, "And you, you are all man."

Pulling her closer, Mark kissed her neck while he unbuttoned her bra.

Laying her down onto the mattress, he removed her underwear and spread her legs.

On cue, Nina Simone's song 'In the Dark' played.

Running his hands along her thighs, his fingertips stopped to be replaced with his lips.

Closing her eyes, she surrendered her thoughts to the lyrics of the song and her body to Mark's touch.

Easily aroused, Inanna's orgasm drowned out Nina's singing and echoed down the hall.

Mark collapsed sweaty and satisfied on top of her moments later.

Wrapping her arms around him, she held him tightly. His back muscles absorbed the pressure.

They lay in each other's juices, listening to the music for a several minutes before Inanna spoke, "Sometimes before you kiss me, you hover for a while. Why do you do that?"

Mark rolled off her, finding comfort on his side. His hand tickled her stomach where a pool of sweat had gathered.

Their noses touched.

"I love the smell of your breath before I kiss you."

Inanna drew breath. Lost for words, she ran her fingertips over his mouth, "Thank you."

"I better get to work. Sleep gorgeous. I'll see you in the morning."

With a kiss goodnight, he sat at his desk, put his reading glasses on and commenced work. The light from the computer monitor highlighted his middle-aged body.

Inanna watched as his long fingers typed on the keyboard and his gaze was lost in invoices. Mark sitting naked while working was the sexiest image Inanna had ever witnessed.

"Sometimes Mark," she interrupted.

Turning, he lifted his eyebrows above the glasses. He was amused at how quickly she interrupted him.

"There are moments of perfection, just snippets. Long enough to remind us that 'only time' has infinite power, not mighty Gods or Goddesses. Just time! Long enough for us to lose breathe in, like an instant photograph capturing beauty amplified."

Rolling over, she added, "I will remember this moment forever, Mark. I promise."

Mark grinned, "One orgasm and you become a philosopher."

CHAPTER 23
June 5th
Fay Ce'Line

Fay Ce'Line assembled in the doctor's surgery waiting room, after being called that afternoon to make another appointment.

The surgery was busy with feverish children, agitated middle aged people, and the elderly who were mostly there for a social outing or for a repeat prescription.

Two senior men who had been friends for a long time, exchanged stories from their childhood or proud announcements of another grandchild being born. Their elderly aged enthusiasm, soaked up the pitiful stench of cleaning product that stung Fay Ce'Line's eyes.

Relieved to have left the twins at home with Oscar, who would have fed and bathed them before reading to them on the couch, she settled in for the long anticipated wait.

Flicking through a multitude of glossy 'Do It Yourself' magazines, Fay Ce'Line was nonchalantly escorted into the consultation room, after one and half hours of waiting.

Walking along the corridor, she giggled, "You wouldn't want to be dying in here."

The joke was wasted on the nurse who only rolled her eyes, knocked on the door, only to fling it open before the doctor said, "Come in."

Entering the familiar room, she sat on the patient chair. Apprehensively, she crossed her ankles and clenched her fists. Grimacing, she hoped the doctor would not notice her nervousness.

The doctor was a handsome Englishman, well into his fifties. He had been her personal doctor for over twenty years, and he had made it his own personal mission to support Fay Ce'Line during her cancer scare, and for this, she was humbled.

Bushy eyebrows and a regal appearance suited his demure personality and professionalism. Fay Ce'Line appreciated his 'gut instinct' approach to medicine with his best advice being in relation to raising children, "Listen to your instincts," and she had.

Crossing his leg, right over left, he settled into the large office chair. Looking up, his eyes twitched.

She sensed he was uncomfortable. He sat too relaxed in his chair. He was a pathetic rogue.

In a poignant manner, he spoke, "So, Fay Ce'Line, we have your blood results back and they show us that there are no signs that the cancer has returned

272

but I think for good measure, just in case, considering the bloating and stomach pain that we should send you immediately to Hobart for more tests."

Fay Ce'Line fought back the tears, sensing that when he was saying one thing, he was insinuating another.

'Just in case', sounded like, 'you're fucked'.

Looking into the blackness of his pupils, she noted that they looked off-centre, preferring the right side. She also noticed the badly concealed expression of pity in his wrinkles that formed a transparent illusion around his mouth. Out of respect, she would play along with him. It was obviously difficult for him.

Sitting up, her spine unusually straight, she smiled, "I'll have to organise the twins as I know Oscar will want to come with me. He has some time at work owing to him, so it should be fine."

Years of doctoring were better than any blood test results. She knew that he knew the cancer had returned. Secondary ovarian cancer was a death sentence. She was going to die for the first time from a disease called Cancer and no Magick concoction was going to save her.

In a silent room, doctor and patient looked at each other. A friendship built on illness, births, viruses, needles and the common flu was now about to end.

How long she had, was in the hands of the Goddesses.

She smiled at him; a gush of water flooded her cheeks, "Thank you. You really are a wonderful man, a great doctor and good friend."

The doctor placed his hand on Fay Ce'Line's knee, "Would you like me to ring Oscar for you? Maybe ask one of the nurses to make you a cup of tea before you drive home."

Fay Ce'Line voice quivered, "I've shared everything with my husband so I'll tell him, but I'll say yes to a cup of tea. Hopefully, I can keep it down."

Turning towards the desk, he began filling out her admittance form to the Hobart Hospital. She watched as his pen pressed down on the starched paper, how his writing was unreadable but somehow romantic in its cursive font, and how proudly he wrote his signature, flicking the last letter up twice as high as the other letters.

All of a sudden the smallest of things mattered to her.

June 6th
Pagan

After a four hour drive to Hobart, Pagan marched up to the unattended counter relieved to finally be out of the car and stretching her legs. The Midland Highway was tedious as usual, and the traffic frustratingly slow.

A young female receptionist looked up from the desk which was positioned on the back wall of the reception area. Pagan was not surprised to be greeted by a new staff member. The changeover of staff was evidence of poor management and a toxic working environment.

"Can I help you?" The receptionist asked through squinting eyes and a tight lipped mouth.

Pagan attempted to be pleasant although it almost emotionally drained her, "I'm here to meet with Priscilla."

The receptionist screwed her face up as if the air suddenly smelt bitter.

Picking up the phone, she dialled the number one and waited for her superior to answer, "Sorry to interrupt you but your eleven o'clock is here."

The receptionist hung up the phone and instead of communicating with Pagan, continued typing on her computer keyboard.

'Probably on social media', Pagan thought.

Wandering over to the coffee pot, Pagan poured the dark bitter liquid into a white plastic cup. She blew over the top, attempting to cool it down before she took a sip.

Several minutes later, Priscilla appeared through the glass sliding doors, well groomed, dressed in her beige work suit. Her red hair was combed back into a loose bun, "Pagan, I'm right to see you now."

Nodding, Pagan placed the coffee cup down on the small table.

Walking past the counter, Pagan sarcastically turned to the receptionist, "Thanks for your help."

The receptionist sarcastically replied, "You're welcome."

Following Priscilla down the carpeted hallway to her office, third door on the left, Pagan jested, "So you're employing muggles now?"

"Seriously Pagan, you can't wait until we're in my office before you start sledging Harry Potter jokes?"

Pagan walked into the office and sat down, "I'm just saying Priscilla it wouldn't hurt the youth of today to smile. They have electricity. What more is there to want?"

Priscilla ignored the comment while sitting down at her desk.

Looking around the office at the new décor, Pagan snarled, "Nice to see our taxes are being well spent."

Tapping a pen on the desk, Priscilla asked, "What can I do for you, Pagan?"

Not waiting for a reply, Priscilla continued, "Let me guess you have more petitions against the Awakening ritual? Or some bullshit plan to overthrow the Monarchy? Or you want to establish more rights for Witches on low incomes? Bla, bla, bla. I have another appointment at 12:00, Pagan so make it snappy."

"I don't think you can call lunch an appointment, Priscilla."

Squinting, Priscilla increased the speed in which she tapped her pen on the desk.

"You see I have a lot more free time now I don't have my Magick or status. Bummer for you really."

A long deep breath helped Priscilla to concentrate, "What is it that you want, Pagan? And can I just remind you that you are not Royalty anymore before you start throwing your ego around *my* office."

Priscilla laughed, "Actually the only thing royal about you, is that you are royal pain in my arse. Now why are you here?"

Enjoying Priscilla's sarcastic qualities; two alpha Witches battling their wit against each other in playful banter, Pagan focused, "I'm here for several reasons but one in particular."

Pagan reached for her neck, untying the scarf to reveal the yellowing-black bruises, the shape of little hands around her neck.

Repulsed by the injury, Priscilla shuffled backwards on her chair.

A vulnerable Pagan spoke, "I saw the Darkness. It's returned and it's here in Tasmania. It tried to enter my body via my stomach. Where my Magick *should* be."

Confused, Priscilla tilted her neck. She had been told the Darkness was a myth, a story to scare Maiden's before bedtime but she could see fear in Pagan's eyes, an uncertainty that she had never witnessed from Pagan before, she was telling the truth.

Out of her depth, Priscilla tried to bluff her way through the revelation, "Times have changed. Everything is red tape now. I will need you to fill in a Statutory Declaration Form before I can further discuss this matter with you, Pagan."

Pagan rolled her eyes in protest.

"It's in everyone's best interests if we deal with this matter professionally."

Slamming her palms down on the desk, Pagan's voice bellowed down the hall, "Fuck your red tape bullshit and get Aggie here now! She took my fucking Magick. She can deal with the fucking mess. The Darkness is powerful. So powerful it will rip your Non-Ancient arse in half. More powerful than all the Witches put together and it's back! You need to make this a priority. The Darkness won't give a shit about your paper work!"

Priscilla's heart raced. Where once she would have obeyed an Ancient Witch without hesitation, she was now the authority in the room but nevertheless she was petrified of Pagan. She could not let Pagan bully her however. Composing herself, she thought it best to deflate the situation as quickly as possible.

Gritting her teeth, Priscilla stared at Pagan, "Sit down now or I will have the authorities deal with you."

Pagan knew that she was not dealing with the situation properly but Non-Ancient Witches had no idea what they were dealing with. The Darkness was a threat to humanity and the Witches.

Once again, Priscilla saw fear in Pagan's eyes. She reminded herself that Pagan was an excellent actress; perhaps this was a trick?

"How do I know that this isn't some ploy to get Aggie here? When you submit the Statutory Declaration Form and it's processed through the correct channels, then and only then, will I consider contacting the Crone Monarchy."

A nervous giggle escaped Pagan's lips, "What? You don't have Aggie on speed dial?"

"How about you just leave it in the lap of the Goddesses, Pagan."

"The lap of the establishment, you mean."

Morghana

Morghana was introduced to grief counsellor, Lyndsay. After their initial meeting, Morghana told her mother that she had, "Immediately liked her."

Wearing dark prescription reading glasses, Inanna had masked her relief from her daughter as a single tear had dropped.

Lyndsay had jotted down on a small piece of paper to remind herself to ask Morghana 'why she touched her ears' so frequently. She wondered, if Morghana was partially deaf or was suffering from an inner ear infection?' It would explain her fits of frustration, although it was uncommon for such a disability like deafness not to be found earlier in life.

Inanna had bullied Morghana into counselling, thinking it would be a terrific idea to help her deal with the loss of Hensley. Lyndsay was the fourth counsellor Morghana had now seen over two weeks. Each counsellor recommending after one session that Morghana should be transferred to someone else. Someone more qualified.

'Qualified for what?'

Hiding a bruise on her cheek by applying thick foundation, a bruise obtained during one of Morghana's rages, one and a half weeks ago, Inanna was worried for her daughter's mental state.

Fits of frustration were increasing instead of decreasing, and Mark was fed up with trying to deal with a step-daughter who was obviously experiencing a mental breakdown.

Sitting Inanna down, handing her a glass of scotch with four ice cubes, Mark persuaded Inanna that Morghana needed professional help. That as parents, they were limited to how best to deal with a grieving teenager.

Since Hensley's suicide, Morghana had been on a destructive bender, falling deeper into depression right in front of them.

As Mark described it, "It's our parental duty to find the best support for Morghana during this time."

Inanna agreed, kissing Mark on the cheek, "What would I do without you? You're right, Morghana needs external help."

Sitting in another waiting room, Inanna watched her daughter walk off with a stranger, a stranger who could 'apparently' help her daughter more than she could. Inanna could not help but feel that she had let her daughter down as a mother and as a Witch.

Lyndsay walked beside Morghana to the office. Holding her breath, the stench of the unwashed teenager made Lyndsay unwell.

Entering the room, Morghana's held her breath. The room looked like a playpen for toddlers. She felt insulted. Lyndsay obviously did not understand her grief at all?

Grudgingly, she sat down on a child's wooden chair, barely one bum cheek fitting on it. A wooden play table sat in front of her.

Lyndsay spoke calmly, patronisingly in fact, "Ok! Morghana I've spoken at some length with your mum but in today's session I thought it would be good to tell you a little about grief and then try to help you to understand where you are on a personal level in relation to grief? Ok?"

Morghana chewed on her tongue as a way of concealing her amusement.

"Right, firstly I am going to draw you a diagram on the smart-board. I find this diagram to be very helpful."

Drawing a river with a long island in the middle of it, she then added two canoes at one end of the river, explaining to Morghana that she was in one canoe and Hensley was in the other canoe and that both canoes would travelled down the river until they hit rapids, where consequently both canoes would be separated and travel around the island on opposite sides.

"You see Morghana, Hensley is just travelling along another path now. Her essence is still here!"

Lyndsay shook her head enthusiastically at Morghana, "And the awesome news is that one day your paths will join back up."

Lyndsay waited for Morghana to respond. Morghana turned to look out the window, wondering how long she had to sit listening to all the university crap.

Intuitively, Lyndsay realised that Morghana was struggling with more than just grief.

"Morghana, the next activity might seem a little strange to you at first but I promise that if you just trust me, you will find it very beneficial. It is also a wonderful tool for me to better understand where you are in the grief process."

Walking over to the little table, her high heels imprinting the freshly laid carpet, Lyndsay removed the lid, "Now this table is not just a table, it's also a sandpit, so basically I want you to imagine the sand is a blank canvas."

Pointing around the room, Lyndsay showcased the overcrowded shelving, "Around the room there are lots of different toys. What I would like you to do, in your own time is choose certain toys that represent how you feel and place them on your blank canvas. You can choose lots or just a few. It' really up to you. Now, I also have a container of water here."

She picked up a container of water, "That you can use in manipulating your sand."

Morghana sat rigid. The counsellor was treating her like a child, and the chatting in her ears was getting louder.

As if her plan was 'fool proof', arrogantly Lyndsay walked towards the door, "I'm going to leave the room for a while. I know it sounds silly but it really is a good exercise."

Left in the room on her own, Morghana felt vulnerable and annoyed. The whole exercise was a waste of her time. Had Lyndsay ever lost her only friend? A friend who understood how lonely it was to be a Maiden, to be facing a ceremony that ultimately led to her friend's suicide? Was she hearing voices constantly in her ears? None of these mental health professionals have a clue what they are dealing with.

A burst of anger burned in her stomach.

Glaring at the table; the blank canvas, Morghana channelled her anger at the small beads of sand. Leaning towards it, she swirled her index finger through the sand, making deep trails that swirled, collided and turn back on themselves.

Energized, she jumped up from her seat to look at the abundance of toys on the shelves. There had to be easily a thousand toys. Children would love this room: she hated it.

Spotting a tiny metal ambulance on the second shelf to the left of her, Morghana stared at it for some time before grabbing it and placing in the sandpit. Then a Barbie doll that reminded her of Hensley, a school building, a 'Happy Birthday' sign. Strategically, she placed the toys in the sandpit, each time jamming the next toy a little harder into the sand.

There was room for one more toy. Searching the shelves, she spotted a Witch- a modern Witch with a large floppy hat, a dress that barely went past her bottom, and black and orange stripped stockings.

Digging a hole with the side of her palm, she buried it, splashing the container of water over it.

"Drown Witch, drown."

In one large livid heave, Morghana grabbed the edges of the sandpit, flipping the entire contents onto the floor. Then she started picking the toys off the shelves and smashing them against the opposite wall.

Lyndsay who was watching the ordeal on a security camera asked one of her colleagues to join her. They both watched in dismay as Morghana tore the room apart.

Calling security, Lyndsay shook her head. In five years, no one had ever erupted into a rage.

Pulling her small pad out of her pocket, she wrote down that Morghana had played with her ears, twenty three times in the last ten minutes.

Amelie

They drove for one and half hours in Marcus's 1999 sedan. The vehicle was in pristine condition but Amelie still felt uncomfortable sitting in a tank.

"You're a snob, Amelie."

"Commit to an old classic or a modern car, but honey, choosing a car without refinement is perilously common. You should know better."

Marcus snorted from laughter.

Amelie continued, "Are you sure you're a doctor because you must be able to afford a better car than this?"

Taking his hand off the steering wheel, Marcus reached over to maul his date's knee.

His smile made her soften.

He teased, "I can afford you."

Pushing his hand off her knee, it was Amelie's turn to jest; she sang, "Keep your eyes on the road and your hand upon the wheel."

Marcus belly laughed, "I love that about you, Amelie. You keep me on my toes."

Frozen, Amelie contemplated what Marcus had just said. He said the 'love' word, mindful that it was strategically placed within a friend based sentence, she still felt uncomfortable.

"I prefer you on your back," she buffered.

Marcus refused to tell her where he was driving her. He wanted to surprise her, even after she told him she hated surprises.

Amelie looked outside the car's window. Dusk was settling in.

They had reached Lilydale and were now heading up into the remote Mount Arthur region.

Her hips were aching and she was bored.

'It better be worth it', she thought.

Amelie reminded herself that she was a self-confessed control-freak and she should attempt to chill-out but she was still nervous.

Amelie grew more fearful, "How far up the mountain are we going?"

"Just relax, Amelie, I would never put you in danger. Just enjoy my gift to you."

She studied him. He was very handsome. He kept himself fit, and for age forty nine his general health was exceptional. His black skin highlighted his luscious lips and kind eyes. Aesthetically, he really was an exceptional human.

Amelie took a deep breath, doubt quickly establishing itself. Forty nine years! He had lived a whole lifetime that she knew nothing about. She tried to ignore her pessimism but she felt ambiguous towards her date.

The dirt road was narrowing.

She was relieved that she was wearing sturdy walking boots. Amelie hated bush walking and now she was about to walk into the bush in the dark with a man, she was having sex with but knew nothing about.

Unlike Pagan, Amelie enjoyed modern comforts. She was glad Witches had evolved, moved into the cities and forgot their innate relationship with nature. Pagan could romanticise about the 'past' all she liked, but Amelie knew Pagan would not last two days if she was to return to Ancient times.

Amelie fidgeted on her seat, "Do you actually know where you are going because I could do with a glass of chardonnay right now, and we missed the wine district about half an hour ago."

Marcus responded by pointing out in front of them, "In about ten metres, we'll be there."

Amelie looked ahead. Gigantic overhanging trees arched the road. They were driving into the pitch black.

"Oh Marcus, you are not serious. We've just driven for nearly two hours to bring me here?"

Marcus ignored her, parked the vehicle, jumped out of the car and unlocked the boot, while Amelie sat safety in the car.

'What if Marcus was a serial killer?' Surely not! 'Maybe, he was going to hack her to death, leaving her to rot in a shallow grave?' If she listened to her instinct, she would run for safety but if she listened to her heart she would trust him. She felt confused! 'How could she not trust Marcus? Why was she so frightened to 'let him in?'

Her gut instinct and mind were in conflict.

He knocked on the car roof, "Come on, Amelie. This is going to be amazing."

She sheepishly exited the car, stretching her hips before attempting to walk anywhere.

Wearing a 'led Lenser' head torch on his head, he blinded her.

Amelie giggled, "Are you using that to 'go down' on me later?"

He ignored her, grabbing her hand and leading her into the thick native bush.

Desperately grabbing the back of his jumper, Amelie stayed uncomfortably close to him. That way, she lessoned the chances of him leaving her to fend on her own in the blackness.

Talking excessively about the trees and why no light filtered through, Amelie wondered how come he knew so much about Tasmania's wilderness. And he knew his way through the bush. This only increased her feelings of fear and unease. She wondered how many times he had brought someone to this place and why it had to be at night.

Wanting to tell him that she was scared and that she wanted to head back to the car, especially after Pagan was attacked, she hesitated, ignoring her instinct, again.

Stopping, Marcus abruptly swung his hand behind him, grabbing her hand, "Amelie, here is your gift."

With his other hand, he pushed back a bunch of large bushy branches from a Wattle Tree revealing scenery so breathtaking, so awe-inspiring that for the first time in Amelie's life, she experienced a feeling so overwhelming that it must have been Stendhal syndrome; an overwhelming sense of beauty housed in nature's own artwork.

She cried. Tears of uncontrollable gratitude dropped onto her cold cheeks.

Marcus stood smug, "I told you it was worth the long drive."

Amelie stepped down into the Fern Tree cathedral. The moonlight sprinkled through the giant Man Ferns lighting up the glittery mist. Nature's Magick resided here, skipping and giggling like ancient fairies amongst the echoes of voices past.

It lured her into its haunting web. She trod softly, embracing the smells, the sounds and the untouched beauty that enhanced her own immortality.

Marcus strolled behind her enjoying her enchantment.

Finding a small waterfall cascading down the side of the mountain, she bent down, scooping the fresh mountain water into her cupped palms. She drank the sweet water.

She wanted to stay here forever, frolicking with the fairies, forest nymphs and naughty goblins.

Amelie swung around to face Marcus. Her face lit up as if she was a child again, abundant with possibilities and hope.

Did Marcus know that she was a Witch, and why had he brought her to such a wondrous place?

Kissing him passionately, she tasted his breath.

Pulling away, Marcus placed his hands around her upper arms, "Why do you treat every man like he has already broken your heart?"

Amelie pulled away, overwhelmed and delicate, her lip quavered, "Because they always do."

Pagan

Pagan forgot to pull the handbrake on or move the gear stick into 'park' as she parked in the driveway. The car slowly moved backwards until she felt the movement. Slamming her foot on the brake, she yanked the handbrake on and put the gearstick into 'Park', before scolding herself.

"Wake up, Pagan!"

Although exhausted, Pagan was thrilled to finally be home. She had departed from Hobart disenchanted with the day's enterprise and then spent the duration of the next three hours critiquing her conversation with Priscilla, concluding that it had been a wasted trip.

Non-Ancients did not have the herstory to comprehend what it meant to have the Darkness coming through the portal at will, again.

Opening the car door a familiar smell irritated her nostrils. Henry sat slumped on the rustic bench inside the back patio.

"Shit! What did her Fuckboy want?"

Grabbing her slouch bag, she stepped out of the car, slamming the door shut, loud enough to warn Henry she was upset with the intrusion.

Storming up the back steps to where he was sitting, she did not greet him before firing contempt at him.

"Seriously, how dare you come to my house uninvited?"

Pouting, Henry replied, "I sent you a text."

Remembering that she had turned the mobile phone off once she exited Hobart, she angered because she could have dealt with Henry hours ago.

"Um didn't reply, so maybe, you should have waited at home?"

Surprised by her annoyance, Henry missed the point.

"Look! I've had a really stressful couple of weeks and I really just need to be on my own tonight. I just don't have the energy for you."

His eyes pleaded with her.

"Don't give me puppy dog eyes, Henry, I fucking hate it."

"Please Pagan, I just need to say a few things and I'll leave, I promise."

She laughed, knowing how little a promise from a human meant. Staring out the window into the backyard, she weighed up her options. Rubbing her eyes, she wondered why she had started a sexual relationship with a boy. She answered her 'own' question honestly. It had been boredom mostly, and a desire to be in control and now she had to deal with the consequences of her stupidity.

"Ok! But can we go inside so people don't see you here?"

Pagan unlocked the back door, "I'm old enough to be your mother."

"Now our age difference worries you?"

Truth be known, anytime, he spoke their age difference worried her.

Walking inside, she slammed the backdoor shut behind them. Registering that the dining room light had been switched on and a familiar aroma tickled her nose, she could not believe the irony that she had two uninvited males in her home at once.

Throwing the slouch bag on the dining room table, she patted her two cats, using them as a timewaster.

Placing her hands on her hips, she snapped, "Ok, what's so important, Henry?"

He braced himself, uncomfortable in his own skin, "My girlfriend wants to get married so I am going to have to stop seeing you."

Pagan giggled, which quickly developed into a hysterical cackle.

Through snorts, she said, "You couldn't just text me that?"

Offended, he struggled to keep his voice at a respectable level, "You can be a real heartless bitch, when you want to be."

Pagan rolled her eyes, "You can leave now."

She was not about to waste precious energy on a situation she did not value.

Searching Pagan's face for any sign of compassion and only finding aloofness, Henry erupted into a rage, smashing a hole into the dining room wall. The thick horse hair plaster crumbled under the impact and his hand instantly swelled.

Outraged by Henry's tantrum, Pagan grabbed his right elbow, forcing it behind his back, lifting it up towards his left shoulder blade. She then threw his 'unwilling' submissive body up against the wall, squashing the side of his face.

Only inches away from the hole, bent in, her lips almost touching his ear lobe, she warned, "Listen, you little shit! Don't go changing the rules and then getting pissed off because I don't care to play anymore."

She released him, "Now run home to mummy and daddy and put a ring on your girlfriend's finger and don't be surprised when you're divorced in ten years."

Henry scrambled to the back door, looking back at Pagan for a brief moment before leaving.

"And their love affair ended," she jested as if she was writing the end of a long and tedious prologue.

Needing to balance her energies, she turned the tap on and drank directly from the stream of water. It tasted of chlorine. It was not her day.

Bed seemed the best option, plus it was time for her to confront the 'other' intruder in her home, but not before she examined the damage to the wall.

Running her fingers over the bristly horse hair exposed through the plaster, she cursed Henry. Then she cursed herself for getting involved with him. She should have known better. He was a mere child, so how could she be mad at his immaturity?

'Now to deal with the other intruder', she thought.

Sneaking down the hallway towards her bedroom, she struggled not to giggle. Satisfied that she had snuck up on her intruder, Pagan flipped the bedroom light on and jumped into the bedroom like a child playing 'peekaboo' with her parents.

Resting his head against the wrought iron bedhead, Dante raised his right eyebrow. Smugness protected his amusement.

Playfully, Pagan returned his raised eyebrow.

Pushing the doona cover off his body in one flick, Dante revealed his nakedness; a large erect penis pointed at her.

"Hmmm. Subtle Dante."

"What can I say, I've missed you."

"I must admit, Dante, you have impeccable timing."

The Sarcasm was not wasted on him. He was used to Pagan's use of mockery as a coping mechanism. Witnessing her vulnerable side, a vast hole so deep that even he worried that one day she would fully succumb to it, lost forever inside her own torment, he often wished he could open up to her fully, perhaps together they could help mend some holes.

Leaning against the door frame, Pagan pulled her shoes off. The day's activities weighed heavily upon her, but somehow removing the heaviness from her feet did helped, if only symbolically.

"Did you hear all that? You know with the kid?" Her cheeks flushed from embarrassment.

Dante smirked, "Yes! Yes! Of course. But you seemed to have had the situation under control. I thought for a moment I may have to save the boy though."

Pagan looked at Dante, a snort escaped her nose.

"I'm so embarrassed. I really don't know why I was fucking a boy."

Dante's memories flooded back to when he lay with Pagan, seventeen and still a Maiden. He had been aroused, intoxicated by her delicate smooth skin, her pale brown freckles and 'hard-on inducing' breasts.

Youth is for a long time a powerful aphrodisiac until mental compatibility replaces it and a desire to connect on a higher frequency becomes the new sexuality.

"He was not a boy, Pagan. Wet behind the ears, yes, but he was a man non-the-less. It's just men are boys for much longer now."

Her heart skipped a beat, even when exhausted she desired him. Her thirst for him growing beyond sensibilities: his long dark hair, sprinkled with grey highlights, shoulders uneven from years of broomstick travel, olive skin aging with the occasional sun spots, alluring cracking lips; a breath that once repulsed her, now enticed and teased, while his enigmatic eyes still protected his secretive nature, even after all these years.

"Who are you, Tristan Dante?"

"Does it matter?"

"Why do you always answer a question with a question? Who or what are you protecting?"

The answer was 'himself' but now was not the time to let his guard down.

Composed, he shielded his true feelings, "Pagan, come to bed. I've missed you."

His deflection annoyed her but Dante had always preferred to stay mysterious. After all these years, she knew no more of his nature than when he had kidnapped her at age seventeen.

Walking towards the bed, she undressed slowly. Pagan had always enjoyed being looked at, admired by her lovers. She liked the way that their eyes focused and their lips curled.

Jumper, singlet, bra, trousers and then knickers, Dante noted every twist of fabric as it dropped to the floor, while also registering the bruises on her neck and torso. Dante knew what creature had made those marks. Shivering, he chose to ignore her bruises but he could not ignore that the Darkness was gaining its strength, growing stronger each decade. While dormant, it had been planning its revenge.

The Witches were not strong enough to defeat the Darkness again. Over the centuries they had lost a substantial proportion of their Magick, reduced to fancy party tricks, if that. Degenerate from toxins, he feared for their survival.

Dante pursed his lips together. He had to remain in the moment. Focus on Pagan, after all, he could only offer her 'now'. Moments, were all they had.

Scooting beside him in the bed, she wedged herself tightly around his body.

"What are you doing here really, Dante? I just stop thinking about you and you appear. What is with that?"

Sinking into the mattress, he pulled the doona cover up over her shoulders, tucking her in as if she was a child.

Pagan rested her head on his hairy chest.

Their palms quickly found each other, and their legs entwined into a human knot.

Dante jested, "Well, I've started seeing someone and we are getting married."

Closing her eyes, she laughed, "What's he like?"

Dante squeezed her, "He snores but I think he could be the one."

Chuckling, she snuggled closer to him. Her ear hunted for his heartbeat, "A snorer is never the one."

Pagan would never capture Dante's heart but he was her soft place to fall, sometimes, and in a time of uncertainty it seemed enough.

Within seconds, she had fallen asleep in his arms.

Dante ran his fingertips down her neck. The welts were still prominent. He listened to her shallow breath. Their time was limited and he wanted to remember as much of her as he could. His instinct warned him that she would lose her head soon.

CHAPTER 24
June 12th
Ruby

Cassandrea jumped up from the seat, knocking over an empty glass. It rolled approximately thirty centimetres across the desk before she grabbed it, placing it upright.

She had not seen Ruby since Graham's funeral which she had been forced to attend by her work colleagues, and now Ruby had entered his old office and was swiftly walking towards her. There was nowhere to escape. Guilt attacked her chest and neck, a sign of discomfort as blotches covered her otherwise flawless complexion.

At age twenty three, Cassandrea had not learned the skill of social diplomacy, especially in relation to mourning etiquette, so she had put all her energy into avoiding Ruby instead. Crossing the road if she had seen Ruby walking towards her on the footpath, she had evaded contact several times. Even after Hensley's death, she had not even mustered up the strength to send a card of commiseration, hoping that she could plead ignorance if reproached for her behaviour.

Only working for Graham as a trainee receptionist for four months before he had suddenly died, Cassandrea crossed her fingers that Ruby would not remember her, let alone be offended by the lack of thoughtfulness.

"Good morning, can I help you?"

Ruby smiled out of politeness.

Entering the work place where her husband had died was difficult enough without having to deal with the receptionist who was pretending not to know who she was.

"Cassandrea, I'm sorry to arrive unannounced but I was hoping I could ask a favour?"

The room suddenly felt claustrophobic. Fidgeting, Cassandrea clenched her hands together as if she was about to recite a passage from the Bible.

Shocked by how Ruby had aged in the last few years, dark bags as large as teabags cushioned her already smallish eyes and wrinkles that once had defined her personality now sketched across her face like a sinister portrait.

"What can I do for you, Ruby?"

Moving closer to the desk it was now Ruby who appeared apprehensive, "I know this is a strange request but I was hoping I could just sit in Graham's office for a little while? I mean, I know it's not his office now."

Noticing Cassandrea's tenseness, Ruby continued, "It would only be for a few minutes. I promise, I won't touch anything. I just need to gather my thoughts."

Tears welled in her eyes, "I need to feel close to him."

Not sure how sitting in an office would make Ruby feel closer to her dead husband, Cassandrea thought about the consequences, finally deciding she could clear her conscience by helping Ruby. She looked at the clock on the wall opposite them. It was 10:08.

"Mr Johnson is in a meeting until ten thirty. I'm sure he won't mind as long as you don't touch anything."

Walking around the desk, Cassandrea led Ruby to Graham's old office. Turning the door handle, she pushed the door open and stood aside to let Ruby pass.

As if she was afraid the door was booby trapped, Ruby scanned the doorway before walking in. She closed the door behind her.

The office had certainly changed. Coffee coloured carpet had replaced the worn brown coiled carpet, and the walls had been painted a pale olive green where once a peach palette had depressed even the most positive of clients. Graham would have liked the crispness and modernisation of the room. A few new prints hung on the wall but the desk, bookcase and chair remained the same.

Smiling, Ruby remembered how Graham had hated the chair. Years of computer work had damaged his eyes while the constant sitting for hours each day had weakened his lower and upper back. Muscle spasms were a daily occurrence. It had taken her five months to pay off the brown leather chair (to suit the brown carpet and peach walls) with adjustable arms and guaranteed back support.

The sharp pain of grief jolted any advancements of Ruby's daydreaming and she quickly focused on the main objective for being there which was to analyse the room for any evidence that the Darkness had killed her husband.

The idea that the Darkness may have attributed to Graham's death had woken her from a dream after Pagan had been attacked. A massive heart attack had been the cause of death and the cleaner had said that the look on Graham's face had, "Chilled him to the bone", as if Graham had been scared to death.

'But what would the Darkness want with Graham?' Ruby scratched her chin.

There were too many possibilities and no one to help her figure the truth out; even Amelie would struggle to link the answers.

Pulling the chair out from the desk, she sat down and swivelled on it. It only seemed like yesterday that Graham had sat on the chair and Hensley on his lap. She had been a 'daddy's girl' enslaving Graham to all her childish requests.

Hensley, a Witch, and Graham, a human, meant that they would never meet again. It was a gloomy truth made even sadder that Hensley when Awoken in the next life, would feel the pain of losing Graham again. Their lives were grief 'on repeat'.

Morghana

The thick curtains dimmed the office while the room's musky odour with a hint of perfume attempted to mask the room's antiquity.

'It would help lighten the mood if the windows were opened, even slightly', Morghana thought. Perhaps, the psychologist was worried that the patients would attempt suicide if the windows were opened.

'Nothing a few prison bars would not fix, surely?' The irony made Morghana snigger.

The interior was bawdy; expensive but out-of-date furniture: a desk, two chairs, a bookshelf, and in an attempt to create a sense of homeliness a pot plant was placed in the corner of the room. The plant was plastic. If a room could influence a person's suicidal tendencies, it was certainly this one. Thoughts of suicide entertained Morghana for a few minutes while the psychologist fluffed around with some loose paperwork.

Analysing the psychologist, Morghana disliked what she saw. A middle-aged female, crossed legged, with a navy blue clipboard, an expensive black and gold pen, and an aura of superiority.

Morghana sensed she was bluffing. Probably studied at University to search for answers about her own mental health. Skin coloured stockings contrasted the blue court heel shoes and a dark brown suit. A skirt and jacket layered over a white blouse suggested that she had not fitted into University, in fact, she probably did not fit in anywhere.

Morghana sat, open-legged, slouched, a baby blue beanie pulled down over her knotty hair with a dismissive attitude.

Inanna had excelled herself, paying top dollar for Morghana's mental health. Her mother's health insurance would surely cover the expenses? Insurance certainly was a rich person's acquaintance.

It had only taken seventeen years for her mother to realise that her daughter needed someone to talk to. Aunty Pagan was too consumed with her own troubles to be of any help. Maybe her mother was right about Aunty Pagan's selfishness?

Struggling to concentrate on what the psychologist was saying due to a second voice interrupting and irritating her, Morghana stuck her index finger in her right ear to muffle the chatter.

"Morghana, what the results from the questionnaire show is that you are feeling high amounts of anxiety and depression which is not uncommon during the grief process, however after talking at great length with your mother, I think that we should also concentrate on other contributing factors."

The psychologist paused, waiting prematurely for Morghana to respond.

Morghana panicked. Had her mother told the psychologists that she was a Maiden?

The psychologist continued, "For the next few sessions, I think it's best if we start to examine your word usage, basic techniques on mindfulness, and really start to focus on your fear of death. I think these techniques will be a useful tool for you, especially dealing with the loss of your friend."

Morghana interrupted, "Her name was Hensley."

The psychologist apologised, "Hensley, and 'your' own immortality."

Morghana straightened her spine in an awkward attempt to engage, "So, you want to reprogram me?"

Alarmed, the psychologist quickly replied, however sensing Morghana seemed pleased with the idea of reprogramming, "Oh no, Morghana, I simply want to teach you effective techniques to help you deal with your anxiety and depression through education and mindfulness techniques."

Morghana slump back down on her chair, "Whatever!"

Fay Ce'Line

Fay Ce'Line held tightly onto Oscar's hand.

Closing her eyes, she committed his touch to memory: his coarse and dry labouring skin, his short and stumpy fingers and how they wrapped around her delicate hands, and his natural warmth that make her hands sweat.

It had been a tiresome twenty four hours for them both.

The doctor had organised for Fay Ce'Line to be flown by helicopter to the Hobart Hospital, concerned that her symptoms were far more advanced than first thought.

Fay Ce'Line's pain threshold was unlike any other patient's. If she was in extreme pain, something was terribly wrong.

She had never flown in a helicopter before, noting that it was considerably more comfortable than a broomstick, and although for most of the trip she had vomited, which the cabin crew had kindly taken in their stride, the view of Tasmania, particularly Cradle Mountain was still breathtakingly beautiful.

Closing her eyes, she prayed that in the next reincarnation that she would be born in Australia again. She had enjoyed the heat and the relaxed vibe, committing Tasmania's demographics to memory.

Arriving at the hospital, she was dangerously dehydrated, swallowing the hospital food only to regurgitate it. None of the Western medicine provided by the hospital reduced her chronic vomiting. Somewhat relieved to be in the safety of health care professionals, she had hoped that modern medicine would give her some amnesty, as none of her potions or lotions had reduced the symptoms.

Cancer was beyond the Magick of Witchcraft. Perhaps, a few thousand years before their Magick would have been strong enough to cure her but not now.

Oscar organised the twins to stay with his sister and then he had frantically driven to Hobart, arriving three hours after Fay Ce'Line had landed and was allocated a bed.

Forbidding Oscar to contact Pagan, Amelie, Roberta or Ruby, because she did not want them to worry, he had unwillingly agreed. Her friends had enough going on in their lives without having to worry about her as well. Well at least, that is what she told herself. Lying to herself was her only coping mechanism. While the Witches were blissfully ignorant, believing the cancer was in remission, just for a moment, she could pretend her reality was a delusion.

It had been traumatic telling Oscar, who had sobbed uncontrollably for several hours, bursting into sharp moans periodically throughout the night while he slept. As a broken man, he had fallen to her feet, grabbing at her toes as if he was somehow clawing away from his pain.

It was important to her to be a strong role-model for the twins in the future, for those moments of weakness when they wished that they had their mother to support and love them unconditionally, they would remember her strength. As far as Fay Ce'Line was concerned, having strength, strength to face the next chapter, strength that gives others strength, was true conviction of character.

Nauseous, she let go of Oscar's hand, grabbing the white plastic vomit bag that sat on the bedside table, she vomited again.

Oscar tried to help by rubbing her back. He knew it was not helping but he felt useless, and doing anything seemed better than doing nothing.

Heaving, her frail body buckling under the strain and she collapsed on the bed. Vomit covered her chest and lap. She heaved again, feeling the yellow bile travel from her stomach, past her chest and into her mouth, using all her strength she managed to aim the vomit into the plastic bag. Again, she heaved. This time, only water sprayed inside the plastic bag.

"Why the hell aren't the drugs helping?" Oscar screamed at the day nurse, "There has to be more that you can do than this?"

Wishing that her dayshift was already over, the nurse impatiently responded, "Until the results are back we are not sure what we are dealing with. She has the drip in. This will help with her dehydration."

The nurse grabbed a cloth, wiping Fay Ce'Line's chin and mouth. She used another cloth to wipe the densely salty tears away from her cheeks.

Exhausted, Fay Ce'Line looked up at the nurse who had barely graduated from University. Her skin was softly freckled and her eyes were tired from the lack of sleep.

Fay Ce'Line smiled at the young woman and then grabbed the nurse's hand to squeezed it.

The nurse tensed. Uncomfortable, and unsure how best to respond to the patient's sudden intimacy, the nurse waited for a cue from the patient.

Fay Ce'Line read her name tag; she spoke kindly, "Thank you, Ava. You will be a wonderful nurse."

Unsure how best to reply, Ava decided to squeezed the patient's hand, after all, how much energy should she waste on a dying woman?

Pagan

Pagan plonked herself down in front of the crackling fire. Slowly the angry flickers extracted the cold from her frozen body. The unforgiving wind and the fallen snow on the mountain only added to Tasmania's wintery bluster.

Demeter sat on the couch, curled up under a blanket with Nanna's laptop on his lap. Concentrating on a computer game, he rejected any interaction that Pagan encouraged.

Deity busied herself on the floor, crayoning in a colouring book that she had found in Nanna's art drawer.

Listening to her mother singing in the kitchen, Pagan noted how the evening seemed surprisingly normal and mundane considering the menacing undercurrent.

Aislyn was the happiest Pagan had ever seen her mother. Warranted, she had only been privileged to spend one reincarnation as her daughter but from what Pagan could tell, single life seemed to suit her.

Pagan looked around at Aislyn's brightly coloured lounge room: a large zodiac mat hung on the wall, a broomstick proudly displayed horizontally along two lion head hinges, second hand furniture, a piano, and Asian décor, complimented a round stained glass window which only filtered in moderate light.

Growing up, their lounge room had been best described as dingy with expressionless furnishings. How quickly life can change.

Memories of her father brought feelings of disenchantment. Guilt, ego and pride, battling it out for the moral high ground, usually 'agreeing to disagree', in the end. Always referring to him in 'past tense', Pagan had forgotten she had a father. It was only when he was mentioned did the pain of their estranged relationships affect her.

In previous lives, she had encountered fathers who 'used' her, 'manipulated' her, 'hit' her, 'molested' her, and so on, but there was something about Cain that she purely hated. Perhaps, it was because when she saw him, somewhere hidden deep in his eyes, she saw herself? He was weak, and weakness was what she hated in herself.

In her mind, Cain died the night he threw her brother onto the street. How that moment had come back to slap them all in the face.

Entering the room, carrying two trays, consisting of a bowl of pumpkin soup and freshly made bread (crunchy crust and a steaming hot loaf), Aislyn handed the first tray to Demeter who scolded his Grandmother for interrupting his game.

"No Nanna, I can't pause an online game."

Helpful, Deity sat up, grabbing the second tray from Nanna. She then dipped the bread into the soup, squashing the entire piece into her mouth and grinned.

Aislyn disappeared into the kitchen, returning with two more trays.

Gratefully accepting her meal, Pagan thanked her mother, "The best thing about winter is your soup, Aislyn."

"Any meal cooked by someone else is a good meal I think, Pagan."

Aislyn relaxed into the recliner, the aching in her lower back eventually easing.

Keen to move onto the main reason for Pagan's visit (the Darkness), she gulped down the meal, burning her tongue and throat.

"So you think the creature that attacked you was perhaps, Norman?"

Hoping that her daughter had not heard, Pagan glanced at Deity. Satisfied that Deity was focused on her colouring, she answered, "Where did Norman go that night? Do you know? Have you heard from him?"

Aislyn scooped up the last of her soup, placing the tray down on the floor, she replied, "I think we may need a glass of wine for this conversation."

Aislyn giggled, "It' always time for wine, I find."

Moments later, she reappeared from the kitchen with two glasses of Pinot Noir, "Cherries and raspberries to tantalise your palate."

Aislyn sat down, "A mother, albeit a Witch always knows that at some stage they will lose their sons, either to a partner, to their employment or to an adventure, but losing a son because I didn't provide a safe home for him will haunt me forever."

Surprised by Aislyn's honesty, Pagan looked at Demeter, a son that she had already lost to an imaginary world on a computer screen. She wondered what the world had in store for him.

"Norman was a quiet boy. Kept to himself. He had a few mates but no one he would confide in. I suppose when you have an authoritarian father and a submissive mother you're bound to be pretty messed up. He bottled it all up until he found a way to release it all."

Pagan closed her eyes. Norman had been aloof but she had loved him.

"So darling daughter, it does not surprise me that he has, somehow, found a way to return to us seeking revenge. What this means for you, for him, I wouldn't hazard a guess. Is he the Darkness? It chills my blood to think about it."

Pagan weighed up the possibilities that Norman had made contact with the Darkness (which they, the Witches, had foolishly thought was dormant), found the portal and managed to survive once inside. It truly was incredible.

Pagan looked deeply into her mother's eyes, "Do you know where the Ancient Doctrine is? I mean you were alive when it disappeared and I'm not really in a position to find it or even explore any possibilities."

The Ancient Witch Doctrine had been written during the Black and Red War in an attempt to document Witch Lore and lineage just in case they were defeated by the Red Haired Men. It was written in a dialect so old that even the Ancient Witches struggled to interpret it but Pagan knew that if it was placed in the hands of a good Ruler, like her daughter again, perhaps the future for the Witches would be secured.

Fixed in stare and posture, Aislyn remained composed, "No, Pagan I don't."

"I need the Ancient Doctrine. It could save my life. It could save Norman."

Looking at her daughter, Pagan felt a wave of maternal instinct suffocate her. She loved Deity's straight red hair, freckly face and long slender feet, but most of all she loved and respected her daughter as a wise Witch (a Crone, Witch and Maiden, all wrapped into a calm and caring personality). If only Deity had taken her Magick, rather than Aggie. She would be indestructible.

She continued, "And it could save Deity. She has always been an excellent Ruler, bringing peace to not only us but to the humans."

Aislyn angered as she also felt a maternal instinct to protect her son, "You don't know the future, Pagan, yes my vision saw great danger, and yes, I believe it was the Darkness but you don't know for sure if Norman wants to hurt you. He tried to burrow into your Magickal void, perhaps he wants to help you? Perhaps he isn't working with the Darkness but against it?"

Pagan felt her blood pressure rise. Taking a large breath, she exhaled loudly. She wondered if they shared the same desires; after all how loyal was their bond, as mother and daughter? As Non-Ancient to Ancient?

Aislyn interrupted Pagan's thoughts, "I haven't always been a good mum. We all have secrets. Things we're not happy about. You need to trust me that the Ancient Witch Doctrine is better off lost. It's only a matter of time before all Witches lose their Magick. You just happened to be the first."

Pagan snapped, "I haven't lost my Magick, and the Doctrine isn't lost, is it? It's hidden! Someone knows where it is and therefore is a potential threat. It needs to be found. If the Darkness is planning on another attack, Witches and humans will need to unite and that means we need all the help we can muster."

Alarmed by the raised voices, Demeter muted his game and listened, and Deity stopped colouring in.

Aislyn placed her empty glass on the piano next to the chair, careless if it stained the veneer, "Life has got so complicated. So many twists and turns that I don't know what to do for the best. I think the only motto humans and Witches should abide by is, 'Be happy to wake up in the morning'. I might not be as old as you but I wasn't born yesterday. The only certainty is uncertainty. Flexibility is real power. The Darkness feeds off fear so let's dry up its food source?"

Pagan ran her finger around the rim of the half-drunk wine glass, the humming sound amused her for a mere second, "It's easy for you. You're not an Ancient. My herstory is different from yours and as much as it pains me to admit it, our Magick is different. Therefore 'we' are different. Ancients and Non-Ancients are not the same. Each thread is mutating at different speeds. The moment Witches left the forest, everything we stood for, believed in, what connected us to each other, to ourselves and to the Goddesses disappeared. We might as well be living in the shadows with the Darkness."

Noticing that Demeter had paled, Pagan placed the wine glass on the floor, hopped up and walked over to him, wrapping her arms around him and then continued the conversation, "Ancients are so far removed from our authentic self, we don't even exist in any form. Non-Ancients are far surpassing any 'resilience' needed to move forward. Let's face the facts. The Red Haired Men didn't dilute the Witch strain they actually made it stronger. Ancients are the inbred."

Pagan looked at Deity. Most of the Goddess' Magick was inside of her, in its purest form.

Aislyn tucked her feet underneath her bottom and then asked Deity to share the recliner with her.

Deity enthusiastically snuggled into the warmth of Aislyn's body.

Their foreheads touched: love, intimacy, comfort and an unspoken loyalty between grandmother and granddaughter, a bond formed in one reincarnation

"If only we could connect with the fourth moon again!"

Aislyn shivered, "Perhaps, your brother already has?"

Pagan shuddered. Norman must have used the Fourth moon's Magick to enter the Darkness.

The Fourth moon, also known as a Darkmoon, is an invisible moon present during the day. Spells and rituals performed during the day are forbidden by Witch Lore. Practised by the Red Haired Men during their reign, Darkmoons were used against the Witches.

Fear augmenting Pagan's imagination. 'Witches must have been helped him, Ancient Witches. Thirteen Witches who have betrayed their own kind, but why? What did they gain from their betrayal?'

It was plausible that thirteen Witches could betray their own kind. It seemed everyone was betraying someone these days.

CHAPTER 25
Fay Ce'Line

Dressed in blue theatre clothes, the specialist strode into Fay Ce'Line's hospital room; ward six, room fourteen with a view over North Hobart, after a sixteen hour shift.

The room was a ghastly mauve colour. Appreciated only by Fay Ce'Line because of her innate nature to see the positive in every situation. A pastel coloured painting that had been hung too high on the wall behind the bed, failed to make the room look contemporary.

Knuckles, whitening from holding the clipboard too tightly, a technique she had learned over twenty years to hide anxiety, Pam scanned Fay Ce'Line's results. Sipping bad tasting coffee as she analysed the results, Pam ignored the nurse who stood patiently behind her.

Fay Ce'Line was relieved to see Pam. A specialist in women's cancers, she had diagnosed Fay Ce'Line's cancer two years previously. An exceptional woman, she was upfront and honest. A personality trait only shared by a few, and during stressful times it was a beneficial attribute. A bedside manner matched by none, Pam's heartfelt kindness settled even the worst of upset tummies and Fay Ce'Line noted that she did, indeed, feel better for seeing Pam.

Intelligence more abundant than her wealth and her wealth was ample, Pam demanded respect by simply walking into a room. Pearls and diamonds decorated her moisturised neck. Tanned skin confirmed a recent holiday, and her manicured nails displayed a lavish lifestyle away from the horrors of hospital life.

It was easy to admired Pam as a woman, as an intellect and as a good person.

Recognising Fay Ce'Line immediately, only added to Pam's disappointment that another patient was about to hear the 'concluding' news of their life's chapter.

Best described as an atheist, Pam shuddered at the thought of another 'good' person being the next victim of cancer.

"Can I sit down, Fay Ce'Line?"

Waiting until her frail patient responded, which was no more than a tired blink, she sat down at the end of the bed. Straightening out the white bed sheets, mostly from habit, Pam was struggling to relay the results and a few stolen seconds were a blessing.

Pam lost herself for a moment in Fay Ce'Line's dimming eyes, "Had a rough trot today, yeah?"

Fatigued, Fay Ce'Line nodded, even attempting a half smile.

Pam reached out, patting Fay Ce'Line on her leg. Then she paused for an extended time. Closing her eyes, she looked as if she had fallen asleep. Reopening them she began, "Well, I'm glad you're both here."

Looking up at Oscar, Pam winked, not a happy 'nice to see you' wink but a condolences 'pity' wink.

"What I have to tell you isn't great."

Oscar sat down next to Fay Ce'Line, wrapping his arm around her bony shoulders. Pam noticed that he had started shaking, not from the cold but from shock.

"Nurse, can you please grab an extra blanket."

The nurse obeyed.

"Although your bloods showed no irregularity, the M.R.I showed us a very different story."

Frowning, Pam continued, "Unfortunately, the chemotherapy didn't work. Primarily due to weakness, we could only give you a small percentage of the full treatment."

Pam held her breath as if the words had stopped midway, caught in her throat, "The cancer has now spread thoroughly throughout your small intestines and this is why you are unable to hold food down. It's now secondary."

Agitated by the news, Oscar yelled at Pam, "How can you say that the cancer's returned when the result showed that Fay Ce'Line was in remission? I'm sorry, but I don't understand what you're saying."

Fay Ce'Line pleaded with Oscar, "Please calm down. I'm trying to listen."

Turning towards Pam, it was Fay Ce'Line's turn to plead, "It will be ok, won't it?"

Pam searched for the right words, "Fay Ce'Line where the cancer is. Well. It's inoperable. We can feed you for a while on the drip but eventually we will have to take you off the drip."

Oscar stood up, pacing the room, as if somehow, he was outside of himself. As the grief numbed his emotions, his thoughts spiralled out of control.

Reaching out Fay Ce'Line held Pam's hand, "Please go on. You will need to slow down and repeat what you're saying. For some reason, I'm hearing you but I'm not making out the words."

Deflating, Pam unconsciously looked at her watch, "I'll have the nurse bring you some pamphlets on palliative care to read, and I think its best that we send you back to Latrobe where you can be closer to family and friends."

Resting her eyes, Fay Ce'Line blanketed the pain with thoughts of her daughters.

Oscar's voice echoed down the hall, "Why do you doctors always talk in riddles? Are you saying there is nothing we can do?"

Pam stood up from the bed, ignoring Oscar's aggression, "I am truly sorry Fay Ce'Line."

Pagan

Holding hands, Dante and Pagan ran for shelter underneath the church's entrance. It was an enclosed porch entry with only enough room for two people, which they used to their benefit.

Dante was unamused by the sudden down pour, "This bloody weather. Four seasons in one day. Why do I stay here?"

"You're very cute when you have a tantrum," Pagan laughed.

"I am not having a tantrum, Pagan. You mistake me for a child."

She brushed his wet hair off his face, "Yes, of course the great, Tristan Dante doesn't have tantrums, doesn't have a sense of humour either," she teased.

The blustery weather seduced the hanging chimes that were securely attached to the weatherboards on the outside of the church

"It's a good thing we drove. I wouldn't fancy flying in this."

"You're getting boring, Old Man. Where has your sense of adventure gone?"

"Young, old, make up your mind, Little Witch!"

The retiring white weatherboard church with its weary red galvanised roof had been built on Pagan's, Grandfather's land. Donated to the Catholic Church early in the 1900's, it had been forgotten about, except for a few elderly community members who tended to the graves and general maintenance.

Pagan had driven her Kombi cautiously along the gravel country road, avoiding several fallen trees that had been viciously attacked by the gusty wind, some pulled out from their roots, leaving large holes in the muddy ground, others snapped at the trunks, leaving them traumatised.

Parking at the rusted and mouldy wrought iron gates, she sat reflective for a few minutes.

Needing to touch base with the part of her childhood that she had enjoyed, the part of her lineage that was not a Witch, she had begged Dante to brave the weather with her for the afternoon.

Warranted, her lineage was as complex as a thousand intricate spider webs, she wanted to share some of it with Dante, regardless. It had become important for her to share the forgotten part of her blood line with a man she was privileged to call a friend and lover.

The grave sites were overgrown with knee-high grass and weeds. The large arch tombstones had, after fifty years, succumbed to the erosion of the ground while vandals had completed the degradation. Tombstone inscriptions that once paid homage to the tear-filled imagination were now smudged by the apathy of time. An array of red haze from the decomposing wrought iron fencing, reminded Pagan of a baby cradle.

Pagan felt Dante rest his hand on her spine, his fingertips gently rubbing the arch of her back to remind her she was not alone.

"Did you ever want children, Dante?"

"I cannot have children even if I had wanted them."

Composing herself from his blunt reply, Pagan pulled Dante back out into the rain. Running across to the far end of the graveyard to a double tombstone where a husband and wife shared an afterlife together, they halted to a slippery stop.

Half parched in the sunken earth and partially shaded from the squeaking trees on the property next to them, the tombstones were hauntingly beautiful.

"This woman," Pagan pointed down, "Was my Great…Great….Great Grandmother, on my dad's side or something like that. She was German, so his family never spoke about her. I think that's sad, don't you?"

Struggling to hear Pagan due to the wild wind, Dante just nodded, unsure of what he was nodding for.

Pagan shrugged her shoulders, signalling that she acknowledged that he could not hear her.

Leaping joyfully back towards the church, enjoying the rain on her face, Pagan forgot that Dante was fifteen years her senior. Her enthusiasm and zest for life bequeathed him his youth but at times it also exhausted him.

Her personality was contradictory, either juvenile or solemn, strong and then vulnerable, which was probably why Dante kept coming back for more. She was the slap in the face that infuriated him as well as aroused him.

This time, Pagan opened the large brown painted arch doors, pushing them open with two hands, she was eager to enter the dainty naturally lit church.

Soaking and cold, Dante hovered at the entrance. A feeling of disrespect sabotaged his fun. Apologising, he walked in after Pagan, who had already skipped up the aisle.

The interior was simple, two rows of ten wooden pews, cream walls and a wooden panel ceiling.

Pagan stood at the small altar, lighting twelve large white candles that were randomly positioned in front of the free-standing copper cross. Matches sat beside them.

Dante inspected his date. Pagan's beauty was magnified by the candlelight; long dark straight hair now fizzy from the rain, a white dress clinging to her breasts, and tanned boots covered in mud, she was a Goddess, wondering aimlessly through time, like a lost child looking for a mother's safety and a father's embrace.

"Dante come here."

He obeyed.

Taking his hand, she led him to the mahogany confessional. Sitting him in the main compartment, she pulled the curtain across, leaving a water trail behind her on the floor, Dante was alarmed at her unusual behaviour.

"You are acting very strange, Little Witch."

Pagan cackled, "I'm feeling a little impulsive, Dante. Trust me."

He heard her sit down in the other dual compartment. Waiting for instructions, he became impatient.

Sitting up straight on the confessional seat, Pagan looked through the wire window, "Forgive me father, for I have sinned."

Quickly calculating her plans, he played along, "What worries you my child?"

Pagan fighting back the laughter continued, "You see father, I have been unfaithful."

Dante theatrically gasped, "That's it? I am surprised that you haven't committed more serious sins than that."

Resuming his composure, he continued, "This is a very bad though. Who have you been unfaithful to and by all means, please tell me with whom and in graphic detail?"

Squashing her nose against the wire, she looked like a trapped chicken, "Many years ago father, I watched with my innocent eyes, a man 'make love' to a woman. They made love for a very long time."

Confused, Dante asked, "But who have you been unfaithful to?"

Pagan stood up walking around into Dante's compartment, sliding the curtain to the side, she grinned, "Every man since."

Dante reached out, pulling her towards him. Resting his face on her stomach, he bit her dress, sucking in the moisture.

Pulling her even closer, he grabbed her round buttocks, squeezing them until it hurt her.

Undressing Pagan, he fought the temptation to rip her dress off.

Rushing, she removed her under garments.

Placing each muddy boot on his lap, he untied the laces, throwing the boots across the room.

He carried Pagan to the carpeted area in front of the altar. There, he stripped his soaking pants and shirt off, throwing them over the closest pew.

They knelt before each other. Their lips touched, rescuing the others from the cold. Both sets of eyes locked into the other.

"We are safe here, in this church. Rules are obeyed here. The Monarchy can't hear what we say to each other."

She ran her fingertips down past his chest and around to his back. "Here we can speak, freely."

He ran his fingertips along her breast, "What have you brought me here to tell me?"

"Everything."

They pulled each other closer as if skin next to skin was not enough.

Pagan desperately caressed Dante's sculpted body, "What I tell you must never leave your lips."

Dante lay down offering his body and ears to her, "I promise."

She lowered herself onto him.

He had never seen her so intense, vacant but acutely attached.

Hunting and determined to make the kill, she clawed his chest. Her eyes flickered as if she was searching for a redundant sentiment. Her hips moved back and forth. Tonight, she would confess more than her faithfulness to him.

He fought the urge to delve into sentiment.

She wanted him, all of him. It would never happen but it did not stop her wanting it. Travelling deeper within her senses, she grabbed his hands placing them on her breasts, "Dante, tonight, I trust you with my daughter's life."

England

Aggie

Aggie fumbled with the keys. Stomping her feet like a bad-tempered toddler the keys fell out of her hands and onto the floor.

"Fuck! Shit! Balls!"

Squinting, she ran her fingers randomly along the floor until she found the keys, which were hiding only a foot away from her bare feet: four dull metal keys, one car key, one green, two red, one blue and one skeleton key.

"There you are."

Not wanting to make the same mistake again, Aggie carefully separated the skeleton key from the rest. Holding it firmly in between her thumb and index finger, she pushed the gold plated skeleton key into the lock. Wiggling it until it unlatched, she decided to leave the key inside the lock, twisting the door handle instead.

"Open!"

The original key, she had flung, tear stricken into the Thames River.

A musky smell mixed with methylated spirits and paint fumes closed up her throat, and stung her eyes, which only added to her apprehension.

Stumbling across the room until she reached the window, Aggie desperately rummaged for the window latch, flicked it up, and slid the window open. Gasping for fresh air, she let the breeze dance over her face.

Fresh air circulated the room but failed to lessen the stifling panic, Aggie was experiencing.

Her art studio was as she had left it. Shut up in the late 1970's, it had haunted her, like a ghost hovering above her bed. She could pretend the room did not exist but deep down underneath the controlled emotions, it existed.

The easel stood taller than she remembered. Running her shaking hands along the top the dust gathered until it fell onto the carpet. She sneezed.

Her flat bottom struggled to find relief on the wooden stool.

Looking into the glass jar, she was amazed to see the water had formed a mould top which was still active.

"Incredible."

The paintbrush had hardened and a flexi-board palette that she had thrown onto the table next to the easel had become a piece of art work. Blobs of dried paint sporadically dotted upon it, like rainbow volcanoes in prehistoric times.

Aggie pushed the hardened paintbrush bristles into the top of the paint mounds. The selection of paint tubes consisted of; green, orange, yellow, blue, red and black.

Hastily, she grabbed the black Gouache acrylic tube. Struggling to take the lid off, she squeezed a large portion of it onto the palette, dipping the dried bristles into the black paint.

She stared at the half painted face, a man she knew well once, half sketched, half a life time ago.

Squashing the dried paintbrush onto the browned paper, Aggie added jowls to his chin, hooded his eyelids, wrinkled his protruding forehead, tightened his lips and darkened his cheeks to lengthen his face, thinning it off. Changing his expression, where once he looked smug, he was now vacant and void of feeling. Aggie felt she had successfully captured his elderly self.

It was now midday. Ignoring her hunger pains, she continued to paint. Painting spoke to her. It has always been a dear friend, one she had missed.

Finally, she finished. Her aching hand reached out to him, or at least the one dimensional version of him, as if somehow, if she willed it, he would walk from the paper and into her arms.

"I miss you."

The painting was amateurish. Her eyesight was almost at thirty percent. Blotches and flashes owned her sight now. She would never take her sight for granted again, declaring in the next reincarnation, she would paint twice as much.

Surprised by her moment of happiness, Aggie laughed, "My first abstract."

Then she wiped a single tear from her cheek, "You sentimental, Crone."

Surprised that she could still cry, she tasted her salty finger.

Standing up, she stretched, "Must be time for a cup of tea and something to eat," before she packed for the flight. It would probably be the last flight she would ever take in this aging body. Her personal assistant Lauren had booked

Qantas Airlines which would fly her to Singapore and then onto Sydney. In Sydney, she would join her connecting flight to Melbourne where she was booked into a hotel close to Tullamarine Airport. Hopefully there, she would catch up on some sleep. Early the next morning, she would fly to Hobart, Tasmania where she would be picked up by Priscilla.

It would be the first and last time she would fly to Tasmania.

Australia
Michelle

Following the blue cord from the internet modem out of the study and into the hallway, Michelle finally stopped outside of Demeter's bedroom. The bedroom door was ajar and the lights were turned off but common sense suggested that Demeter was not asleep. Suspicion suggested that Demeter was still on his laptop, probably hiding underneath the bed covers, hoping not to be discovered.

Hovering outside of the room, Michelle considered what to do for the best: catch him out-right and discipline him which could lead to a probable and traumatic evening, or she could let it slide, just once, so that she could enjoy some serenity in the house, after all, he was only doing exactly what children of his age do.

At his age, she had been sneaking out of the bedroom window to spend the night with a male friend who lived two blocks away, who had moved out to the shed when his dad married a woman who already had three children. As the eldest, he had the privilege of first bids on some privacy, which he had spent mostly with Michelle, cuddling in his smelly unmade bed. If her parents had found out, she would have been grounded until she was eighteen.

Knocking on the door, Michelle heard erratic movements coming from his bed.

"Night, Demeter."

She paused, "Sweet dreams."

Panicking, Demeter pulled the laptop screen down gently to hide the glow. He then popped his sweaty face out of the bed covers to replied, "Night."

Smug that she freaked her stepson out a little, a parental technique based on anxiety which seemed to work in its own special way, she headed to bed. After a long day, her only motivation was to snuggle with John. Something about resting her face against John's chin made everything else seem trivial. Taking on a partner with two young children limited their 'alone' time, so every chance they got to indulge in intimacy they did and tonight would be no exception.

Listening for a few minutes until he heard Michelle close the upstairs bedroom door, Demeter returned to his internet game. Flipping the laptop screen back up, he was instantly 'pissed off' his character had been killed. He would have to wait now until he could re-join the game.

Noticing he had lost internet connection, he tried to reconnect via home but it failed.

"Oh, man."

Distrustful if Michelle had disconnected the internet via the modem on her way to bed, he checked that the cord was still connected to the USB connection, and then thought of sneaking out of bed to check it at the modem when he heard movement in his room and a low growling sound.

An unexpected shiver rushed through his body. His eyes dilated to full capacity, and his breathing rapidly increased as all his senses alerted him to the immediate danger that the shadow man was somewhere in his room again.

Slowly and quietly, he pulled the screen down closing his laptop.

Preparing to face the shadow man, he reminded himself that the shadow man was not there to hurt him. The shadow man's visits had become more frequent, once a week now. Demeter almost looked forward to the visitor who seemed harmless enough. Just staring at Demeter, he got the feeling that the shadow man was actually guarding him, like a soldier protecting a Prince, a duty rather than an intimidation. Occasionally, the shadow man would walk towards him, only to stop and return to the corner of the bedroom. Once frightening with his pitiless black eyes and foul odour, Demeter now found the shadow man intriguing, dimming any potential risk he had initially felt.

Some nights, Demeter just sat up in bed, locking in on the shadow man, seeing who would look away first. It was hard to tell who won as the shadow man had no eyes.

Contemplating pulling the covers down so he could return the shadow man's stare, he hesitated as he felt something heavy jump onto the end of the bed, pinning his feet to the mattress. It was heavy, tilting the bed downwards. The bed started to buckle underneath the weight.

Demeter held his breath as fear paralysed him, which consequently kept him from yelling out for help.

A low growling sound indicated that whatever was at the end of his bed was an animal or a creature of some kind. Could the shadow man 'shape shift' and why now, after all this time?

Glad that his knees and laptop created a wall between his face and whatever sat at the end of the bed, he was, however, at the mercy of the creature, vulnerable to its unpredictability.

If he could just scream, surely the creature would disappear otherwise it would jeopardise its cover.

If he was a character from one of his computer games what would he do? He may be twelve but even he knew that he did not have several lives to gamble with.

The creature moved, startling Demeter, who then considered running for the door, if only he was not so scared.

A whiff of ammonia blocked Demeter's nose, forcing him to cough, which alerted the creature he was indeed awake. The creature reacted by turning around on the bed as if it was a dog chasing its tail, excited but menacing in its movement.

Making a split decision to escape, Demeter threw his laptop off his stomach and flipped out of bed.

The creature reacted by slicing Demeter's calf with its claws.

Screaming, Demeter crawled along the floor determined to reach the light switch. He wanted to see the creature before it killed him. It swiped him again, this time across the arch of his back. Adrenaline numbed the flesh wound.

Reaching up, Demeter flicked the light switch on. He spun around to face the creature.

As large as a tiger, the creature was hideous. Comparable to a dog left to die in a gutter after days of torture, its hair was patchy and clots of blood coated its scaly skin. One eye hung from his eye socket, resting on its scarred cheek while the other eye hosted an enlarged pupil that stared at Demeter. But most shocking was its mouth that had been sewn together with wire. Drool escaped from the small slits in the wire. Then the creature vanished leaving Demeter relieved but bloody from the deep wounds.

Pagan

Their wet clothes hung over the back of the pews.

The ambience of the church relaxed them. The mild glow of light from the candles and the shine of the moon penetrating through the rain, humbled their existence. They certainly did rent this place called Earth.

Once the moonlight reached the windows, it collaborated with the window seal making the shadows dance upon their naked bodies.

Just finishing, after a long and intense love-making session, their energies entwined were liberated and tension free. Words that once got caught on the edge of their tongues suddenly were free to pass.

Facing each other, Pagan and Dante sat uncomfortably on the wooden church pew while chatting and re-telling colourful and avid accounts of stories they had experienced during their life. Each story leaving them exhausted from laughter.

Flushed cheek bones, pale pink from the release of dopamine complimented Pagan's sparkling eyes which were now vibrant blue. Her head rested on her elbow, "Dante, I am going to call you, Raven."

"Why, Raven?"

Pagan reached out to Dante, touching the stubble on his face, "You just are."

Dissatisfied with her answer, he asked her again, "Why Raven, there are so many animals I could be, Little Witch?"

Dante wondered if he could handle anymore of Pagan's honesty tonight, especially when he could not reciprocate fully. His mind was already spinning from the revelations during sex.

Running her tongue along her lips, she replied, "Ravens are intelligent, they fly, opportunists, thrive in varied climates, playful, they're black, and you suit black."

She laughed, and then a solemn discourse followed, "And Ravens live successfully among humans."

Predicting where Pagan's commentary was heading, Dante shuffled uncomfortably on the pew.

Powerfully, she fired the question, "You are human aren't you, Dante? Mother was a Witch and your father was human, yes? You don't speak of your father."

Silence exhausted the questioning, but Pagan stubbornly held her stare.

Dante dodged the question, "Why did you bring me here other than to bombard me with your requests and questions?"

She noted his defensiveness but strangely relaxed and changed the direction of the conversation, "Because I need you to know that I am more than just a Witch, I am also a mother, a sister, and a daughter."

Sensing her defences were down, he changed the direction of the conversation again, "What do you need me to be?"

Listening to the sound of the angry wind circulating the church, she pulled Dante closer to her. Turning around, she slid in between his legs. His arms reached around her while his chin found comfort on her right shoulder.

"People assume I'm complicated, that all my relationships need to be complicated and therefore my life becomes a rollercoaster of ups and downs, even when I don't want them to. It's tiring, Dante. What I want is simplicity and that's what you give me. I don't want to have to think about everything all the time. I don't want to have to think. I just want to lie in your arms and feel safe."

Feeling embarrassed, Pagan cupped her own face, "Wow, I'm such a cliché. I just want to feel safe. Safe to trust another person completely."

"I understand what you are saying. Go on, Little Witch."

Pagan swung around, this time cupping Dante's face, "You make no promises, so therefore you never break them, but what I've asked of you tonight, if you accept, will change your life. I'm asking you to sacrifice your own existence. I'm asking you to become *complicated*. The karma will affect me in the next reincarnation."

Dante looked at the copper cross screwed perfectly to the wall above the altar. His mind was already made up but now was not the time to tell her.

"Sometimes, I miss home, Little Witch, but in some cases you can never go back home and if you can, it has changed somehow. I can only compare it to a Witch Awakening, once you are 'Awakened' it is impossible for you to forget what it is you miss. So we create journeys for ourselves to compensate for our loss, tests to convince ourselves that we are actually achieving something. I've done this my whole life, made journeys to compensate that I do not have a home to return to. What you ask of me, if I accept it, I promise you I will honour my complicated life and I will not allow the karma of my 'free will' to affect you. I set you free from the karma, Little Witch."

Running his hand down Pagan's cooling face, Dante asked, "Who were you in your last reincarnation?"

Pagan jolted. As if she was opening up a filing cabinet, she remembered, "Olympe de Gouge. I was French Witch, a writer and political protagonist. Oh, how much energy I had in my last reincarnation. To be honest, I think I stole some of my energy from this life to pull it off. I bleached my hair white, I married a man I did not care for, had a son that I discarded. No daughter, no Soul-mate. Free to cause trouble at will and I loved supporting my human sisters in their fight to be liberated. It felt so good Dante, to run wild. To write what I actually thought for people to read. For them to criticise and condemn me. It was liberating in itself. It was the first reincarnation when I was not chosen by the Goddesses to be a Royal. I think they were preparing me for this life. For the dulling, the beautiful dullness."

Dante shrugged, "I do not know of this name, Olympe."

She cackled, "You wouldn't. The books forgot about me. Books only ever care about *his*tory not *her*story."

Lost in thought for a moment, she continued, "My dear friend, Mary Wollstonecraft was a famous feminist writer. I believe she changed the world, the female world at least. Females, be it Witches or humans are linked by a feminine cord. When the world changes, even slightly, it affects both Witches and humans. As much as I wish we were not, it is undeniable. Our fate is linked to humans."

Dante sighed, a breath that journeyed to the pit of his stomach, "You were betrayed by a Witch, Pagan, a close Witch. She undid the Obscurity spell in her last reincarnation, so that each time you are born your identity is known before you are Awakened. It will leave you vulnerable, each time you are reincarnated, those in power will manipulate your life before you even know who you are. I am sorry to tell you this. I have known this for a long time. It is common knowledge by the hierarchy."

Pagan search her memories for details, "You see Dante, being born a Witch is about role playing, choosing a character, playing it to the best of your ability and within the era you were born and hope no-one figures it out and calls your bluff. You told me once that I had no friends in the world and you were right but the present is only for setting the pawns up for the next life. And eventually 'checkmate'. I only wish, you were my mate when I checked in."

Yawning as the early hours of the morning approached, Pagan declared, "Dante, I'm tired of role-playing. I want nothing more than to become a recluse living in a hut hidden deep within a forest."

Pausing for dramatic effect, she added, "But it seems no matter what role I play, how different the plot is, I still manage to lose my head, every single time. At least if I lost my head in the forest it would remind me of the first time."

Standing up, Dante replied, "Everyone is role-playing, Little Witch but some people are just better at it than others."

CHAPTER 26
June 15th

Pagan

Pagan felt apprehensive as she reluctantly welcomed her sister into her cluttered home. It had been at least three years since Inanna had voluntarily visited and over six months since they had spoken to each other at length, usually sour coated niceties, direct and short.

Arriving unexpectedly at the front door at 09:00, frazzled and wearing a mask of anxiety, Pagan had jumped out of bed, surprised and annoyed, wearing no more than sleep wear; loose shorts and singlet.

Leaning on the door frame, she hoped she would find balance from the support of the hard material; it also helped hide her awkwardness.

Pagan had set her alarm for 09:30, planning to catch up on some much needed sleep. After several nights of staying behind at the hospital with Fay Ce'Line, she was in need of an energy recharge. It had been another long night watching Fay Ce'Line drift in and out of consciousness, waking only to vomit, apologise and then float back into a sleep so deep that several times, she checked Fay Ce'Line was breathing.

Inanna was noticeably anxious, so Pagan gathered the 'left overs' of compassion and welcomed her sister inside.

Judgementally, Inanna peered into all the bedrooms as she passed them. Each room revealed Pagan's lack of discipline.

Inanna sat on the edge of the couch, a clear indication that she was not planning on staying for too long. Her fingers entwined around each other was a failed attempt to hide the sweat that rinsed her palms.

Relieved by the body language, Pagan hoped that Inanna would leave almost immediately so she could go back to bed.

"Would you like a coffee, Inanna? It's only instant coffee. I know you don't drink it. I can make you some tea?"

Inanna shook her head, "No thank you, Pagan, I've just had a coffee."

Sitting furthest away from her sister on a chair usually vacant, Pagan waited for Inanna to start the conversation, after all, she was clueless to what the visitation meant and she was not eager to find out. The grimace on her face confirmed that Inanna was indeed stressed about something.

Studying the chaotic lounge room, Inanna tried to hide her disdain for Pagan's decor: mismatched Mediterranean, and rustic décor. Probably all bought from a tacky mass-made factory in a third world country. Oil burners, paintings of empowered women, a blackboard with positive quotes, and a bookcase with feminist and historical memorabilia to give the impression she was cultured, and photographs of Demeter and Deity, and dusty floorboards which screamed- 'good mum, terrible housekeeper'.

Inanna was not entirely sure Pagan could call herself a 'good mum'.

"So why have you come here?"

"It's Morghana."

Pagan sat up straight, "Why? Is she ok?"

Inanna was uncomfortable due to the lumpiness of the second hand couch but also because trying to communicate with Pagan was always difficult. She would rather present an hour speech in front of a room of intellectuals than speak directly to her sister on any subject.

"Inanna, you're clearly distressed. Take your time."

Her voice softened, "They want to admit her into a heath care clinic."

"Who are 'they?'"

Inanna closed her eyes, struggling to maintain her composure. Choosing her words carefully, she lifted her right hand, waving it as if she was swatting a fly away, "Please Pagan, let me finish."

Pagan angered. How dare Inanna come to her home dictating the 'terms and conditions' of a conversation she had no desire to have, with a sister she could barely tolerate.

A long-standing tension exuded between them, the verbal argument inside their heads far more vile and cruel. Thoughts fired across the room like bullets glazed in arsenic.

Desperate for Pagan's help, Inanna pushed her anger aside, "It could be Morghana's anxiety towards her own Awakening but she truly believes that Hensley talks to her, warning her, telling her to suicide before the monsters get her. That she is actually inside of her, sharing the same body, two energies in one body?"

Pagan frowned, "Deja Vu?"

Inanna replied, "Sometimes Morghana can hear what people are thinking. It is similar to your acute smell. She has acute hearing. Hensley's energies have attached to Morghana somehow. Hensley obviously found a way to stay in the void so that she won't be reincarnated. Pretty smart actually. She was a high achiever."

Pagan was impressed, "Clever."

Inanna burst into tears, bending over as if she was about to miscarry, "I've lost my daughter before she is even Awakened!"

Pagan felt uncomfortable. It was unusual for Inanna to show her vulnerable side, and 'vulnerability', looked bad on her.

Gaining some composure and a little bit of her dignity, Inanna wiped the tears from her cheeks, "I need your help, Pagan. I don't know what to do. I've tried to deal with the situation without Witchcraft but it hasn't helped. The doctors want to lock her up in some mental hospital and feed her drugs. It's all a huge mess."

Pagan studied her sister; her healthy voluminous golden hair, her wrinkle free skin and her immaculate attire. If it was not for Morghana, Pagan would have asked her to leave, insulted that she was the last person Inanna had asked for help, especially knowing how much she loved her niece.

"Wow, that must have hurt asking me for help?"

Pagan began to slowly clap, exaggerated, sarcastic and hurtful, "Not once in all our reincarnations have you asked me for help. Your pride, unwavering, even after everything we have been through together."

Inanna angered, humiliated and heartbroken, she feared Pagan would deny Morghana the help she needed. Fighting the urge to leave, her fingers wrapped around the edge of the pillows. Anger and exhaustion creating a dissonance she could not manage or control.

"Why do you always have to be so damn difficult, Pagan? If you need me to beg, I will."

A surge of power poisoned Pagan's blood. Better than any drug rush, Pagan enjoyed the feeling; chest expanding and an arousal deep within her stomach.

"Then beg, sister!"

Inanna straightened her torso, a look of shock and panic intertwined, tightening the muscles around her mouth.

"That's right, I want you to beg. Beg for your daughter."

Standing up, Pagan swaggered towards Inanna, her hips extending further than usual and as if she was about to strike Inanna, she suddenly stopped a metre away.

Pagan was amused, so much for Inanna's money and education which was of no help to her now.

"Show me how much you love, Morghana."

Placing her palm on top of Inanna's head, Pagan pushed her head down, ushering her to get on her hands and knees.

"Lower yourself to the floor and bow before me."

Wanting to either run for the door, or push Pagan so hard that she would fall onto the floorboards, Inanna submitted instead. She was at the mercy of a more powerful Witch, even without her Magick. Recognising the rush of power in Pagan's eyes, Inanna knew from past experiences not to rebel at such times. Cruel and unyielding in the past, Pagan had commanded the slaughter of hundreds of Witches and humans in the past and then feasted on their flesh.

"I said bow, Inanna! Remember where you come from Aphrodite."

Slipping onto her knees, the dust from the floorboards covered her trouser pants; she would have to change before being seen in public like that.

Fearful that her lower back, already weakened, may snap, Inanna pulled her stomach muscles in to take the pressure.

"Now kiss my feet."

Inanna closed her eyes, memories of submission sweeping over her like a nightmare.

Bending down to kiss Pagan's feet, her clean lips upon her unwashed skin, Pagan suddenly pulled her foot back.

"Get up, Inanna."

Inanna sat up, leaning back on her heals.

"Of course I'll help my niece but that was a reminder that I'm not the Witch I used to be but I could easily be her again."

Priscilla

Priscilla glanced into the rear view mirror. The Supreme Femineity sat directly behind her.

Tired from her long trip, Aggie remained quiet for most of the journey, which gave Priscilla ample time to gather her thoughts. Thoughts that were densely rooted in the past.

Peering through the tinted, double glazed security glass, left Aggie feeling vulnerable, an emotion that she had not felt in some time. Even the ever-changing Tasmanian landscape could not comfort her insecurities.

Respectful towards the Supreme Femineity, Priscilla could not deny an overwhelming dislike of her, especially since arriving in Tasmania, Aggie had treated Priscilla like a servant, reminding her of her dreadful childhood.

Growing up on the remote West Coast of Tasmania, Priscilla had explored the untouched wilderness while experiencing unpredictable extreme weather, and the harsh realities of loneliness. It had prepared her for all the unpredictability life offers but had left her bitter and suspicious in all situations.

At age five, Priscilla's mother, Maltyeda died. Running underneath the house where she hid for three days, Priscilla had cried until she was unable to shed another tear. She had not cried again, ever. Eating dirt to sustain her strength, she had shit gravel for a week afterwards.

Her father, Grayson, had dealt with his grief by ignoring it. Spending endless weeks 'gone bush', he left his heartbroken daughter to fend for herself.

At age seven, Priscilla discovered a box containing her mother's Witchcraft tools hidden behind several cardboard boxes in the tin shed: a brown leather note book full of spells scribbled down with blue pen, a blunt knife that many years later Priscilla discovered was an Athame, a small gold plated bell that she broke by vigorously ringing it, a moth chewed cloth, and a wand carved from a white wood, or perhaps some drift wood her mother would have collected on one of their many trips to the beach.

Positioning her body just inside the doorway days later, she had crouched down behind a chair. Her knees knocked together as she waited for her father to return home. Pointing the wand at her father as he walked through the door, she shouted, "Make him go away!"

Reacting quickly, he tackled his daughter to the ground, snatching the wand out of her tight grip. Without hesitation, he snapped the wand in half. A spark flashed, blinding Priscilla who fell to the ground, inconsolable.

Unbuckling his belt buckle, he removed the belt in one motion, whipping it into the air like a hose on full blast. The clothing accessory was now a disciplinary tool, one that Priscilla had experienced many times before.

The seven year old ran around the house avoiding the sharp sting of the belt. Twice as large as her, he easily navigated the room, whipping her thighs, back and stomach. Blood splattered the walls, clotting on the dust that had gathered due to months of filthy living.

Exhausted, he slumped to the floor, a wave of regret and guilt overwhelmed him. It was the not the last time he would take to his daughter with his belt.

Five years later, Priscilla was sent to a boarding school in Hobart where she had been an astute student, topping her class in all the main subjects; Math, Science, English and Humanities, spending only the necessary amount of effort on peripheral subjects. In her opinion, true intelligence was assigning the perfect amount of energy for the required affect. Uninterested in making friends, she spent most of her spare time in the library researching Witchcraft. Since finding her mother's craft tools, Witchcraft had become an obsession.

Peers suspected she suffered from Aspergers due to her quietness and disinterest in other people.

She would reply, "I simply dislike you."

After blowing out the candle on a supermarket cake, her seventeen year old 'solo' birthday celebration was abruptly interrupted when government officials, the Tasmanian Crone Alliance entered the building to collect her.

She had been hesitant but a certain 'knowing' encouraged her to leave with the two Crones.

Home schooled by a Crone, named Sooz only fortified her enthusiasm for educational achievement and for the first time since her mother had died, she developed a meaningful relationship with another female, albeit a Crone.

One year later, when it was time for Priscilla to leave for her Witch Awakening, Sooz cried on the veranda, and finally Priscilla understood what true love was- letting go of another person when it is better for them to go, even if it pains you, and it pains them.

Priscilla flew alone, by broomstick, to her own Witch Awakening fully aware of what the evening entailed. Several weeks earlier, Priscilla had picked the lock into Sooz's study. A folder entitled 'Top Secret' exposed her to classified information. Although it was initially a traumatic read, afterwards, Priscilla felt liberated, aware. After all, some slimy old men drooling over her body for some 'sick kick' would lead to her reuniting with her Magick, "So be it."

Memorising each detail of the nine men, cowardly hidden underneath their cloaks- the smell of their breath, the jewellery they wore, and the way their lips curled when they ejaculated helped her several years later track them down and confirm them as her targets. Watching each one of them bleed-out over their expensive flooring after slitting their throats inside of their own homes, with wives and children to discover their tortured bodies, resolved any deep seeded resentment she had towards her own kind; the Witches.

Working for the Tasmanian Crone Alliance allowed her to hide any evidence that she was the culprit of such horrendous crimes.

The new era she had been born into had given Priscilla an abundance of power she had never experienced before and she revelled in it. Never before had a Non-Ancient risen to such heights of employment and esteem. Aggie was her idol. Aggie a Non-Ancient Witch had claimed absolute power, single-handedly manipulated the ego-driven, lazy and disengaged Ancient Witches. Worshipping Aggie, she had been nothing but disappointed on meeting her.

"Don't interrupt me," Aggie had barked at Priscilla when she had attempted to bond with her idol. Aggie's lack of etiquette was starting to exasperate Priscilla who had held her tongue several times since picking the Supreme Femineity up from the Hobart airport.

Relieved that Aggie had demanded to sit in the back seat, Priscilla took the opportunity to centre her thoughts. Why did the Supreme Femineity want to visit an Aged Care facility? There were more important issues at hand, the Darkness returning for instance.

Aggie's security guard, Svenana travelled with Aggie from London and now sat rigidly beside Priscilla in the front seat. Svenana was an attractive Witch, so much so Priscilla had chocked on her breath when they had met.

Platinum blond hair that was pulled back tightly into a bun, complimented her pale white skin and pink lips. Her teeth were unnaturally white, and her large almond size brown eyes were heavily decorated with black eyeliner and fake eyelashes, and a small amount of regrowth revealed Svenana was a natural red head.

A cockney accent lessened her credibility, but still, it was undeniable that Svenana had more sex appeal than most Witches, even for a Non-Ancient.

Regardless of her chemistry with Svenana, she would remain guarded. Most Witches had their own agenda and therefore could not be trusted.

"I need a toilet stop and I'll grab some coffee."

Parking in the main street of Campbell Town, Priscilla asked Svenana and the Supreme Femineity if they would like sugar in their coffee. They declined.

"No sugar it is then. I won't be long."

Aggie responded by grunting.

"Kiss my arse," Priscilla said under her breath.

'It was alarming how similar Aggie and Pagan were. Rivals in every aspect but both as self-centred and stubborn as the other. It was no wonder they had clashed', Priscilla thought.

After the toilet stop, Priscilla entered her favourite coffee shop. As usual it was busy but after three minutes, she ordered three coffees while grabbing three home-made biscuits.

"One with sugar and two without," she added.

Feeling the vibration of her mobile in her bag, she frantically searched for the mobile but missed the call. Just as she found it, it rang again. It was Aquarius.

She chose to ignore it, placing it on 'silent'.

Pagan

The red mud squished up through Pagan's already pinkish red toes. Stinging the soles of her feet the cold felt good. Compensating for her seriousness, she rolled her trousers up above her Achilles heels, as she had done as a child.

The only protection from the dreary weather was an already dirty raincoat that she had found in the back of the Kombi. Throwing it over her, she zipped it up until she felt the raincoat tighten around her neck. Allowing several seconds to enjoy the cold sting of the drizzle on her face, the rain soon burned her skin reminding her that she was indeed alive in a place of death.

Looking around the lawn cemetery, she was relieved to be alone which was one of the perks of visiting in winter. During summer the cemetery was an enjoyable place to visit. Uniformed rows of blossoming flowers, angel statues staring off into the heavenly abyss, and an abundance of personalised mementos; soggy teddy bears, unopened beer cans and faded letters.

"Sentimental rubbish!"

Pagan enjoyed scanning the graves, calculating how long it had been since the grave had been visited by how faded the plastic flowers were.

"Lazy. Graves deserve fresh flowers."

Possum excrement and soggy overgrown grass covered the older plaques while the newer sections were well landscaped and inviting.

Rogan's gravesite was in the newer area, lifted off the ground by a cement plinth. Five rows up and nine gravesites along, his decayed body had been laid to rest.

"Rest from what? Oxygen?"

Visiting his grave several times a year; mostly due to guilt, Pagan found an intense 'pull' to visit him again. Today, unlike other days, she missed him, a crippling loneliness that she could not explain. His death had stolen a large part of her happiness with it.

It was the first time in their reincarnations together that she had outlived Rogan and now she finally understood his lament of losing his Soul-mate each life time, except the last reincarnation when he had married Jane Seymour that same year, 1536.

She wanted to believe she had only killed him to assure Deity's safety but she knew that it had been much more than that. It had been 'payback' for his betrayal. Was their love fading? She hoped so.

It was the rawness of finding Dante that had challenged her. Made her lustful, and feel more alive than she had ever felt.

Rogan had always been her 'constant', not that he had ever known that and his personality certainly changed due to the era he was born in. Rogan had been the gentlest she had ever seen him but she had still desperately wanted some space from him.

Loving Dante was fresh and exciting to her but he was not hers to have. She sensed, he had loved someone, so hard it broke him.

Her love for Rogan, somehow tainted, was still indeed simmering. Rogan was her favourite chair; lumpy in all the right places but he had broken her heart in the last reincarnation and she had not forgiven him. Hopefully in the next reincarnation, she would reunite with him without fear that they would be under threat or surveillance from the Crone Monarchy. They could live a simple life; a small house, mundane jobs, have lots of children, and then grandchildren. Pagan had never been alive to see her Grandchildren. If only the Witch community would let her. She finally understood how the Non-Ancient Witches had felt for centuries-terrorised by the Ancient Witches.

'What a ghastly affair'.

If the opportunity was to arise where Pagan would once again rule, she would govern rather than dictate. Create equal opportunities for all Witches.

The irony of never resolving issues was that she was guaranteed to spend another reincarnation with the same Witches, even Inanna; learning the same life lessons. She may not like Inanna, but she loved her; after all, they had been sisters for what felt like an eternity.

Life was amazing; its pain, its love, its laughter, and its darkness. Why would she want to ever evolve, why because she had to?

Dropping down on top of Rogan's grave, Pagan's knees squished into the ground. The wet grass stained her trousers. Raindrops fell off her eye lashes.

His blue plaque was covered with rotting leaves that had fallen from the trees only twenty metres behind her. Pagan wiped the leaves off with her hand. Mud smudged across his name. Annoyed that she had not brought cleaning products with her, she cursed his wife who should be keeping his grave clean.

Rogan's decaying body lay only six feet below her. His energy was now with the Goddesses but somehow visiting his gravesite made her feel closer to him.

When she had first visited him, she would curl up above the loose dirt, clawing at it, yearning to lay with him, to hold his dead body in her arms. She still wanted to dig him up and hold him, but for what?

Turning onto her side, Pagan pushed her hip into the ground to balance herself, "She's beautiful Rogan. Deity is so beautiful and smart. She will be powerful, very Magickal. She has your cheeky smile. The way she giggles at silly jokes, or always dips her finger into the cooking to taste it, reminds me of you."

Pagan quietly cried.

"How could I have killed you? You didn't deserve to die. You were an innocent. It's me who deserves to die. I'm a horrible Witch who is aware of what was happening, the past, the future. You had a young family, a wife, and I killed you."

She picked up a soft toy bear that his children had left for him and held it to her lips and sobbed. The grief was unbearable. All she had wanted was his sperm.

Aggie

Aggie sat in the car waiting for Priscilla to return from the reception area where she was filling in paperwork.

Svenana sat in the front seat, aloof and exhausted from the boredom.

Aggie ignored Svenana. She had 'put off' this moment for far too long to be concerned by her employee's sulkiness.

Experiencing the sensation of pins and needles in her limbs from the journey from one end of the island to the other, Aggie wiggled her body, hoping that when she exited the car, she would not fall over and break a hip. The irony amused her. The only man she had ever obsessed over, lay in one of the rooms, perhaps a mental vegetable and she could die metres before she reached the entrance. It would make one 'hell of' an ending.

Priscilla opened the door, "Supreme Femineity, you can visit him now."

Loosely holding Aggie's hand, Priscilla escorted the Supreme Femineity through the front doors and down the corridor. Scanning the area for any potential threat, Svenana marched behind them. Her rigidness obvious to all who saw her.

Shuffling along slowly, Aggie's heart raced. Her brittle fingernails cut into Priscilla's youthful skin but out of fear, Priscilla said nothing.

Instantly, Aggie searched for him as they entered the room.

Svenana turned the lights on and opened the curtains so Aggie could see.

Hierarchically, Priscilla ordered Svenana to grab the chair nearest the window and bring it to the bed for the Supreme Femineity to sit on.

Svenana threw Priscilla an angry glance. In defiance, she pulled the chair along the carpet to where they stood, rather than carrying it.

Once Aggie was settled, Priscilla and Svenana left the room, finding a bench seat to sit at in the sitting room.

Aggie moved her seat in closer and stared at Cain.

Pulling the thin white blanket off his torso, she placed her shaking hand on top of his, twisting her arthritic fingers around his fingers. His hands were cold. Hands that once had built them a room, a long time ago. His arms which had once held her so tight were now worn away, wasted.

She moved her hand along to his bony shoulder and up along his saggy neck.

Smiling, she remembered when he had thrown her over his shoulder, spanking her bottom. They both had laughed so hard that their stomachs had hurt. It had been the happiest and worst time of her life.

His lips were blue.

"Why do they not have more blankets on you? Surely, you deserved more respect than this?"

Bending in, she kissed him. The sharpness of his chaffed skin prickled her.

Reaching for his cheek, she longed to be held by him again, just once. She prayed to the Goddesses to wake him up but they were not listening.

She was going to die soon, after living more than two previous reincarnations a Witch sensed when her time was almost up, but first she wanted to tell him that she missed him, that although, he had broken her heart, he had in fact taught her how to love and that she regretted the choices she had made, all of them.

"Who am I kidding? You never wanted me did you?"

He had chosen Aislyn over her, every single time. Every time, he decided to fly back to Tasmania to be with his wife and children, Cain took with him, a part of Aggie's kindness, softness and compassion until she was dried up. The love he gave to Aggie was unlimited, far surpassing any other lover but it had not been enough. Having to share him with another woman, another Witch, was too much for her to cope with. Realistically, she had not been enough for him.

'Why was she not his 'number one?'

Gently grabbing his hand, she positioned it against her face, kissing his palm repeatedly.

For the next thirty minutes she sat in silence. The past filling her up like a helium balloon, lifting her up, only to pop every few minutes.

Cain had not chosen Alzheimer's, and in fact, Aggie knew that it was a hex that condemned him to the bed.

It was early February, 1976 when Aggie hexed him. Cain was a

319

'contaminated' man but she made sure she had the final say in their love affair. She always had to win, but winning only made her feel great in the moment of impact.

But Cain had been killing her, slowly, since the day they meet. An emotional slow-releasing arsenic that had paled every part of her body. Her inflamed vagina was evidence of their volatile chemistry.

"But you get to live forever," he had said, circling her tiny ankles in between his large hand as if 'eternity' was the ultimate gift.

The word 'forever' had flown around her thoughts like a flock of birds soaring towards the shore before the storm.

"I don't want to live without you," Aggie had said, as her eyes succumbed to tears.

Cain had his suspicions that Aggie had bewitched him in the beginning of their romance but it was Cain who had cast the enchantment. He had not used a wand, a spell, or the moon, he had done nothing but stand before her and the spell had been cast.

Cain and Aggie had spoken of 'true love' in the beginning. Perhaps, even a soulmate connection but Aggie soon concluded that their romantic connection was merely centuries of evolution. Two chemicals combining to create a reaction, a bomb that had left them both tattered.

Warranted, the perfect combination of chemicals meeting could be called 'serendipity' but Aggie knew that their meeting had been nothing more than a scientific experiment and there is nothing romantic about that.

A magnetic suicide.

She fell inlove with a man she could not tame. The man that left her crazy from rejection. The man that stripped her from herself, leaving her abandoned and bitter.

Standing before her, naked, he was physically only metres away from her but his heart was half a world away, with his wife, always.

Tonight Aggie had planned to conceive a child before declaring Cain a prisoner in the room he had built for her, them. The concept had entertained her as she watched him labouring for months building his own prison, not that he knew that, or maybe he did?

He had thought he was travelling back to Australia in the morning, back to his wife, Aislyn but he would never step outside of that room again. He would live the rest of his life as Aggie's prisoner, a pet for her to feed at will. Starvation made men rather submissive, she had found.

But her time was running out. Menopause was her next hurdle.

He had begun the evening passionately making love to her, as he had done in the past, enticing her into an erotic illusion but unlike previous times he baulked. Slapping her face would have been less painful then pulling his penis out of her vagina, leaving her naked and rejected on the bed.

Standing, he had almost cowered in fear. This enraged Aggie. How dare he be scared of her, after everything he had done?

Springing from the bed, she lashed out at him. Repetitively smacking his face until it welted, he struggled to regain the upper hand. She was petite but her thirst for winning could not be quantified in body size.

Cain finally clasped Aggie's wrists together, a technique she was sure little boys were taught in pre-school.

Wild, her feet climbed his legs. Ripping more flesh from his cheeks, he held back from head-butting her.

"You crazy, bitch!"

Throwing her back onto the bed, he stepped backwards several steps, so he could attend to his bleeding face.

As if tranquillity washed over her, Aggie calmed. The muscles in her face relaxed and her posture loosened.

"Cain, all I ask is that you give me a child? You owe me that much. After all these years, you owe me that!"

Aggie sat up, liken to a leopard before pouncing on its prey, she slithered to the edge of the bed.

Cain sensed she was purring.

"Please Cain. I'm begging you. Please, before you go back to her, give me a child. Our child, a child for me to love."

"Aggie. How many babies must die for you to stop this madness?"

A heaviness perched upon Aggie's busty chest as if she was able to read his mind, "They were your babies as well, Cain. They were our babies. Babies we made together."

Cain had not wanted to look into Aggie's eyes. It was as if his autobiography had been written in them. Open pages to contradict his newly reconstructed reality but now he was trapped within her gaze.

He softened, "Aggie, you're too old now. We tried. You can't carry babies to full term. You need to let this go. This obsession with carrying a child has ruined us."

Switching positions onto her knees, her face tightened, "You ruined us, Cain. You lying unfaithful prick. YOU ruined us. Everything that comes out of your mouth is fucking lies."

Why did she want his child? Deep down she hated him but she had invested so much in him, she was owed the profit.

Aged forty five, this was her last chance to carry a child to full term before she would be classified a Crone for another reincarnation. Desperate, she considered raping Cain. Tie him to the bed, suck him off, and ride him until, he ejaculated.

"I will have your baby, Cain. I found a new spell. I will conceive and give birth. I will push a breathing baby out, even if it kills me."

Cain shaking with rage, screamed at Aggie, "It has already killed you. You've rotted from the inside out. Anything that I once found kind in you has died."

Adrenaline igniting her body, Aggie gathered a lifetime of rejection and bitterness. Lifting her head towards the Fused Quartz ceiling of the room, she looked into the darkness of the night sky. *The critiquing waning moon looked down upon her. The words he had just sprayed across the room, now lay dormant.*

Thousands of unkind words had left their lips, attacking and judging in righteous contradiction. Their motivation was to hurt the other as much as they felt hurt, as much as they had loved. It was an endless cycle of hatred that neither one could stop.

A Witch unable to have a child was not unheard of but none-the-less she had never met another and it had made her twisted with jealousy and internal rage that Aislyn fell pregnant so easily.

Aggie saw her own reflection in the ceiling. She looked tired and she was. Tired of fighting for everything she had and would achieve.

Ancient Witches were born with wealth, power and esteem, a golden broomstick placed firmly up their bottoms.

Ancient Witches had been born to fight and they had fought well in the beginning but Non-Ancient Witches had been born to fight harder, a necessary counterattack when experiencing prejudice and discrimination from their own kind, and Aggie would not back down now. Her life was only just about to start. She was on the edge of menopause. It was a sign to attack, take everything she had learned and fight with such ferocity that the world would stop.

Unconcerned with the tensions between Ancient and Non-Ancient Witches, Aggie wanted everything that she had been denied, not because she had been discriminated against, or for revenge sake but because it had been prophesised.

Aggie, the petite auburn haired Non-Ancient Witch would become the most powerful Witch that ever existed. She would bring down the Ancients and rule all Witches but… she had to birth a breathing child first.

Cain wanted to leave now. Fly back to Australia, to his country town in Tasmania, to his gentle, Aislyn and his two beautiful children, Norman and Inanna.

Mid-thirties, he was too old for the drama. It was time for him to grow up. Be accountable, and finally faithful to his wife and family. He had jeopardised everything for a wicked and manipulative Witch, to lust. It was time to break the spell.

"I'm leaving now."

"No, you're fucking not."

Cain's voiced raised an octave, "Yes I am Aggie. I'm going home."

He looked around the room searching for his clothes.

As if she had flown to him, Aggie, only inches now from his face, stood a WITCH-red eyes, mouth wide open, sharp teeth and tangled hair.

Reactive, he shoved her away.

"Get away from my face! Aggie get me out of this room. I've had enough."

Every cell in his body rejected her, "I'VE HAD ENOUGH OF US!"

The earth felt as if it had suddenly stopped spinning- a defence mechanism where Aggie would shut down all her emotions, and as if a new Witch stood before him, Aggie straightened up and stared coldly at him. Her hands dropped to her side.

"And how do you suppose you're going to leave this room, Cain?"

As he looked around the room, she smelt fear in him.

She giggled, "A lion who walked willingly into its own cage."

"Let me go, Aggie. People will notice me missing."

Cain noticed her flinch, "They will look for me, Aggie. I'm booked on the flight in the morning."

Aggie laughed, "I'm a Witch. I can make shit happen and make shit disappear. I can make you disappear."

"But I'm married to a Witch, Aggie. She has the same Magick as you."

"Don't insult me, Cain. Your wife is pathetic and mild and sweet and ugly. I would fucking crush her. It's not the Magick in me, it's the thirst that makes me stronger. Precious Aislyn, so kind and innocent. Crawl back to your wife, Cain."

"So now you're saying I can go. You're fucking loony."

Cain hated to admit it but he was trapped. He had ignored his suspicions that Aggie might entrap him inside the Magickally sealed room. He knew she was evil and capable of monstrous things but still he had stayed, still he loved her.

"I have a gift for you," she chuckled.

Nervous by what she said, he struggled to find a response.

The Witch stood up and then as if to remind him of her Magickal superiority her toes lifted off the floor and glided effortlessly towards the mahogany chest of drawers where she produced a large glass jar that was filled with a clear liquid. Turning towards him, her eyes widened, as if she had been injected with adrenaline.

"This jar is filled with my tears. Tears I've cried over you. Kept to remind me that one day, I must finally admit to myself that we are finished. It's full, so now is the time to stop all this and set myself free from this love, if this is love?"

Predicting that he would only make matters worse if he spoke, he also sensed that by not speaking would seal his fate, however, it would be at least, a quick and decisive death.

Crying loudly now, her heart screamed to be held by him while wanting to cut his throat open. It had been like this for years.

"I fucking hate her, and I fucking hate you, and tonight I promise to ruin both your lives but not before I take a baby from your groin to throw in your face. You couldn't leave her because of your children together, well that is my motivation."

Quickly, she flew towards him. From a backwards swing, she hit him several times until his face welted, again and he fell down upon the floor. With one motion, she smashed the glass jar across the floor, the tears splashing over him, burning as if it was acid. Glass splintered his skin. And the liquid was acid, years of bitterness combined into a single litre.

"I HEX YOU!"

Covering his bleeding face with his hand, he felt the hex enter his body, and then as quickly as it surged through his body, it fizzed and then left his body.

Jumping to his feet, he gathered his clothes.

"You think she really loves you, Cain? Like I do...did?"

Aggie slithered closer to Cain, placing her index finger on his chin, "No one will ever love you like I did."

And there it was, the twinkle in her eye. The same twinkle that had seduced him hundreds of time and although he fought the urge, his penis hardened.

He wanted to bite her finger off. Rip her apart, one bone at a time but he also wanted to fuck her one last time.

"Cain, a wife that ignores her husband's infidelity doesn't really care about him, doesn't really care about herself. Doesn't even know who you really are. She's never met the man I loved. She loves only a portion of you."

Standing on the tips of her toes, Aggie rubbed his groan, her lips barely reaching his chin, "Does she fuck you, the way I fuck you?"

Pleased that his penis was already hard, Aggie felt satisfied that she would win him over, voluntarily.

"No Cain, not like this! I want to take the child from you, unwillingly. I want you to feel violated."

He frowned, what did she mean?

She picked up her wand from the side table and pointed it at Cain. With a flick of her wrist, she lifted Cain off the floor, and with another flick, she threw him across the room and onto her bed.

Catatonic, he watched as she Magickally erected his penis, mounted him until he ejaculated inside of her and then emotionally dismounted.

Putting her clothes on, she stared at her victim; hopeless, helpless, and at her mercy.

Dressed, she sat at the edge of the bed. Her fingers walked across his forehead and then she sighed, "What is love, Cain, when it so easily turns into this?"

Then she kissed his lips, goodbye.

With a twist of her wrist again, she released Cain from his catatonic state.

He rolled off the bed and stood up, "I don't want anything to do with this child. As far as I'm concerned, it's already dead."

Aggie had only ever wanted Cain. To have his arms around her every night as she fell asleep and to wake every morning to his tender kiss but Aislyn had that privilege.

Cain gathered his clothes, roughly putting them on. His only intention was to leave Aggie, get on the plane and forget her.

Mumbling something, Cain asked her to repeat herself.

"You can't hurt me anymore," as if possessed by a demonic entity her voice deepened, "I hexed you."

Smirking, he turned to her, "It didn't work."

"I hope you truly love her, as I cursed you both. Every time, I pass through your thoughts, even for a fleeting moment, I'll steal some of your happiness and memories until you are a shell, an empty shell. A walking skeleton, just like you've left me. We'll see how much you don't love me. Your love for me, will kill you."

She saw fear in his eyes as she grabbed for her wand, and with intent, vanished him from the room.

Instantly regretting what she had done, Aggie burst into tears. The curse would be irreversible. She had cursed herself as well.

Three days later, Aggie felt the child inside of her. The rip across her stomach had bent her over. This child was fierce. Her Magick was strong. This Maiden will want to live.

Cain ejaculated inside of his wife, Aislyn.

The flight home had seemed like an eternity and he had held Aislyn for a long time at the airport. Insisting that the Norman and Inanna be put to bed early that night, he had held his wife's hand walking her to their bedroom. Undressing her slowly, he had been tender with her. Missionary style, her favourite meant he could gaze into his wife's eyes.

"I love you. I love you so goddam much."

He had held Aislyn until she fell asleep, and just as Aggie had predicted, Cain thought of her. An unusual feeling stirred inside of him, as if a wave of melancholy lodged itself in his chest.

Six weeks later, Aislyn was thrilled to tell her grumpy husband that they had conceived their third child.

And now, Aggie sat beside him.

Aggie felt his fingers move. Sitting up, her chest expanded from excitement, "Cain, its Aggie."

He did not respond.

"Cain, wake up."

She shook his head. His eyes that once held her glance were now vacant.

Frantically, Aggie slapped his cheek, "Wake up Cain, just for a minute. Wake up. Please."

The hex had worked, and after all these years, she finally understood how much he had actually loved her. His Alzheimer's was evidence of it. He had gone home to his family, to his wife but he could not forget her, even to his detriment. Every time his heart pined for her the hex got stronger, and he got sicker until he was a shell, until he became what she predicted, a skeleton.

Had she really won?

Rummaging through her bag, she pulled out a small sketching pad and pencil. Flipping the book open, she started drawing his face or at least what she could see of it which was mere shadows and outlines. It would be the last time that she would draw him.

Amelie

Amelie readjusted her knickers, wiggled the hem of her cotton skirt down to where it was meant to be (below her knees), grabbed the bottle of white wine off Marcus's work station, and slammed the door shut behind her, leaving Marcus with a smirk on his face.

It was wrong to have sex with Marcus in his office, on his desk, but he was just so damn irresistible and a cliché she had fantasised about for weeks.

Strutting along the corridor into B block, room seven, she closed the door, placing the bottle of white wine on the table. Producing two plastic wine cups from her bag, Amelie unscrewed the lid and poured the wine to the top of each cup. Two gulps and she had drunk the entire plastic cup full.

Unlatching the balcony door (ignoring the sign 'No Exit'), Amelie needed some fresh air to cool off from straddling Marcus only minutes before. Sex certainly demanded a different type of fitness.

The cold air whipped her face.

Lighting a cigarette, she took a large drag, sucking the smoke into her lungs until they felt as if they might burst.

Dozens of cars on the highway drove past, the passengers oblivious to the anguish the internal walls of the hospital housed.

Amelie threw her cigarette butt onto the ground, squashing it under her foot.

She stopped as the sound of crows deafened her. Swiftly turning to look into the cloudy sky, two crows flew towards her.

"No!"

Amelie quickly entered the hospital room, slamming the balcony door shut behind her.

Landing on the balcony the crows cawed, aggressively tapping with their beaks on the window sill.

Amelie glared at Fay Ce'Line. The Goddesses had sent their death carriers to collect her.

"Fuck you crows, she isn't ready to leave us yet. The Goddesses will need to wait."

Looking up into the sky, Amelie stuck her middle finger up, "Fuck you, Goddesses."

Amelie walked over to the wine, sculling its contents directly from the bottle and then returned to the window to close the curtains, "Fuck off birds, she's ours for now."

Sitting down on the end of the bed, Amelie studied the hospital equipment that monitored Fay Ce'Line statistics. Her heartbeat looked stable but she looked like a sleeping zombie.

Fay Ce'Line's feet were still warm, "Surely, you're days away from dying Fay Ce'Line with warm tootsies like that?"

The larger crow found the gap between the curtains and tapped on the window again. His yellow eyes stared on Fay Ce'Line. Amelie stormed over to the window pulling the curtains shut.

Fay Ce'Line whimpered.

Instinctively, Amelie helped Fay Ce'Line to sit up, "Honey, I've brought wine but I've already drunk half of it. Sorry."

Sunken eyes and skin the colour of four day old paste, her only prominent facial features were her pouty lips that had cracked and bled, and her high cheekbones that only accentuated her death mask.

Amelie kissed Fay Ce'Line's forehead, "Would you like a drink, Honey?"

Fay Ce'Line nodded.

"You're a go'er Fay, that's for sure."

Placing a straw into the plastic cup, Amelie held it for her as Fay Ce'Line was too weak to hold the cup. Most of the wine ran down her chin. Amelie wiped most of it off using a tissue.

Fay Ce'Line struggled to speak but somehow found the strength, "Should I have wine in the hospital?"

Amelie laughed, "Honey! What are they going to do? Kill you? It's a bit fucking late for that."

Managing a grin, Amelie enjoyed the sparkle in Fay Ce'Line's eyes.

Amelie grabbed Fay Ce'Line's hand and squeezed it tightly, "I've been thinking Fay Ce'Line. You don't have to die like this. I could discharge you. Buy the best bottle of wine. A shit load of drugs! I'll drive you to your favourite place and we can all watch the sunset. Together?"

Inhaling, Amelie fought back the need to cry, "Pagan, Ruby and Oscar, they could all be there. Just Oscar, if you prefer. It would be beautiful, unlike this fucking place. You deserve more than this Fay Ce'Line. There is no dignity here."

Fay Ce'Line squeezed Amelie's hand, "No."

She needed to die, normally, like this, for Oscar.

Pagan

Pagan looked into the rear view mirror, sucked on her index finger and wiped the smeared mascara from underneath her eyes.

"You need to be strong for Fay Ce'Line. You can mourn her death after she's died. It's not like you haven't had to cope with death before."

Modern medicine could now predict a person's estimated time of death. That meant that Fay Ce'Line only had a few days left according to 'their' estimate.

Although, she was dying of cancer, it was starvation that would eventually kill her as the cancer had travelled into her intestines and bowel. The intravenous drip had prolonged her life but could not sustain it.

Fay Ce'Line had given the news surprisingly well, "You have to die of something, I suppose."

In other reincarnations, Fay Ce'Line had lived well into her sixties. A great injustice had occurred.

It had been an emotional day already; Inanna, then Rogan, and now, she had to care for Fay Ce'Line while Oscar looked after the twins. Oscar had aged in the last few weeks. Clumps of hair had fallen out from stress, leaving his once scruffy mane, matted and patchy.

Looking up at the third level of the hospital, two crows stood on Fay Ce'Line's balcony. Pagan blew a raspberry with her lips as she tried to hold back the tears.

"Be strong," she whispered to herself.

Jumping out of the Kombi, Pagan slowly walked towards the entrance.

Smiling at the two receptionists, she bypassed the elevator and chose the staircase instead. She was stalling. Once she was on the third floor, she walked into the employee's kiosk and grabbed an orange juice from the fridge. It cost two dollars and twenty cents. She decided to drink it there. She watched several of the nursing staff chat amongst themselves at a table. Pagan wondered how long it took them to desensitise to death due to being surrounded by it every day.

Throwing the plastic container into the bin, she exited the room. Lost in thought, she walked straight into a man. Embarrassed, she hid her botchy face from him, keeping it facing down towards the floor.

"Sorry."

"No worries."

Her nose smelt something familiar. She sniffed again. 'What did the smell remind her of?'

Amelie was sitting in the brown coloured vinyl recliner with a cup of wine, when Pagan entered the room.

Out of habit, Pagan checked Fay Ce'Line's temperature by placing her palm across her forehead. She was warm.

Amelie sat up, "She's sleeping again. I suspect she will fall into a coma in a few days. The nurse keeps coming in and asking if I think she needs more morphine."

Amelie shrugged her shoulders "I'm like, 'hell yeah' and the nurse increases the dosage. It's like legalised euthanasia."

Pagan grabbed Fay Ce'Line's cup of wine and drunk the remainder of it, "I'm surprised you haven't asked for some morphine yourself."

She was relieved the curtains were drawn, "I take it you've noticed the crows outside."

"The fuckers won't stop tapping on the window. I'm seriously thinking about blowing them up. Smash them like the pumpkins."

"I'm surprised we haven't been reprimanded for using Magick that day to smash the pumpkins."

"I would say, the authorities have more to worry about then our vendetta against vegetables."

Laughing, Pagan sat down next to Amelie on the arm of the recliner, "When do you think she might wake up? I need to ask her to do something for Morghana. Something that only Fay Ce'Line can do."

Amelie screwed her face up, "Hmmm, maybe in a few hours."

Suddenly sitting up, Pagan looked at Amelie, "Have you just had sex?"

Amelie laughed, "Is it that obvious?"

"Ha, I think I just bumped into your boyfriend at the kiosk. I knew he smelt familiar."

Peony

Peony heard the backdoor close. Carl was home.

She had waited six weeks for this night, carefully planning what she would say to him. She had not slept most nights due to her anticipation of taking back her power. When she had slept, her dreams had been heavily occupied by vivid characters and unforeseen catastrophe.

Carl would take his boots off, leaving them at the backdoor for people to trip over, strip his clothes off, placing them into the laundry basket for Peony to wash, and lastly, he would pat the dog (the only affection he would display), and then he would enter the dining room where tea would be ready for him, usually.

This evening Peony sat at the dining table, drinking from a tumbler filled with two nips of scotch and ice.

An Elvis Presley vinyl played on their second hand record player and dinner was not prepared nor would she wash his clothes.

Carl stood at the doorway in his underwear. The mere sight of her husband repulsed her. How had she spent nearly twenty years of her life with him?

He was surprised to find Peony stiffly positioned at the dining table.

Flipping the light switch on, Carl barked at her, "What the heck are you doing, Peony?"

Never dropping her gaze, Peony took another sip of scotch.

Dramatically, she kicked her suitcase out from underneath the table. That strategic move, she had thought of at 02:00, Tuesday morning, several weeks ago.

Slamming the tumbler down on the glass dining table, she replied, "Sit down, Carl. We need to talk. No! You need to listen. I know the concept is new to you but you will quickly catch on."

He walked towards the kitchen bench, grabbing the bottle of scotch, taking a long and exaggerated swig from it.

"Fucking oath, Peony, this sounds serious."

"Mock all you like, Carl. Nothing you can say to me affects me anymore. Tonight you cannot bully me."

Choosing to sit opposite Peony, he sat back, crossing one leg over the other. His ankle sat at his opposite knee. Both hands placed behind his head.

Peony smirked, 'Cocky bastard'.

"Is this going to take long Peony because I'm hungry?"

Peony straightened up, "It won't take long, Carl. To be honest you've wasted enough of my life as it is."

She pushed a letter across the table towards him, "Please read."

He quickly guessed her point, "A Dear John letter? Really? You're too pathetic to leave me, Peony. You really think you can cope out in the real world. Geez, you don't even have a job."

Peony gentle smiled, "No Carl, it's a 'you gave me herpes sleeping with some slut' letter and for your information, I have a job in Spain. It doesn't take long to organise a passport and visa with your money. You see, I'm off to see the world, backpacking or couch surfing. Anywhere but here, Carl!"

Surely, she was bluffing, and the suitcase was purely for dramatic effect?

He stood up, "I'm having a shower."

She stood up, "Sit down Carl! I haven't finished."

Hesitant to play-out whatever scenario she had concocted in her warped mind, Carl grudgingly sat down. He would control how this conversation would play-out, not her.

He pointed his ring finger at her, "What I do when I'm in Western Australia is none of your fucking business. I didn't marry you because you were beautiful or intelligent. I married you because you were obedient. So stay fucking obedient."

Not surprised that he had not even tried to deny it, Peony chuckled.

"You married a little girl. She doesn't exist anymore. She settled for a man who offered her beer and T.V and who fucks like a robot. But I meet someone. With a passion for life. Divine timing, I reckon."

Carl laughed, "You're 'nothing' without me."

"You see Carl. You gave me herpes, obviously after sleeping with some desperate whore and she would have to be 'desperate'. So therefore I pity her. The herpes put me into hospital. I ended up with a kidney and bladder infection. It took me a month to get over the physical effects but I'm still not over the emotional. I kept it from you. Scared that you would accuse me of sleeping with another man, giving you the excuse to hit me again."

Disrespectfully, Carl turned away from her and yawned.

Peony ignored his technique of contempt and continued, "The sad truth is Carl, you're not my enemy. You're 'nothing'. I'm my worst enemy, and while you've given me the opportunity to think, well, I've decided to start liking myself. I'm putting myself first and you, well, you've become irrelevant. I think for most women catching herpes would have destroyed their sexual power but lucky for me, you already had."

Carl stood up, flinging the chair across the room, "Fuck off then, Cunt!"

Peony slowly stood up. Walking around the table, she paused for a moment before pushing him. Carl stumbled backwards a few steps. The look of shock amused her. She had never fought back. Suddenly, she realised why he fancied Pagan. She always fought back.

He raised his fist at her.

"Do it!"

His fist hovered above her face but he was unable to make contact.

Peony raised her voice, "Do it, you weakling! Not so much fun when I want you to do it, is it?"

Blood rushed to his fist. He wanted to smack her face in. 'How dare she challenge him? How dare she speak to him like that?' His fist dropped.

Without any warning, Peony pulled out a pair of garden secateurs from her back pocket and smiled.

"Bruises heal," and then she cut her ring finger off. Never again would she marry.

CHAPTER 27
Pagan

Pagan could not ignore the urge to spend more time with Demeter and Deity, even if it was not 'her' kid week.

Annoyed by the intrusion at dinner time, John obligingly asked his ex-partner to join them. Assuming Pagan was unnerved by Fay Ce'Line's illness, he sympathised with her sentiment to spend some extra time with their children, even if her timing was off.

Awkwardly, Pagan wedged herself between Michelle and Demeter, avoiding eye contact with John, who habitually clenched his jaw. Pagan noted that John sat at the end of the table while Michelle the other. Interesting.

Excited to see her mother join them for dinner, Deity kicked Pagan underneath the dining table. Infectious with laughter, Deity kicked her mother again, only to be scolded by John.

"Settle down, young lady."

Uncomfortable to have his past and future partners in the present, John remained quiet throughout the meal.

After a few glasses of Baileys the conversation between Michelle and Pagan flowed and as usual it led to them both teasing John about his serious personality, a conversation they both seemed to enjoy. After all, they were not rivals. They had just loved the same man and it was difficult not to like, if not admire Michelle. Young, intelligent, attractive, emotionally well-balanced and kind, Pagan could see why John had fallen-in-love with her. She seemed to have her 'shit together' and she appeared to truly love her stepchildren.

Michelle had once told Pagan at Demeter's birthday party, "That to truly love John was to fully accept his children, even his ex."

They had laughed, forming a strong female bond that day, much to John's dismay.

Michelle was indeed an excellent role model for Demeter and Deity who were lucky to have a wonderful second mum.

Pagan felt a wince of jealousy soar through her body and then a wave of guilt that she had allowed ego and pride to consume her. There was no need for her to be jealous that another woman loved her children. In fact, it showed that she loved them more due to her acceptance.

Pagan rubbed Demeter's leg, "Do you think I could spend some alone time with you and Deity for a while, up in your room?"

Demeter shrugged his shoulder, "I suppose."

Michelle looked at John, "Help me with the dishes, John. I'm sure the kids can have one night off from their chores?"

It was tempting to snoop into each room as Pagan walked to Demeter's room.

Michelle and John seemed to have a cosy existence. Holiday photographs of their time spent in Bali, decorated the wall. Beige coloured walls, matched the carpet and curtains.

Pagan was not surprised that Inanna and Mark spent a considerable amount of leisurely time with Michelle and John, often catching up for the movies and late evening walks.

Enthusiastically, Deity held her mother's hand, pulling her down the hallway and into Demeter's room.

"Sit here, mummy."

Deity sat on Pagan's lap as Demeter characteristically sat at his Xbox, grabbing the controller.

Reading a few nursery books and losing three games on the Xbox, Pagan left.

Her hugs were exaggerated but she strangely found the strength to leave, never knowing if she would ever see them again.

"Always remember that mummy loves you and will always be close, no matter what."

Closing the door as she left, her heart ached.

At the front door, John had been surprised by an unexpected hug from Pagan.

"Everything alright, Pagan?"

"You're a good dad, John. Just remember that, and thank you."

He did not reciprocate her affections.

Arriving home, Pagan walked to the lounge room in the dark where she fell onto the couch, hiding her face in the pillows. An overwhelming melancholy consumed her.

Dante had disappeared again, Fay Ce'Line was dying, her brother had reappeared as the Darkness, Morghana was unwell, there was talk of a secret uprising that threatened to kill her, and in several days, Pagan was scheduled to meet Aggie, the Crone who had destroyed her life. Spending the evening with the children had only increased the pressure.

Exhausted, she slept.

Alert, she sat up!

"Dante?" She asked quietly.

Silence.

'Yes, she could smell something'.

Tiptoeing through the house, she followed the smell until she stood in front of her bedroom window. Luckily, the curtains were open and she had a clear view down the street, each way. Fog blanketed the wet road. The grey haze spread evenly along the street, motionless it appeared dormant.

'Was it fog?' She wondered.

Reaching up, she ran her fingertips over her bruised neck. Almost healed, it was a reminder of what Norman had done to her. Had Don not chased him away, she may have died that night.

The front gate shut. Someone was in her front yard.

Inhaling, she recognised the smell. Relieved, she ran to the front door. Turning the door handle, she quickly opened the front door to a frail Oscar.

"Quickly come inside. I think the Darkness is out there."

Pulling him through the door, she double checked the lock before ushering him to the lounge room, turning all the lights on as she went.

Slouched, Oscar sat down on the couch.

Switching the lounge room light on, Pagan was shocked by how unwell Oscar looked.

"I'll make us a cup of tea with a dash of scotch."

Entering the kitchen, Pagan slipped on the floor.

"Fuck! Can this day get any worse?"

She loved Oscar but she was depleted and he needed as much support as he could receive.

Turning the kettle on, she made two cups of tea; two sugars and small drop of milk. Grabbing the scotch bottle from the cupboard, she poured roughly a nip in each cup and a large amount directly down her throat.

"Here you go, Oscar."

Shaking, his hand struggled to hold the cup.

"You look shit, Oscar. When did you have a shower last, or some sleep?"

His hair was unwashed, his face unshaven, his eyes merely slits and his aura a dirty brown colour.

"The moment they told me Fay Ce'Line was inoperable my life ended. I'm just helping it along."

Unsure what to say to Oscar, Pagan ignored his dramatics. He needed a hug but she was emotionally drained and wished he had not woken her from a much needed sleep.

"The pain will decrease over time, and then one day, you will find yourself laughing again. A real laugh and then you will feel guilty for having a moment of happiness. I know you're not ready to hear this yet but over time it will get easier. You need to be strong for the twins."

Oscar sipped his drink. Vacant, he had not heard a word Pagan had said to him.

"She went into a coma tonight."

Pagan clenched her fists. Hoping that Oscar would not see, she hid her hands behind her back.

Oscar wrapped his hands around the cup. The heat burned him but the pain seemed irrelevant.

"Fay Ce'Line sat up and hugged the twins. Touched her chest and then lay back down. She hasn't woken since."

Without hesitation, Pagan sat beside him, wrapping her arms around his shoulders.

Rigid, he ignored her failed attempt to console him, instead he pulled out a piece of paper from his shirt pocket.

"She gave me this map several days ago."

As if it had been folded and unfolded a hundred times, it appeared old and tattered.

"Open it, Pagan."

It was indeed a map. A black spot marked an area close to Oscar's home, a few kilometres into dense bush.

"She wants me to bury photos, and a diary about the twins. You know major life stuff, so in her next life she can have information about them. Know how their lives turned out."

Pagan brushed his hair back from his forehead, "How do you feel about this?"

As if awoken from his own coma, Oscar suddenly energised and clawed at Pagan, "How do I feel. I don't feel anything, that's the fucking problem, Pagan. I don't feel anything."

His hands desperately searched for her, "Please Pagan, you can't let her die!"

Scratching at Pagan's pale face, his coarse hands felt like sandpaper.

She pulled away from him.

Raging, he jumped on top of Pagan, "You need to do a spell, you have to make her live. I'll kill, Aggie. I'll do anything. I'll die without her."

Pagan pushed Oscar off. His sudden outburst scared her. Stumbling backwards all the stress released from her body. Dropping to the floor, she wailed, "I can't do *it* all."

If she saved Fay Ce'Line, she would lose Morghana.

CHAPTER 28
Hobart, June 20th, 09:00
Pagan

Priscilla held the conference door open with one hand while the other hand waved at Pagan to enter.

Pagan deliberately bumped shoulders with Priscilla as she passed.

Amused by Pagan's childish antics, Priscilla smiled.

Swaggering down the corridor, Priscilla was aware that Svenana was perving on her meaty bottom.

Priscilla thought she heard a whistle but was too eager to catch up on paper work to see who had made the noise.

Nine chairs positioned around a horse shoe shaped table, only one chair housed her nemesis, Aggie.

Sensing movement, Aggie straightened her back to signal that she was ready for company. No, not ready, prepared.

Pagan struggled to find a seat that would maximise her empowerment in the room, after all, she was not a seventeen year old Maiden anymore and Aggie was certainly not in her prime. What was important was that Aggie would hear what Pagan had to say, regardless if she could see her or not.

Choosing to sit three chairs from Aggie, Pagan sunk into the large purple cushioned chair.

Two walls were covered with a whiteboard and professional glamour shots photography of the Tasmanian Crone Alliance. The third wall was made up of large windows that harboured a misty view of Hobart. The dull morning sunlight shone through the dark clouds. A large flat screen television hung on the back wall behind Aggie.

"Are you intending on inviting the Crone Monarchy to join us via satellite?"

"No!" Aggie grumbled.

Pagan may be in her early thirties, old by any teenage standard, but Pagan was in her physical prime.

Pagan studied Aggie. She was certainly a Crone now. Old and fragile.

Suddenly feeling confident, she moved one chair closer to Aggie.

Aggie slapped her wrinkly hand on the table, "Come here."

Humouring the Crone, Pagan slid onto the next chair. She now sat only a ruler length from the Crone Monarch who had almost killed her and stole her Magick. Aggie's mothball breath made Pagan turn her head slightly to avoid full coverage.

The smell of Aggie's body internally rotting discharged from Aggie's pores. Aggie was dying, the smell was undeniable.

Poking her head out, Aggie's hands fumbled along Pagan's body until she found her hair. Aggie had done the same thing when they had first met.

Tugging on it, she pulled Pagan's head down. Sniffing Pagan's long dark curls as if she was confirming Pagan's identity, then pushed Pagan away in disgust.

Aggie's harsh voice broke the tension, "You smell like your father."

Insulted, Pagan chose to remain silent.

Aggie waved her hand, "Sit!"

"It's fascinating how a petite Non-Ancient Witch, single-handedly brought down the Ancient Witches? It really is a great story. I'm very disappointed I wasn't sitting on the throne when you attempted it."

Snorting, Aggie rejoiced in the recognition, "You'd be dead like the rest."

Pagan interrupted, "Had we ruled together we would have made the most powerful force Witches had ever witnessed. My Magick and your brains?"

The room suddenly became electric.

Aggie squinted at Pagan. Her eyesight was certainly limited, "A political duet? I don't think your friend, Amelie would have coped due to jealousy."

"Can I ask you why you travelled to Tasmania alone? I could kill you. I passed your security guard in the hallway, not really that scary is she? And you've left the Crone Monarchy safely, behind in London. It was either very calculated or stupid. A smart Crone like you would have her reasons surely for flying willingly into potential danger unprotected?"

"There comes a time when you stop fearing fear itself, and for those who then welcome fear, well, they must be the happiest of all," Aggie proclaimed.

Aggie was withholding information from Pagan. She could sense it. There had to be an agenda.

Aggie snapped, "Firstly, you will call me the Supreme Femineity and only speak when asked to. Do you understand?"

Pagan grinned, and then sarcastically answered, "Yes, Supreme Femineity. I did always believe Highest Priestess was a bit churchy for my liking."

She caught Aggie off guard who had anticipated resilience from Pagan, "You are a deceitful Witch. A personality trait you also inherited from your father."

Aggie repositioned herself on the chair. Her heavy red velvet dress and brown cloak were a hindrance, and her deep seeded love of her humble home, only added to her homesickness.

Regaining her composure, although her voice vibrated and her body twitched at random, she spoke, "The Darkness has awoken from its slumber. It has been active for almost a century now. This is a major concern to the Crone Monarchy who is assessing the situation. We can confirm that it is your brother Norman who is now the Darkness or is 'himself' being controlled by them.

Regardless, he has an alliance with them and is able to enter both worlds at will. We cannot confirm his reasons for it or how he possesses the knowledge. Therefore, we are all at risk. There is a Darkness taskforce, although I'm not sure they are doing a damn thing to help."

Aggie made an exaggerated hum as if she was releasing negativity from her aging body.

Pagan sensed that Aggie knew more than what she was willing to reveal but she was surprised that Aggie had revealed as much as she already had, after all they were enemies and Aggie had every right to remain suspicious. The irony that they would need to work together to face the Darkness was humorous.

Aggie snarled, "We are now a political duet. My Magick and your knowledge."

Sitting back on her seat, Pagan replied, "The Darkness can only possess a human on a Darkmoon. The spell to awaken the Darkness is in the Ancient Doctrine and must be performed by a Coven of thirteen Witches. Norman must know where the Ancient Doctrine is hidden?"

Aggie yelled, "I did not ask you what your thoughts are on this situation? You bloody Ancient's think you know everything. We get it, you're really old. Really, really, really old!"

Angering, Pagan replied, "Beg your pardon, Supreme Femineity but fuck you! I'm in danger because you stole my Magick. You left me vulnerable to my own brother, and to be honest, I've read the Ancient Doctrine where you haven't even laid eyes on it."

Pagan had several reasons for directing her comment towards Aggie's incompetence. There were loose ends she had to tie up or at least take responsibility for. She was not as clever as she thought.

Aggie rubbed her chin. Regret plagued her. Lowering her defences only enough so that she could reduce some of the karma, she had gathered up in one reincarnation, she spoke earnestly, "I thought about Awakening you, so that we could rule together but I'm not one for sharing. My thirst for power was, let's say... too intense. I had things to prove. When you are pushed down your entire life the thirst for climbing ladders is all empowering. So desperate to see the view from the top."

Aggie cackled. Her wrinkly face lit up, "I suppose, I proved myself."

Fury buried so deep encouraged a knee jerk reaction, "So to prove yourself, you ruined my life? I could kill you now, Aggie."

"I asked Svenana to leave us be. Without a sword or your Magick? You're not a common murderer. Knives do not become you and revenge is only satisfactory when your victim wants to live. You would be doing this Crone a favour. Make sure you bury your fury with me."

Wisdom supported Pagan, "We both know our mistakes carry onto the next reincarnation. Trust me, it will never leave us. Our hatred for each other will carry over."

"Spoken like a true pessimist."

"You see Aggie, you did me a favour by taking my Magick. You stole my Magick but gave me 'life'. You gave me the simple things. Pleasures, I had never experienced before. I suppose humans call it, normality. As an Ancient it was my duty to rule. Not my choice. So I come here today to thank you, warranted you have left me with quite a legacy where I am now vulnerable to the Darkness but you have given me more than I could have imagined. There is something comforting about being a bee and not the queen."

Demoralised, Aggie twisted on her chair. Pagan's words burned deep within her.

"If it's any consolation once I am dead you regain your Magick. It was a waste really. I could never conquer the damn thing. I suspect you will have a laugh at my expense when you realise the torment that it has caused me."

The urge to kill Aggie surged through Pagan's body. She could kill Aggie and regain her Magick. Aggie was tempting her but she was not about to take the bait.

"You think I'm prodding the bear, maybe my request is real. Maybe not?"

"Maybe Supreme Femineity, you're scared to face the Darkness. Fuck, it took an entire army of Magickally powerful Ancient Witches to beat it last time. I very much doubt your Non-Ancient defences will make much impact. You don't have a clue when it comes to the Darkness. If the Darkness gets through the portal at full capacity, it means the end of the world for humans and Witches. It feeds off sorrow, fear and anger and the world is full of it. The world is ripe for the picking. You see the Darkness cares very little for anything other than itself. Our little differences will mean nothing."

Pagan stood up and walked behind Aggie, placing both hands on her round shoulders. Her hands wrapped around Aggie's throat. Pagan bent inwards, her lips touching Aggie's right ear, "Maybe it's time to drop the bullshit and start telling each other the truth. It's obvious that I need you and you need me…Mother."

Aggie heard her daughter say the words. The word 'mother' echoed inside her head.

Crisp and collected, Aggie remained composed, "How did you know?"

Pagan shook her head, "You left me clues. Subconscious or not, deep down you wanted me to know."

It was true, Aggie had left Pagan clues.

Pagan continued, "The glass room where you kept me prisoner, the walls were plastered with drawings of my father. I never told Jaide I recognised him

339

because I didn't recognise the man. Cain looked different. Not the father I remember at all. He looked, almost happy."

Aggie stiffened. Memories of Jaide, her half-sister flooded back.

"The only way that you could steal my Magick was by sharing the same blood. Your power is 'acute smell' as is mine. It really was not that hard to figure out. Your loathing towards me…well I admit, I haven't figured that out."

"It was prophesised that I must birth a child before I achieved my destiny. It happened very quickly after I conceived you."

Aggie turned to Pagan. Her hands desperately tugged on Pagan's jumper, "Why did you remain silent?"

Pagan inhaled "Because I always did like a good secret."

Fay Ce'Line

Oscar slept very little in the hospital recliner and finally after the night nurse completed her rounds and the hospital fell into a clinical slumber, he climbed in beside Fay Ce'Line, gentle placing one arm over her, leaving the rest of his body only an inch away from hers as to not break her bones accidently.

His breath warmed her chilled face but he doubted she knew he was even there.

Starving to death, Fay Ce'Line had thinned quickly. Her breath was shallow and she lay so still that he thought she could die at any moment. Her cheeks were flushed but she radiated no heat. The rest of her face was wraithlike pale.

The nurse's attitude had changed towards him the last few days. Where once they would send him home at night or order him around as if he was a child, they now supported him, allowing him to make a coffee across the hall in their kitchen rather than at the kiosk. He sensed that they knew through experience that Fay Ce'Line would be leaving him soon. Their orderly professionalism had transformed into subtle pity.

As far as Oscar was concerned, Fay Ce'Line had already left him. She had succumbed to a death sleep that he would not see her wake from, transient and foreboding.

Trapped in transit, Oscar was exhausted, he had to mourn his wife's death twice and then he would have to 'suck it up' to organise her funeral. Guilty, he wished she would die soon so he could busy himself with anything actually, anything other than waiting. Numb; he felt everything. He dreaded the daylight loneliness but what he feared most was lying in an empty bed.

The nurses told him, "They had all grown fond of Fay Ce'Line and that it was a real shame that such a beautiful soul was leaving the earth so quickly."

Of course Fay Ce'Line would reincarnate in several hundred years. The thought gave him little comfort. The only legacy he would leave was an imprint of the soles of his boots where he would leave her mementos of a life, she exited too quickly from.

Oscar watched the sunrise peek through the blinds. More crows had landed on the balcony and he felt more alone than he had in his entire life.

The day nurse woke him. She was pleased he had slept a little, even if he had slept in the hospital bed.

She increased Fay Ce'Line's morphine.

The Doctor arrived at 09:00, briefly predicting that she would die very soon. He offered his professional condolences. Oscar did not hear a word he said, only politely shaking his hand for his services.

Mid-morning, Ruby arrived checking Fay Ce'Line's feet. They were still warm.

Ruby messaged Pagan, Roberta and Amelie to let them know that it was time for them to make their way to the hospital, "It's time to say goodbye."

Ruby feared that Pagan would not make it back from Hobart in time.

By eleven o'clock Ruby, Roberta and Amelie sat in silence in the hospital room. Their eyes engrossed on Fay Ce'Line. Struggling with their own grief, they all sat engrossed in memory. They were bonded through the centuries as Witch sisters. Cancer had affected them all.

Amelie broke the silence with a giggle, "Do you remember when you and Fay Ce'Line got married?"

Oscar nodded.

Amelie covered her face to hide the laughter, "And your mum called Fay Ce'Line a Witch who had stolen her son and we all accused you of telling your mum the truth."

Oscar smiled, "Fay Ce'Line nearly called the wedding off."

Ruby piped up, "What about the time when we bought her a vibrator on one of our group holidays and it went off in her luggage at the airport."

"I had never seen her so bright red. I think Pagan got the number of the airport security man," Amelie laughed.

"Yes, she dated him for about three weeks until she bored of him," Oscar scowled.

"If it's any consolation, we think of you as one of us, Oscar."

Roberta wiped tears from her eyes, "Gee, we've had some funny times. I wonder what the next reincarnation will give us."

They all silenced.

Roberta glared at Oscar who heard the comment. What Roberta had said stung him but he did not have time to indulge as Fay Ce'Line's head moved as if she was waking.

Ruby jumped up, grabbing Fay Ce'Line's feet. Icy cold suggested that they had been for quite some time.

Amelie and Roberta saw the panic in Ruby's eyes.

Surrounding the bed, Fay Ce'Line began choking.

Oscar pressed the red emergency button, pushing it several times for the nurse to come. The nurse arrived several seconds later. She immediately placed her hands on Oscar's shoulder, "It won't be long now."

They all stood helplessly beside Fay Ce'Line as she struggled to work through her last breath. Her chin lay open and her jaw moved unnaturally. One last exhale; a foul smell left her body.

Oscar stood still. He had never seen anyone die before. It happened so quickly. One breathe and she was gone. How could a whole life be gone – just like that?

Oscar and the nurse did not witness Fay Ce'Line's purple energy leave her body, or her Magick, four totem horses (a chocolate Clydesdale, a gray Arabian, a dun Mustang and a black Morgan Arabian) galloped from her stomach, disappearing before they reached the window.

Roberta and Ruby hugged each other in quiet hysteria while the nurse busied herself with the final care.

Oscar leaned in, his lips touching Fay Ce'Line's lips, "You sleep, my baby girl!"

Amelie walked to the window where the crows pecked wildly on the window, "You will need to wait, little birds. She's not ready."

12:10
Inanna

Inanna sat stiffly on a wooden chair - a chair that she had carried from the dining room to Morghana's bedroom, placing it on the inside of Morghana's door.

The bedroom door was locked from the outside by Mark.

Inanna was unsure if she was protecting her daughter or keeping her a prisoner, either way, something had to be done to assure everyone's safety, even if it meant putting herself in danger.

Morghana had violently attacked Inanna five times, once knocking Inanna down the stairwell where it had taken her several minutes to stand up.

Ashamed, Inanna was now scared of her daughter.

"No! I'm scared of Hensley."

'Why had the Goddesses reincarnated Hensley to be Ruby's daughter?' Ruby had in the past helped burn Hensley's family alive in a church. Inanna had watched the church burn, she herself taking pleasure in their cruelty. Hensley lost her three children; a three year old boy and two girls aged nine and fourteen that

342

day. The smell of their burning flesh still haunted Inanna who stood by and did nothing to prevent the tragedy.

In those days, nobody challenged Pagan. It had been a hot summer and tensions between Ancients and Non-Ancients were increasing. Pagan had been particularly angry that day and had decided to take a ride to clear her thoughts when she came across a church in the forest. As far as Pagan was concerned, the forest belonged to the Witches not humans. Riddled with a sickness of revenge, Pagan had sanctioned the destruction of the building. Ruby had locked the church doors trapping people inside. Amelie had raised her hand, shooting a fireball from her palm at the church, sparking the fire.

Many reincarnations later, Inanna closed her eyes, guilty of what they had done.

'Perhaps the Goddesses thought Ruby and Hensley could work through the pain and resentment? There would never be enough time to heal wounds that run that deeply'.

A Maiden is chosen specifically for the Witch; dependent of course on what the Witch has to offer the Maiden or how badly a Witch yearns for a particular Maiden. The Goddesses had chosen Morghana to be her daughter. Why the Goddesses chose Morghana baffled Inanna. Morghana suited Pagan's personality more. Inanna feared that the Goddesses had also paired her to a Witch she had wronged in the past. They had wronged so many Witches they would be running out of karmic free children to choose from.

Regardless of their tensions, she loved Morghana as she had loved all the rest and the thought of her possessed by an embittered energy only increased her innate need to protect the Maiden.

Hearing Morghana whimper, Inanna walked towards her sleeping daughter who lay sleeping on top of her doona cover. Beads of sweat covered her forehead. Knotted hair fell over her olive skin and her eyelids so soft and delicate, twitched.

"You look so peaceful. Hensley has such a firm grip on you, I fear you will be dead before your eighteenth birthday. We must make you well again."

Inanna had never witnessed a possession before. It frightened her.

Possessions were for the humans not Witches. How had Hensley managed to connect her energies to Morghana's? Was Morghana feeble of mind? Perhaps, they were Coven sisters?

Stretching, Inanna felt a breeze. The gust of wind was subtle but undoubtable.

Checking the window, she was surprised to find it was locked.

The second gust of wind was stronger. Energy was present.

Suddenly alert, Inanna's heart raced.

An electric purple miasma sparkling with flashes of golden flakes zoomed round the room.

"Fay Ce'Line?" Inanna yelled.

Unaware that she had started crying, Inanna jumped for joy. Hope, poisoned any doubt now.

The energy entered Morghana's body, heaving her off the bed. Morghana released a scream so deep and primitive that Inanna ran to her side.

Three energies now battled inside of Morghana's body. A squealing sound intensified as Morghana's body raised a metre from her bed, twisting, spinning and smashing into the furniture, walls and the ceiling. Books and make-up become missiles.

Foaming from the mouth, Morghana looked like she was having a seizure. Morghana's arms snapped backwards. The sound made Inanna dry-wretch.

Morghana's body heaved again, this time her body violently smashed into the ceiling, only to float down to smash into the ceiling again. Plaster broke and fell down, covering them both in white dust.

Two energies exited Morghana's body; one purple and the other a murky green, vanishing out the window. A murder of crows swooped and cawed outside the bedroom.

Inanna caught Morghana as she fell from the ceiling, both hurdled onto the bed in a bundle of limbs.

Cradling Morghana, Inanna wrapped her up into the foetal position.

Awake and aware, Morghana howled wildly. The pain of her broken arms, induced shock.

Inanna rocked Morghana back and forth, "Hensley's with the Goddesses. Everything is ok now."

Pagan's plan had worked. Fay Ce'Line an Ancient Witch had managed to connect to Hensley's energies, pulling her out of Morghana.

Inanna allowed herself to cry as she was ecstatic to have her daughter back.

'Thank goodness for Magick!"

22:00
Amelie

Marcus gently kissed Amelie's back.

Each kiss hummed through Amelie's body, reducing her to tears with each touch. Tears sat on her cheek and on her pillow.

The pain of losing one of her best friend only intensified her need to experience a certain amount of intimacy with Marcus. He entered her vagina. Arching her back to accommodate his reach and rhythm, he moved slowly inside of her. One hand cupped her left breast while the other hand buried deeply into her waist. His nose nestled into her hair, and randomly he would bite at the fleshy part of her neck. She enjoyed the pain.

Amelie humped backwards towards him, desperately needing him to fill the void Fay Ce'Line had left behind.

Pagan dies first, usually in her mid-thirties followed by Ruby and Roberta and then Fay Ce'Line. Inanna usually made it well into her seventies and she lived well into her nineties. Unlike humans, Witches life spans were not prolonged by hygiene practises and medical advancements.

Marcus pinched her breast. His movement was quickening and his desire for each her, intensifying.

He had been unselfish after hearing the news of Fay Ce'Line's death, understanding that he was a peripheral person in her life and that she needed to be with her friends, he had willingly urged her to spend the day with them. Once she reached his home, he had insisted she nap late into the afternoon. Feeding her a warm meal and a glass of chardonnay, Amelie drifted in and out of sleep, eventually falling into an exhausted sleep. After dinner, he had sat and held her while she cried.

Usually during times of stress and sadness, Pagan would be her support, and together they would find the strength and wisdom to move forward, even find the humour in the situation but Pagan wanted to grieve on her own.

Amelie was falling in love with Marcus, so much so, she had chosen him over Pagan to spend the evening with. It was hard to resist his charm. He made her feel safe. He softened her.

His large arms wrapped her up as if she was a child, a delicate heart, desperate to be protected. He had become her unexpected guardian over the last few months, reintroduced her to love-making, challenging her trust issues, and now she was safe in the knowledge that she was capable of loving again.

Marcus ejaculated quietly.

It pleased Amelie that he had reach a place where he had orgasmed. Under the circumstances it was very unlikely she would.

Pulling her close, she snuggled into him. Fighting the urge to tell him, she was falling in love with him, she pursed her lips together. Grief had made her vulnerable and needy.

Compensating for ejaculating, he jested with her, "Can we just lay here forever?"

She patted his hand, "But Marcus you better lift your game if you want that."

Uncharacteristically, he pulled away from her, "You know what? I'm hungry again. Are you hungry? I make a mean Green Thai Curry. In fact, it's my favourite. It won't take long. I'll grab you a chardonnay."

Disappointed, he felt the need to leave her side so soon after their love-making, she shook her head, "No. Thank you. I just can't eat right now."

A cold breeze snuck under the doona as he pulled the covers back and hopped out of bed.

Amelie sat up, "Can I have a cigarette?"

"Knock yourself out."

Marcus lived in a rental unit that the hospital had organised for him prior to his flight from Heathrow.

Suddenly the realisation that Marcus would return to England once his working visa expired, scared her. Pushing the fear into the shadows of her mind, she leaned over the bed to grab a cigarette and lighter from her bag.

She sat back up in bed and lit the cigarette. The instant rush, superficially calmed her.

Thoughts floated to Oscar. 'Should she have left him alone with the twins?'

Amelie dropped the cigarette. It bounced onto the bed, finally resting on the carpet.

Panicking, Amelie bounced out of bed to pick the cigarette up, squashing it into her bag to put it out.

"Oh no! Oh no!"

The cigarette had singed the carpet. Marcus was going to be really 'pissed off'.

In vain, she licked her finger and tried to rub the burn mark off.

"Scissors?"

Turning her bag upside down, Amelie poured the contents over the carpet. Finding a pair of scissors, she cut the burnt carpet off and was relieved that it was almost unnoticeable. Shoving the contents back into the bag, she spotted a box underneath the bed. Not just a box, but a wooden box with strange markings on it. Markings, she recognised. Witch markings.

Her stomach flipped and a waves of nausea warned her that something was not right. Leaning further down, she reached out to grab the box which was closest to Marcus' side of the bed.

"Shit!"

Amelie felt another wave of nausea rush over her. 'What was in the box?' 'Did she have enough time before Marcus come back?' Curiosity and fear, overwhelmed her.

She jumped over the bed, sticking her hand under the bed to pull the box out.

Amelie suddenly felt as if her head had caught on fire. Jealousy and betrayal a deadly mixture, one she had hoped she would never feel towards Marcus.

She opened it, flipping the wooden top up, she stared at an amulet on a red velvet cloth. Amelie had never seen one like this before but she has heard about an amulet of the same description. Anger tore through her body as her heart broke into a million pieces.

Her hand touched the amulet. Pagan's description of the amulet that Dante had given her before the Witch Awakening was spot on. Pagan had longed for its return. Searching pawn shops online for years, even paying for one of her bohemian artist friends to draw it for her. She had never stopped looking for it.

'Had Marcus deliberately left it for her to find? Had he left it underneath his bed as a constant reminder of his sexual conquests? Was everything that they had shared a plot to seek revenge on Pagan? Had she been his guinea pig?'

Amelie slammed her fists on the doona.

Dizzy, she cursed the Goddesses. 'Why could she not enjoy one moment of happiness without something to ruin it? Why did everything have to be about Pagan?'

Hearing movement behind her, she swung around. Marcus stood at the door. He already looked different. His body once inviting now stood aloof, as if it was ready for battle, ready to defend his lies. Where once stood kindness, only arrogance remained.

Amelie flung the box at Marcus, "You lying fucking cunt!"

All witty sarcasms numbed as the heartache raged through her body.

The amulet landed behind him. Desperately, he chased the rolling jewellery until it was safely in his hand. For the first time, Amelie witnessed a true emotion from Marcus. His affection for the amulet was unbalanced, if not damn creepy.

Amelie steadied herself. Ready for an attack, after all, rape was his thing. Suddenly, she wished, she was dressed.

"You've picked the wrong Witch to fuck with!"

Marcus laughed, "I've already fucked you, many times."

"Fucked me over, you mean?" The one-liners were back.

His body now relaxing into smug cockiness, he snarled, "Your precious Pagan doesn't seem to like a good fucking as much as you do. It's a pity you live in her shadow. I think you're the Witch people should bow down to."

"Why me? Why did you choose me? I was happy."

He knew the answer. Amelie was Pagan's best friend. Only an idiot would approach the target. Infiltrate the Coven by befriending the protector of the Coven and she will do all the work for him. Better to blow it up from the inside than the outside.

"Because you think you're the Alpha and so do I! I have a plan, Amelie. It's where you're the Coven leader and Pagan follows you?"

22:30

Kramer

Since Aggie had given him a detailed description of Pagan's biography, Kramer had become obsessed with her. She was a magnificent creature; her beauty incomparable to any other Witch, even without her Magick, she oozed power. Whatever she oozed, she had been born with, and it certainly was not something one could obtain through training.

Before hiding in Pagan's daughter's bedroom, he had placed a piece of cloth in between the door and the frame so he could open it later without alerting her. Wearing Deity's clothes, he hoped to mask his smell. Pagan had already picked up on his scent several times. Barely escaping detection, he had been relieved.

Feeding the cats on a regular basis had lured the cats into a false alliance. As usual Pagan would greet the cats and then put them to bed in the laundry with a bowl of fresh water and dried cat biscuits. Only in the morning, she fed her familiars with wet cat food, consisting of tuna and an array of meaty casserole dishes. On special occasions, Pagan would feed the cats salmon which they ate quickly, making sure to lick their whiskers clean.

Using the spare key that she lazily hid behind the clothes drier, at arm's length so the children could reach it, he had entered her home at will. The early mornings were his favourite time. Sleeping underneath her home in a one metre square room, he could easily come and go as he pleased. Creeping through the house, he enjoyed watching Pagan sleep. Her sense of smell did not work when she slept. She made short wispy grunts in deep sleep that made him want to cum all over her face.

The last few months, he had watched Pagan's every move and she had sensed nothing. This had intrigued him. Too preoccupied with the Darkness and Witchy endeavours, she had not sensed that she was being hunted, right within the same walls where she slept.

He had witnessed the Darkness also stalk her house. It had entered his territory, only visiting for a few minutes and then disappearing into the night sky.

The young boy, Henry who had visited her, now lay in a shallow grave while the foreigner, Dante would shortly join him if he visited again. He owned Pagan, not him.

Returning home at 21:00, after sitting with Ruby and Roberta at the pub, Pagan had slammed the backdoor shut.

Putting his hand down his pants, he had pulled on his penis. He had already leaked onto his underwear, just knowing she was in the house.

Pagan patted the cats, ate some cold meat in the fridge, and then opted for a shower before heading to bed.

Imagining her naked body in the shower, the way the soap slid over her silky skin and how she closed her eyes as the hot water fell over her breast, made him climax. He looked forward to feasting on her skin and ripping the flesh from her neck, in vampire fashion.

The solace of bed reduced her to tears. Unaware that she could be heard, Pagan howled. The loss of Fay Ce'Line had broken her. The past had taught her how to mourn but tonight it seemed as if she had forgotten all that she had learned.

Kramer waited half an hour, just in case she stirred. Instinct told him it was safe to make his move. Slowly unlatching the door, he slipped easily through the small gap. He had already chosen the exact route he would walk after previously testing the floorboards: five steps across the hallway and another seven to her bed. She slept on the left side of her bed and never in the middle.

He wore sneakers that had never squeaked. Clothes that did not rub and he had practised over twenty times.

Five steps, he now entered her bedroom. He could see her figure in the bed. Ignoring his instant arousal, he focused on his task. The second step into her bedroom was tricky. There was a chance that if he placed his foot in the wrong position the board would creak. Carefully placing his right foot down, his foot slipped. It creaked! Holding his breath, he waited to see if Pagan had woken. Two smaller steps and he froze as Pagan's mobile phone lit up as a phone call came through. Luckily, it was on 'silent'. He would need to be swift if she woke. He tightened his palm around the weapon. Another three steps and now he stood beside her. He put his left hand out as if he was touching her. His fingers hovered only centimetres away from her face.

Snoring quietly, he wished that he did not have to kill her. He had wanted to torture her. Watch her blood decorate her skin. He would smile as she begged for mercy but instructions had to be followed and his orders were to kill her tonight.

'You would have been fierce under torture my Highest Priestess'.

The sword was not his weapon of choice but Aquarius had insisted.

Raising the sword above her neck, he closed his eyes. Self-assured that he would make a clean cut, he celebrated that he may be able to keep her head as a souvenir.

Hesitating, he longed to touch her warm skin but he had to follow orders.

Lifting the sword higher, another text message come through, lighting the room up.

Panicking, he brought the sword down with enough force he cut right through her neck as if he was slicing a cabbage. Soaring, it cut off her head, continued through the mattress and lodged in the bed frame. Her head rolled down, landing on the floor.

Aggie woke! Her body hovered above the mattress. Her body dropped as Pagan's Magick left her. Her daughter was dead.

When the call came through that Kramer had sliced Pagan's head off, Aquarius and Priscilla rejoiced by opening up a bottle of champagne and a jar of oysters which they fed to each other in a freak lovers ritual.

Kramer was now flying to Aggie, with Pagan's head in his backpack.

Svenana would willingly step aside to allow him to enter the secure building to murder Aggie. It had not taken much persuasion by Priscilla, who had used Svenana's obvious lust for her to recruit Svenana to their side.

Kramer had been granted ownership of Pagan's body and would betray anyone to have it, even Aggie. He had no loyalties to Aggie. He had no loyalties to anyone.

Aquarius laughed, "Finally, I have my revenge on both Bitches. Good riddance, Aunty Aggie, and Pagan."

Aquarius was unaware that he had managed to not only kill-off one family member, but two, as Pagan was his first cousin by blood.

Priscilla smiled, while noting that a 'patient man' was the most dangerous, and Aquarius was a very patient man.

Seductively, she lifted her champagne flute to her mouth, "Cheers, to the Age of Aquarius."

CHAPTER 29
John

Erratically, John threw as many clothes as he could find into a large backpack.

"What the hell's going on John?" Michelle asked.

He feared this day would happen. Stumbling out of bed after a loud knock had woken him at 22:30, he had marched down the stairs to be greeted by a strange man at the front door. He had been very persistent that Deity needed to leave with him immediately.

His sleepy daughter now sat on the end of her bed. Legs swinging as she waited.

Deity had dressed herself; thermals; top and pants, and woollen jumper and cosy trousers. Finally a beanie over her head, gloves for her hands, and thick socks and shoes for her feet, as mummy had instructed.

Singing her favourite pop songs, John was unnerved by his daughter's calmness.

He was relieved that Deity was a keen broomstick rider. Pagan had made sure Deity flew from an early age. It had frightened John at the beginning but now he realised why Pagan had been so adamant about how Deity was raised.

"She's a Witch, John. Not a human. And not just a Witch! She is my daughter and the offspring of Gorr. Anything happens to me and they will hunt her down and falling off a broomstick will be the least of her problems."

Deity may not be his blood daughter but he loved her like she was his own. He brushed the heartache away. He had to remain strong for Deity. His daughter was clever and soon she would be able to control her Magick.

John held his daughter's hand, "You're a survivor, and daddy's little girl. Never forget that."

Zipping up her backpack, he quickly ran to the bathroom to collect toothpaste, a tooth brush and Deity's favourite hairbrush. She was nearly ready to go.

Stopping at the kitchen cabinet, he grabbed four muesli bars for when she got hungry and a water bottle for when she got thirsty.

He had no idea where the man was taking her but he could see in his eyes that he would take care of his daughter. He had also said the correct password. He could only trust that Pagan had chosen the right person to look after their daughter.

Fearful, he would never see Deity again, he hugged her until her bones popped. Moments away from an emotional breakdown, John squeezed her even tighter.

"Stop, you're squashing me."

Walking Deity to the front door, with Michelle weeping behind them, he could not believe how little Deity was and he was about to hand her over to a very physically large foreign man, who he had never met but knew existed.

Holding both of John's hands, Deity smiled, "Daddy, everything will be ok. My Nanna told me so, she's psychic you know. She saw it in a vision…I win."

John choked on his breath, "Nanna, knows best."

Regally, Deity strolled towards the man. She looked at him. He was tall and funny looking. She ushered him to bend down so she could be on the same eye level.

Deity put her hand out, resting it against his cheek, "I like you. You have kind eyes. Mummy liked you too. She told me to be brave when she dies, like all the other times. I remember her dying lots. But I'll see her again."

She pinched his cheek, "What's your name?"

He laughed. She was her mother's daughter, "My name is Dante, but you can call me Raven."

Deity nodded, "Merry Winter Solstice, Raven."

One week ago, her mother had spoken of Raven. Warning Deity that danger was coming and if anything was to happen to her that a Raven would swoop down and pick her up, flying her to safety.

Dante slowly stood up. He was much older now and his body took longer to stretch out.

The little Witch looked at him. Her eyes searching for truth. The full moon lit up the night sky.

She asked, "Did mummy know that you are half Witch and half Darkness?"

Taken aback, Dante struggled to respond. Deity was wise and was remembering quickly.

"Your mum knew, deep down, but never said."

Dante put his large hand out to the little Witch who willingly took hold of it.

"Where are you taking me?"

Dante picked her up. She instantly snuggled into him.

"Somewhere special, where you can't be found. There is a book there you need to read, again."

Two broomsticks rested against the house. Unlike her mother, Deity would fly beside him.

Dante turned to John, whose tears dripped from his chin, "I'll keep her safe, John. I made a promise to Pagan. One in which I intend to keep."

Message from the Author

I have no idea what I am doing, and I suppose S^ORD was always going to be the 'learning' book for the series. Proudly Tasmanian, it seemed only fitting that I would self-publish, and work with artists who I personally know from this beautiful Island I call home. I admit I am bad at spelling, and what is grammar? I spent most of my education 'day dreaming', but there was always one underlying trait that stood out, I was and am passionate, to the point of exhaustion. I love hard, and I hate hard. My entire life is within this book, a melting pot of everything I've witnessed, or heard, and felt- the tears, the laughter, the friends, my family, and everything I treasure about life and everything that makes me furious. I may never write again once I have completed this series, but it has meant the world to me that I have given myself enough respect to listen to the 'pull' to write it, and now with one book finished, I am proud that I am inspiring others to follow their dreams, or at least, day dream about the 'what if'. Writing S^ORD on a dinosaur laptop, working many jobs, losing my mum to cancer, raising two children split-share, single, and battling health issues, I hope readers believe that if 'Jo Green' can accomplish something great during troubled times, than so can I.

Jo Green.

WAND^
Book Two

***

^CUP
Book Three

***

PEN^TACLE
Book Four

www.ingramcontent.com/pod-product-compliance
Lightning Source LLC
Chambersburg PA
CBHW031428240626
47154CB00001B/247